WHISKEY & LIES

E.A. HARPER

For the good girls who read smut like scripture.
For the good girls who bend when told and beg when needed.
For the good girls who blush at praise and sin on command.
For the good girls who can't keep quiet. Especially when they should.
To the good girls who know that "yes, sir" gets them exactly what they want.

CONTENT & TRIGGER WARNINGS
FOR WHISKEY & LIES

This book is intended for adult readers **18+** and contains dark themes, explicit content, and potentially distressing material. Please read with care.

Content includes, but is not limited to

Physical abuse

Emotional and psychological abuse (referenced)

Sexual assault and harassment (referenced, not graphic)

Consensual non-consent (CNC) scenes involving explicit consent and prior discussion between characters

Somnophilia (sexual acts initiated while one partner is asleep)

Obsessive and possessive behavior (on-page, romanticized through morally gray dynamics)

Controlling/territorial tendencies in romantic relationships

Toxic relationship patterns

Power imbalances (boss/employee dynamic)

Murder and vigilante justice

Graphic violence and torture

Gun violence and threats with firearms

Knife violence and implied torture with sharp objects

Use of physical restraint

Fear-based manipulation and intimidation

Discussion and depictions of panic attacks

Heart disease / heart condition

Stalking and invasive behavior

Character death

False identity/fraudulent résumé

Criminal activity

Mild substance use (alcohol, smoking)

Explicit sexual content (includes rough sex, degradation, power play, oral, use of fingers, and public teasing)

Language that may be triggering or offensive (explicit, aggressive, and raw)

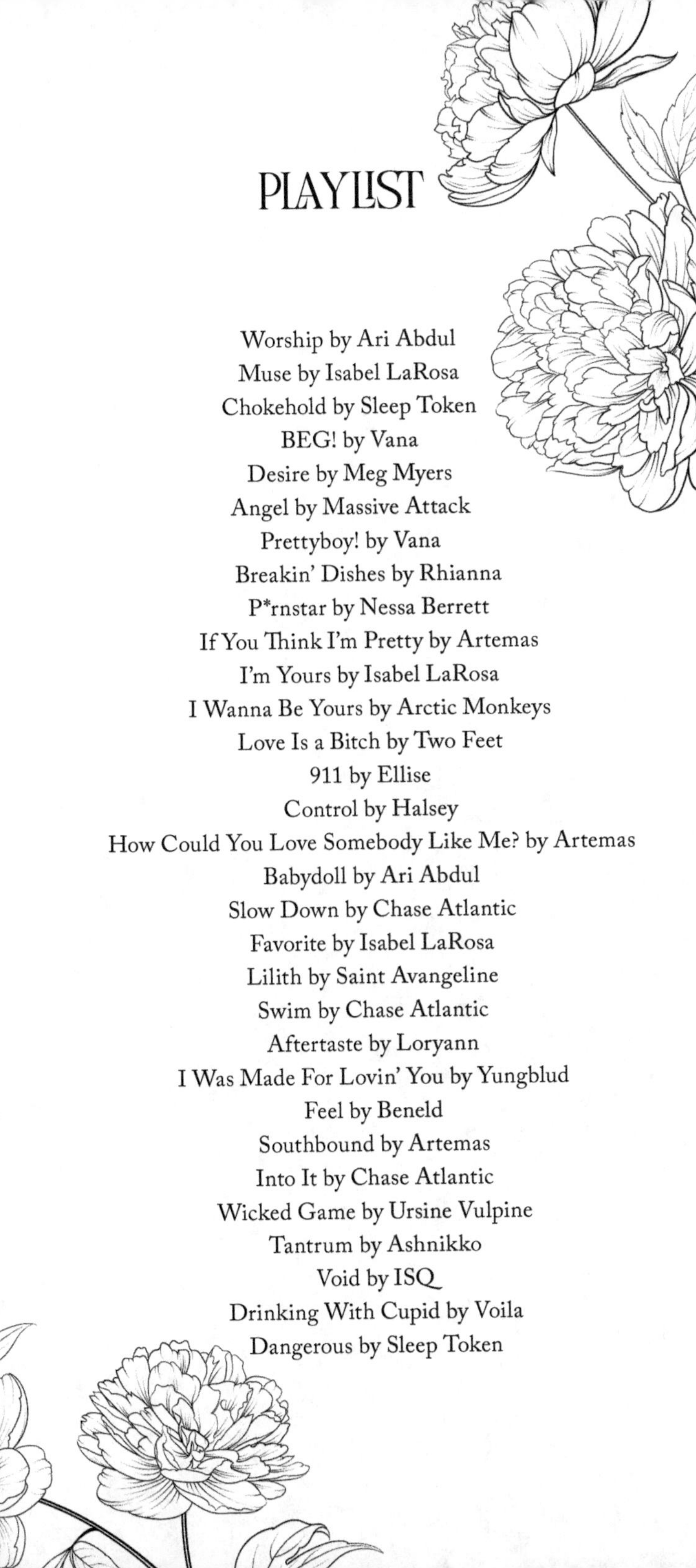

PLAYLIST

Worship by Ari Abdul
Muse by Isabel LaRosa
Chokehold by Sleep Token
BEG! by Vana
Desire by Meg Myers
Angel by Massive Attack
Prettyboy! by Vana
Breakin' Dishes by Rhianna
P*rnstar by Nessa Berrett
If You Think I'm Pretty by Artemas
I'm Yours by Isabel LaRosa
I Wanna Be Yours by Arctic Monkeys
Love Is a Bitch by Two Feet
911 by Ellise
Control by Halsey
How Could You Love Somebody Like Me? by Artemas
Babydoll by Ari Abdul
Slow Down by Chase Atlantic
Favorite by Isabel LaRosa
Lilith by Saint Avangeline
Swim by Chase Atlantic
Aftertaste by Loryann
I Was Made For Lovin' You by Yungblud
Feel by Beneld
Southbound by Artemas
Into It by Chase Atlantic
Wicked Game by Ursine Vulpine
Tantrum by Ashnikko
Void by ISQ
Drinking With Cupid by Voila
Dangerous by Sleep Token

CHAPTER ONE
Octavia

It is 4 AM, and I am tired of forcing myself to sleep. I start a new job with Digi Pulse Marketing today and my anxiety is through the roof. I never imagined I would get this job. I may or may not have lied on my resume. Whatever. It's not like I claimed to be a brain surgeon—I just gave myself a little upgrade. If men can exaggerate their dick size, I can inflate my skill set. Fair is fair. Besides, my ex once told me I'd never amount to anything. Said I'd always be stuck, barely scraping by. So yeah, maybe I fudged a few details. And now that I *have* the job? Even better. Every exaggeration was worth it just to prove him wrong. Every. Damn. Word.

Tyler said that shit two years ago, and I walked out like the badass I should have been all along. Never once looking back. He's married now—not that I care. I only know this because his wedding photo with his smug face popped up on a mutual friend's Facebook post a couple of months ago. Honestly? It lit a fire under my ass. If he can move on and play house, I can damn sure get my life together. It was time to stop surviving and actually *do* something.

I climb out of bed, get my morning coffee going, and aimlessly

scroll my newsfeed. I haven't told anyone in my group of friends about my new job except my best friend, Lena. They won't find out either unless they happen to visit the Rustic Harbor Bar & Grill and notice that I am no longer on staff. But let's be realistic, they probably won't because they only visited once when I invited them. It's not exactly an affordable place, so I don't blame them.

When I handed in my two weeks notice, my old boss, Ciara, laughed, full on *laughed*. She didn't believe I landed a huge gig at Digi Pulse. My hands damn near curled into fists. People have always doubted me, acted like I was aiming too high. But not me. I've *never* doubted what I'm capable of. I'm going to be great whether they like it or not.

And honestly? Why the hell do I care what Ciara thinks? It's not like we were friends. We barely spoke outside of passive-aggressive emails. She's just background noise. A nobody.

As I sip my coffee, I catch a glimpse of myself in the mirror. My hair is a mess, and dark circles frame my eyes. I look nothing like the polished marketing professional I'm supposed to be in a few hours. Anxiety grips my heart as I walk into the room. Will they be able to see through my façade? Can I keep up this act or will it all come crumbling down?

I force myself to take a deep breath. No, I can do this. I *have* to do this. I've spent the last two weeks cramming every marketing book and online course I could find. I may not have the experience, but I have the determination. And sometimes, that's enough.

I shower and put on the new blazer I bought for this job - it still has the price tag on it. As I put on my makeup, I practice my introduction in the mirror. "Hi, I'm Octavia. I'm excited to join the team." My voice wavers.

I clear my throat and try again, this time with more conviction.

"Hi, I'm Octavia. I'm excited to join the team." Better, but still not quite there. As I finish getting ready, my phone buzzes with a text from Lena.

LENA

Good luck today, girl! You've got this!

I smile, grateful for her support, even though she doesn't know the whole truth about how I landed this job. My phone vibrates, notifying me that my Uber driver is outside waiting for me. The ride to Digi Pulse's office feels surreal. The city streets are quiet at this early hour, and I find myself constantly smoothing my hands over my skirt. I tell the driver to drop me in front of the building and tip her.

As I walk towards the sleek, modern building towering above me, my heels click against the pavement, each step bringing me closer to a new chapter in my life, or possibly, my downfall. I pause at the entrance, my hand hovering over the door handle. This is it, the moment of truth.

I take one last deep breath and step inside.

The lobby is massive, and with the building being all glass, sunlight pours in like it's trying to show off. I definitely feel out of my element here. I walk over to the receptionist, a young man wearing thick black-framed glasses and a nice smile. "Good morning," I say, hoping my voice doesn't reveal how nervous I actually am. "I'm Octavia. I'm starting today on the marketing team." He nods, as he is still busy typing on his computer. "Ah, yes! Welcome! Let me just get you a visitor's badge for now. HR will sort out getting you a permanent one later today." As he hands me the badge, I notice my hand trembling slightly. I clip it to my blazer, telling myself to calm down. "The marketing team is on the top floor," the receptionist says, gesturing towards the elevators. "Marissa from HR will meet you up there." I thank him and make my way to the elevators, my heart pounding so hard I feel like my chest is about to explode.

As I wait, I catch a glimpse of myself in the mirrored doors and I look... surprisingly put together. I don't look like I'm not meant to be here. Maybe I *can* pull this off. The elevator dings, and I am thankful I am alone so I can take a second to breathe and shake off the nerves that keep coming in waves.

This is my chance to reinvent myself, to become the person I've always wanted to be. The person Tyler said I could never be.

When the doors open on the third floor, I'm greeted by a woman with a warm smile and a tablet in her hand. "Octavia?" she asks, extending her hand. "I'm Marissa from HR. Welcome to Digi Pulse Marketing," Marissa finishes, shaking my hand. Her grip is firm and confident, everything I'm pretending to be. "Let's get you settled in."

She leads me through an open-expansive office, past rows of desks that have dual monitors. The air hums with quiet conversation and the clacking of keyboards. I try not to stare, but it's a far cry from the noisy kitchen and asshole customers I'm used to.

"This will be your desk," Marissa says, showing me to a bare workspace. "IT will be by shortly to set up your computer and get you on the network."

I nod, setting my bag down like I own the place, and roll my shoulders back—because why not pretend I belong here until they believe I do? A man in a crisp button-down approaches us, his smile wide but his eyes sharp.

"Ah, you must be our new marketing strategist," he says, extending his hand. "I'm Derek, the lead marketing director. Welcome to the team."

I shake his hand, hoping he can't feel how clammy my palm is. "Thank you, I'm excited to be here," I manage to say with conviction.

Derek nods with what seems like approval. "We're excited to have you. Your experience at those smaller firms will bring a fresh perspective to our team."

My stomach instantly goes into knots. The lies on my resume flash through my mind, but I force a smile. "I am looking forward to contributing," I say, silently praying I can live up to the expectations.

"Great," Derek says. "We have a team meeting in an hour to discuss our upcoming campaign for Tech Nova. I'd love for you to sit in and share any initial thoughts."

My mind races. Tech Nova? Campaign?

My mind races and I am filled with anxiety as I try to figure out how to make this work. Calling Lena for advice would be a relief, but she has no clue about the lies on my resume, nor does she know a damn thing about marketing. She believes I got this job because of my connection to the CEO, who used to visit Rustic Harbor. But does he even remember me? Will he find out the truth about my qualifications?

As Derek walks away, I sink into my chair, my mind still reeling. Tech Nova? I vaguely remember seeing their logo on some billboards around the city, but that's the only thing I know. I have less than an hour to prepare for this meeting, and I have no idea where to even begin.

I pull out my phone, Googling "Tech Nova" in a frenzy under my desk. It's a tech startup specializing in smart home devices. I can work with this. I search through their website, trying to absorb as much information as possible.

The IT guy arrives to set up my computer, and I try to look busy while he works. Once he's done, I log in and immediately open a blank document. I write down ideas, anything that comes to mind about marketing for a tech company. Social media campaigns, influencer partnerships, and interactive demos at tech conventions. I have no clue if any of these ideas are any good, but it's all I've got. As the hour ticks by, my anxiety builds. I can feel sweat forming at the small of my back.

What if they ask me a question I can't answer? What if they realize I'm a complete fraud?

I take a deep breath, trying to calm my racing heart.

When Derek comes over to grab me for the meeting, I follow him on shaky legs. We enter the conference room, where ten people are already sitting. I scan their faces, wondering if any of them can see that I'm walking on a tightrope with no safety net. "Everyone, this is Octavia, our new marketing strategist," Derek announces. "Why don't you tell us a bit about yourself, Octavia?"

I swallow hard, hoping my voice doesn't shake. "Hi everyone," I begin, mustering all the confidence I can fake.

"I am very excited to join the team," my voice is strong and confident, unlike how I am feeling. "I have worked with a couple smaller firms in the past, focusing on original digital marketing strategies to boost their brands awareness and engagement."

The lies taste bitter on my tongue, but I force myself to keep going. "I'm especially interested in using the leverage that emerging platforms and technologies offer to reach new demographics."

Derek nods and smiles. "Excellent. We can't wait to hear what you come up with for the Tech Nova campaign. Thank you, Octavia. Let's get into this, shall we?"

He turns to the screen at the front of the room, pulling up a presentation. As he outlines the campaign objectives, I take all the notes I can, trying to remember every detail. The team around me chimes in with ideas and feedback. Their expertise is clear in every word.

My palms are sweating as I listen intently, with my thoughts racing at a million miles per minute. And then, suddenly, the door to the boardroom opens. It's him—Dominic fucking Callahan! Why didn't I expect to see him so soon? My stomach churns as he strides confidently to the front of the room, his presence filling every inch of space, making it hard to breathe. As his eyes scan the faces around the table, his eyes meet mine, and there is a moment of recognition. I hold my breath, waiting for the ball to drop, but he says nothing.

"Good morning, everyone. I hope you don't mind me dropping in on your meeting. I'm particularly interested in our approach to Tech Nova." His voice is deep and authoritative. It shouldn't affect me like this. But the way he speaks—confident, composed—sends a rush of heat through me, and suddenly I am painfully aware of every inch of skin he's not touching.

Derek gives an enthusiastic nod. "Of course, Mr. Callahan. We are just getting started, we are happy to have you join in. In fact, we have a new team member joining us today. Octavia, would you like to introduce yourself to Mr. Callahan?" My mouth goes dry as all eyes turn to me. This is it. The moment of truth. Will he remember me from the bar? Will he expose me and send my ass packing?

I stand up slowly, my legs feeling like jello beneath me. His piercing green eyes lock onto mine, and for a moment, I'm transported back to Rustic Harbor, sliding him his usual whiskey neat across the polished bar top.

"It's nice to see you again, Octavia," he says with a hint of a smile playing across his lips. "I hope you are finding the transition to be going smoothly?"

Relief floods over me. He remembers me, but he isn't calling me out on my bullshit. I take the lifeline he's thrown at me. "Yes, I am, Mr. Callahan," my voice coming out more confident than I feel. "It's been a very exciting change. I'm looking forward to using my experience in customer engagement and seeing how I can work it into digital strategies." He nods with satisfaction. "Outstanding. Fresh perspectives are always a vital key in this industry. I look forward to seeing what you bring to this campaign."

As he takes his seat at the head of the table, I sink back into my chair. I can feel my heart pounding through my entire body. I've dodged a bullet for now, but for how long? The meeting continues, with team members discussing various aspects of the campaign. I listen intently, scribbling notes, still trying to grasp everything that is going on.

Derek turns to me suddenly. "Octavia, you had mentioned experience with some emerging platforms. Any thoughts on how we could use those for Tech Nova?"

All eyes are on me again, and I feel like a fish stuck in a pet store. I take a deep breath, my mind racing through the ideas I quickly researched earlier. "Well," I begin, hoping my voice stays steady, "given that their focus is on smart home devices, I think there is an amazing opportunity to use augmented reality platforms." I pause, gauging the room's reaction. Seeing no objections, I continue. "We could create an AR application that allows the potential customer to visualize the devices in their homes. It would provide an interactive experience and help consumers to overcome the struggle of trying to imagine how these products would fit into their lives."

There's a brief silence, and I feel my pulse pounding. Did I say something completely off-base? Then Mr. Callahan leans forward, his eyes bright with interest. "That's an intriguing idea, Octavia. How would you see us implementing something like that?"

I clear my throat. "Maybe we start simple—an app that lets people see the top-selling products in 3D," I say, voice a little shaky but steadying with each word. "They could point their phones at a table or wall and actually see what it would look like in their space. We could even make it interactive—like showing the thermostat adjusting in real-time, or a smart speaker actually playing music. If we tie it into a social campaign, maybe something shareable, users could show off their setups and it might even go viral."

I finish speaking and immediately regret opening my mouth. But then—heads nod. Actual nods. Derek leans forward, eyebrows raised. "That's a fresh angle. We haven't touched anything like that yet. Could really help people *feel* the product."

My pulse is pounding in my ears, but I nod like this is totally normal.

Then Callahan speaks.

"I like it," he says. No expression, just that unreadable intensity. "Innovative. In line with the Tech Nova brand."

He doesn't look away. "Octavia, I want you to develop this further. Bring a more detailed version to our next meeting."

I try to play it cool, even as my chest tightens like I just sprinted ten floors. "Of course, Mr. Callahan. I'd be happy to."

When the meeting wraps, people file out of the boardroom. I'm riding the high of not totally bombing when I catch movement from the corner of my eye.

Callahan, again.

"Octavia," he says quietly as he steps closer to me. "Do you have a moment?"

His tone is low. Not demanding, not exactly gentle. Just... definite.

Suddenly, I'm not so sure this is about AR anymore.

My stomach drops. This is it. He is going to confront me about my lies. I give him a tight smile, trying to keep my face neutral as I follow him to a quiet corner of the office.

"I have to say, I'm very impressed," and I brace myself for the 'but' that is sure to follow. "Your idea for the AR app shows some real potential. It's exactly the fresh thinking we need here at Digi Pulse."

The words catch me off guard, confusion blooming at the unexpected praise, "Thank you, Mr. Callahan. I'm glad you think so."

He leans in slightly, his voice lowering to a tone that is so authoritative but so sexy. "I'll be honest, when I recognized you from the bar, I was skeptical about how you'd fit in here. But you've proven me wrong. Keep this up, and you'll go far."

My heart races. He knows, and the bastard is testing me. I force a smile, trying to keep my voice steady. "I appreciate the opportunity, Sir. I am committed to giving it my all."

He nods, satisfied. "Good. I look forward to seeing your proposal. And Octavia?" He pauses, his gaze is so intense the way he looks at me. "Don't let me down," he says with a wink.

As he walks away, I let out a shaky breath. The mixture of praise and veiled threat leaves me reeling.

CHAPTER TWO

Dominic

My heart skips the moment our eyes meet. Ice-blue and unblinking, and they lock onto mine with the same piercing look I remember.

It's her, the bartender from Rustic Harbor. The one I can't forget, no matter how many nights I'd tried.

I knew she was starting this week, but I didn't expect to see her sitting in the conference room, notebook in hand, pretending not to notice me while every part of me snapped to attention.

Somehow, she looks even better now, which is really un-fucking fair. The delicate curve of her jaw, the scatter of freckles across her nose, the red waves of her hair like fire spilling down her back. She looks more polished, but she is still the same woman who served me whiskey with a smirk that made my mouth go dry.

I force myself to look away, to stay collected. There are a dozen eyes on me, and none of them need to know what's rushing through my head. I'm the CEO. I'm supposed to be in control. But right now? I'm not even fucking close to being in control.

When her resume landed on my desk, I read her name twice.

Octavia Moore.

I didn't even need to see the rest. I knew it was her. It was extremely obvious the resume wasn't entirely honest. Part of that was because I knew who she was. If this had landed on someone else's desk, they may have believed it. But I didn't care. I don't need her qualifications. I need her close.

I slid the file to Alexis and told her to move forward. Told her to keep the interview short, just enough to make it look like protocol, then offer Octavia the job and make sure she's stationed on my floor. Alexis gave me that look, the one that says I'm impossible and maybe a little insane, but I don't give a fuck.

I need her back in my space. I want her where I can track every step, every breath, where she can't slip past me unnoticed.

She shifts in her seat, scribbling a note. The buttons on her blouse look like they're clinging for dear life, and my sanity's hanging on just as tight. Every time she leans forward to look at something Derek is showing her; I feel my control slip a little more.

This is dangerous. I already knew that it would be before she even stepped foot in this building. But it doesn't stop me from looking.

Remembering the sound of her laugh over music, the way she used to lean across the bar when it got loud, speaking close so she would be heard. The vanilla with a hint of spice in her perfume. The way she called me sir before she even knew who I was.

I told myself I wasn't obsessed, that looking through her Instagram at midnight with my dick in my hand didn't mean anything. She was just a woman I found interesting.

But now she's here, and it's all unraveling.

Checking my watch, I still have two more hours. I'm supposed to be reviewing quarterly projections, but I can barely keep my eyes on the screen. My mind keeps going back to her and the way her hips sway when she walks, making my cock twitch uncomfortably against my zipper.

The phone rings, bringing me back to reality.

"Mr. Callahan, marketing is waiting for your final approval on the campaign visuals," Alexis says.

"Send them in," I reply, grateful for something, anything, to ground me.

The door opens.

And it's not the team.

It's her. Of course, it is because the world wants to tease me. I don't have anyone to blame but myself.

"Sorry to interrupt," she says, holding a folder against her chest, covering her perfect tits. "Derek asked me to bring these to you for signature."

I clear my throat. "Thank you, Miss Moore, you can leave them on the desk."

She moves in closer, sliding the folder toward me. I reach out to grab it and her fingers brush mine—barely a touch, but it might as well be a lightning strike.

"Anything else you need, Mr. Callahan?" she asks, her tone careful.

Yes. So many things. Like you, bent over this desk while I fist your hair and tell you to take all of me like a good girl. You cumming all over my dick. But I shake my head instead.

"No. That's all."

She gives a small nod, turning to leave. But I stop her because I can't just leave well enough alone.

"Octavia."

She turns and her eyes are wide like she's seen a ghost.

"How was your first day?"

Her lips quirk up at the corners. "It's been really good. Everyone has been very nice to me."

I quickly nod. "Good, I am glad to hear that. I expect you'll settle in rather quickly."

There's something in her eyes that I can't quite read. Something that I hope isn't disappointment.

She opens the door again, and I almost let her go.

"One more thing," I say. "I want a full report on your current role by eight tomorrow morning."

She blinks and takes an exasperated breath. "You got it, Mr. Callahan."

The door closes behind her.

Now, I am sitting here, dick straining against my pants, pulse pounding, and I am wondering what the hell I just did. Why did I tell her I want a full report on her current role? What kind of asshole boss does that shit? Oh well, I guess it is better that she thinks I am just a prick rather than her knowing what is really going on in my head.

But really, what the hell am I thinking? I've built this company from the ground up, every contract, every win, carved out with time, blood, and too many sleepless nights to count. I didn't get here by luck or clean hands; I've made choices that don't exactly shine in the light.

And I sure as hell didn't get here by getting distracted by women I can't have.

But then there's her.

The way she looked at me like she remembered every second at Rustic Harbor, every glance, every word.

I grab my phone, thumb hovering over Alexis's contact. I should move Octavia to a different team. Put her upstairs, minimizing contact. I should be smart about this.

Instead, I toss the phone aside and turn to look out the window. The city glows beneath me, stretching out, people walking along the streets in their own worlds.

And here I am, shaken by a woman who used to pour my drinks and now sits ten feet from my fucking office.

I try to get back to work. I pull the folder she brought in closer and pretend I'm reading. But my nose is invaded with her perfume, and her eyes linger in my mind, vivid and impossible to outrun. I've never let someone under my skin like this. Women were a distraction, sure. A way to blow off steam. But Octavia?

Octavia is different.

When the end of the day finally rolls around, I wait until the office thins out. The quiet is deafening, and she catches my eye. She is still at her desk, typing, probably that bullshit report I told her to write.

I should leave.

I pause… then cross the floor anyway.

"Working late on your first day?" I ask, crossing the floor.

She startles slightly, clearly caught off guard. Her gaze lifts and locks on mine.

"Mr. Callahan," she says quickly, smoothing her skirt. "Just wanted to get a head start on that report."

I step in closer. "That's… very thorough of you."

She offers a small smile. "I am trying to make a good impression."

"You already have," I blurt out before I can stop myself.

The blush that creeps into her cheeks is almost my undoing.

"You should wrap it up for tonight," I tell her. "Get some rest. You've done enough for your first day."

She hesitates. "But you said—"

"I know what I said," I interrupt, softer now. "Take your time. I'd rather see something thoughtful than rushed."

Exhaling, the tension in her shoulders eases. "Thank you."

There's a pause. Too long. Too charged.

"Did you drive?" I ask.

She shakes her head. "Took an uber."

I bite back a curse. "I'll take you home."

"That's really not necessary"

"I insist, it is company policy"

She lets a small smile slip. "If it's company policy…"

"Page forty-three," I mutter, sounding too serious.

She laughs—and it's the first real one I've heard from her all day. I wait while she shuts down her computer. I try not to be too obvious when I stare at her perfect ass as she bends over to grab her purse from under her desk.

My hand drifts toward the small of her back as we step into the hallway, a reflex more than anything else. I feel her tense just slightly— then relax into it. The heat from her body seeps through the fabric of her blouse, grounding me in a way that feels both dangerous and necessary.

The elevator opens and we step inside, just the two of us. The doors close with a hush, sealing us into the quiet hum of the descent. The air feels heavier in here, more dense. Like it knows we're holding something back.

She's the first to speak.

"You didn't seem to be surprised to see me today," she says. Her eyes are fixed on the lights above the door, tracking each floor we go down.

I think about deflecting, about pretending. But there's no point.

"I knew you were starting," keeping my voice even. "I approved your hire."

She turns her head then, her eyes searching mine. "Even though my resume was a little… creative?"

I don't hesitate. "Because of that."

Her lips twitch, but it's not quite a smile. "Creative initiative. Got it."

The elevator dings before I have to explain further. The doors slide open into the private garage. We walk together toward my car, our footsteps echoing against the walls.

She slows when she sees it. "This is yours?"

"Just one of them," I say, unlocking the doors with a press of the fob.

I open her door, and she slides in, skirt riding up just enough to test my self-control. I shut it gently and circle to the driver's side, sliding in and starting the engine. The car comes to life, the scent of her perfume filling the air, subtle but impossible to ignore.

"Where to?"

Her address is just on the other side of town, not far from where we met. I put it into the GPS and pull out into traffic.

We don't talk right away. I steal glances at her profile, golden from the glow of the streetlights. It's too intimate.

Then, she breaks the silence again.

"Do you always drive your employees home, Mr. Callahan?"

Her voice is light and teasing. But I can tell there's something beneath it.

"No," I say honestly. "Only the ones I can't stop thinking about."

The words escape before I can stop them.

She looks at me confused. "Why me?"

I grip the wheel tighter. "I think you probably already have an idea of why."

The streetlights fly past. I catch her fingers tracing the seam of her skirt, slowly, like it's helping her think.

"Rustic Harbor," she says after a while. "You remembered me."

"Of course, I did."

"You were always a good tipper."

"You always remembered my drink."

"Whiskey. Neat."

I look over at her. "You used to watch me when you thought I wasn't paying attention. I always noticed"

She lifts a brow. "You weren't exactly subtle with your looking, either."

The tension coils tight again, no hesitation this time, just heat and something neither of us is bothering to hide.

"This is a dangerous game we're playing," I say. "Especially now."

"Because you're my boss now?"

"That, and because I haven't figured out how to stop wanting you."

She goes quiet, and I let the silence fill the car as we turn onto her street. Her building is modest. Almost familiar. I pull up to the curb and shift the car into park.

Neither of us moves.

"What we want doesn't matter," I finally say. "You work for me now. And there are lines we can't cross."

She looks over at me, disappointment showing through, even though she is trying to hide it. "I understand."

The word tastes like shit.

I step out and walk around my car to open her door. She gets out slowly, not making eye contact.

"Thanks for the ride, boss," her tone is clipped. "Next time, I'll call an Uber."

She walks away without waiting for a response. Her heels click up the concrete steps, each sound sharper than the last.

I let her go, even as something in me twists at the sight of her back turned. Something that feels a hell of a lot like regret, but deeper. Like I already know I won't be able to stay away.

CHAPTER THREE
Octavia

The key trembles in my hand as I unlock my apartment door. The hallway light flickers overhead, leaving moving shadows across the worn carpet. I step inside, letting the darkness swallow me before flipping the switch. My place looks exactly as I left it this morning—small, cluttered, mine. Yet somehow it feels different. Or maybe I'm the one who's different.

I slide down the closed door, my legs finally giving out. The ghost of Dominic's cologne still clings to my skin, and I can feel the phantom pressure of his large hands on my waist. God, what have I gotten myself into?

"It's just a job," I whisper to the empty room. "Just a job with the most terrifying, gorgeous man I've ever met."

My phone buzzes in my purse, and my heart leaps into my throat. Fishing it out with shaking fingers, I see his name illuminated on the screen.

DOMINIC

Inside safe, little minx?

Four simple words that shouldn't make my stomach flip. Four

words that shouldn't make me feel both protected and hunted at the same time. I type back quickly.

ME

Yes, Mr. Callahan. Thank you for the ride.

The three dots appear immediately, as if he's been waiting with his phone in hand. The thought makes my cheeks flush.

DOMINIC

Dominic. When we're alone, it's Dominic. Remember that.

His commanding tone translates perfectly through text. I can almost hear his deep voice, the way it caressed my name earlier tonight. The way he'd whispered it against my ear when helping me into his car, his hot breath against my skin.

I bite my lip, fingers hovering over the keyboard. Something about this man makes me want to push boundaries I shouldn't.

Yes, Dominic.

I hit send before I can talk myself out of it. My apartment suddenly feels too quiet, the silence punctuated only by my racing heartbeat.

I text Lena

ME

911. Boss gave me a ride home. In his PORSCHE.

My phone rings—Lena, right on cue.

"Spill it," she demands the moment I answer. "And don't leave out a single detail."

I laugh, feeling lighter than I have all day. "He insisted on driving me home when he saw me working late."

"And?" Lena presses, her voice alive with curiosity. "Did he touch your thigh while shifting gears? Give you smoldering looks at stoplights?"

"No!" I laugh, though my mind flashes to the way his knuckles brushed against my knee when he reached for the gear shift. "Well, not exactly. But Lena, you should've seen this car. The seats alone probably cost more than my rent."

"Forget the car. Tell me about him."

I curl up on my couch, tucking my feet beneath me. "He's... intense. Like he's constantly holding something back. And the way he looks at me sometimes makes me feel like I'm the only person in the room."

"Sounds like someone's crushing on the big boss man," Lena teases.

"It's not like that," I protest, though my cheeks warm at her accusation. "It's professional. Mostly."

"Mostly?" Lena's gleeful tone makes me regret my word choice immediately.

I sigh. "He called me 'little minx.' And just texted to make sure I got inside safely."

Lena's squeal nearly breaks my eardrum. "Octavia Moore, you've been there for one day and already have the CEO wrapped around your finger!"

"That's ridiculous," I argue, but a smile tugs at my lips. "He's just being nice."

"Men like Dominic Callahan aren't 'just nice,'" Lena counters. "They're strategic. Calculated. He wants something from you."

"Yeah, a competent employee," I say, rolling my eyes even though she can't see me.

"And maybe access to what's under that skirt."

"Lena!" I gasp, but can't help laughing. "I've literally just started this job. I'm not going to mess it up by fantasizing about my boss."

"Too late for that," she says smugly. "I can hear it in your voice."

I sigh, unable to deny it. "Fine. He's attractive. Devastatingly so.

But nothing's going to happen."

"We'll see about that," Lena says in a singsong voice. "Anyway, I've got to run. Early shift tomorrow. Text me updates!"

After we hang up, I force myself to stand, legs still wobbly. I make my way to the bathroom. The woman in the mirror looks like me but somehow transformed—cheeks flushed, eyes bright, lips slightly swollen from nervously biting them all evening.

The shower does little to wash away thoughts of him. Water cascades down my body, but I can still feel the weight of his gaze during the drive home. The way his eyes had tracked every movement, how they'd darkened when I'd accidentally brushed against him while reaching for the car door.

Now, in the shower, the water follows the same path I imagine his hands would. Down my arms, across my hips. It's not just hot—it's *him,* burning into me, seeping under my skin like he left something behind I can't rinse off. I press my palms to the tile, trying to steady myself, but it's useless. The water trails his memory, and I let it.

"It's just attraction," I mutter, wrapping myself in a towel. "A perfectly normal biological response to an objectively attractive man." My phone buzzes again on the counter. I reach for it with dripping fingers.

DOMINIC

Sweet dreams, Octavia. I'll send a car for you tomorrow. 8 AM sharp.

Not a request—a statement. The presumption should irritate me, but instead, a thrill runs down my spine. I towel off quickly and crawl into bed. I grab my phone again and before I can overthink it I send him a quick text.

ME

Goodnight, Dominic.

I can't stop thinking about the way he put his hand on the small of my back. This man is so insanely intimidating. The way he called me *Little Minx*, the way his large hand enveloped mine when he helped me out of the car. My body feels like it's on fire just remembering it.

I toss and turn, my sheets tangling around my legs as sleep evades me. Every time I close my eyes, I see his face—those intense green eyes that seem to strip away all my defenses, the slight curl of his lips when he caught me staring at him.

"I need to get a grip," I say to the ceiling, but my mind is already betraying me—stuck on thick veins, tight sleeves and the kind of arms that don't belong in polite company. Lena is right, I am so fucked.

My phone glows again in the darkness. I snatch it up, heart hammering.

DOMINIC

Good girl.

Just two words, but they send a shiver through me that has nothing to do with the temperature. I press the phone against my chest, feeling a warmth spread through me that's equal parts excitement and dread. I can't sleep. Two hours of staring at the ceiling, and all I can think about is Dominic Callahan. How is it possible for someone to consume my thoughts this completely after just one day? I roll over, burying my face in the pillow, trying to smother the burning in my cheeks.

When I served him drinks at Rustic Harbor, he was just a customer—intimidating, yes, with his tailored suits and commanding presence—but still just a customer. I could keep my distance behind the bar, pour his whiskey neat, and pretend that my hands didn't tremble when he looked at me. But now? Now, I'll be seeing him every day, breathing the same air, existing in his orbit.

I reach for my phone again, scrolling back through our brief conversation. "Good girl." The words seem to pulse on the screen.

Something about them makes my stomach tighten in a way that's not entirely unpleasant.

"He's probably like this with everyone. It doesn't mean anything." I mutter, forcing myself to set the phone down.

But even as I say it, I know it's a lie. The way he looked at me tonight wasn't how someone looks at "everyone." It was intense, possessive almost, like he could see right through me.

I throw off my covers and pad to the kitchen for water, my oversized sleep shirt brushing against my thighs. The cool tile against my bare feet grounds me momentarily. I lean against the counter, sipping slowly, trying to cool the heat that seems to have taken permanent residence under my skin.

My reflection in the window above the sink shows a woman I barely recognize—flushed, wide-eyed, hair a wild tangle around my shoulders. This isn't me. I don't get flustered over men, especially men who wouldn't look twice at someone with my curves in broad daylight.

Because that's the truth, isn't it? Men like Dominic Callahan don't end up with women like me. They date supermodels and socialites with perfect bodies and pedigrees. Not former bartenders with thick thighs and insecurities. "Get it together, Octavia," I whisper to my reflection. "This is just a job. An opportunity. Don't ruin it by developing feelings for your boss."

But, I know it's already too late. Something shifted between us tonight. In the close confines of his luxury car, with the city lights painting shadows across his sharp jawline, something dangerous and thrilling had sparked to life.

I drag myself back to bed, setting an early alarm. Whatever this is—this pull, this tension—I need to get it under control before morning. I need to be professional, competent, not the trembling mess I've been since he touched me.

Sleep finally comes, but my dreams are filled with green eyes and large hands unbuttoning my blouse in his office. I wake with a gasp, sheets damp with sweat. The digital clock on my nightstand reads 3:42 AM. Too early to be awake, too late to hope for any meaningful rest before my alarm. I press my thighs together, trying to ignore the ache that lingers there. It was just a dream, but the wetness between my legs tells a different story.

I roll onto my side, hugging my pillow close. What would Dominic think if he knew I was dreaming about him? Those large hands exploring every inch of me, his lips trailing fire across my skin. Would he be disgusted by my curves? Or would he—

No. I can't let myself go there.

I force myself out of bed and into the shower again, this time the need overcomes me as I pull down the shower wand and angle it directly between my legs. The pulsing water hits my aching bud and I gasp, bracing myself against the tile wall with my free hand. I close my eyes and immediately see him— looming over me, those intense green eyes watching me come undone.

"Dominic," I whisper, the name escaping my lips before I can stop it. The water pressure intensifies my pleasure as I adjust the angle, imagining it's his fingers touching me instead. I picture his large hands gripping my thick thighs, spreading them wider as he kneels before me.

My breathing is ragged as I move the shower head in small circles. Heat builds low in my belly, coiling tighter with each passing second. In my mind, Dominic's voice is rough with desire. "That's it, little minx. Show me how much you want me."

The orgasm crashes through me unexpectedly, making my knees buckle. I bite down on my lip to muffle my cry as waves of pleasure pulse through my body. As the aftershocks subside, I slide down to the shower floor, water still cascading over me.

Reality crashes back like a bucket of cold water. What am I doing? Fantasizing about my boss while masturbating in my shower at 4 AM? This is beyond inappropriate. This is career suicide.

I shut off the water and step out, wrapping myself in a towel. My reflection in the foggy mirror looks guilty, cheeks flushed, lips parted. I look thoroughly debauched, and I haven't even been touched.

"Pull yourself together," I whisper to my reflection. "This is just a crush. A wildly inappropriate, potentially disastrous crush."

But the memory of his text message—"Good girl"—sends another wave of heat through me. I've never reacted this way to anyone before. Never felt so completely consumed by desire for a man I barely know.

I dry off and try to focus on getting ready for the day ahead. It takes three outfit changes before I settle on something that feels both professional and flattering—a dark green skirt that hugs my curves without being too tight, paired with a silky cream blouse that shows just a hint of cleavage. I apply my makeup carefully, trying to achieve that perfect balance between "put together" and "not trying too hard."

By the time my alarm finally goes off at 6:30, I've been awake for hours, alternating between anxiety and arousal. I check my phone one last time before leaving—no new messages from him. I'm not sure if I'm relieved or disappointed.

The car arrives precisely at 8 AM, just as he promised. The driver, an older man with a kind smile, holds the door open for me.

"Good morning, Ms. Moore. Mr. Callahan instructed me to take you directly to the office."

Of course he did. I slide into the sleek black car, smoothing my skirt beneath me. The leather seat is cool against my bare legs, sending a shiver up my spine. As the driver pulls away from my apartment building, I take a deep breath, trying to steady my racing heart.

The city slides by outside the window, a blur of colors and shapes that can't penetrate the fog of my thoughts. Every minute brings me closer to him. To Dominic. To those penetrating green eyes that haunt my dreams.

My phone buzzes in my purse, and I nearly jump out of my skin. With trembling fingers, I fish it out, already knowing who it is before I see the screen.

DOMINIC

On your way?

Such a simple question, but it sends butterflies swarming through my stomach. I type back quickly, before I can overthink it.

ME

Yes. The car just picked me up.

Three dots appear immediately. I watch them, hypnotized, as they dance across the screen.

DOMINIC

Good. I'll be waiting.

Heat floods my cheeks. The words themselves are innocent enough, but something about the way he phrases it—like he's been counting the minutes until he sees me again—makes my insides turn to liquid.

The driver catches my eye in the rearview mirror. "First week at Digi Pulse, Ms. Moore?"

"Second day, actually," I say, grateful for the distraction.

He nods knowingly. "Mr. Callahan doesn't usually arrange transportation for new employees."

I swallow hard, unsure how to respond. "I don't have a car," I offer lamely, though I know that doesn't explain Dominic's unusual attention.

"Well, you must have made quite an impression," the driver says with a smile that seems to suggest he knows more than he's letting on.

I turn my attention back to my phone, my pulse quickening as I read his message again. "I'll be waiting." The words echo in my mind, stirring up images from last night's dream—his large hands gripping my waist, his lips at my neck, his voice rough against my ear.

The car pulls up to the imposing glass building of Digi Pulse headquarters far too quickly. I check my reflection in my compact mirror one last time, adjusting a strand of red hair and dab at my lipstick. My blue eyes stare back at me, wide with anticipation and something else—desire, plain and simple.

"Thank you," I tell the driver as he opens my door.

"My pleasure, Ms. Moore. Mr. Callahan asked me to tell you he's in the executive conference room on the top floor."

Of course. Not his office, where others might see us together, but somewhere more private. My stomach flips at the thought.

The elevator ride feels endless. I watch the numbers climb higher, each floor stripping away the distance between us. When the doors finally slide open on the top floor, I'm greeted by an empty hallway of polished marble. My heels click against the floor, the sound echoing in the silence. The conference room door looms ahead, and I pause before it, taking a deep breath to steady myself.

I can do this. It's just a meeting. Just work.

My hand trembles slightly as I reach for the handle, but before I can touch it, the door swings open, and there he is.

Dominic fills the doorway, his broad shoulders blocking the light from behind him. He's dressed impeccably in a charcoal suit that hugs his muscular frame, the top button of his white shirt undone to reveal a tantalizing glimpse of tanned skin beneath. Those green eyes sweep over me slowly, from my face down to my shoes and back up again, lingering on the curves of my hips, the swell of my breasts beneath my cream blouse.

"Octavia," he says, my name rolling off his tongue like a caress.

"Right on time."

I swallow hard, suddenly very aware of how alone we are on this floor. "Good morning, Mr. Callahan—I mean, Dominic."

The corner of his mouth twitches upward. "Come in."

He steps aside, but not far enough. I have to brush past him to enter, and the brief contact sends electricity shooting through me. His cologne envelops me—sandalwood and something darker, more primal—and for a moment, I'm transported back to my shower this morning, to the fantasy that made me unravel.

The conference room is massive, with floor-to-ceiling windows offering a panoramic view of the city sprawled below. A long glass table dominates the space, surrounded by leather chairs. The room is empty except for us.

"Did you sleep well?" Dominic asks, his voice deceptively casual as he closes the door behind me. The soft click of the lock engaging makes my pulse quicken.

"I—yes, thank you." The lie slips out easily. I can hardly tell him I spent half the night fantasizing about him, the other half touching myself to thoughts of him.

He moves closer, his tall frame looming over mine. "You look tired, Octavia. Those shadows under your eyes tell a different story."

My cheeks burn at his observation. "Just first-week jitters, I suppose."

"Hmm." The sound is noncommittal, but his eyes are knowing, as if he can see right through me. He takes another step forward, and I instinctively move backward until my thighs hit the edge of the conference table. There's nowhere else to go.

"I wasn't sure if you'd come today," he says, his voice dropping to a lower register that makes goosebumps rise on my arms.

"Why wouldn't I?" I manage to ask, though my throat feels

suddenly dry.

Dominic tilts his head slightly, studying me with those piercing green eyes. "Most people find me... intimidating. Especially after our little car ride yesterday."

I swallow hard, trying to maintain eye contact despite the heat rising in my cheeks. "I'm not most people."

A slow smile spreads across his face, transforming his features from merely handsome to devastating. "No," he agrees, "you're certainly not."

He reaches out, and for one wild moment, I think he's going to touch me. Instead, he picks up a folder from the table beside me. "The marketing team needs these numbers reviewed by noon. I thought we could go through them together."

Work. Right. That's why I'm here.

"Of course," I say, relief and disappointment warring within me. I accept the folder, careful not to let our fingers brush. "I'll get right on it."

"Sit," he commands, pulling out a chair for me. I obey, sinking into the plush leather chair as he takes the one directly beside me rather than across the table. He's close enough that our knees almost touch, close enough that I can feel the heat radiating off his body.

"Thank you for the car this morning," I say, desperate to break the tension that's building between us. "It wasn't necessary."

"I disagree." His voice is firm, brooking no argument. "I need you here early, and I want to ensure you arrive safely."

"I've been getting myself to work safely for years now," I point out, a hint of defiance creeping into my tone. "Uber works just fine."

Dominic's jaw tightens almost imperceptibly. "Uber is not always reliable, and not to mention dangerous. My employees deserve better."

"Do all your employees get personal car service?" The question slips out before I can stop it.

His green eyes lock with mine, intensity blazing in their depths. "No. They don't."

The implication hangs in the air between us, heavy and undeniable. I break eye contact first, focusing on the folder in my hands. The numbers swim before my eyes, meaningless in the face of his proximity.

"Is there something you want to ask me, Octavia?" His voice has dropped to that dangerous low register again.

My heart hammers against my ribs. "I'm not sure what you mean."

"I think you do." He leans closer, his breath warm against my cheek. "Eyes on me. You've had something brewing behind that look since the second you walked in. Ask it. Or I'll drag it out of you myself."

My mouth goes dry. His proximity makes it hard to think straight, hard to remember all the reasons why I shouldn't be feeling this way about my boss. I gather my courage and meet his gaze.

"Why me?" The words come out barely above a whisper. "Out of all the employees at Digi Pulse, why am I the one getting special treatment?"

A slow smile spreads across his face, transforming his features from intimidating to devastatingly handsome. He doesn't answer immediately, instead reaching out to tuck a strand of hair behind my ear. His fingers brush against my skin, and I suppress a shiver.

"I think you know the answer to that, little minx," he says finally, his voice low and intimate.

I swallow hard. "I'd prefer if you spelled it out for me, Mr. Callahan."

"Dominic," he corrects, his eyes darkening. "And I think clarity between us would be... dangerous."

"Dangerous," I repeat, the word hanging between us like smoke.

He leans back slightly, creating just enough space for me to breathe again. "Let's focus on these numbers, shall we? The marketing team needs them by noon."

The abrupt shift in conversation leaves me rattled. One moment he's looking at me like he wants to devour me, the next he's all business. It's giving me whiplash.

"Of course," I say, straightening in my seat and forcing myself to focus on the spreadsheets he's placed before me. "These quarterly projections seem optimistic. Are you sure the sales team can hit these targets?"

He studies me for a moment, a hint of approval in his eyes. I've managed to surprise him with my quick professional pivot.

"That's exactly what I wanted your opinion on," he says, his voice back to that controlled, CEO tone. "Fresh eyes. You haven't been indoctrinated into our corporate group-think yet."

I scan the numbers more carefully, grateful for the distraction from the heat still lingering in my cheeks.

"The Q3 projections especially seem ambitious given the seasonal trends in this industry." I take a breath.

"Go on." There's genuine interest in his voice now.

I bite my lip, organizing my thoughts. "Based on what I've seen, digital engagement typically dips during summer months when people are outdoors more. Your team is projecting a 15% increase during that period, which seems..."

"Delusional?" he offers, the corner of his mouth quirking up.

"I was going to say 'optimistic' again, but yes." I smile, despite myself. "Unless you have a major campaign planned that I'm not aware of."

Dominic leans back in his chair, regarding me with newfound interest. "No major campaign. Just overeager department heads trying to impress me." He reaches for the spreadsheet, his fingers brushing against mine in the process. "Mark up the areas you think are unrealistic. I want specifics, not just gut feelings."

"Yes, Mr.—Dominic," I correct myself, pulling my hand away from his. The brief contact sends electricity up my arm. I focus on the task, scribbling notes in the margins with the pen he provides.

While I work, I can feel his eyes on me. Not on the spreadsheet, but on my face, my hands, the curve of my neck as I bend over the papers. It's distracting.

"You bite your lip when you concentrate," he observes quietly.

I freeze, suddenly self-conscious. "Bad habit."

"I didn't say it was bad." His voice has that dangerous edge again, the one that makes heat pool low in my belly.

I clear my throat and slide the marked-up spreadsheet toward him. "There. I've highlighted the projections that seem unrealistic and suggested more attainable targets."

Dominic studies my work, his expression unreadable. After a moment, he nods. "Good. Very good, in fact." He looks up at me, and there's something like respect there, mingling with the hunger that's been lingering since I walked in. "Most new hires wouldn't have the courage to question these numbers."

"Most new hires probably didn't tend a bar for three years," I say with a small laugh. "You learn to read people when you're serving them drinks. Know when they're bluffing, when they're showing off."

His eyebrows lift slightly. "And what am I doing right now, bartender? Am I bluffing? Showing off?"

I meet his gaze, feeling a surge of boldness I didn't know I possessed. "Neither. You're testing me. Seeing if I'm as smart as you thought I was when you hired me."

A slow smile spreads across his face, genuine and almost boyish in its delight. It transforms him from intimidating CEO to something far more dangerous—a man I could actually fall for.

"And am I going to be disappointed?" he asks, voice low.

I straighten in my chair. "I don't think so."

"Good." He stands abruptly, towering over me. "Because I hate being disappointed, Octavia."

The way he says my name—like it's something forbidden on his tongue—sends a shiver down my spine. I rise too, needing to feel at less of a disadvantage, though, even standing, the top of my head barely reaches his shoulders.

"I should get back to my desk," I say, though there's a part of me that doesn't want to leave this charged atmosphere, this private bubble.

"Actually," Dominic says, checking his watch, "I need you to join me for a meeting with the marketing department in ten minutes. They should see for themselves what you've found." He gathers the spreadsheets, sliding them into a leather portfolio. "I want you to present your analysis."

My stomach drops. "Present? To the entire marketing department? Today?"

"Is that a problem?" His tone is casual, but there's a challenge in his eyes.

"I—no, it's just—I've been here exactly one day." I take a deep breath, trying to calm my racing heart. "They're going to wonder why the new girl is critiquing their work."

Dominic steps closer, close enough that I have to tilt my head back to maintain eye contact. "They'll wonder because I told them to listen. That's all they need to know."

The power he wields so effortlessly is Intimidating as hell, but there's a pull to him—like gravity laced with danger. The kind that makes you lean in when you know you shouldn't. I've never been the type to fall for the alpha male routine, but there's something about the absolute certainty with which he moves through the world that makes my knees weak.

"Fine," I concede. "But don't blame me if they hate me by lunchtime."

A small smile plays at his lips. "They won't hate you. They might fear you a little, being associated with me, but that's not a bad thing in this company."

"Associated with you?" I repeat, my voice higher than I'd like.

"My protégée," he clarifies, though something in his eyes suggests he's enjoying my discomfort. "Unless you'd prefer another title?"

My cheeks flush at the implication. "Protégée is fine."

"Good." His hand comes to rest at the small of my back as he guides me toward the door. It's a casual touch, the kind that could be explained away as professional courtesy, but the heat of his palm burns through the thin fabric of my blouse, branding me. "Let's go show them what you can do."

The walk to the meeting room feels like a march to my execution. Dominic's hand remains at my back, a constant reminder of his presence, his power, his apparent faith in me. Employees we pass in the hallway watch us with curious eyes, their gazes lingering on his hand at my back. I can practically hear the whispers that will follow.

"Nervous?" he asks as we approach the glass-walled conference room where the marketing team is already gathered.

"Terrified," I admit, seeing no point in lying when my trembling hands would betray me anyway.

Dominic leans down, his lips close to my ear. "Don't be. I wouldn't put you in this position if I didn't think you could handle it." His breath is warm against my skin, sending goosebumps racing down my arm. "Besides, I'll be right beside you."

Somehow, that's both reassuring and terrifying in equal measure.

CHAPTER FOUR

Octavia

The room falls silent as we enter, a dozen pairs of eyes tracking our movement. I recognize a few faces from my brief orientation yesterday, but most are strangers, their expressions varying from mild curiosity to barely-concealed judgment. I smooth my skirt nervously, grateful that I spent the extra time on my appearance this morning.

"Team, this is Octavia Moore," Dominic's voice carries effortlessly through the conference room. "She joined our marketing department yesterday. I trust you'll all to make her feel welcome." There's something in the way he says 'welcome' that makes my stomach flutter, though his face reveals nothing.

I offer a small wave and a smile that feels too tight. "Looking forward to working with everyone."

Dominic gestures to an empty chair halfway down the table. "You can sit there for now." As I move toward it, he adds, just loud enough for me to hear, "Unless you'd prefer the hot seat next to me."

I pause, glancing at him. His expression is professionally neutral, but there's a glint in his eyes that makes me wonder if I imagined the

comment. Two can play this game.

"I think I'll work my way up to the hot seat," I reply quietly, matching his tone. "Best not to peak too early."

A flicker of surprise crosses his face, but he masks it quickly with a smirk aimed in my direction.

The meeting begins, and I try to focus on the quarterly projections being displayed, but my awareness of Dominic is distracting. He commands the room with an easy confidence, occasionally tossing questions that cut through rehearsed answers and force people to think on their feet. I take notes diligently, determined to appear competent despite the nervous energy thrumming through me.

When someone mentions the Hartwell campaign—the project I was hired to help with—Dominic turns to me.

"Octavia, any initial thoughts on their social media strategy?"

I wasn't expecting to be put on the spot so soon. Everyone's attention shifts to me, and for a moment, my mind goes blank. I take a deep breath, recalling the research I'd stayed up late reviewing.

"Their current approach lacks cohesion," I say, my voice steadier than I feel. "They're trying to appeal to too many demographics without a clear brand voice. I think we should narrow their focus to millennials with disposable income who value sustainability, then build authentic storytelling around that."

Dominic studies me for a beat longer than necessary. "Not bad for day two," he says finally. "Though, I'm curious what makes you think millennials are their key demographic?"

The challenge in his tone is unmistakable. Is he testing me or undermining me? Either way, I refuse to shrink.

"Their pricing point and product design," I respond, meeting his gaze. "Plus, the data shows their highest conversion rates come from Instagram campaigns targeting the 25-38 age range. We could double those numbers with the right approach."

A hint of approval flashes across his face. "Bold claim."

"Bold strategies get results," I counter. As soon as I say the words I can feel my whole body flush with heat.

Dominic's eyes darken slightly, and his lips curve into a smile that doesn't quite reach professional territory. "Indeed they do, Ms. Moore." He holds my gaze a beat longer than necessary before turning back to the group. "Let's break for fifteen minutes."

As the room empties, I gather my notes, trying to calm my racing heart. What is it about this man that makes every interaction feel like stepping onto a high wire?

"You handled that well," comes his voice from behind me, closer than I expected.

I turn to find him leaning against the table, tie slightly loosened, those penetrating eyes focused entirely on me. The conference room suddenly feels too small, too warm.

"Thank you," I say, proud that my voice comes out steady. "Though, I get the feeling you were deliberately testing me."

"Testing you?" He chuckles, the sound rich and low. "I prefer to think of it as... creating opportunities for you to shine."

"How generous of you," I reply dryly, tucking a wayward curl behind my ear.

His eyes track the movement. "I'm known for my generosity."

"Is that what you're known for?" The words slip out before I can stop them, tinged with a playfulness I hadn't intended.

Dominic straightens, taking a step closer. Not enough to be inappropriate, but enough that I can smell his cologne – something woodsy and expensive that makes my pulse quicken.

"Among other things," he says, voice dropping slightly. "I prefer to let people discover my... qualities on their own."

The way he says it makes warmth blossom low in my belly. I shift my weight, suddenly very aware of how my pencil skirt hugs my curves.

"Well, I've always been a quick study," I respond, raising my chin slightly. "Though I find hands-on learning most effective."

His eyes flicker with something dangerous before he masks it with professional distance. "Your enthusiasm for the job is noted, Octavia."

"Octavia," he repeats, my name sounding richer in his deep voice. "Latin origin. Means 'eighth'."

I blink in surprise. "You know etymology?"

"I know many things that might surprise you." A slight smile plays at the corner of his mouth. "I make it a point to understand what's valuable."

The way his eyes linger on me suggests he's not just talking about my professional skills. Heat crawls up my neck, and I find myself wishing I'd worn something less constricting. I shift my weight again, and he notices—of course he notices.

"Uncomfortable?" he asks, his voice a perfect blend of professional concern and something much less appropriate.

"Not at all," I reply, gathering my composure. "Just... processing all the new information. It's only day two, after all."

"And you're already making quite the impression." His eyes drop briefly to my lips before returning to meet my gaze. "The Hartwell team specifically requested someone with fresh ideas. I think you might be exactly what they've been looking for."

"And what about you?" The question escapes before I can censor it. "What are you looking for, Dominic?"

A slow smile spreads across his face, transforming his features from merely handsome to devastating. "Excellence," he says simply. "In all things."

The way he says it sends a shiver down my spine that has nothing to do with the office air conditioning.

"Well," I manage, "I've never been one to aim for mediocrity."

"I suspected as much." He straightens suddenly, creating distance between us as voices approach the conference room.

As the meeting breaks, I grab my phone, discovering a text from Lena.

LENA

How's day 2 with Mr. Gorgeous Boss Man? Has he ravished you on his desk yet? 😈

I nearly choke, glancing around to make sure no one can see my screen. My fingers fly across the keyboard:

ME

OMG stop! People can see my phone! And NO. It's professional. Mostly. I think? Call you later.

I slide my phone back into my pocket just as Dominic approaches again, a stack of folders in his hands.

"These are the previous campaign materials for Hartwell," he says, placing them in front of me. "I'd like your analysis by tomorrow morning."

"All of these?" I ask, eyeing the substantial pile.

One corner of his mouth quirks up. "Problem, Ms. Moore? I thought you weren't aiming for mediocrity."

"Just clarifying expectations," I counter, meeting his challenge with a smile. "I'll have it on your desk first thing."

"I have no doubt." He closes the space between us, voice barely above a murmur. "You strike me as someone who delivers... thoroughly."

My cheeks warm at the double entendre, but I refuse to be flustered. "I believe in exceeding expectations, Mr. Callahan."

His eyes darken slightly, and for a moment, we're locked in a silent exchange that makes my heart race. Then, as if remembering where we are, he steps back and adjusts his tie.

"Good. I'll look forward to seeing what you come up with." With that, he turns and walks off, and no—I don't miss the way those muscles move under his shirt. The man is a walking distraction, and he damn well knows it.

I exhale slowly, not realizing I'd been holding my breath. What is it about this man that makes every interaction feel like verbal foreplay?

Back at my desk, I dive into the Hartwell files, determined to prove myself professionally despite the distracting thoughts that keep intruding. The afternoon passes in a blur of market research and campaign analytics. I'm so absorbed that I barely notice when people begin packing up for the day.

"Still here?"

I look up to find Dominic leaning against the partition of my cubicle, jacket discarded and sleeves rolled up to reveal tanned tattooed forearms. Of course he looks hotter like this. Like I needed *another* reason to struggle through this workday without combusting.

"Just finishing up with these files," I say, gesturing to the organized chaos I've created. "There's a lot to digest."

"Most people would have taken that pile home and claimed they needed more time." He sounds impressed, which sends a ridiculous flutter through my chest.

"Most people aren't me." I straighten in my chair, stretching my neck slightly. "Besides, I work better with fewer distractions."

His eyes drift over my desk, taking in the color-coded sticky notes and organized stacks. "And what distracts you, Octavia?"

The way he says my name makes it sound like he's savoring every syllable. I swallow hard, trying to maintain my professional demeanor.

"The usual things," I say vaguely, shuffling some papers.

"Background noise, interruptions..." I look up at him through my lashes. "Intimidating bosses hovering over my workspace."

A slow smile spreads across his face. "Intimidating? Is that how you see me?"

"Among other things," I echo his earlier words, enjoying the flash of recognition in his eyes.

"Interesting." He moves closer, examining the notes I've spread across my desk. "You've already identified the three main weaknesses in their previous campaign." He sounds genuinely impressed, which sends a ridiculous thrill through me.

"It wasn't difficult to spot. Their messaging is scattered, their visuals inconsistent, and they're completely missing the emotional connection with their audience." I point to my analysis, suddenly eager to show him my thought process. "See here? They're selling sustainability as a feature, not as a lifestyle their customers can feel good about embracing."

He leans in, shoulder nearly brushing mine. That same scent—woodsy, dark, unmistakably him, wraps around me like a memory I never shook. My focus doesn't stand a chance.

"You've got good instincts," he murmurs, close enough that I can feel his breath on my cheek. I try not to visibly shiver.

"Thank you," I say, attempting to focus on the papers instead of his proximity. "I think with the right approach, we could transform their entire brand perception."

"Bold strategies," he murmurs, his voice a low rumble that I feel more than hear.

I turn my head slightly, suddenly aware of how close our faces are. "Like I said earlier, they get results."

For a moment, something electric passes between us. His gaze drops to my lips for just a heartbeat before he straightens.

"You've done good work here, Octavia. I'm impressed." He takes a step back, creating a respectable distance between us. "It's past seven. Let's go, I'll take you home now."

My heart skips. "Oh, that's not necessary. I can just grab an Uber—"

"An Uber, little minx? You know how I feel about Uber."

I freeze, my eyes widening at the nickname. The way he says it sends a dangerous shiver down my spine that I try desperately to ignore.

"Little minx?" I repeat, raising an eyebrow and trying to sound indignant rather than flustered.

Dominic's eyes glint with amusement. "If the shoe fits." He gestures to my organized chaos of notes. "Meticulous and mischievous in equal measure, I'd say."

I feel my cheeks flush with heat, but I refuse to be rattled by his teasing. I'm not about to let his teasing get to me. He thinks I'm just being playful? That's cute. I am a lot more calculating than I let on.

"I prefer to think of it as thorough and forthright," I counter, gathering my things with deliberate movements. "Though, I suppose 'meticulous and mischievous' has a better ring to it."

"It certainly does." He watches me slide the files into my bag. "And I wasn't asking about taking you home, Octavia. I'm telling you. It's late, you've worked hard, and I'd like to ensure you get home safely."

The authority in his voice should irritate me—I've had enough of controlling men to last a lifetime—but something about the way he says it feels more protective than possessive.

"Fine," I concede, slinging my bag over my shoulder. "But only because I'm too tired to argue, and Ubers are getting expensive."

His smile is triumphant, "A practical decision. I like that."

We walk to the elevator in companionable silence, though I'm acutely aware of his presence beside me—the slight brush of his arm against mine, the way his cologne surrounds me. The elevator doors close, trapping us in the small space together, and my heart rate kicks up a notch.

Suddenly, the elevator jolts to a stop, the lights flickering once before plunging us into darkness. I gasp, my hand instinctively reaching out and finding Dominic's arm.

"Looks like we're stuck," he says, his voice calm in the darkness. I can feel the solid muscle of his forearm under my fingers, and I reluctantly let go, hyper aware of the contact.

The emergency lights flicker on, casting us in a soft blue glow that makes his features look almost ethereal. In this light, the sharpness of his jawline and the intensity of his eyes are somehow magnified.

"Are you okay?" he asks, studying my face with concern.

"Fine," I say, though my heart is racing for reasons that have nothing to do with the stalled elevator. "Just surprised."

He pulls out his phone, the screen illuminating his face as he makes a quick call to building maintenance. I try not to stare at the way the light catches on his cheekbones or how his lips move as he speaks.

"They'll have us out in about fifteen minutes," he says after hanging up. "A minor power surge. Nothing to worry about."

Fifteen minutes alone in a confined space with Dominic Callahan. My pulse quickens.

"So," I say, leaning against the wall of the elevator, trying to appear casual. "Is this how you typically end the workday? Trapping new employees in elevators?"

His laugh is unexpected and genuine, the sound rich and low in the small space. "You've caught me. It's my special onboarding process."

"I knew it," I say, mock serious. "Clever strategy—evaluate how employees handle unexpected crises."

"Something like that." His eyes lock on mine, and in the blue emergency light, they look almost predatory. "You're handling it remarkably well."

"I've been through worse than being stuck in an elevator with an attractive man," I say, then immediately feel heat rush to my cheeks. Did I really just call him attractive out loud?

Dominic's eyebrow raises slightly, a slow smile spreading across his face. "Attractive, hm?"

I lift my chin, refusing to backtrack. "I have functioning eyes, Dominic. It's not exactly a controversial observation."

He takes a step closer, and suddenly the elevator feels much smaller. "What other observations have those functioning eyes made about me, I wonder?"

My breath catches. We're venturing into dangerous territory now. "That you enjoy keeping people off-balance," I say, my voice softer than I intended. "That you notice details others miss. That you're used to being in control."

"All true," he murmurs, his gaze intensifying. "And what about you, Octavia? Do you always need to be in control?"

The question hangs between us, loaded with implications that make my pulse race. "I've learned to be," I answer honestly. "It's safer that way." I'm suddenly aware of how vulnerable I feel in this moment, not just physically trapped in the elevator, but emotionally exposed.

Dominic studies me, his expression softening slightly. "Safer, perhaps. But is it more fulfilling?"

The question hits closer to home than he could possibly know. Before I can formulate a response, the elevator jerks back to life, the regular lights flooding the small space. The moment between us shatters, but something lingers in the air.

We descend to the parking garage in silence, but it's not uncomfortable—it's charged with unspoken words and possibilities. When the doors open, he gestures for me to exit first.

"My car is this way," he says, guiding me with a light touch at the small of my back that makes desire coil low and tight inside me.

The Porsche gleams under the garage lights. He opens the passenger door for me, and I slide into the seat, trying to keep my composure.

"You remember where I live?" I ask as he gets in beside me.

"I remember everything about you," he says simply, starting the engine. The car comes to life with a throaty purr that somehow matches its owner perfectly.

As we pull out of the garage, I steal glances at his profile—the strong line of his jaw, the way his hands rest confidently on the steering wheel. The city lights slide across his features as we drive, creating a kaleidoscope of shadows and light that's mesmerizing.

"You're staring," he says without looking at me, a hint of amusement in his voice.

I quickly look away, heat rising to my cheeks. "Just admiring the car," I lie, smoothing invisible wrinkles from my skirt.

"Just the car?" His voice carries that teasing edge that makes my stomach flip. "I'm wounded."

"Your ego can handle it," I reply, trying to regain my composure. "I'm sure you're not lacking in admiration."

He chuckles, a rich sound that fills the luxury interior. "You'd be surprised."

"Somehow I doubt that." I watch the city blur past, streetlights creating rhythmic patterns across his face. "Men like you rarely go unnoticed."

"Men like me?" Dominic asks, glancing at me briefly before returning his attention to the road. "And what kind of man am I, Octavia?"

My name sounds like a caress on his tongue. I swallow hard.

"Successful. Confident. The kind who knows exactly what he wants and how to get it." I pause, wondering if I'm being too bold. "The kind of man who makes women wonder what it would be like to..." I trail off, realizing I'm venturing into dangerous territory.

"To what?" he prompts, his voice dropping lower, the rumble of it vibrating through me.

I turn to face him fully, emboldened by the darkness of the car and the electricity that's been building between us all day. "To surrender control. Just for a little while."

CHAPTER FIVE

Dominic

God, what is she doing to me? The thought of her relinquishing control, even for a moment, has my insides twisting. If only she realized the depths of my desire, to make her yield every ounce of control to me, to dominate her completely.

I glance over, those blue eyes framed by fiery curls that seem to dance with the setting sun. She's fumbling with her seatbelt, her delicate fingers working the clasp as the leather strap crosses between her breasts. I shouldn't be looking. I shouldn't be noticing how her skirt has ridden up slightly on those thick thighs as she settled into my passenger seat.

"I appreciate the ride again, Mr. Callahan," she says, her voice carrying that hint of playfulness that's becoming dangerously familiar. "Much better than an Uber."

"Dominic," I correct her, my voice rougher than intended. "And it's no trouble."

I hit the gas, feeling the engine's response like an extension of my own racing pulse. The car hugs the curves of the road, and I'm acutely aware of her scent filling the confined space – something floral mixed

with a warmth that's uniquely her.

"This car really suits you," she observes, trailing her fingers over the leather dashboard. I track the movement, imagining those same fingers tracing paths elsewhere.

"How so?" I manage to ask, keeping my eyes firmly on the road.

"Powerful. Precise." She pauses, and I feel her gaze on my profile. "Demanding attention without having to try."

My grip tightens on the steering wheel. "Are we still talking about the car?" I ask, my voice dropping lower.

The corner of her mouth quirks up, and I catch the glint in her eye. "What else would we be talking about, Mr. Callahan?"

That "Mr. Callahan" again. She knows exactly what she's doing, this little minx.

I take a sharp turn, perhaps too aggressively, and her body shifts in the seat. I hear her quick inhale as she steadies herself, her hand accidentally brushing against my thigh. The touch, even through my suit pants, sets my blood on fire.

"Sorry," she murmurs, not sounding sorry at all.

"You should be more careful," I warn, my tone edged with something dangerous. "Distracting the driver can be... risky."

She adjusts herself in the seat, crossing one leg over the other. The movement draws my eye again to those thighs that have been haunting my thoughts since our first meeting.

"I wouldn't want to be a distraction," she says innocently, but there's nothing innocent about the way she's looking at me now. Her blue eyes darken slightly.

The traffic light ahead turns red, and I bring the car to a stop, finally allowing myself to look at her fully. A mistake. Her blouse has the top two buttons undone, revealing the delicate hollow of her throat and the beginning curve of her cleavage. I imagine pressing my lips to that spot, feeling her pulse quicken beneath my lips.

I need to stop thinking like this. This obsession I have had with her needs to stop. A text from Derek pops up on my screen. The contents of it flash on the car's display, momentarily breaking the tension between us.

"Everything okay?" Octavia asks, her voice softer now, genuinely concerned.

I clear my throat and shift in my seat as the light turns green. "Just Derek checking in about tomorrow's meeting."

"He seems nice," she says, settling back into her seat. "Really helped me get oriented yesterday."

"Derek is great," I agree, grateful for the shift in conversation. "Been with me since the beginning of Digi Pulse."

She smiles, and there's something so warm and genuine about it that makes my chest tighten. "I can see why you keep him around. Unlike some bosses, you seem to value loyalty."

"I do," I say, navigating through an intersection. "Loyalty is... everything in business."

"And outside of business?" she asks, her question hanging in the air between us.

I consider her question, feeling the weight of it. "Even more important."

The sun has nearly set now, painting the sky in deep purples and oranges. The light catches in her red curls, making them look like they're on fire. She's looking out the window, her profile illuminated, and I can't help but think she looks like she belongs here, in my car, beside me. When we pull up to her apartment complex, I step out of the car, discreetly adjusting myself to ensure she doesn't notice. When I get to her car door, I can't help but notice she has her phone out texting someone, and I feel an irrational surge of jealousy. Who is she texting?

A boyfriend? Some other man waiting for her upstairs? I have no right to these feelings, but they claw at me nonetheless.

"Home sweet home," she says, looking up at me with those impossibly blue eyes as I open her door. "Thanks again for the ride, Dominic."

My name on her lips sounds different this time—less teasing, more intimate—and it does things to me I can't afford to acknowledge.

"My pleasure," I respond, and I mean it far more than I should.

She steps out, her skirt riding up just a fraction more as she stands, and I have to force myself to look away. When I look back, she's fumbling with her purse, searching for something.

"Everything okay?" I ask.

"Just looking for my keys," she says, then triumphantly pulls them out with a little flourish that makes me smile despite myself. "Got them! Though I should probably attach them to a neon sign or something. I'd lose my head if it wasn't attached."

I chuckle at that, the tension between us momentarily dissolving into something lighter. "That would be a shame. It's a very nice head."

She laughs, a genuine sound that seems to bubble up from somewhere deep inside her. "Well, that's the nicest compliment I've gotten all day. 'Nice head, Octavia.'"

Her impression of my deeper voice makes me laugh, too, the sound unexpected even to myself. When was the last time I laughed this freely?

"I see my compliment skills need work," I say, watching her twirl the keys around her finger.

"Oh, I don't know." She tilts her head, studying me with those perceptive eyes. "You seem quite skilled at many things, Mr. Callahan."

There's that formal address again, but this time I recognize it for what it is—a little game between us, one that sends heat coursing through my veins.

"Would you like to come up for coffee?" she asks suddenly, and I freeze, caught completely off-guard.

The question hangs between us, loaded with possibility. I want to say yes. God, do I want to say yes.

She must see the conflict in my eyes because she quickly adds, "As a thank you for the ride. And the job. Nothing more." But there's a flicker of something in her expression that suggests otherwise. A call interrupts the moment, my phone vibrating in my pocket like an unwelcome alarm.

I glance at the screen and see Marcus's name flashing. "I have to take this," I say, torn between relief and disappointment at the interruption.

"Of course," she nods, stepping back slightly. "CEO stuff never stops, huh?"

"Unfortunately not," I admit, watching her twirl those keys again. "Rain check on the coffee?"

The words are out before I can analyze them, before I can remind myself of all the reasons this is a terrible idea. Her smile widens, genuine and bright. "Rain check it is. Though, fair warning—I make terrible coffee. Like, truly awful. People have been known to dramatically spit it out and run for the nearest sink."

I can't help the laugh that escapes me again. "Is that so?"

"Oh yes. My last boyfriend said it tasted like motor oil filtered through a sweaty gym sock." She wrinkles her nose adorably. "Not that I know what that tastes like, but the visual was... vivid."

"Sounds like your ex had a way with words," I comment, surprised by the sudden flare of dislike for this unknown man.

"Tyler was creative with insults," she says lightly, but I catch something in her tone—a slight dimming of her brightness that makes me want to find this Tyler and throttle him.

My phone won't stop vibrating, demanding attention. Marcus never was patient when it came to business calls.

"Go ahead and answer," Octavia says, nodding toward my still-buzzing phone. "I should head inside anyway. Early morning tomorrow."

I want to tell her to wait, to hold this moment a little longer, but instead, I nod and take a step back. "Right. I'll see you at the office."

She turns to go, then pauses, looking back over her shoulder. "Dominic?"

"Yes?" I respond too quickly, too eagerly.

"Thanks again for the ride." She smiles, and there's something soft and genuine in it that makes my chest ache. "It's nice to know there's more to you than the intimidating CEO everyone at the office whispers about."

Before I can respond, she's walking away, those hips swaying in a rhythm that seems designed to torture me. I don't look away until she slips inside the building without looking back, the phone still vibrating in my hand like it's trying to pull me out of the moment.

"What?" I snap, finally answering.

"Well, hello to you too, sunshine," Marcus drawls. "Bad time?"

I run a hand through my hair, turning back toward my car. "Just dropping an employee home."

"An employee?" Marcus's voice drips with innuendo. "Would this employee happen to be the redhead Derek mentioned? The one you've allegedly been staring at like she's water and you're dying of thirst?"

"Derek needs to learn to keep his mouth shut," I growl into the phone, but there's no real heat in it. Derek has been with me from the beginning, one of the few people I trust implicitly.

"So it is her," Marcus sounds too pleased with himself. "The new marketing hire that's got you all twisted up. Interesting."

"I'm not twisted up," I lie, sliding back into my car and slamming the door harder than necessary. "She needed a ride home. That's all."

"Right. And I'm the Queen of England." Marcus chuckles. "Look, I'm not judging. It's been, what, two years since Sophia? It's about damn time you showed an interest in someone."

The mention of Sophia makes my jaw clench. "What did you call for, Marcus? I doubt it was to discuss my love life."

"Or lack thereof," he quips. "The Westfield deal. Their lawyers sent over some revised terms."

I start the engine, watching the lights of Octavia's building, wondering which window is hers. "And?"

"And they fucked us, Dom. Classic bait and switch."

I pull away from the curb, forcing myself not to look back. "Send me the details. I'll review them tonight."

"Already did," Marcus says, but then his voice drops lower, more serious. "But that's not all."

He hesitates for a second before lowering his voice. "I had Jake dig into Westfield's CFO—Tom Fletcher. Turns out he didn't just fuck a few numbers. He rerouted money from the joint venture fund. The one earmarked for the clinical trial for heart disease, the one your mother was in."

My stomach drops. "The reason the trial stalled," Marcus adds quietly. "The reason she didn't make it. That money never made it to the lab, Dominic. It disappeared, and now we know where it went."

He pauses. "If you want to use it... we've got enough to bury him."

I grip the steering wheel tighter, something dark and familiar stirring in me. "What kind of leverage?"

"The kind that stays between us," Marcus says meaningfully. "The kind that made us successful in the first place."

My jaw clenches so tight it aches. My mind snaps back to the early days—when we were scrappy and ruthless, cutting corners, crossing lines, doing whatever it took to build Digi Pulse into something real. I've made peace with the fact that our success was built on more than clean hands. But this? What Fletcher did? That's different. Most of my employees—Octavia included—don't know that side of me. They see the suits, the success, the surface. They don't see the wreckage we left behind. The lines we crossed. But even at my worst, I never stole hope from dying people. I never gambled with lives.

Fletcher did, and now he's going to learn what happens when you steal from the wrong man.

"Text me his address," I say, my voice dropping to that cold register that Marcus knows well. "I'll pay him a visit tomorrow."

"There he is," Marcus sounds almost proud. "Was starting to worry that redhead had softened you."

I end the call without responding, tossing my phone onto the passenger seat where Octavia sat just minutes ago. Her scent still lingers. The sweet floral scent seems completely at odds with the darkness I'm slipping back into.

For a brief moment with her, I'd forgotten who I really am. What I'm capable of.

I drive home in silence, my thoughts oscillating between the curve of Octavia's smile and the calculated moves I'll need to make tomorrow to ensure Westfield falls in line. The contradiction doesn't escape me— how I can simultaneously want to trace gentle patterns on Octavia's skin with reverent fingertips and also imagine pressing just enough pressure to a man's throat. To make him feel every inch of the warning, to make sure he knows exactly what crossing me will cost. And that the cost won't just be paid. It'll be taken—slowly.

This duality has always existed within me. The public face of Dominic Callahan: successful CEO, ruthless but fair businessman. And the shadow self that does what needs to be done, no matter the cost. It's that darker side that built Digi Pulse from nothing, that protected our interests when conventional methods failed.

I pull into the underground garage, the private gate sliding open without a sound. The elevator opens directly into my penthouse—modern, minimalist, impressive. Empty. Just like me.

As I step inside, dropping my keys on the marble countertop, I check my phone. Marcus has already sent the file on Westfield's CFO, along with his home address and daily schedule. Thorough, as always.

I pour myself two fingers of whiskey, neat, and sink into my leather chair, opening the file. The CFO's face stares back at me from his corporate headshot—mid-50s, balding, practiced smile that doesn't reach his eyes. I recognize the type immediately. Men like him think they're clever, that their schemes are too sophisticated to be detected. They never are.

A notification pops up on my phone—a company-wide email from HR welcoming the new marketing hires. Octavia's professional headshot appears among them, and even in the sterile corporate photo, there's something vibrant about her that reaches through the screen. Her smile seems genuine, reaching her bright blue eyes in a way that makes my chest tighten uncomfortably. I close the email quickly, like I've been caught doing something illicit.

The whiskey burns pleasantly as I swallow, focusing back on the CFO's file. This is what I should be concentrating on—the business, the deal, the next strategic move. Not the way Octavia's voice had softened when she said my name, or how her fingers had brushed against my thigh in the car.

My phone rings again. Derek this time.

"What now?" I answer, more sharply than he deserves.

"Hello to you too," Derek says, unconsciously echoing Marcus's earlier greeting. "Did I catch you at a bad time? Were you busy brooding dramatically while staring out a window?"

Despite myself, I feel the corner of my mouth twitch. "I don't brood."

"Right," Derek chuckles. "And I don't have a receding hairline. We all tell ourselves comfortable lies."

I take another sip of whiskey. "Did you call for a reason, or just to critique my evening activities?"

"Both, actually. I sent over the Q3 projections for your review, and I wanted to give you a heads-up that HR is planning a team building event next month."

I groan audibly, "No."

"Yes," Derek counters cheerfully. "And before you say you're too busy, I've already cleared your schedule. Team chemistry matters, Dom. Especially for the new hires."

"Team chemistry," I repeat flatly, thinking of Octavia and the kind of chemistry I'm trying desperately not to acknowledge. "Fine. But nothing involving trust falls or sharing childhood memories."

"Damn, there goes my suggestion for 'Trauma Bonding: The Workshop,' " Derek quips. "But seriously, I was thinking something more along the lines of an escape room followed by drinks. Low pressure, builds camaraderie, minimal emotional scarring."

I grunt noncommittally, swirling the amber liquid in my glass. "Whatever. Just make it quick and painless."

"Speaking of quick and painless," Derek's tone shifts slightly, "Marcus mentioned the Westfield situation. You sure you want to handle this personally? I could send Jake."

I stare at the CFO's file still open on my screen. "No. This needs a personal touch."

There's a pause on the other end. Derek's been with me long enough to know what that means. He's one of the few who knows about the methods that built our empire, though he keeps his own hands relatively clean.

"Dom," he says finally, his voice unusually serious, "be careful. Not just with Westfield. I saw you leave with Octavia today."

"It was just a ride home," I say defensively, too quickly.

"Right. And that's why you've been drooling over her since she first stepped foot in the building," Derek says dryly. "Look, I'm not saying don't pursue her. God knows you could use someone in your life who makes you smile. I just think you need to be careful about mixing business with pleasure, especially given... your other business methods."

I down the rest of my whiskey in one burning gulp. "I'm not pursuing anyone."

"If you say so," Derek sounds unconvinced. "Just remember, she's not Sophia, and that's a good thing."

My grip tightens on the glass at the mention of Sophia's name twice in one night. "We're done discussing this."

"Fine, fine," Derek concedes. "I'll email you the details for the team building. Try not to look too murderous when I announce it tomorrow."

After we hang up, I pour another drink and walk to the floor-to-ceiling windows overlooking the city. Lights twinkle below like fallen stars, the darkness between them as vast as the space between who I pretend to be and who I actually am.

Would Octavia still look at me with that playful gleam if she knew what I was planning to do tomorrow? If she knew about the threats I've made good on, the competitors I've crushed not just financially but personally? The secrets buried in Digi Pulse's meteoric rise?

I press my forehead against the cool glass. The truth is, I want her. Not just physically—though God knows I want her body under mine. I want her in my bed, writhing beneath me, begging for the release that only I can give her. But more than that, I want her laughter, her wit, her bright perspective that seems to cut through the darkness I've cultivated around myself.

This desire terrifies me more than any business rival ever could.

I drain my second whiskey and set the glass down with more force than necessary. This is ridiculous. I'm Dominic Callahan. I don't pine after employees like some lovesick teenager. I take what I want, when I want it.

Except I can't take Octavia. Not without risking everything I've built.

My phone vibrates with a text from Marcus.

MARCUS

CFO's schedule confirmed. He'll be alone tomorrow evening.

I type back a curt acknowledgment, already mentally preparing for tomorrow's confrontation. This is what I'm good at—the calculated application of pressure until people break. Not... whatever this thing with Octavia is becoming.

I shower quickly, the hot water doing little to wash away the tension coiled inside me. When I finally slide into bed, my mind betrays me again, filled with images of fiery red curls spread across my pillow, blue eyes darkened with desire, those full lips parted on a moan...

"Fuck," I growl into the empty room. It's clear I need a release or my balls might explode. I go to her Instagram page and as I scroll through her feed, my pulse quickens with each image. Most are innocent enough—her hiking with friends, posing with a coffee mug, a sunset at the beach. But there's one from last summer, her in a bikini on some tropical vacation, hair wet and slicked back, droplets of water clinging to her skin like they can't bear to let go. I can relate.

My hand slides beneath the sheets, gripping myself through my boxers. I should stop.

I keep scrolling, finding another photo that makes my breath catch—she's in a form-fitted black dress, the neckline dipping just low enough to make my mouth water, her smile bright and carefree. I imagine peeling that dress off her, revealing inch by inch of creamy skin.

"This is pathetic," I mutter to the empty room, even as I continue to stroke myself. I'm a grown man jerking off to Instagram photos like a teenager. I could have any woman I want with the snap of my fingers. But it's not just any woman I want. It's her.

My pace quickens, my breathing growing ragged as I picture Octavia beneath me, those blue eyes locked on mine, her voice breaking as she cries out my name breathless and needy.

I cum with a strangled groan, shuddering through my release with an intensity that surprises even me. As the pleasure subsides, I'm left with a hollow feeling in my chest, my satisfaction quickly replaced by something dangerously close to shame.

I clean myself up and toss my phone aside, disgusted with my weakness. This isn't me. I don't lose control like this. I'm the one who makes others lose control, who manipulates situations to my advantage. Yet here I am, undone by a marketing hire with bright blue eyes and a laugh that seems to crack something open inside me.

Sleep eludes me for hours, my mind cycling between strategies for tomorrow's confrontation with Westfield's CFO and forbidden images of Octavia. When I finally drift off, my dreams are a confused tangle of power and desire, of her soft curves and whispered pleas mixing with business deals and veiled threats.

I wake before my alarm, the sky outside still dark. My morning routine is military in its precision—cold shower, black coffee, brief workout in my home gym, protein shake. By the time I dress in one of my custom-tailored suits, I've locked away thoughts of Octavia in a compartment labeled, "Deal With Later," and focused my mind on the day ahead.

The drive to the office is mercifully free of traffic at this early hour. I'm usually the first to arrive, savoring the quiet before the chaos of the workday begins.

The elevator doors open to the 30th floor, and I stride across the empty bullpen toward my office, the morning sun painting the sky with streaks of pink and gold. The silence is a welcome companion, allowing me to sort through the day's priorities without distraction.

Or so I thought.

"You're early," a voice says from the break room, startling me.

I turn to find Octavia there, a steaming mug in her hands, wearing a dark green dress that hugs her curves in a way that makes my morning resolve crumble instantly.

"I could say the same to you," I manage, my voice thankfully steady despite the sudden acceleration of my pulse.

She smiles, lifting her mug in a mock toast. "Couldn't sleep. Figured I might as well be productive."

I nod, momentarily unsure of how to proceed. Last night's fantasies are still too fresh, making it difficult to look at her without remembering what I imagined doing to her in the darkness of my bedroom.

"Everything okay?" she asks, concern creeping into her voice as she takes a step closer. "You look... tense."

I clear my throat. "Just a busy day ahead."

"Ah, big boss stuff," she says with that playful lilt that's becoming dangerously familiar. "Very mysterious and important, I'm sure." Despite myself, I feel the corner of my mouth twitch upward. "Very mysterious. Very important."

CHAPTER SIX
Octavia

The way he says *very mysterious* with that smirk on his face sends a chill down my spine, the kind that makes me want to step closer to him, to see what other reactions I can draw out. I'm playing with fire, and I know it.

"How mysterious?" I ask, my voice coming out huskier than I intended. "Like 'I have a collection of rare stamps' mysterious, or 'I have bodies buried in my backyard' mysterious?"

Dominic's smile falters, just for a millisecond, but I catch it. Something flickers behind his eyes—something dark and unreadable—before his mask slips back into place.

"Wouldn't you like to know?" he says, taking a deliberate step back from me. I follow him into his office and laugh, trying to lighten the sudden tension. "I mean, that's why I asked. That's generally how questions work."

He doesn't laugh back. Instead, he turns away, busying himself with straightening a stack of papers on his desk that were already perfectly aligned.

"Octavia," he says my name like it's something fragile. "We should

probably focus on the project."

"Right. The project." I shift my weight from one foot to the other. "Because that's all this is."

The silence between us stretches into something uncomfortable. I hate how we do this dance—stepping close, then retreating like we've been burned. Maybe we have.

Dominic clears his throat. "Look, I didn't mean to—"

"It's fine," I cut him off, waving my hand dismissively while my insides twist. "Really. I get it. Professional boundaries and all that corporate jazz."

His jaw tightens. "It's not that simple."

"Isn't it?" I challenge, surprising myself with my boldness. "Because from where I'm standing, it seems pretty straightforward. You're attracted to me. I'm attracted to you. But you're too... something... to do anything about it."

"Too something?" He raises an eyebrow, and I can see I've sparked that dangerous interest again.

"Too scared. Too professional. Too mysterious," I say, emphasizing the last word with air quotes.

He laughs, but it's hollow. "You have no idea what you're asking for, Octavia."

"Try me," I say, stepping closer again.

His eyes darken. "Do you know what happened to the last person who said that to me?"

I swallow hard. "Let me guess—they're part of your backyard collection?"

That breaks the tension. He laughs genuinely this time, a rich sound that makes my stomach flip. "God, you're impossible."

"I prefer the term 'delightfully persistent,'"

His expression softens, and for a moment, there's a glimpse of something vulnerable behind his carefully constructed walls.

"Delightfully persistent," he repeats, shaking his head. "That's one way to put it."

"I've got others if you'd prefer. Charmingly stubborn? Adorably tenacious?" I offer, tapping my chin thoughtfully. "Spectacularly unwilling to take a hint?"

Dominic runs a hand through his hair, messing up the perfect styling he probably spent twenty minutes on this morning. Something about that small imperfection makes my heart squeeze.

"The hint isn't for you to take, Octavia. It's for me to remember." His voice drops lower. "There are things about me... things I've done..."

"We've all got baggage," I interrupt. "Mine comes with a matching set of daddy issues and an ex who thought I'd never amount to anything so I dumped the asshole."

"It's not the same."

"How would I know?" I cross my arms, suddenly feeling exposed. "For all I know, you could be harboring a terrible secret like... you don't recycle. Or you're one of those people who claps when the plane lands."

He barks out a laugh. "Is that what you think my dark side is? Poor environmental practices and social faux pas?"

"Well, those or you're secretly Batman. The evidence is mounting—wealthy, brooding, mysterious, unreasonably attractive." I tick off the points on my fingers. "Though, I haven't seen any evidence of a butler named Alfred, so maybe you're still in origin story mode."

His smile fades again, and I realize I've hit too close to something real. "Batman had his demons for a reason, Octavia."

"Are we really discussing comic book psychology right now?" I try to keep my tone light, but my heart is racing. Every time I get close to peeling back a layer, he rebuilds his walls faster than I can scale them.

"It's easier than discussing the real thing," he admits, leaning against his desk with his arms crossed. The position pulls his shirt tight across his chest, and I force my eyes back to his face before he catches me staring.

"Okay, let's play it your way." I perch on the edge of his desk, close enough that our arms almost touch. "If you were a superhero, what would your tragic backstory be?"

He stares at me for a long moment, his expression unreadable. "I'm not the hero in this story."

"Anti hero then," I counter. "Those are sexier anyway."

His laugh catches in his throat, turning into something rougher. "You're playing with fire, little minx."

The nickname sends heat spiraling through me. "Maybe I like getting burned."

"No," he says, his voice suddenly serious. "You don't. Trust me on that."

I slide off the desk, irritated by his cryptic warnings. "You know what? Fine. Keep your mysterious aura intact. I'm sure it's very effective on most women."

I grab my bag and head for the door, surprising myself. I'm not usually the one who walks away first.

"Octavia, wait." His voice stops me with my hand on the doorknob. I don't turn around.

"For what, Dominic? More vague warnings about how dangerous you are? More hot-and-cold signals that leave me feeling like I'm on some twisted emotional rollercoaster?" I take a deep breath. "I'm not asking for your life story or a marriage proposal. Just... something real. Anything."

The quiet shift of movement behind me makes my skin prickle. When his hand touches my shoulder, I nearly jump.

"You want something real?" His voice is low, almost a growl. "My last relationship? She didn't just break me, Octavia. She humiliated me. Lied to my face, and then fucked every man who ever shook my hand. Sophia thought she could handle what it meant to be with me. She couldn't. So I stopped letting people in. I buried the emotions. And I buried the men who thought they could cross me. You want to know who I am? I'm not some clean-cut CEO with a perfect track record. I didn't build my company the right way—I built it *my* way. You screw me over; I don't sue you. I end you. Quietly. Permanently. Since her, no one's gotten close. Because I don't give second chances. I give warnings. And if those get ignored, I burn your world to the fucking ground."

His words hang in the air between us, heavy and sharp. I should be terrified. I should be running for the door. Instead, I'm rooted to the spot, my heart pounding against my ribs like it's trying to escape.

"Is this the part where I'm supposed to be scared?" I finally ask, my voice steadier than I feel.

Dominic's eyes narrow. "Most people would be."

"I'm not most people." I turn to face him fully. "And besides, you just told me your big scary secret is that you're... what? Ruthless in business? A man with trust issues? Shocker. I thought you were going to confess to being in a boy band in the 90s or something truly unforgivable."

He blinks, clearly not expecting this reaction. "Did you miss the part about ending people?"

"Oh, please. 'Ending people' could mean anything from getting them fired to making them social pariahs. You're being deliberately vague to sound more dangerous than you are." I roll my eyes. "It's like when guys on dating apps pose with fish they caught to seem rugged and outdoorsy, but all it really says is 'I have no personality beyond this bass.'"

A surprised laugh escapes him. "Are you comparing my dark past to... fish pictures on Tinder?"

"If the overcompensation fits." I shrug, though my heart is still racing. I'm pushing him, and I know it. But something about the way his eyes darken tells me I might be closer to the truth than he wants me to know.

Dominic moves closer, towering over me. "You think you've got me all figured out, don't you?"

"Not even close," I admit. "But I'm getting there. One enigmatic statement at a time."

His fingers brush my cheek, so lightly I almost think I imagined it. "What if I told you I wasn't speaking metaphorically?"

A chill runs through me, but I stand my ground. "Then I'd say you watch too many mafia movies."

"You're impossible," he mutters, but there's a reluctant smile tugging at his lips.

"So you've mentioned." I tilt my head. "Look, we all have baggage. Mine comes with a Tyler-shaped tag on it. Yours comes with... whatever intimidating designer label you prefer. The point is, you don't scare me."

"I should," he says, his voice dropping to that dangerous register that makes my insides liquify.

"Well, I once ate gas station sushi on a dare, so clearly my self-preservation instincts are questionable at best."

That breaks him. The laugh that erupts from him is genuine and unguarded. For a moment, I see the man beneath the armor—someone who's been hurt, who's built walls so high they've become part of his identity.

"Gas station sushi?" he repeats, shaking his head in disbelief. "That's not bravery, that's a death wish."

"And yet I lived to tell the tale," I counter, tapping my temple. "Iron stomach. It's my superpower."

His expression shifts, becoming more serious again. "You joke, but you don't understand what you're getting yourself into with me."

"Then help me understand," I say, softer now. "Give me something real, Dominic. Not these cryptic warnings or vague threats. Just... you."

He studies me for a long moment, and I can almost see the war raging behind his eyes—push me away or let me in. Finally, he sighs, his shoulders dropping slightly.

"I've done things I'm not proud of," he admits. "Built this company on the backs of people who underestimated me, who thought they could take advantage. And when they tried... I didn't just beat them at their own game, I made sure they never played again."

"Business is cutthroat," I say carefully. "That doesn't make you a villain."

"It does when you cross certain lines." His eyes hold mine, searching for judgment. "Lines that can't be uncrossed."

I swallow hard, "Legal lines?"

His silence is answer enough.

"Is that why you keep pushing me away? You think I can't handle knowing that you've... bent the rules?"

Dominic laughs, but there's no humor in it. "Bent the rules is putting it mildly, Octavia. I've buried them."

The way he says it, with such cold certainty, makes me pause. Maybe there's more truth to his warnings than I wanted to believe. But instead of feeling afraid, I feel... intrigued. What does that say about me?

"So, you're what—some kind of corporate hitman?" I ask, trying to keep my voice light despite the heaviness settling in my chest.

He runs a hand through his hair again, messing it up further. "Something like that."

We stand in silence for a moment, the weight of his partial confession hanging between us. I should be running for the door. I should be blocking his number and updating my resume. Instead, I'm calculating how many steps it would take to close the distance between us.

"You're not running," he observes, his voice tinged with confusion.

"My cardio routine is on Tuesdays and Thursdays," I quip automatically. "Today is strictly strength training."

A reluctant smile tugs at his lips. "Are you physically incapable of taking anything seriously?"

"Oh, I'm taking this very seriously," I counter. "I just process existential crises through inappropriate humor. It's cheaper than therapy."

"This isn't a joke, Octavia."

"I know." I take a deep breath. "But here's the thing—you keep warning me about how dangerous you are, about these terrible things you've done—but you never actually tell me what they are. If you want me out of your life, tell me the truth. All of it. And then let me decide if I'm running or staying."

His jaw tightens. "You think you want the truth, but you don't."

"Try me." I cross my arms, holding my ground. "What's the worst thing you've done, Dominic? Because from where I'm standing, the most frightening thing about you is how desperately you're trying to push away someone who actually sees you."

Something flashes in his eyes—vulnerability, maybe, or resignation. He steps closer, close enough that I can smell his cologne, feel the heat radiating off his body.

"The man who tried to blackmail me three years ago?" His voice is so quiet I have to strain to hear him. "He's not filing lawsuits anymore. He's not doing anything anymore."

My breath catches. "You mean—"

"I mean he made a choice, and it was the wrong one." Dominic's eyes never leave mine.

"People like to test boundaries. They smile to your face while reaching for what isn't theirs—thinking they're smart enough, subtle enough, untouchable enough to get away with it. Just like the ones who tried to slip into my company. Whispering in boardrooms. Making backdoor deals. Thinking I wouldn't notice. I noticed. And Sophia's lovers? They were no different. Thought they could fuck what was mine and walk away unscathed. They didn't walk away. No one does. Not when they mistake me for a man who forgets."

A chill runs through me, but I stand my ground. "Are you confessing to murder right now? Because I feel like I should point out that's not typically third-date material."

He doesn't laugh this time.

"Is that what you want to hear?" he asks, his voice dangerously low. "That I've made people disappear? That I've ruined lives? That the man who thought he could steal my company's trade secrets woke up one morning to find his career, his reputation, and his future gone—not because I sued him, but because I destroyed him so thoroughly there was nothing left to salvage?"

I should be disturbed. Maybe even scared. But I'm not. He's holding back, I can feel it. There's more he's not saying, darker things he's done that he won't speak aloud. And yet... my pulse doesn't quicken out of fear. It's something else entirely. A warmth that pulses through me, steady and undeniable. It should make me question everything. Instead, it just makes me want to know how far he'd go for me. What lines he'd cross, what lines he already has.

And fuck me... maybe I don't need all the answers. Not if the truth feels like this.

I swallow hard, my mouth suddenly dry. "Are you trying to scare me off?"

"I'm trying to make you understand." His hand comes up to cup my face, his touch surprisingly gentle for a man confessing to such darkness. "This isn't a game, Octavia. I am not a good man."

"I don't believe that," I whisper, even as doubt creeps in. "Good men don't warn people away. They don't... care enough to try to protect them."

His thumb brushes my cheek. "Or maybe I'm selfish enough to want you despite knowing better."

"So you admit you want me?" I can't help the small smile that forms, despite the heaviness of the moment.

He closes his eyes briefly, like he's in pain. "God, help me, I do. More than I should. More than is safe for either of us."

"Well, that's something," I say, trying to lighten the mood. "Though, I have to say, this whole 'I'm too dangerous for you' routine is giving major Edward Cullen vibes."

Next thing I know, I'm pinned against the wall, his eyes burning into mine like twin flames.

"Don't," he growls, his face inches from mine. "Don't make light of this."

"Sorry," I breathe, though I'm not entirely sure I am. My heart is hammering so hard I wonder if he can feel it. "Dark humor defense mechanism. Activates automatically in the presence of emotional intensity or men who look like they could be cast in a reboot of 'American Psycho.'"

A reluctant smile tugs at his lips, but disappears just as quickly. "You're infuriating."

"I prefer 'enigmatic,'" I counter, mimicking his earlier tone. "Keeps people guessing."

His hands slide from the wall to frame my face, tilting it up toward his. "Do you have any idea what I want to do to you right now?"

"I have several theories," I manage to say, my voice embarrassingly breathy. "Most of them would violate at least three workplace conduct policies."

"And that doesn't scare you?" His thumb traces my lower lip, igniting a slow, aching heat that drips down my spine. "After everything I just told you?"

I consider lying, but decide against it. "Parts of it terrify me. Not in the way you think, though."

"Enlighten me." His voice is rough, demanding.

"I'm not scared of what you've done," I admit. "I'm scared of what it means that I still want you anyway. What kind of person does that make me?"

His gaze turns lethal, searching mine for any sign of deception. "It makes you either very brave or very foolish."

"Can't I be both?" I challenge. "Bravely foolish? Foolishly brave?"

"This isn't a joke, Octavia," he says, but his grip on me softens slightly.

"I know it's not. But if I don't laugh, I might do something else. Like kiss you. Or run away. Or both, in rapid succession."

Something shifts in his expression—a crack in the armor. "You should run."

"Probably," I agree, making no move to do so. "But I've never been very good at doing what I should."

His forehead rests against mine, and we stand there for a moment, breathing each other's air, teetering on the edge of something that feels both dangerous and inevitable.

"I will ruin you," he whispers, but it sounds more like a plea than a threat.

"Bold of you to assume I'm not already a little ruined," I counter. "Tyler did a number on me, you know. Made me feel small. Worthless.

Like I'd never amount to anything without him."

Dominic pulls back slightly, his eyes flashing with anger. "He was wrong."

"I know that now. But for a while..." I shrug, trying to seem casual. "For a while, I believed him. That I was nothing special. That I'd be lucky if anyone else wanted me."

Dominic's jaw tightens, his hands moving to grip my shoulders. "Tyler is a fucking idiot."

"Well, obviously," I laugh, but it comes out shaky. "My point is, we all have damage, Dominic. Mine makes me doubt myself. Yours makes you push people away. Different symptoms, same disease."

He stares at me for a long moment, his expression unreadable. "You make it sound so simple."

"It's not simple at all," I admit. "But maybe it doesn't need to be as complicated as you're making it. Maybe we could just... see where this goes. No promises, no expectations. Just two slightly damaged people figuring things out."

His eyes search mine, looking for any trace of hesitation or fear. Finding none, he releases a heavy sigh that seems to carry the weight of every secret he's been keeping.

"You make it sound so reasonable," he murmurs. "Like we're just two people with typical baggage—you have trust issues, I have... homicidal tendencies."

I can't help but laugh, which earns me a raised eyebrow. "I'm sorry, but when you put it that way, it does sound like a really twisted rom-com. 'She's a plucky redhead with daddy issues! He's a brooding CEO who occasionally makes people disappear! Can these crazy kids make it work?'"

For a moment, he just stares at me like I've grown a second head. Then, unexpectedly, he laughs—a genuine laugh that transforms his entire face, making him look younger, lighter.

"You're absolutely insane," he says, but there's something like wonder in his voice.

"Probably," I agree. "But at least I'm honest about it."

His laughter fades, replaced by an intensity that makes my pulse quicken. "I have never met anyone like you."

"Is that a good thing or a bad thing?"

"I haven't decided yet." His fingers trace the line of my jaw, feather-light. "You should be running for the door right now."

"And yet, here I am." I lean into his touch, defying every instinct for self-preservation I probably should have. "Maybe I'm just as dangerous as you are."

His eyes darken at that, something primal flickering in their depths. "You have no idea what you're saying."

He throws out another warning like it's supposed to scare me. Like the darkness in him is some big, bad secret I haven't already seen written all over the way he looks at me.

Cute.

I should walk away. Should cool it, be smart, keep my head down and stay out of whatever storm he's trying to shield me from. But I don't. I stay exactly where I am—back to his desk, heat radiating off him like he's daring me to step closer.He looks at me like he's two seconds from doing something reckless. Like he's already done it in his head a hundred times.

My pulse kicks. Not from fear. From want. From the way his gaze dips to my mouth like he's already decided what he wants to do with it.

And maybe I should be nervous. Maybe I should be scared. But all I can think is—fuck it.

I lift my chin, meet his stare head-on. "Then show me," I say, steadily. "Stop with the scare tactics and just show me what you're so damn afraid I'll see."

For a heartbeat, we stand frozen, the air between us buzzing with tension that threatens to snap. I can see the war raging behind his eyes—desire versus restraint, need versus caution. I don't know which will win, but I'm holding my breath either way.

And then his control snaps.

His mouth crashes down on mine with a ferocity that makes my knees buckle. His hands tangle in my hair, pulling just enough to make me gasp. I clutch at his shoulders, his chest, anywhere I can reach, as he pushes me against the wall, rough and possessive.

This isn't a gentle first kiss. It's not tentative or exploring. It's consuming, desperate, like he's been starving for this and can't get enough now that he's had a taste. His tongue sweeps against mine, demanding a response I'm all too willing to give.

I moan against his mouth, and the sound only seems to push him further—like it sets something off.

I feel the hard length of him, undeniable, demanding.

One hand grips my hip, rough and possessive, fingers digging into my skin like he wants to claim it—like he wants to own me.

But the other...

The other cups my face with a tenderness that doesn't match the way he's holding me. Doesn't match the tension rippling through his body.

The contrast is dizzying—like he can't decide whether to ruin me or worship me.

Maybe he plans to do both—the contradictions tear me apart and I hate how much I want more of it.

When he finally pulls back, we're both breathing hard. His pupils are blown wide, only a thin ring of color remaining around the edges. I can feel his heart hammering against my palm.

"That..." I gasp, trying to find my voice. "That didn't feel like you're trying to push me away."

"I'm not a good man, Octavia," he says, his voice rough with desire, "and I never claimed to be a strong one."

I laugh, breathlessly. "If that's you being weak, I'm not sure I'd survive you at full strength."

His thumb traces my lower lip, now swollen from his kiss. "You have no idea what you're getting yourself into."

"Neither do you," I counter, feeling bolder than I ever have. "I might be the one who ruins you."

Something flashes in his eyes—amusement, interest, maybe even a hint of fear. Good. Let him be the one off-balance for once.

"Is that a threat, little minx?" he asks, the nickname sending a fresh wave of heat through me.

"It's a possibility." I reach up to straighten his tie, purposely letting my fingers linger. "One of many I'm willing to explore if you are."

He captures my wrist, his grip firm but not painful. "There's no reset button here. No undo."

"I never said there was." I meet his gaze steadily. "But I'm starting to think that whatever this is between us, it might be worth the risk."

His hand slides from my wrist to interlace with my fingers, the gesture unexpectedly intimate. "You should go," he says, but his body language contradicts his words. He's still close, still looking at me like he wants to devour me whole.

"Is that what you want?" I challenge.

"What I want..." He closes his eyes briefly, as if in pain. "What I want and what should happen are two very different things."

"Always so cryptic," I sigh, but there's no real frustration in it. I've gotten more from him today than I expected. More than I think he intended to give. That feels like progress.

I untangle my fingers from his and step away, needing the distance to think clearly. My lips still tingle from his kiss, my body humming with unfulfilled desire. But rushing this—whatever it is—would be a mistake. We both know it.

"I should go," I say, surprising myself. "Not because I'm scared, but because we both need to think. You've got some... intense revelations to process, and I need to figure out why I'm not running for the hills like any sane person would."

A reluctant smile tugs at his lips. "That's actually... reasonable."

"Don't sound so surprised," I quip, grabbing my bag from where I dropped it earlier. "I have my moments of maturity. They're rare, like solar eclipses or a decent Adam Sandler movie, but they do happen."

His laugh surprises both of us, a rich sound that makes something in my chest tighten. "You're impossible."

"So I've been told." I pause at the door, my hand on the knob. "For what it's worth, Dominic... I'm not afraid of your darkness. Maybe I should be, but I'm not."

His expression turns serious again. "Maybe that's what scares me the most."

I offer him a small smile before slipping out the door, closing it softly behind me.

In the hallway, I lean against the wall, my legs suddenly wobbly. What the hell just happened? Did Dominic just confess to... what, exactly? Corporate espionage? Ruining people's lives? Something worse? And did I just kiss him, anyway?

I press my fingers to my lips, still feeling the ghost of his touch. My heart is racing like I've just sprinted up ten flights of stairs.

What kind of person hears a man hint at possibly ending people— literally ending them—and responds by kissing him senseless?

Me, apparently. Octavia Moore: terrible at self-preservation, excellent at making questionable life choices.

I push off the wall and head toward the elevator, not to leave—just to breathe. I need a minute. A moment to clear my head before I lose it completely.

There's a very real possibility I just made out with a man whose past could fill an entire true crime docuseries. And the worst part? I want to do it again. Desperately.

The elevator arrives with a cheerful ding that feels completely at odds with my inner turmoil. As I step inside, I catch my reflection in the mirrored wall—flushed cheeks, wild eyes, hair mussed where Dominic's fingers tangled in it. I look... claimed. Like someone who's been thoroughly kissed by a man who knows exactly what he wants.

"Get it together, Octavia," I mutter to my reflection. "Just because he kisses like a god doesn't mean you should ignore the red flags. And they're not even flags at this point—they're giant blinking neon signs saying 'DANGER: PROCEED AT YOUR OWN RISK.' "

But as the elevator descends, I can't help but replay the way his control snapped, the hunger in his eyes when he finally gave in.

CHAPTER SEVEN
Dominic

What the hell was I thinking? I cracked. Let her in. Told her more than I've ever told anyone—laid it all bare like it wouldn't cost me. And then I kissed her. Not by accident. Not in a moment of weakness. I *wanted* to.

That's the problem.

I've spent years building walls, controlling every variable, every risk. But with her? I'm reckless. And with paying a visit to Westfield's CFO tonight and my head spinning with her taste still on my mouth…

Hours slip by while I bury myself in work—half out of necessity, half out of desperation to hold on to something I can control.

But my control is slipping. And I don't know how to stop it.

Eventually, I shut my laptop with more force than necessary and push to my feet. I've stalled long enough.

I head down the hall toward the elevator, every step sharp, deliberate.

Then, I see Octavia—rounding the corner and walking straight into my path like she hasn't spent the entire day under my skin. She slows when she sees me, like she might say something. Like she *wants*

to. But I don't give her the chance. I brush past her, close enough that my shoulder nearly grazes hers. I don't speak. I don't look. Because if I do, I'll forget what matters. And I can't afford that. Not tonight.

Not when I have to walk into that asshole's house tonight and remind him exactly who he fucked with. Not when I need my head clear to bury him—quietly, completely, and without hesitation.

I finally get to my car after what feels like an eternity. I slide into the driver's seat, gripping the wheel until my knuckles are bleach white. Without another thought, I pull out of the garage—too fast, too angry, too far gone to care. The headlights cut through the darkness, illuminating the empty road ahead– empty like my fucking soul used to be before Octavia came along and filled it with... complications.

My phone buzzes. Her name lights up the screen.

OCTAVIA

You left so quickly. Are you okay?

Am I okay? I almost laugh out loud at that. No, I'm not fucking okay. I'm waiting to go to a man's house with a gun in my glove compartment... and the taste of the woman I can't have is still on my lips.

I pull over abruptly, tires screeching against the asphalt. I need to focus. Tonight isn't about the red hair and blue eyes that haunt my dreams. It's about business. Cold, calculated business.

OCTAVIA

I can't stop thinking about that kiss.

"Fuck!" I slam my palm against the steering wheel, accidentally honking the horn, startling someone enough they jump back with a muttered curse. Great. Now I'm scaring innocent pedestrians.

What's next? Crying during shampoo ads? Scribbling poetry in the margins of takeout menus?

I text back.

ME

We need to forget it happened. Professional boundaries. I'm your boss.

Her response is immediate.

OCTAVIA

Is that really all you want to be?

The question hangs in the air like a physical thing. I stare at the screen, thumbs hovering over the keyboard. My mind conjures images of her bent over my desk, those fiery curls spilling down her back as I take her from behind. My cock stiffens painfully against my zipper at the thought.

No, I decide. I won't respond. Can't respond. Not tonight.

I toss the phone onto the passenger seat and pull back onto the road, forcing myself to focus on the task at hand. Westfield's CFO. The numbers he fucked. The money he stole. The deals he sabotaged.

Three hours later, I'm parked a block away from his suburban McMansion, watching the lights inside dim as his family settles in for the night. My phone buzzes again. I ignore it. It buzzes three more times in rapid succession.

Against my better judgment, I glance at the screen.

OCTAVIA

Fine. Message received, boss man.

OCTAVIA

Though I should probably mention that Tyler and I broke up months ago.

OCTAVIA

But whatever. Enjoy your evening of brooding and emotional constipation.

A laugh escapes me before I can stop it. Emotional constipation. Jesus Christ. Only Octavia would dare talk to me like that.

I type back before I can stop myself.

ME

I'm not brooding.

Three dots appear immediately.

OCTAVIA

Oh, please. You're probably sitting alone in the dark somewhere right now, glaring at nothing while dramatic music plays in your head.

My eyes dart around the dark interior of my car, to the streetlight creating dramatic shadows across my dashboard, and I scowl. How the fuck does she know me so well already?

I toss the phone aside again and exit the car, the cool night air doing nothing to calm the fire raging inside me. The gun sits heavy against the small of my back, tucked into my waistband—not that I plan on using it. It's not a weapon. It's insurance. A reminder that this isn't just business. It's personal.

Westfield's CFO, Tom Fletcher. The man who thought he could embezzle from my company's joint venture fund and get away with it. Three million dollars. Gone. Siphoned through a maze of shell companies I spent weeks tracing back to him.

I approach the house, my footsteps silent on the manicured lawn. Through the large bay window, I can see him in his living room, nursing a glass of what's probably expensive scotch. My scotch, technically, since I paid for it with the money he stole from me.

My phone buzzes again. I shouldn't look. I know I shouldn't.

I do anyway.

OCTAVIA

Be careful tonight. Whatever you're doing.

I stare at her message, a strange tightness constricting my chest. How does she know I'm up to something? Am I that transparent to her? The thought is both terrifying and oddly comforting.

I slide the phone into my pocket without responding and approach Fletcher's front door. My finger hovers over the doorbell for a moment before I press it. The chime echoes inside, followed by footsteps. I straighten my shoulders, donning the mask of Dominic Callahan, ruthless CEO, the man everyone fears in the boardroom.

The door swings open, and Fletcher's smug face transforms into shock when he sees me standing on his porch.

"Callahan? What the hell are you doing here?" His eyes dart nervously behind me, checking for witnesses, perhaps.

"We need to talk, Tom." My voice is ice, controlled and deadly. "May I come in?"

He hesitates, the wheels turning behind his eyes. "It's late. My family—"

"Is this how you want to do this? On your doorstep, where the neighbors might hear?" I lean in slightly. "Three million reasons why that's a bad idea."

The color drains from his face. He steps back, allowing me entry into his pristine foyer with its marble floors and pretentious artwork. Money well spent—*my money.*

"My office," he mutters, leading me down a hallway.

Once inside, he locks the door behind us, his hands shaking slightly. The room reeks of privilege—leather-bound books he's never read, awards he didn't earn, a desk worth more than what most of my employees make in a month.

"What's this about?" he asks, trying to sound confident but failing miserably.

I take my time before answering, circling his desk like a predator.

My fingers trail over the polished mahogany, over framed photos of his perfect family—his blonde wife with the too-white smile, two children with private school uniforms and vacant eyes. The American fucking dream, built on stolen money.

"Three million dollars," I say finally, my voice dangerously soft. "Transferred through seven different shell companies before landing in an offshore account in the Caymans. Account number 7729-584, to be precise."

His Adam's apple bobs as he swallows hard. "I don't know what you're talking about."

"Don't insult my intelligence, Tom." I lean against his desk, casual, as if we're discussing the weather. "The money you stole wasn't just company funds. It was earmarked for the Palmer Medical Initiative."

His eyes widen slightly. Good. He remembers.

"My mother," I continue, each word precise, "was supposed to be part of that trial. The one that could have extended her life and many others who have heart disease by years. The one that got delayed because of 'unexpected budget constraints.'" I make air quotes with my fingers. "Those 'budget constraints' were you, taking what wasn't yours and watching people die for it."

Fletcher's face contorts, first with fear, then with something like indignation. "You can't prove anything."

I laugh, but there's no humor in it, just cold, calculated rage. "Can't I? I have the paper trail, Tom. Every transaction, every transfer. I know which days you moved the money, which accounts you used." I pull out my phone, scrolling through files I've memorized but brought for effect. "I even know what you spent it on. The vacation home in Aspen. The boat. The diamond necklace for your mistress—yes, I know about her, too."

"This is ridiculous," he sputters, but his face has gone ashen. "You're making wild accusations—"

In one fluid motion, I'm across the room, my hand around his throat, backing him against the bookshelf. Books tumble to the floor as his head slams into the hardwood.

"My mother died in pain," I growl, my face inches from his. "While you were sipping champagne on a boat I paid for."

"Dominic, please," he chokes out, clawing at my hand. "I have a family—"

"So did I." I tighten my grip slightly, just enough to make his eyes bulge. "And now, I don't."

Fear floods his eyes—real fear, primal and desperate—as I hold his life in my hands. For a moment, I consider ending it right here. One quick motion. Snap. Problem solved. He'd be gone, and no one would connect it to me. Just another home invasion in a nice neighborhood.

I decide against it.

I release him suddenly, and he collapses to his knees, coughing and gasping for air, rubbing his throat where my fingers left angry red marks.

"I'm not here to kill you, Tom," I say, straightening my cuffs. "Though, God knows, you deserve it."

"Then what do you want?" he croaks, still on his knees. Pathetic.

I crouch down to his level, meeting his terrified gaze. "I want you to confess. Tomorrow morning, you're going to walk into the board meeting and tell everyone exactly what you did. You're going to return every penny—with interest—and you're going to resign."

He shakes his head frantically. "I can't. They'll prosecute me. I'll go to prison."

"Yes," I agree coldly. "You will. Actions have consequences, Tom."

"Please," he begs, actual tears forming in his eyes now. "My kids—"

"Should have a father who isn't a thief," I finish for him. "My mother should have had a fighting chance at treatment. We don't always get what we deserve, do we?"

I stand, towering over his crumpled form. The gun presses against my back, a constant reminder of how easily this could have gone differently. How easily it still could.

"You have until tomorrow morning," I say, my voice returning to its usual controlled timbre. "Nine AM sharp. If you're not there, confessing everything, I'll release the evidence to the board, the SEC, and the police. And then I'll pay a visit to your wife." I pick up a photo from his desk, studying the blonde woman's artificial smile. "I wonder how she'll feel about the apartment you bought for Melanie in Tribeca?"

Fletcher's face crumples. "How did you—"

"I know everything, Tom." I place the photo back on his desk, facing it deliberately toward him. "That's the difference between us. You thought you were clever, but I'm thorough."

He remains on the floor, broken and pathetic, as I walk toward the door. I pause with my hand on the knob. "Oh, and Tom? Don't even think about running. There isn't a place on this Earth you could hide that I wouldn't find you."

The threat hangs in the air between us, heavy and real. He knows I mean it. I can see it in his eyes—the realization that his comfortable life is over. That everything he's built on lies and theft is about to come crashing down.

Good. Let him suffer through the night, wondering if prison or my wrath would be worse.

I leave without another word, closing the door behind me. The air outside feels cleaner somehow, despite the weight still pressing on my chest. I pull out my phone as I walk back to my car, my thumb hovering over Octavia's last message.

Be careful tonight. Whatever you're doing.

I type out a response, delete it, try again.

ME

I'm always careful.

The response comes almost immediately.

OCTAVIA

Bullshit.

I can't help the smile that tugs at my lips. Even through text, she sees right through me. I slide into my car and sit for a moment, letting the adrenaline slowly ebb away. The gun at my back digs uncomfortably into my spine. I remove it, placing it in the glovebox where it belongs.

My phone buzzes again.

OCTAVIA

Where are you?

I stare at the screen, debating how to respond. The rational part of my brain, the businessman, the fucking adult—says to ignore it. To drive home to my empty penthouse and drown the evening in whiskey until I can sleep without seeing red hair behind my eyelids.

Instead, I type:

ME

Where are you?

Three dots appear, disappear, appear again.

OCTAVIA

Home. Alone.

CHAPTER EIGHT
Octavia

I can't believe I'm still doing this. Still chasing him. Still wanting more, even after everything he's said. Everything he's *shown* me.

He keeps pushing me away—warning me off like he's some villain in a story I don't want to be part of. And I should listen. I *should*.

But I don't.

I keep coming back.

And the worst part? The more he pushes, the more I want him.

What the fuck is wrong with me?

Why does the danger pull me closer instead of sending me running?

Is it because of the way he protects what's his? The way he looks at me like I'm already claimed—even if he won't admit it?

Maybe I'm not drawn to the darkness. Maybe I'm just desperate for someone who'd actually go to war for me.

And that's fucked up. Right?

That I feel safer in his chaos than I ever did in someone else's calm?

A text comes in and pulls me out of my spiral.

Dominic's name lights up my screen, and my heart does that stupid flutter thing again.

DOMINIC

Going to bed?

Three simple words that shouldn't make my stomach twist with longing. I stare at the message, trying to decode what he really means. Is he actually asking about my sleep schedule, or is this his way of testing waters he keeps claiming are too dangerous to wade into?

I type back before I can overthink it.

ME

Not yet. Too wound up.

I watch the three dots appear, disappear, then reappear. He's deliberating. Choosing his words carefully, as always. The man never says anything without calculating its impact first.

DOMINIC

What has you so wound up, little minx?

My fingers hover over the keyboard. The honest answer would be "you," but I'm not brave enough for that level of vulnerability. Not when he keeps this careful distance between us—close enough to feel the heat, never close enough to touch the flame.

ME

Just one of those nights. Brain won't shut off.

What about you? Why are you still up?

His response comes faster this time.

DOMINIC

Work. Always work.

I can picture him in his penthouse office, suit jacket discarded, sleeves rolled up to reveal those powerful tattooed forearms, hair slightly mussed from running his hands through it in frustration. The image makes my body ache in places it shouldn't.

ME

All work and no play makes
Dominic a dull boy.

I hit send before my better judgment can talk me out of it. A moment of boldness, a flash of the person I used to be before Tyler systematically dismantled my confidence.

The three dots appear immediately. My heart thunders in my chest.

DOMINIC

Careful, Octavia. I might think you're inviting me to play.

Heat rushes to my face, spreading down my neck and pooling low in my belly. This is the game we've been playing since day one—advance and retreat, push and pull. He draws me in with one breath and pushes me away with the next.

ME

Maybe I am.

My fingers tremble as I hit send. I'm crossing a line, and I know it. Professional boundaries crumbling with three simple words. But I'm tired of pretending I don't feel this pull between us, this magnetic force that makes me forget all the reasons why this is a terrible idea.

Three dots. Disappear. Three dots again. He's struggling with how to respond, and I find a certain satisfaction in knowing I've thrown the always-composed Dominic Callahan off balance.

DOMINIC

You don't know what you're asking for.

I sit up straighter in bed, suddenly emboldened.

ME

I think I do.

His response is almost immediate.

DOMINIC

No, you don't. Because if I came over right now, I wouldn't be gentle. I wouldn't be sweet. I'd take what I want, how I want it. And you're not ready for that.

My breath catches in my throat. I cross my legs, and the pressure only reminds me how wet I already am—from a *single* message. He's not even here, and my body's already begging for him.

I don't want slow. I don't want sweet.

I want his hands on me—rough, greedy, unapologetic.

I want him to take what's his.

I'll give him everything. However, he wants me… I'm his to ruin.

I type before courage deserts me.

ME

Then ruin me.

The message sits there, naked and raw on the screen. Three seconds. Five. Ten. No immediate response. No three dots. Nothing.

Oh God. I've gone too far. Pushed too hard. My stomach twists with humiliation, and I toss the phone onto the bed as if it's suddenly burning my fingers. What was I thinking? He's my boss. My impossibly complex, frustratingly cryptic boss who has made it clear—repeatedly—that whatever this is between us is a bad idea.

I pace my small bedroom, hugging myself tightly. The silence from my phone is deafening. I should take it back. Send another message laughing it off as a joke. Say I've had too much wine. Anything to salvage what's left of my dignity.

But before I can reach for my phone, it lights up with an incoming call. Not a text. A call.

Dominic.

My hand trembles as I answer, but I can't make my voice work.

"Octavia." His voice is deeper over the phone, rougher around the edges.

"Yes?" I manage to whisper, sinking down onto the edge of my bed.

"Do you have any idea what you're doing to me right now?" His voice is controlled, but I can hear the strain beneath it, like a dam about to break.

I swallow hard. "I—"

"No," he cuts me off. "Don't answer that. You don't know. You can't possibly know what it takes for me to keep my distance from you. The restraint I have to exercise every time you walk into a room."

My heart hammers against my ribs so hard I'm certain he can hear it through the phone. "Then stop restraining yourself."

A harsh laugh escapes him. "You make it sound so simple."

"Isn't it?"

"No, Octavia, it isn't." There's a rustling sound on his end, like he's moving. "Do you know where I am right now?"

I bite my lip. "Your office? Your penthouse?"

"I'm in my car, parked outside your building."

My breath catches. "What?"

"I've been sitting here, telling myself to drive away." His voice drops lower. "And then you send me that text."

I stand on shaky legs and move to my window, pulling back the curtain to peer down at the street below. Sure enough, there's his sleek black Porsche, engine off, parked in the shadows across from my building.

"How long have you been there?" I ask, my voice barely audible even to my own ears.

"Long enough to talk myself out of coming up three different times." He pauses, and I can almost see him running a hand through his hair in frustration. "This is a mistake, Octavia. A mistake I've been avoiding since the moment I saw you."

I press my forehead against the cool glass of the window, eyes fixed on his car. "Then why are you here?"

"Because I'm weak when it comes to you." The raw honesty in his voice makes my knees buckle. "Because every time I think I've built my walls high enough, you find a way to climb them."

"Come upstairs," I whisper.

The silence that follows hangs between us, heavy with possibility and danger.

"If I come up those stairs, there's no going back," he finally says, his voice like gravel. "You understand that, don't you? This changes everything."

I close my eyes, weighing his words against the ache that's been building inside me since the day we met. The rational part of my brain is screaming warnings—he's my boss, he's dangerous, he's made it clear he's not the kind of man who stays.

But the part of me that's been awakened by his touch, his gaze, his presence—that part is louder.

"I understand," I tell him, surprised by the steadiness in my voice. "I still want you to come up."

I hear him exhale slowly on the other end of the line. "Apartment number?"

"4C," I whisper, my heart threatening to beat right out of my chest.

"Five minutes." He ends the call abruptly, and his car door swings open. Even from this distance, his movements are deliberate—powerful, controlled. A predator finally giving in to the hunt.

Five minutes. The words echo in my empty apartment as I frantically look around. What am I doing? My place is a mess—clothes draped over chairs, dishes in the sink, bed unmade. Not that the state of my housekeeping should matter when I've just invited my boss up for what will definitely not be a professional conversation.

I rush to the bathroom, splashing cold water on my face and checking my reflection. My cheeks are flushed, eyes bright with anticipation and fear. I'm wearing an oversized t-shirt and sleep shorts—not exactly the seductive outfit I would have chosen for this moment. But there's no time to change, no time to become someone else.

This is me. Messy apartment, bare face, wild red curls. If he wants me, he'll have to want this version.

A knock at the door sends a jolt through my system. Five minutes on the dot. Of course he's punctual, even for this.

I take one last steadying breath before crossing to the door. My hand hesitates on the deadbolt. This is my last chance to be smart, to back away from the fire before I get burned. But my body moves of its own accord, unlatching the lock and pulling the door open.

And there he is.

Dominic fills the doorframe, his broad shoulders blocking the hallway light. He's still in his work clothes—dark tailored pants and a white button-down with the sleeves rolled up, exposing those forearms that have starred in too many of my fantasies. His tie is loosened, hair slightly disheveled, as if he's been running his hands through it. But it's his eyes that stop my breath—dark, hungry, almost feral in their intensity.

We stand frozen for several heartbeats, neither speaking. The air between us crackles with electricity, with all the things we've left unsaid.

"Last chance to send me away," he says, his voice rougher than I've ever heard it.

I shake my head, stepping back to let him in. "I don't want to send you away."

He enters slowly, deliberately, like a wolf crossing a threshold. His eyes never leave mine as he closes the door behind him, the soft click of the latch echoing in the silence. My apartment suddenly feels too small, too intimate with him in it. His presence consumes everything—the air, the space, my ability to think clearly.

"You should be afraid of me right now," he says, still maintaining that careful distance between us.

"Why?" I manage to ask, my voice barely a whisper.

"Because I've been fighting this for weeks. Fighting what I want to do to you." He takes a step closer, and I instinctively back up until my shoulders hit the wall. "And I'm done fighting."

Before I can respond, he's on me. One hand cups my face while the other grips my hip, pinning me against the wall as his mouth claims mine. There's nothing gentle about it—it's all hunger and possession, tongue and barely restrained violence. I gasp against his lips, and he takes advantage, deepening the kiss until I'm dizzy with want.

His body presses against mine, hard planes against soft curves, and I can feel every inch of him—hard and undeniable—pressing against my stomach, showing just how much he wants me. My grip tightens on his shoulders, fists twisting in the fine fabric like I'll lose myself if I let go.

When he finally breaks away, we're both breathing hard. His forehead rests against mine, eyes closed as if he's gathering the last shreds of his control.

"Tell me to stop," he says roughly. "Tell me this isn't what you want."

I shake my head, unable to form words with my heart hammering in my throat. Instead, I slide my hands up to cup his face, pulling him back down to me. This time, I initiate, pouring every ounce of my longing into it.

A growl rumbles deep in his chest as he lifts me in one fluid motion, hands gripping my thighs as he wraps my legs around his waist. I cling to him, gasping as he carries me through my apartment, somehow knowing exactly where my bedroom is without asking.

"You have no idea how many times I've imagined this," he murmurs against my neck, his teeth grazing the tender skin there. "Having you like this. At my mercy."

He lays me onto the bed with a softness that doesn't match the storm in his eyes, then straightens to look down at me. The intensity in his gaze leaves me feeling both vulnerable and powerful. His fingers move to his shirt, unfastening each button slowly and deliberately, never breaking eye contact as inch after inch of sun-warmed skin and hard muscle is revealed.

"Take that off," he commands, nodding toward my oversized t-shirt. "I want to see you."

My hands tremble as I grasp the hem, suddenly self-conscious. This isn't the body men like Dominic typically desire—I'm all soft curves and thick thighs, not the willowy model type I imagine he's used to.

"Now, Octavia." His voice brooks no argument.

I pull the shirt over my head, resisting the urge to cover myself as his gaze travels over my exposed skin, lingering on my breasts, barely contained in a simple cotton bra.

"Beautiful," he breathes, and the reverence in his voice has my insecurities momentarily retreating. "Even more perfect than I imagined."

His shirt falls to the floor, revealing a torso sculpted as if it were carved from marble—broad shoulders tapering to a narrow waist, abs defined beneath skin decorated with intricate tattoos that disappear into the waistband of his pants. I want to trace every line of ink with my tongue, learn the stories written on his body.

Dominic climbs onto the bed, his weight causing the mattress to dip as he hovers above me, one knee between my thighs. "I need you to understand something," he says, voice tight with restraint. "I don't do gentle. I don't do sweet. If that's what you're looking for, tell me now."

I reach up to touch his face, tracing the sharp line of his jaw. "I told you what I wanted."

His gaze turns molten, heavy with need. "Say it again. I need to hear it."

"Ruin me," I whisper, the words a confession and a plea.

Something dangerous flashes in his eyes—possession, hunger, something darker I can't name. "Remember, you asked for this."

His mouth crashes down on mine again, demanding and relentless. His hands are everywhere—tangling in my hair, gripping my waist, sliding beneath the elastic of my sleep shorts. I arch into his touch, desperate for more, for everything he's willing to give me.

He pulls back just enough to look down at me, his breathing ragged. "You've been driving me crazy since the first time I saw you at Rustic Harbor," he growls, tracing the curve of my hip with the kind of touch that doesn't ask—it takes. "Every time you walk into a room, I can think of nothing but bending you over the nearest surface and making you scream my name."

His words send liquid heat pooling between my thighs. No one has ever spoken to me like this—raw, honest, unapologetically carnal. It's intoxicating.

"Then do it," I challenge, surprising myself with my boldness.

A dark smile curves his lips. "Oh, little minx, I plan to."

His hand slides up my ribs to cup my breast, thumb brushing over the fabric covering my nipple. Even this light touch sends sparks shooting through me. I arch into his hand, silently begging for more.

"So responsive," he murmurs, lowering his head to replace his thumb with his mouth, hot and wet through the cotton of my bra. "I've wondered if your body would be as honest as your eyes."

I gasp as he nips at the taut peak, the sharp mixture of pleasure and pain making me writhe beneath him. His other hand slides down to grip my thigh, fingers digging into the soft flesh there.

"I want these wrapped around my waist while I fuck you," he says, squeezing my thigh. "Around my head while I taste you."

The crude words in his refined voice make me whimper. I've never been spoken to like this—never been wanted like this. It's overwhelming and exhilarating all at once.

He unclasps my bra smooth and sure, like muscle memory, drawing it down my arms and tossing it aside. His eyes darken as he takes in my naked breasts, heavy and flushed with arousal.

"Perfect," he breathes, lowering his head to take one nipple into his mouth. The sensation is electric, his tongue circling the exposed peak before sucking hard enough to make me cry out. My hands fly to his hair, fingers tangling in the thick strands, holding him to me.

Dominic growls against my skin, the vibration sending shivers through my body. His hand slides down my stomach, dipping beneath the waistband of my shorts. When his fingers brush against the soaked fabric of my panties, we both groan.

"So wet for me already," he murmurs, pressing his fingers against me through the thin cotton. "Is this all for me, little minx?"

"Yes," I gasp, hips lifting involuntarily to increase the pressure. "Only you."

He captures my mouth in another bruising kiss as his fingers push my panties aside, finally touching me where I'm aching for him. I moan into his mouth as he slides one long finger through my folds, gathering my wetness before circling my clit with maddening perfection.

"Do you know how many times I've thought about this?" he asks against my lips. "How many meetings I've sat through, hard and aching for you, imagining these perfect thighs around me?" His finger circles my entrance teasingly. "How many nights I've spent with my hand on my cock, wishing it was your tight little pussy instead?"

His crude words send a fresh wave of heat through me. I've never been spoken to like this—never been wanted with such raw, unfiltered hunger. It makes me feel powerful and vulnerable all at once.

"Please," I whimper, unable to form more coherent thoughts as his skilled fingers continue their torturous exploration.

"Please what?" he demands, pressing just the tip of his finger inside me, then withdrawing. "Use your words, Octavia. Tell me exactly what you want."

I swallow hard, fighting through the haze of arousal. "I want you inside me."

His eyes flash with approval. "Good girl. But not yet."

Before I can protest, he's moving down my body, trailing open-mouthed kisses across my stomach, my hip bones. He hooks his fingers in the waistband of my shorts and panties, dragging them down my legs in one swift movement.

I'm completely naked now, exposed to his hungry gaze. My thighs try to close instinctively, but his broad shoulders are already between them.

"Don't hide from me," he commands, his hot breath ghosting over my most intimate place. "I want to see all of you."

My face burns with embarrassment, but Dominic doesn't give me time to dwell on my insecurities. His mouth is on me in an instant, his tongue parting my folds with devastating intent. I cry out, my hands flying to his hair, not sure if I'm surrendering or trying to claw my way back from the edge he's throwing me off.

"God, you taste even better than I imagined," he groans against me, the vibration of his voice sending shockwaves through my body. His large hands grip my thighs, spreading them wider as he devours me like a man starved.

My back arches off the bed when he sucks my clit between his lips, applying just the right amount of pressure. It has me teetering on the edge already. One of his hands slides up my body to palm my breast roughly, pinching my nipple between his fingers as his tongue works magic below.

"Dominic," I gasp, my hips moving of their own accord against his mouth. "I'm going to—"

"Not yet," he growls, pulling back just enough to deny me release. His eyes meet mine from between my thighs, dark and dangerous. "Not until I say so."

I whimper in frustration, my body trembling with need. He smirks, clearly enjoying the power he holds over me.

"Patience, little minx," he says, pressing a surprisingly gentle kiss to my inner thigh before rising to his knees. His hands move to his belt, undoing it with tantalizing slowness. My breath catches in my throat as he unzips his pants, pushing them down along with his boxer briefs to free himself.

I can't help the gasp that escapes me. He's huge—thick and long, the head already glistening with pre-cum. I've never seen anything like him before. Tyler was average at best, but Dominic...there's nothing average about him.

"See something you like?" he asks, a knowing smirk playing at his lips as he strokes himself lazily.

"I..." Words fail me as I stare, equal parts intimidated and desperate to feel him inside me.

"Don't worry, baby," he says, reading my expression. "I'll make sure you're ready for me."

He lowers himself over me again, his hard length pressing against my thigh as he captures my mouth in another searing kiss. I feel small beneath him, completely surrounded by his size and strength. His hand slides between us, fingers finding my entrance and pressing inside—first one, then two, with just enough pressure that makes me whimper.

I moan into his mouth as his thumb circles my clit, his fingers curling to find that spot inside me that has stars exploding behind my eyelids. He swallows my cries, his kiss growing more demanding as his fingers work me higher.

"That's it," he murmurs against my lips. "Let go for me. I want to feel you cum around my fingers before I fuck you."

His crude words push me over the edge. I shatter around his fingers, my body convulsing as waves of pleasure crash over me. He works me through it, never stopping his movements until I'm quivering with aftershocks.

"Beautiful," he murmurs, kissing my neck as I come down from the high. "But we're just getting started."

He withdraws his fingers, bringing them to his mouth and sucking them clean while maintaining eye contact. The sight is so erotic I feel desire building again already.

"Are you on birth control?" he asks suddenly, his voice serious despite the hunger in his eyes.

I nod, grateful for my responsible past self. "Yes, the pill. I take it regularly."

Relief flickers in his expression. "Good. Because I want to feel every inch of you—no barriers, no limits." His hand dips down again, sliding his hard cock through my folds, as he coats himself in my arousal. "I want to fill you with my cum. Would you like that?"

The question sends a fresh wave of heat through me. "Yes," I breathe, spreading my thighs wider in invitation.

Dominic positions himself at my entrance, the blunt head of his cock pressing against me. "Look at me," he commands. "I want to see your face when I fuck you. I want every reaction. Every second."

I obey, meeting his intense gaze as he presses inside. The intrusion is immediate and overwhelming—he's so much bigger than anyone I've ever been with. My breath hitches as he pushes deeper, the pleasure-pain making me dig my nails into his shoulders.

"That's it," he murmurs, his voice strained with restraint. "Feel every inch, baby. All of me."

He inches forward slowly, allowing my body to adjust to his size. I feel impossibly full already, and he's only halfway inside. A small whimper escapes me as he pushes deeper.

"Breathe," he commands, one hand coming up to grip my throat lightly. The unexpected gesture sends a thrill through me as his thumb caresses my pulse point. "Relax for me."

The weight of his hand at my neck sends a shockwave through me, my body surrendering before I can think. He thrusts again, forcing me to take more of him, every nerve screaming as I adjust to the overwhelming fullness.

"Fuck," he growls when he's finally fully seated inside me. "So tight. So perfect."

I feel impaled, stretched to my limit around him. He holds still, giving me time to adjust, his eyes never leaving mine. The intensity of his gaze strips me bare in ways my naked body never could.

"Mine," he whispers, and I'm not sure if he means to say it aloud. His hand tightens slightly just enough to make me breathless as he begins to move, pulling out almost completely before thrusting back in with controlled force.

"Oh god," I gasp, the sensation overwhelming. My legs wrap around his waist instinctively, opening myself further to him.

"That's it," he mutters darkly, losing rhythm. "I'll never get enough of you."

His hand tightens at the base of my neck, just enough to make my pulse race, the slight restriction sending an unexpected surge of arousal through me. I've never been touched like this before—never been wanted with such raw, consuming need.

His thrusts grow harder, more demanding, the sound of skin against skin filling my small bedroom. Each powerful stroke hits places inside me I didn't know existed, sending sparks of pleasure shooting up my spine.

"You feel that?" he demands, his voice rough with exertion. "How perfect your pussy wraps around me? Like you were made for my cock."

"Yes," I moan, unable to form more coherent thoughts as he drives into me relentlessly. My hands slide down his sweat-slicked back, nails digging into the hard muscle there.

Without warning, he withdraws completely, leaving me empty and aching. Before I can protest, he flips me onto my stomach with surprising ease, pulling my hips up while pushing my shoulders down. The position leaves me completely exposed to him, vulnerable in a way that should terrify me but only increases my arousal.

"I want to see these perfect curves while I'm buried deep inside you," he says, one large hand running appreciatively over the swell of my ass. "So goddamn beautiful."

His hand comes down suddenly in a sharp slap across my right cheek, the sting making me cry out in surprised pleasure. "Is this okay?" he asks, his voice tight with restraint.

"Yes," I gasp, pushing back against him. "Please, don't stop."

He rewards me with another slap, this one harder, the pain blooming into pleasure that makes me moan shamelessly into the pillow. His hand soothes over the heated skin before he positions himself at my entrance again.

"Spread wider," he commands, pushing back inside me in one powerful thrust that steals the breath from my lungs.

The new angle allows him to penetrate even deeper, hitting spots that make my vision blur. His hands grip my hips with bruising force as he sets a punishing rhythm, each thrust pushing me further up the bed until I have to brace myself against the headboard.

"Fuck, you're taking all of me like you can't get enough." He growls, one hand sliding up my spine to tangle in my hair. He pulls, forcing my head back, arching my spine into an even more vulnerable position. "Such a good girl for me. So fucking perfect."

The praise combined with the rough treatment sends me spiraling toward another orgasm. I'm making sounds I've never heard myself make before—desperate, animalistic noises that would embarrass me if I had any capacity for shame left.

"Are you going to cum for me again?" Dominic demands, his voice strained with the effort of maintaining control. "Going to cum all over my cock like the good little minx you are?"

"Yes," I moan, my walls already tightening around him. "Please, Dominic—"

His hand tightens in my hair, pulling harder as his thrusts become more erratic. "Not yet," he growls. "Not until I say."

The command sends a fresh wave of arousal through me. This control he has over my body is intoxicating—terrifying and thrilling all at once. His free hand slides around to find my clit, circling the overloaded bundle of nerves with devastating accuracy.

"Oh god," I gasp, my arms trembling as they struggle to support me against the force of his thrusts. "I can't—I need—"

"Tell me," he demands, his fingers pressing harder against my clit. "Tell me what you need."

"You," I manage to choke out. "Please, let me cum, Dominic. Please."

He leans over me, his chest pressed against my back, his lips at my ear. "Cum for me," he commands, his fingers working my clit mercilessly as his cock drives into me. "Now, Octavia."

The permission breaks the dam. I shatter around him, my entire body convulsing as the most intense orgasm of my life tears through me. I scream his name; the sound muffled by the pillow as Dominic's powerful body drives me through wave after wave of pleasure.

His control snaps. I feel it happen—the moment his restraint shatters completely. His thrusts become wild, almost brutal in their intensity as he chases his own release. His fingers dig into my hips hard enough to leave marks, claiming me, branding me as his.

"Fuck," he growls, the sound primal and raw. "I'm going to fill you up, little minx. Make you take every drop."

"Yes," I gasp, my body still trembling from aftershocks. "Please, Dominic."

With a final, punishing thrust, he buries himself to the hilt inside me and groans my name like a prayer and a curse. I feel him pulsing, flooding me with his release, the sensation triggering another smaller orgasm that has me whimpering beneath him.

For several long moments, the only sound in the room is our ragged breathing. Dominic's weight presses me into the mattress, his body covering mine completely. I should feel trapped, but instead, I feel... protected. Safe in a way I've never experienced before.

He presses a surprisingly tender kiss to my shoulder before carefully withdrawing from me. The loss of him leaves me feeling empty, and I can't help the small whimper that escapes me. He turns me over gently, his eyes roaming my face with an intensity that should frighten me. I expect to see regret there, or worse, dismissal. Instead, I find something that looks almost like wonder.

"You okay?" he asks, voice gentler than I've ever heard it. His thumb brushes across my cheekbone, wiping away tears I didn't realize I'd shed.

I nod, not trusting my voice. My body feels thoroughly used, pleasantly sore in places I've never been sore before. There will be bruises tomorrow—on my hips, my thighs, perhaps even my neck. The thought sends an unexpected thrill through me.

Dominic rises from the bed, and for one heart-stopping moment, I think he's going to leave. Instead, he disappears into my bathroom. The sound of water running drifts out a moment later, and he returns with a warm washcloth. The tenderness with which he cleans between my thighs—so at odds with the man who just fucked me senseless—has tears threatening to rise all over again.

"Did I hurt you?" he asks, misreading my expression.

"No," I whisper, finding my voice at last. "Just the opposite."

A small smile tugs at the corner of his mouth. "Good." He finishes his ministrations and tosses the washcloth aside before sliding back into bed beside me. Without hesitation, he pulls me against his chest, one strong arm wrapping around my waist. "Because I'm not nearly done with you tonight."

CHAPTER NINE
Octavia

The words send a thrill through my exhausted body. My muscles ache like my body's still echoing his touch, but the thought of him touching me again makes my heart damn near punch its way out of my chest.

"I need a minute to recover," I admit, my voice hoarse from screaming his name.

He chuckles, the sound vibrating against my cheek. "We have all night, little minx." His fingers trace lazy patterns on my hip, sending shivers across my sensitized skin. "I'm not going anywhere."

There's something in his tone that makes me look up at him. His expression is softer than I've ever seen it, though that dangerous edge still lurks beneath the surface.

"What changed?" I ask before I can stop myself. "It's only been a few days, and you've already mastered the art of keeping your distance."

That flicker of tension in his jaw says what he won't—he's barely holding it together. His fingers continue their gentle exploration of my skin, drifting up my ribs, making my breath catch.

"I told myself I could resist you," he says finally. "That I was strong

enough to keep my distance." His hand slides up to cup my face, thumb brushing across my swollen bottom lip. "I was wrong."

"I'm glad you were wrong," I whisper against his thumb.

Something dark and territorial flashes in his eyes. "Are you? Because there's no going back from this, Octavia. You understand that, don't you? You're mine now."

The declaration should terrify me. Instead, it settles in my chest like a vow. The dominance in his voice has my core clenching with renewed desire.

"Yours," I agree, meeting his gaze without hesitation.

His eyes shift to midnight, pupils dilating until only a thin ring of green remains. "Say it again." His voice is rough, commanding.

"I'm yours, Dominic." The words echo through me, an admission that ignites something fierce and unspoken between us.

He moves so quickly I barely register it—flipping me onto my back, pinning my wrists above my head with one large hand. His body hovers over mine, his erection already hard against my thigh.

"Again," he growls, his free hand sliding down my body, fingers finding me slick and ready despite my earlier exhaustion.

"Yours," I gasp as he pushes two thick fingers inside me, my walls clenching around the intrusion. "Oh god, Dominic—"

"Mine," he confirms, his thumb circling my clit with ruthless focus. "Every inch of this perfect body belongs to me now."

I arch beneath him, helpless against the rush of pleasure climbing fast. His fingers curl just right, and my vision sparks white-hot behind my eyelids.

"Please," I whimper, not even sure what I'm begging for.

"Please what, little minx? Tell me what you need." His voice is velvet-wrapped steel, commanding yet tender.

"I need you inside me again," I pant, rolling my hips against his hand. "Please, Dominic."

His eyes flash with carnal satisfaction. "Already? So greedy for my cock." He withdraws his fingers, making me whimper at the loss. "Turn over. Hands and knees."

I comply without hesitation, my body trembling with anticipation as I present myself to him. His large hands grip my hips, positioning me exactly how he wants me. I feel the blunt head of his impressive length pressing against my entrance, and I bite my lip, bracing myself for the satisfying sting.

"Remember who you belong to," he growls, then slams into me in one powerful thrust.

I cry out, the sensation overwhelming—pain and pleasure blurring into something transcendent. He's so big, it's a violation I welcome, pressure mounting so hard I forget how to breathe. My arms give out, and I collapse onto my elbows, my face pressed against the sheets as he establishes a punishing rhythm.

"So eager for my fucking cock, aren't you?" He groans, one hand sliding up my spine to tangle in my hair. He pulls, arching my back at a severe angle. "Such a perfect little pussy, so tight around my dick."

Heat floods through me. I've never been with someone who talks like this, who claims me so completely. Each thrust drives me closer to the edge, the new angle letting him hit spots deep inside that shatters every thought.

"Dominic—" I gasp his name as he drives deeper, his thickness stretching me almost painfully. "Oh god, I can't—it's too much—"

"You can take it," he growls against my ear, his chest pressing against my back as he maintains his bruising pace. "Every part of you screams for me."

His hand slides around to find my clit, teasing the swollen bud with a ruthless control. The dual stimulation is overwhelming, building a pressure inside me that threatens to shatter me completely.

"That's it, baby," he encourages as my walls flutter, needy and desperate around him. "Let go for me. Show me how much you love my cock."

My climax hits with devastating force, tearing a scream from my throat as waves of pleasure crash through me. Dominic doesn't slow, fucking me through it, prolonging the intense sensations until I'm sobbing his name, begging incoherently.

"Not done with you yet," he warns, his voice strained with his own restraint. He pulls out suddenly, leaving me empty and aching, then flips me onto my back. "I want to see your face when I fill you with my cum."

His words crack through the haze of fatigue, dragging desire right back to the surface like it never left. He positions himself between my trembling thighs, the head of his cock nudging at my entrance again. This time, he enters me slowly, his eyes locked on mine as he fills me with deliberate pressure that borders on blissful torment.

"Watch yourself give in to me," he commands, his voice rough with desire. "Watch me claim what's mine."

I force my heavy eyelids open, looking down to where our bodies join. The sight of his thick length disappearing inside me, forcing my body to surrender to his size, drowns me in more need, even with every nerve raw and frayed.

"So beautiful," he groans, one hand gripping my hip while the other moves to my throat, applying just enough pressure to make my pulse race. "So fucking perfect for me."

His thrusts grow more forceful, more desperate, the controlled rhythm faltering as his own release approaches. His thumb presses against my bottom lip, and I instinctively open for him, sucking it into my mouth.

"That's it, baby," he growls, his eyes dark with desire. "Such a good girl for me."

The praise washes over me like a physical caress, igniting something fierce and all-consuming inside me. I wrap my legs around his waist, pulling him deeper, wanting—needing—to feel every inch of him. He groans my name, his release spilling deep inside me, claiming me all over again.

The intensity of my climax crashes through me, pulling me under waves of pleasure as Dominic collapses beside me, his breathing ragged. He pulls me against his chest, one strong arm wrapped tightly around my waist.

"Sleep now, little minx," he murmurs into my hair, his voice a drowsy rumble. "You'll need your strength for round three."

I smile against his skin, too exhausted to form words. The steady rhythm of his heartbeat lulls me into darkness, my body utterly spent and satisfied.

I'm floating in that hazy space between sleeping and waking when I feel it—strong hands sliding up my thighs, parting them with gentle insistence. Still caught in dreams, I sigh and shift, allowing access without opening my eyes.

"You're so beautiful when you sleep," Dominic's voice whispers in the darkness. "So peaceful. So mine."

His fingers trace delicate patterns up my inner thighs, gradually moving higher until they brush against my center. Even in sleep, my body responds to him, growing wet and ready.

"That's it, baby," he murmurs. "Open for me."

I feel the bed dip as he positions himself between my legs. The blunt head of his cock presses against my entrance, and I moan softly, still drifting in that twilight state where dreams and reality blur together.

"So perfect," he groans as he pushes inside me, the slow press of his length lighting me up from the inside. The intoxicating friction sends waves of pleasure through me, even as I hover at the edge of consciousness.

"That's it," he whispers, his voice thick with desire. "You're going to feel me for days."

He fills me completely, his thickness forcing me open in a way that makes my nerves sing. I arch beneath him, my body responding instinctively to his claim. His hips fall into a steady rhythm, each thrust pushing me higher into pleasure. His hands grip my thighs, spreading me wider, forcing himself so deep it knocks the breath right out of my lungs.

"You feel so good around me," he groans, his pace increasing. "So tight. So perfect."

I moan, my head thrashing against the pillow as he hits that perfect spot inside me. His mouth finds my breast, teeth grazing my nipple before sucking it between his lips. The dual sensation makes me cry out, my back arching off the bed.

"That's it, baby," he encourages, one hand sliding between us to circle my clit. "Cum for me. Let me feel you."

The pressure builds rapidly, his expert touches pushing me toward a blinding climax. My walls clench around him as the pleasure crests, washing over me in powerful waves. I scream his name as I shatter, my nails digging into his shoulders.

"Fuck, Octavia," he growls, his thrusts becoming erratic. "I'm cumming again."

I gasp and bolt upright, my heart racing, my body flushed with heat. The sheets are tangled around my legs, damp with sweat. I blink in confusion, my hand instinctively reaching beside me, finding only empty space.

"Dominic?" I whisper into the darkness.

Silence answers me. My bedroom slowly comes into focus as my eyes adjust to the dim light filtering through my curtains. I'm alone. Completely alone.

It was just a dream. An incredibly vivid, toe-curling dream that has left me aching and frustrated. I slip out of bed, my eyes landing on Dominic's shirt and pants still crumpled on the floor. He hasn't left. So where the hell is he?

I tug on his shirt and pad into the kitchen—only to find him making breakfast like he owns the place. Seriously? What time is it? And how the hell did I sleep through all of this?

"Well, good morning, beautiful," Dominic says, his voice a low rumble that sends tingles through my still-sensitized body. He's wearing only his boxer briefs, the fabric doing little to hide his impressive morning situation. His hair is tousled, his jaw darkened with stubble that I can still feel burning between my thighs.

"You made breakfast?" I ask, stupidly, as if the pancakes flipping in the pan and the coffee brewing aren't obvious enough.

He raises an eyebrow, a smirk playing at his lips. "I worked up quite an appetite last night. Figured you might need sustenance, too."

The memories of last night flood back in vivid detail, making heat pool low in my belly. My thighs press together instinctively.

"I thought you'd left," I admit, leaning against the doorframe. His shirt hangs loosely on my frame, barely covering the essentials.

"Without saying goodbye?" He turns fully toward me, his eyes darkening as they travel down my body. "Not a chance, little minx."

"Don't you have some important CEO things to do today? Emergency board meetings? Hostile takeovers? Crushing the souls of competitors?"

He laughs, the sound rich and genuine. "All that can wait." He flips a pancake smooth as hell. "Besides, it's Saturday."

"Oh." I'd completely lost track of time. That's what mind-blowing sex does to a girl, apparently. I push away from the doorframe, moving toward the coffee pot. Dominic's arm snakes around my waist before I can reach it, pulling me against his hard chest.

"Good morning," he murmurs against my neck, his stubble scraping intoxicatingly against my delicate skin. His hand slips under the shirt I'm wearing—his shirt—fingers splaying across my bare stomach.

"Morning," I reply, my voice embarrassingly breathy. I should be playing it cool, not melting into him like chocolate in the sun, but my body has other ideas. It remembers exactly what those hands can do.

"You were talking in your sleep," he says, his lips brushing the shell of my ear. "Something about wanting me inside you again."

My cheeks flame. "I was not."

"You absolutely were." His hand slides lower, fingers dipping between my thighs. "And you're soaked, little minx. Were you dreaming about me?"

I squirm against him, caught between embarrassment and arousal. "Maybe."

"Tell me," he demands softly, his fingers circling my entrance without pushing inside. "Tell me what you were dreaming about."

"You," I admit, my hips involuntarily pushing against his hand, seeking more pressure. "You were... waking me up."

"Like this?" His fingers push inside me, making me gasp. "Were my fingers inside you in your dream, Octavia?"

"N-No," I stammer, my breath hitching as his skilled fingers curl inside me. "It was your... your cock."

His low growl of approval vibrates against my back. "Tell me more," he commands, adding a second finger, making me ache in the best possible way. "What was I doing to you with my cock?"

My head falls back against his shoulder as his thumb finds my clit, circling with mind-numbing accuracy. "You were... oh god... you were taking me while I was half-asleep. Slow at first, then—" I gasp as he presses against that perfect spot inside me. "Then harder."

"Like this?" He withdraws his fingers suddenly, leaving me empty and aching. Before I can protest, he spins me around, lifting me onto the kitchen counter. The cool surface against my bare ass makes me gasp. Dominic steps between my spread thighs, his boxer briefs tented impressively.

"Is this what you want, little minx?" he asks, his voice rough with desire as he frees himself from the confining fabric. "You want me to fuck you right here in your kitchen?"

"Yes," I breathe, beyond caring about anything but having him inside me again. "Please, Dominic."

He smirks, positioning himself at my entrance. "Such pretty manners." He pushes forward slowly, just the tip breaching me. "But I think you can beg prettier than that."

I should be offended by his arrogance, but something about his dominance makes me wild with need. I tighten my legs around his waist, trying to pull him deeper. He resists, holding back with infuriating control.

"Please fuck me," I whimper, my pride abandoned in the face of my desperate need. "I need you inside me. I need to feel you filling me until I can't think."

His eyes darken to midnight. "Good girl," he growls, then thrusts forward in one powerful stroke, burying himself to the hilt.

I cry out, my back arching as he fills me completely. It's overwhelming—too much and somehow not enough. He gives me no time to adjust, setting a punishing rhythm that has me clinging to his shoulders.

"This what you dreamed about?" he asks, his voice strained as he drives into me. "Me taking you hard and fast? Claiming what's mine?"

"Yes," I gasp, each thrust pushing me closer to the edge. "God, yes!"

"Look at me," he commands, one hand tangling in my hair to tilt my face up. "Let me see how fucking ruined you look when you cum for me."

I force myself to look up, and for a second, everything stills. The way he looks at me—it's not just physical. It's like he's reaching for something more. His rhythm falters slightly, and I know he feels it too—this is more than just incredible sex.

"Dominic," I breathe his name like a prayer as the pressure builds inside me, coiling tighter with each thrust. "I'm so close—"

"Don't hold back," he growls, thumb relentless against my clit. "Make a fucking mess for me, Octavia."

My orgasm crashes through me with such force that I scream, my inner walls clamping down around him as wave after wave of pleasure pulses through my body. He groans, his rhythm faltering as my orgasm triggers his own. He buries himself deep, his cock pulsing inside me as he fills me with his release.

For a moment, we stay locked together, breathing hard, his forehead pressed against mine. The intimacy of the moment threatens to overwhelm me. This isn't just sex anymore—it's something deeper, more dangerous.

"So," I say when I can finally form words again, desperate to lighten the mood before I drown in the intensity. "Is this how you treat all your new employees, or am I getting special onboarding perks?"

He laughs, the sound rumbling through his chest. "Only the redheaded marketing specialists with smart mouths and brilliant minds."

"That's quite the specific category," I tease, wincing slightly as he withdraws from me. My body already misses his fullness.

"You're in a category all your own, little minx." He kisses me softly, then steps back, tucking himself away. "Now eat your breakfast before it gets too cold. I didn't spend twenty minutes making these pancakes just to let them go to waste."

I slide off the counter on shaky legs, tugging his shirt down to cover myself. "Didn't know CEOs could cook."

"There's a lot you don't know about me yet." The way he says 'yet' sends a pleasant shiver down my spine. It implies a future, more mornings like this.

I hop onto one of my barstools, wincing slightly at the soreness between my thighs. Dominic notices—of course he does—and a satisfied smirk plays across his lips.

"Sore?" he asks, sliding a plate of pancakes in front of me.

"Don't look so smug," I mutter, but can't help smiling. "It's unbecoming."

"Liar," he counters, pouring coffee into a mug and placing it beside my plate. "You like it when I'm smug."

"I tolerate it," I correct, taking a bite of pancake. The buttery sweetness explodes on my tongue, and I can't hold back an appreciative moan. "Oh my god, these are amazing."

"I excel at everything I do, Octavia." The double meaning isn't lost on me, and warmth spreads across my skin.

My phone buzzes on the counter, and I reach for it automatically. Lena's name flashes on the screen.

LENA

Did you die? Or just get laid?

Shit I forgot to call her last night. I snatch the phone up before

Dominic can see it, but I'm too late. He raises an eyebrow, amusement dancing in his eyes.

"Friend of yours?" he asks.

"Best friend," I reply, quickly typing back.

ME

Still alive. Details later. Having breakfast. 😈

"The same friend who was asking about me ravishing you on my desk?" Dominic asks casually, sipping his coffee.

I nearly choke on my pancake. "You saw that?"

"I catch glimpses of things," he says with that infuriating smirk. "Good peripheral vision. Comes in handy in business."

"I'm sure it does," I mutter, feeling my cheeks burn. "Her name is Lena. She's... protective."

"Protective?" He raises an eyebrow. "Of what, exactly?"

"Me," I say simply. "She's been there through... everything."

Something in my tone must alert him because his expression shifts, becoming more serious. "Everything, meaning?"

I hesitate, not wanting to kill the mood with talk of Tyler and my past disasters. "Just life. Bad relationships. Good ones, too, I guess, though those have been rarer."

Dominic studies me over the rim of his coffee mug, his green eyes intense. "This Lena sounds like someone I should meet."

"God, no," I laugh, nearly spitting out my coffee. "She'd interrogate you like a serial killer on trial."

"I'm not afraid of interrogations, little minx." His confidence is both irritating and sexy.

"You would be," I insist, stabbing a piece of pancake with my fork. "Lena once made my college boyfriend cry during what was supposed to be a casual brunch. The poor guy transferred schools."

Dominic laughs, a rich sound that does ridiculous things to my insides. "I've faced down billion-dollar corporate raiders and hostile boards. I think I can handle your friend."

"Your funeral," I sing-song, taking another bite. "She'll ask you about your intentions, your five-year plan for us, your views on feminism, and probably demand to see your STD test results."

"All reasonable questions," he says with maddening confidence. "My intentions are to keep you in my bed as often as possible. My five-year plan involves you continuing to challenge me professionally and personally. My views on feminism are that any man threatened by a woman's equality isn't much of a man. And I get tested regularly—all clear, in case you were wondering."

I blink, taken aback by his straightforward answers. "That was... thorough."

"I told you, I excel at everything." He leans across the counter, his eyes locked on mine. "Including answering difficult questions."

My phone buzzes again. I glance down to see another text from Lena.

LENA

OMG YOU'RE STILL WITH HIM?? Is he as good as he looks? Scale of 1-10? DETAILS WOMAN!!!

I quickly flip my phone over and look up to find Dominic watching me with amusement.

"Your friend is persistent," he observes, taking another sip of coffee.

"You have no idea." I set my phone face-down on the counter. "She won't let this go until I give her something."

"By all means." He gestures toward my phone with a casual wave. "Don't let me stop you."

I narrow my eyes at him. "You want me to tell her about... this?" I gesture between us.

"Is there something to tell?" His expression is infuriatingly neutral, but there's a challenge in his eyes.

"I don't know, is there?" I counter, crossing my arms. "We haven't exactly defined... whatever this is."

Dominic sets down his coffee mug and rounds the counter, coming to stand between my knees as I perch on the barstool. His hands settle on my thighs, warm and greedy.

"Would you like me to define it for you, Octavia?" His voice drops to that commanding tone that makes my insides liquify.

"I'd like to hear your thoughts on the matter," I manage, trying to sound casual despite the heat building between my legs again.

He leans in closer, lips brushing against my ear. "You're mine now. I don't share what's mine. And I have no intention of letting you go anytime soon."

CHAPTER TEN

Dominic

She trembles against me, her breath catching in her throat. For a moment, she's perfectly still, and I wonder if I've finally pushed too far, crossed a line that can't be uncrossed. Then, she pulls back just enough to look me in the eyes, that fire I've come to crave dancing in her gaze.

"Interesting theory, Mr. Callahan," she says, her voice lower than usual, husky with something that makes my blood run hot. "But I don't recall signing ownership papers when I accepted this job. Was that in the fine print I missed?"

I can't help the dark chuckle that escapes me. Even now, with tension thick enough to cut between us, she challenges me. It's intoxicating.

"Not in the contract," I murmur, reaching up to twist one of her fiery curls around my finger. "Consider it more of a... mutual understanding we're developing."

"Mutual?" She arches one perfect eyebrow. "That implies I get something out of this arrangement, too. What exactly would that be?"

My hand slides from her hair to cup her cheek, thumb brushing across her bottom lip. Her eyes darken, pupils dilating as she parts her

lips slightly.

"Everything," I promise, my voice rough with desire. "Everything you need. Everything you want. Everything you didn't even know you were craving."

She leans into my touch, just barely, but it's enough to make triumph surge through me.

"Pretty confident for someone I barely know," she whispers, but there's no real resistance in her voice. Her kitchen counter presses against her back as I move closer, eliminating any space between us.

"I know enough," I tell her, my free hand finding her waist, feeling the warmth of her skin through the thin fabric of her dress. "I know how your breath catches when I touch you here—" My fingers drift lower, tracing the curve of her hip. "I know how your eyes darken when I use that tone of voice you pretend to hate."

"I do hate it," she lies, her hands coming up to rest against my chest, not pushing me away but not pulling me closer either. "It's arrogant and presumptuous and—"

"And it makes you wet," I finish for her, watching her cheeks flush with color. "Doesn't it, Octavia?"

She bites her lip, a gesture so innocently seductive it nearly undoes me. "You think you know everything?"

"Not everything," I admit, leaning down to press my lips to the pulse point at her neck, feeling it race beneath my touch. "I'm going to learn everything about you, Octavia—and I won't stop until I do."

Her breath hitches as she tilts her head, giving me better access to her neck. "And what if I don't want to be figured out?" she challenges, even as her fingers curl into the fabric of my shirt. "What if I prefer to remain a mystery?"

I smile against her skin, teeth grazing lightly over her pulse point before soothing it with my tongue. "Too late," I murmur. "I've already gotten a taste. And I'm not a man who stops at just a sample."

Her laugh is breathy, half desire and half genuine amusement. "God, do you practice these lines in the mirror? 'I'm Dominic Callahan, and I don't stop at samples,'" she mimics, lowering her voice in an exaggerated impression of mine.

I pull back just enough to see her face, letting out a small laugh. "You're impossible."

"And yet here you are," she points out, her hands sliding up to my shoulders. My shirt—still clinging to her—rides up with every shift, revealing more of those thighs that won't stop haunting me.

"Here I am," I agree, my hands finding her bare legs, skin impossibly soft beneath my palms. "Though, I should be heading home to change."

Her eyes flicker with something—disappointment?—before she masks it with a teasing smile. "I've got to get some clean clothes, baby," I say, voice low and steady, "But don't get comfortable thinking I'm gone for long. I'll be back— *you're mine*, and I'm not finished with you yet." I pause, smirking as my eyes linger on the way my shirt clings to her curves. "Not when you look that fucking good in something that belongs to me."

She rolls her eyes, but I catch the way her thighs press together, the slight hitch in her breathing. "Don't flatter yourself, Callahan. I'm only wearing it because it was convenient."

"Is that so?" I step closer again, backing her fully against the counter. My hands slide beneath the shirt, finding her bare hips. "Then you won't mind if I take it back right now?"

Her eyes widen slightly, that delicious blush spreading across her cheeks again. "In my kitchen? Really?"

"Really. It's not like I didn't already fuck you in here, Octavia" I confirm, enjoying the way she squirms slightly under my gaze. "Unless you'd prefer to admit you like wearing my clothes?"

She narrows her eyes at the challenge. "Fine. I like wearing your shirt. It smells like you. Happy now?"

The simple admission hits me with an unexpected force, a territorial satisfaction unfurling in my chest. "Extremely."

"You're insufferable," she mutters, but there's no heat behind it.

"And you're beautiful," I counter, watching surprise flicker across her features before she can mask it. Has no one ever told her that before? The thought makes something protective and dangerous stir within me.

"I should get going," I say, even though every part of me is screaming to stay—*to take my time with her, to claim her all over again.* "I need clean clothes, and you need... well, clothes in general."

Her laugh is bright and genuine, a melody I find myself craving more and more. "So, your master plan is to go home, change clothes, and come right back?"

"Is that a problem?" I lean closer, my breath mingling with hers.

"Not at all," she says, trying to sound casual but failing to hide the anticipation in her voice. "I just think it's funny that the great Dominic Callahan, who probably has meetings scheduled down to the minute, is spending his precious Saturday shuttling back and forth to my apartment."

"I can think of worse ways to spend my time." My fingers trace lazy patterns on her thigh, just below where my shirt ends. "Much worse."

She shivers under my touch, then suddenly ducks under my arm, creating space between us. The loss of contact is immediate and frustrating.

"Well, while you're gone, I should probably shower," she says, stretching her arms above her head. Her shirt rides up dangerously high. I catch a glimpse of the curve of her ass and have to physically restrain myself from reaching for her. "Maybe even put on some actual clothes."

"That seems unnecessary," I growl, eyes locked on her as she backs toward the hallway.

"Oh?" she fires back, the challenge in her voice sharp and unmissable. "Did you have other plans for me today besides playing dress-up?"

I take a slow, deliberate step toward her. "I have *plenty* of plans for you, Octavia. Most of them don't require clothing…"

I pause, letting my gaze drag down her body before lifting back to meet her eyes.

"…But when I come back, you're going to need *pants*. And *tennis shoes.*"

Her brow lifts, curious.

I smirk. "We're not taking the car."

"Not taking the car?" She blinks, confusion adorably evident on her face. "What are we doing? Going for a jog?" She scrunches her nose at the thought.

"You'll find out when I get back," I say, enjoying the way her curiosity clearly wars with her desire to appear nonchalant. "Consider it a surprise."

"I hate surprises," she declares, crossing her arms over her chest, which only serves to push her breasts up against the thin fabric of my shirt. "They're usually disappointing."

I step forward, closing the distance between us in two strides. My hand slides around the back of her neck, fingers threading through those wild red curls as I tilt her face up to mine.

"I promise you," I murmur against her lips, "disappointment is not in my vocabulary."

Her breath catches, her body instinctively leaning into mine. For a moment, I consider forgetting my plans, forgetting clean clothes, forgetting everything but taking her back to bed right now. But no—I want more than just her body today. I want to see her laugh, to watch her experience something new with me, to create memories that extend beyond her bedroom walls.

"One hour," I tell her, reluctantly pulling away. "Be ready."

She narrows her eyes, challenge sparking in that blue gaze. "And if I'm not?"

"Then I'll dress you myself," I promise, my voice dropping to that register that makes her shiver. That familiar flush creeps across her cheeks, the subtle tightening of her thighs as she shifts her weight from one foot to the other.

"That sounds more like incentive than a threat," she quips, but her voice has that breathy quality that tells me exactly how affected she is.

I lean in, letting my lips graze the shell of her ear. "That wasn't a threat, baby. Just a promise"

Before she can respond, I step back and slide my shirt off her shoulders, letting the fabric fall away and reveal her—bare, waiting, beautiful. Her nipples are peaked, her breath shallow as she stares at me like she doesn't know whether to run or melt.

I don't give her the chance to choose.

I kiss her—slow, deep—then turn away, pulling my shirt on as I head toward her room where my pants are still crumpled on the floor.

She trails after me with a huff, and I smile to myself.

"What if I don't want to let you leave?" she asks, leaning against the doorframe of her bedroom, watching as I pull my pants on. Her naked body is a masterpiece—every curve, every inch of soft skin still bearing the marks of everything I did to her this morning.

"You could always try to stop me," I challenge, zipping my fly and buckling my belt. I can feel her eyes tracking each movement of my hands.

She pushes off the doorframe and saunters towards me, a predatory gleam in her eyes that makes my cock stir again despite myself. "I have my methods"

When she reaches me, she runs her hands up my chest, fingers playing with the buttons of my shirt. "I could make you forget all about your plans"

"I don't doubt it," I admit, catching her wandering hands in mine. "Which is exactly why I need to leave now"

She pouts, and the expression is so adorably conflicting with her naked state that I can't help but laugh. I give her ass a playful swat, making her yelp in surprise.

"One hour," I remind her, pressing a quick kiss to her forehead. "Wear something comfortable and practical."

"Practical?" She wrinkles her nose. "Now I'm definitely concerned."

I'm still chuckling as I head for the door, pausing only to look back at her standing there — wild-haired, kiss-swollen lips, naked and glowing.

I step outside and head for my car, unlocking it with a sigh. As I check my phone, my chest tightens—five missed calls, ten texts. All from Derek and Marcus.

All about fucking Tom.

How the hell did I forget so easily?

I check the most recent text from Marcus.

MARCUS

Tom's talking. A lot. Get your ass over here ASAP.

"Fuck," I mutter, sliding into the driver's seat and starting the engine. I had completely compartmentalized the Tom situation the moment I'd seen Octavia in my shirt this morning. How is it possible that one woman could make me forget about a potentially company-ending crisis?

I dial Marcus as I pull away from her apartment.

"Finally," he answers on the first ring. "Where the hell have you been? I've been calling you all morning."

"Handling something," I say vaguely. "What's happening with Tom?"

"He's singing like a fucking canary. Derek's with him now at the office, but we need to move quickly. He's talking about going to the board."

My grip tightens on the steering wheel. "What exactly does he know?"

"Enough," Marcus says grimly. "The Harrington deal, for starters. And he's got documentation on the Chen acquisition that could be... problematic."

"Shit." I change lanes aggressively, cutting off a minivan whose driver honks angrily. "I'll be there in twenty. Don't let him leave."

"Already ahead of you. Derek's playing good cop, keeping him comfortable." Marcus pauses. "Just how far do you want to take this, Dom?"

The question hangs between us, loaded with implication. We've crossed certain lines, but it has been years.

"Whatever it takes," I say coldly, a familiar darkness settling over me like an old coat. "I didn't build this company from nothing just to have some self-righteous accountant tear it all down."

"Understood," Marcus says, his tone shifting to business. "I'll prepare the conference room. Soundproof, no cameras."

I end the call and immediately dial Octavia's number, cursing under my breath as I weave through traffic. She answers on the third ring, her voice still carrying that breathless quality that would normally make my blood rush south.

"Miss me already?" she teases.

"I need to postpone," I say, keeping my voice neutral, controlled.

"Something's come up at work."

There's a pause, and I can almost see her expression falling before she masks it with casual indifference. "On a Saturday? Must be important."

"It is," I confirm, taking the exit toward Digi Pulse's headquarters. "I'll make it up to you."

"Don't worry about it," she says quickly, too quickly. "It's fine. I have plenty to do today anyway."

The slight stiffness in her tone tells me it's not fine, but I don't have time to navigate her disappointment right now. Not with Tom threatening everything I've built.

"I'll call you later," I promise, then hesitate before adding, "I meant what I said earlier, Octavia. This isn't just sex for me."

"Right," she says, but I can hear the doubt creeping into her voice. "Look, you don't owe me explanations, Dominic. We're both adults. Go handle your big important crisis."

"Octavia—" I start, but she cuts me off.

"I'll talk to you later, okay? Bye."

The line goes dead before I can respond. I slam my palm against the steering wheel, frustration boiling through me. This thing with her is too new, too fragile to withstand my sudden disappearance after what just happened between us. But Tom is an immediate threat that needs handling.

I pull into the underground parking garage of Digi Pulse, my mind shifting into a darker gear as I step out of the car. By the time the elevator doors open to the executive floor, I've locked away thoughts of Octavia's disappointment and naked body. The man who steps into the conference room is not the same man who left her apartment twenty minutes ago.

Marcus and Derek look up as I enter. Tom sits between them, his face pale and sweaty, eyes darting nervously around the room.

"Dominic," he stammers, half-rising from his chair. "I was just explaining to Marcus and Derek that—"

"Sit down."

My voice is quiet, calm. But Tom hears something in it—*finally* hears it—and his body obeys before his brain can catch up. He drops into the chair like the floor's been ripped out from under him.

I unbutton my suit jacket slowly, deliberately, and lower myself into the seat across from him. Hands folded. Controlled. Measured.

For now.

"Tell me, Tom…" I say, my tone casual, almost conversational. "What made you think it was a good idea to threaten going to your board about our little visit last night?"

He opens his mouth, but I don't let him speak. I'm already moving.

One moment we're talking—

The next, the table slams as I drive it back into him with enough force to knock the breath from his lungs. His eyes go wide, panicked, and mine… mine don't waver.

"You were warned." I lean in, voice still even. "But you didn't listen. And now you've confirmed what I already knew…"

My gaze hardens.

"You're a fucking liability I should have handled the moment I found out what you did."

Tom's face drains of all color, and I can see the moment it clicks— the realization that this isn't just business intimidation anymore. This is something far more dangerous.

"What I did?" he whispers, voice trembling. "I was just doing my job, looking at the books—"

"Your job?" I snarl, leaning in, eyes locked on his. "Was it your job to siphon company funds through Shell Corps? To doctor financials and bury the theft? To funnel money offshore like no one would notice?"

Tom's face pales, but he tries to rally. His voice cracks with disbelief.

"Now you're threatening me? You're going to turn *me* in—for what I did... to *you*?" I let the silence stretch, watching the panic flicker in his eyes. I don't raise my voice. I don't have to.

I adjust my cuffs, smooth my jacket, and lean back in my chair like this is just business. Just another item on my list.

"You misunderstood something, Tom," I say, my tone flat, almost bored. "I'm not threatening you."

He shifts uncomfortably, but I keep my eyes on him, unblinking.

"I'm informing you."

His lips part, maybe to beg, maybe to lie. I don't give a fuck.

"You stole from me. You buried the trial. You funneled money out of the one thing that could have given her more time."

I lean forward, slow and deliberate, my voice dropping to something lethal.

"My mother is *dead* because of you."

He tries to speak, but it's already too late. The moment's passed. The damage is done.

"You were sloppy. You were greedy. And now you're in my way."

I pause, letting that truth settle between us like a loaded gun.

"And you already know how I deal with problems." Tom's mouth opens again, desperation finally catching up to denial.

"Dominic—"

I move before he can finish.

One fluid motion.

No hesitation.

The suppressed pistol I keep beneath the table is in my hand, silencer already threaded.

He doesn't even have time to stand.

One shot—low and clean—rips through his thigh. Not fatal. Not yet.

He screams, slumping sideways, clutching at the leg that won't support him anymore.

"You think this is revenge?" I ask quietly, standing and stepping around the obstacle between us.

"No. This is a correction."

He tries to crawl back, blood slicking his palms. He's babbling now—promises, apologies, useless noise. I crouch in front of him, tilting my head.

"You stole time from her," I say, and it's not anger that laces my voice now—it's grief sharpened into something deadly.

"So I'm taking the rest of yours."

I raise the weapon.

This time, I don't aim to wound.

The shot is quiet. Final.

Tom slumps to the floor, eyes still open like he didn't believe it would actually happen. Like somewhere in his pathetic little mind, he thought I'd let him walk away.

I exhale slowly and stand, sliding the gun back into its hiding place.

Blood pools beneath his body, spreading like ink across the tile. I don't look away. I *want* this to be burned into me.

"Clean this up," I say to Marcus, my voice steady despite the corpse at my feet. "No traces."

"Already on it," he replies, pulling out his phone. "The usual crew?"

I nod, straightening my cuffs. Blood has splattered across my shoes—Italian leather, custom-made. They'll need to be replaced.

Derek stands motionless, staring at Tom's body. He's been with me through everything, but he's never been comfortable with this side of the business. The necessary side.

"Derek," I say, and his eyes snap to mine. "You good?"

He swallows hard, then nods once. "Always am."

"Good. I need you to handle the financial side. Make it look like Tom embezzled more than we initially thought, then fled the country. Drain his accounts, route the money through the Caymans. Leave a trail."

"Consider it done," Derek says, already pulling himself together, compartmentalizing like I taught him years ago.

I check my watch. Barely forty minutes since I left Octavia's apartment.

"I'll be unavailable for the rest of the day," I tell them, my decision already made.

The darkness that consumed me moments ago recedes like a tide, leaving me hollow but focused. "Handle the cleanup. I have somewhere to be."

Marcus gives me a knowing look. "The redhead?"

I don't dignify that with a response. "Call me if there are complications."

"There won't be," Marcus assures me, already on his phone arranging for the disposal team. "Go. We've got this."

I stride toward the private executive bathroom, my movements mechanical and precise. Blood has spattered across the cuffs of my shirt—tiny crimson droplets barely visible against the dark fabric, but there nonetheless. I remove my jacket, roll up my sleeves, and methodically wash my hands, watching Tom's blood swirl down the drain.

My body still carries her scent, my lips still remember her taste. The contradiction should disturb me—how I can go from fucking her to putting a bullet in a man's head without missing a beat.

But it doesn't. This is who I am. This is what made Digi Pulse possible.

The face that stares back at me in the mirror is unreadable, eyes cold and distant. This is the real Dominic Callahan – not the man who whispered promises against Octavia's skin this morning, but the man who built an empire on ruthless decisions and calculated risks. The man who just executed someone without hesitation.

Would she look at me the same way if she knew?

The question lingers as I dry my hands and check my appearance. I look composed, controlled—nothing like a man who just took a life. Years of practice.

My phone buzzes with a text from Octavia.

OCTAVIA

For what it's worth, I was looking forward to our surprise. Rain check?

Something shifts in my chest—a strange tightness I don't immediately recognize. Regret? No, something else. Something dangerously close to longing.

I stare at her message, thumbs hovering over the screen. I should cut this off now. Someone like her doesn't belong in my world—a world where I can transition from lover to killer without breaking stride. She deserves better than a man with blood on his hands.

But I'm not a good man. I've never claimed to be. And I want her anyway.

I type back.

ME

Be ready in 40.

Her response comes quickly.

OCTAVIA

Bossy. But I'll be waiting.

I check my reflection once more, ensuring every trace of what just happened is gone. I've spent a lifetime perfecting this mask—the successful, controlled CEO that everyone sees. Only a select few know what lurks beneath the surface.

As I exit the building, Derek is leaning against my car, looking far too pleased with himself. He was supposed to be upstairs. Apparently, doing what he is told is optional now.

"You sure about this, Dom?" he asks quietly. "Mixing her up in your life right now might not be the wisest move."

"She's already mixed up in it," I reply, straightening my cuffs. "She just doesn't know it yet."

Derek sighs, rubbing his forehead. "Just... be careful. For both your sakes."

I nod once, not bothering to explain further. Derek understands better than most what's at stake. For all his reluctance about our methods, he's loyal to the core. He's seen all the sacrifices required to reach these heights.

I drive back to my penthouse first, stripping off my blood-spattered clothes and stepping into a scalding shower. I scrub my skin until it's red and raw, watching the water swirl down the drain. There's no visible trace of Tom left on me, but I feel the weight of what I've done settling into my bones like a familiar ache.

I used to care. Then I learned how useless that was. Tom crossed a line that was unforgivable. A quick death was mercy—one he didn't earn. I won't waste a single ounce of regret on a piece of shit like him.

CHAPTER ELEVEN

Dominic

I dress in clean clothes—dark jeans, a gray t-shirt, and a black hoodie. Casual, but still me. I check my reflection one last time, noting the hardness in my eyes that never quite disappears these days. Will Octavia see it? Will she sense the blood on my hands when I touch her? Will she feel it the way I do—thick and clinging, seeping beneath her skin the moment I lay my fingers on her? I wonder if she'll notice how it stains, how no matter how gentle I try to be, I'll still leave something behind. Something she can't wash off.

I shake my head, trying to dispel these thoughts. Tonight isn't about who I am or what I've done. It's about her.

I grab my helmet and keys, heading down to the garage where my collection waits in silence.

I pass over the Porsche. That wasn't tonight's plan.

Before Tom fucked everything up, I was going to take Octavia on the backroads—ride out past the city, maybe through the twisting hills above Snoqualmie. Wind in her hair, her arms around me, nothing but the sound of the engine and the blur of trees. Just us. Something simple. Something good.

It's later than I planned. But I'm still taking her.

My BMW S1000RR waits where I left it, its body catching the light with a quiet, lethal shine. There's no mistaking it—this night was made for speed and silence.

Perfect.

My phone buzzes in my pocket.

DEREK

You sure about this?

Boss dating employee never ends well.

I don't bother responding. Derek means well, but he doesn't understand. This isn't dating. This is... hell, I don't know what this is. An obsession. A compulsion. A need I can't seem to shake no matter how many times I tell myself to walk away.

The bike roars to life beneath me, vibrating between my thighs. The sensation grounds me, reminds me I'm still human despite everything. I peel out of the garage, the cool night air slicing through the clothes against my skin. It clears my head, if only temporarily.

Fifteen minutes later, I'm parked outside Octavia's apartment building, engine idling.

I kill the ignition, remove my helmet, and get off the bike. My heart pounds against my ribs like it's trying to escape. I haven't felt this nervous since I pitched my business plan to investors eight years ago. Back then, my entire future hinged on that moment. Tonight feels just as pivotal, though I can't articulate why.

I send her a text.

ME

I'm outside.

Simple. Direct. No room for misinterpretation.

Three minutes later, the building's front door swings open, and she steps out into the night. My breath catches in my throat. She's wearing a simple outfit—fitted black jeans that hug those curves I can't stop thinking about, a white crop top that makes her hair look like living flame, and a leather jacket that's slightly too big for her frame. It's not the kind of outfit that should stop traffic, but on her, it's devastating.

Her eyes find mine, and for a moment, neither of us moves.

"You came," she says, approaching cautiously, like I might change my mind and speed away.

"I said I would." My voice sounds rougher than I intended.

She stops a few feet from me, her eyes drifting to the motorcycle. "That's... not what I was expecting."

"Disappointed?" I ask, unable to keep the edge from my voice. I'm giving her an out, even now. A chance to walk away from whatever dangerous game we're playing.

But she surprises me with a slow smile that lights up her entire face,

"Are you kidding? It's beautiful," she says, approaching the bike with an almost reverent expression. Her fingers trace the sleek lines of the frame, and I watch, transfixed, as she circles it slowly. "I've never been on one before."

"First time for everything," I say, holding out the spare helmet I brought. Our fingers brush as she takes it, and that familiar electricity shoots through me. She looks uncertain as she weighs the helmet in her hands.

"Is it safe?" she asks, her voice small.

I want to lie, to tell her nothing bad could ever happen, but I've done enough lying in my life. "No," I admit. "But I won't let anything happen to you."

A strange promise from a man like me. I've spent years honing my ability to inflict damage, to control and destroy when necessary. But the thought of anything hurting her makes my blood run cold.

She nods, as if my honesty satisfies her more than false reassurance would have. She pulls the helmet over her head, fumbling with the strap until I step forward.

"Let me," I murmur, my fingers deftly securing the buckle beneath her chin. I'm close enough to see the faint freckles dusting her nose, to count each individual eyelash. Her breath hitches.

I step back, putting on my own helmet.

I swing my leg over the bike, settling into the seat. "Climb on behind me," I instruct, my voice muffled by the helmet. "Put your feet on the pegs and hold onto me. Tight."

She hesitates for just a moment before approaching. I feel the bike dip slightly as she mounts it, her body warm against my back as she slides into position. Her thighs press against mine, her chest flush against my spine. Her arms circle my waist tentatively at first, then tighten when I start the engine.

The bike roars to life between us, and I feel her jump slightly at the vibration. Her grip around my middle becomes almost desperate, her fingers digging into my abdomen. My body responds instantly to her touch, and I'm grateful for the dark jeans hiding my growing arousal.

"Ready?" I call over my shoulder.

"No," she shouts back, but I can hear the smile in her voice, the excitement warring with fear. "But do it anyway."

I ease us away from the curb, deliberately gentle with the throttle. Her arms tighten further, her body molding perfectly against mine. I take the first few turns slowly, letting her get used to the sensation of leaning with the bike. By the third turn, I feel her beginning to relax, to move with me rather than against me.

I gradually increase our speed, weaving us out of the city and into the hush of the backroads. The wind is sharp against me, but her warmth at my back never falters.

By the time we hit the long stretch past Fall City, I can feel her relaxing fully—her grip shifting from cautious to something far more deliberate.

Her hands slide a little lower around my waist. Then lower still.

My jaw tightens as her fingers skim just under the edge of my hoodie, palms spreading across my abs like she's testing how much she can get away with while we're flying down a dark winding road.

She's laughing—I can feel it against my back.

Dangerous little thing.

I roll the throttle, just enough to remind her who's in control. Her grip tightens again, this time less teasing and more breathless.

Good.

By the time we pull into the lot near the trail, the bike's humming low and steady beneath us. I kill the engine and swing my leg off, heart still pounding for reasons that have nothing to do with speed.

She climbs off behind me, tugging the helmet from her head, red curls a wild mess around flushed cheeks.

"So, where's this big surprise?" she asks, breathless and grinning.

I smirk, grabbing her hand without answering. "Come on."

The trail is dimly lit and quiet at this hour, the sound of the falls getting louder with every step we take. Trees arch over us, shadows dancing in the moonlight.

When the overlook finally opens before us, she stops dead in her tracks.

The roar of Snoqualmie Falls is thunderous, mist curling in the air and catching the glow from the lamps lining the rails. It's raw, wild—untouched.

She exhales softly. "Okay... wow."

I take her in for a moment, how the silver light kisses her skin, how her chest still rises and falls from the ride.

"This was your plan?" she says without looking at me, voice quieter now.

"Part of it." I move behind her, slipping my arms around her waist. "You needed out of the city. I needed to remind myself there's still shit in this world worth slowing down for."

She leans back into me. Doesn't speak. Doesn't have to.

The water crashes in the distance, but in this moment, all I can hear is her.

And I'm not in a rush to leave it behind.

She's quiet, warm, perfect. The spray from the falls cools the air, but her skin is fever-hot against mine. I lower my head, breathing her in—a mix of lavender, vanilla and spice and something only she carries.

I turn her in my arms, and when our eyes meet, that softness lingering from before is still there. But beneath it?

Want.

She opens her mouth to speak, but I don't let her.

I crash my lips onto hers, hard, greedy, dragging a low moan from her throat. She doesn't hesitate—doesn't flinch. Her hands tangle in my hair like she's been waiting for this.

I walk her back her up until she's pressed against the barrier. The metal groans behind her, but I don't stop. My hands slide up her sides, under her jacket, finding bare skin and soft curves I already crave again.

"You drive me fucking insane," I murmur against her lips, biting down just enough to hear her gasp.

She pulls back just enough to whisper, "Then do something about it."

And just like that—my control snaps.

I take her mouth again, rougher this time, hands fisting in her hair, dragging another moan from her that punches through me like a live wire. I devour her until we're both breathless, until the only thing keeping me from taking her right here is the goddamn railing.

I break the kiss but don't let her go.

"Come with me," I say, voice low and gritty.

Her eyes are glassy, lips swollen, and I don't wait for an answer. I take her hand and lead her back through the trees, down the trail, away from the falls and the last sliver of self-control I had left.

By the time we reach the bike, the parking lot is still empty. Quiet. Private.

I stop just in front of it and turn to her.

Her crop top clings to her chest, rising and falling with every shallow breath. That leather jacket's still open. Her pants—tight, black, and painted on—don't leave much to the imagination.

And all I can think about is bending her over the seat and making her mine all over again. I hand her the helmet, the weight of it nothing compared to what I'm holding back.

She doesn't ask questions—just climbs on behind me, legs hugging my sides like she knows exactly where this is going. Her hands slide under my jacket as I start the engine, fingertips skimming over my abs like she *wants* to distract me.

She's doing a damn good job of it.

I don't speak as I pull us out of the lot. I just ride—fast, hard, cutting through the dark like we're chasing something we can't name.

Fifteen minutes later, I turn off onto a narrow, unmarked road just past a line of evergreens. It's the kind of place that doesn't show up on GPS. One I've used before when I needed silence. Or space. Or to lose my fucking mind.

Tonight, I need all three.

The road winds through the trees, secluded and perfect. No lights. No interruptions. Just the growl of the engine and her body pressed against mine like it's always belonged there.

The clearing opens up around us, quiet and waiting. I cut the engine, and everything stills—except the pulse between us. The air is thick with pine and promises I haven't said out loud.

She swings her leg off the bike slowly, peeling the helmet off like she knows I'm watching her every move—and she's *giving me a show.*

I get off and close the distance between us in two steps.

I reach out and tug her closer by the belt loop.

"You know exactly what you're doing to me, don't you?"

She tilts her head, all tease and trouble. "You're the one who told me to come."

I growl under my breath and spin her gently toward the bike.

"Bend over the seat little minx"

She hesitates for a second—then obeys.

She leans forward, red hair spilling down her back like liquid fire. The curve of her ass in those tight pants has me gripping her hips hard enough to bruise. I press against her from behind, letting her feel exactly what she does to me.

"Is this what you wanted?" I growl in her ear, one hand sliding up her spine to tangle in her hair. "To drive me fucking crazy all night?"

She pushes back against me, a soft moan escaping her lips. "Maybe."

I tug her hair just enough to arch her back further. "Maybe isn't good enough, Octavia."

My free hand slides around to her front, fingers dipping beneath the waistband of her pants. She's already wet, already ready for me, and the knowledge sends a surge of fervent satisfaction through my veins.

"Tell me what you want," I demand, my voice rough against her ear.

"You," she gasps as my fingers find her center, circling slowly. "I want you."

I undo her pants, tugging them down just enough to expose her to the cool night air. She shivers, but not from cold. My hand works between her thighs, stroking, teasing, building her up until she's whimpering and pressing back against me.

"Please," she begs, voice breaking. "Dom, please."

The sound of my name on her lips like that—desperate, wanting—nearly rips through my restraint like it's nothing. I unzip my jeans, freeing myself from the confines that have been torturing me since she first climbed on the bike.

"Tell me again," I command, positioning myself at her entrance. "Tell me what you want."

"You," she moans, arching further, offering herself to me. "Only you, Dom."

I enter her in one swift thrust, driving in until there's nothing left between us. We both cry out—her from pleasure, me from the overwhelming sensation of her tight pussy surrounding me. For a moment, I don't move, savoring the connection, the way she pulses around me.

Then, I start to move.

Each thrust is deliberate, powerful, claiming. My fingers dig into her hips, holding her steady as I take her against the bike. The machine rocks beneath us, the leather seat creaking with our movements. Her moans echo through the clearing, unrestrained and beautiful.

"God, you feel so good," I groan, leaning forward to press my chest against her back. One hand slides up under her shirt, finding her breast, teasing her nipple until she cries out. "So perfect for me."

"Harder," she begs, pushing back to meet each thrust. "Please, Dom, harder."

I pull out of her, chest heaving, every muscle in my body strung tight.

She's not done. Not even close.

Neither am I.

I grab her by the hips and flip her toward me, hauling her up into my arms like she weighs nothing. Her legs wrap around my waist, breath hitching as I carry her the few steps to the tree. When her back hits the rough bark with a soft, stunned grunt, I feel her body jolt against mine—and fuck, it only makes me want more.

I don't give her a second to adjust.

I drive into her again, *hard*, my grip bruising, my mouth right at her ear.

"You wanted it harder?" I growl. "You'll take everything I give you, baby. Every. Fucking. Inch."

She claws at my shoulders, head falling back, a broken moan slipping past her lips—and it unravels every ounce of control I've got left.

Because this? This is mine. *She* is mine.

The way she melts for me. The way she shatters and begs and holds on like I'm the only thing keeping her standing—fuck, it's addictive.

I fuck her like I need to burn her into my skin.

Like she's the only goddamn thing that matters.

Every thrust is punishment and worship. A warning and a promise.

I bury myself deeper, growling against her throat. "No one else gets you like this. No one else ever will."

And when she tightens around me, gasping my name like a prayer—

I lose the last thread of restraint I had left.

Her walls clench around me, taking every inch as she comes undone. I follow her over the edge, my release hitting me like a freight train. I bite down on her shoulder to muffle the roar that tears from my throat, hips still pumping, grinding her into the rough bark of the tree as I empty myself inside her.

For several moments, we stay frozen like that—her legs wrapped around me, my face buried in her neck, both of us gasping for air. The forest is quiet around us, save for our ragged breathing and the distant rush of the falls.

"Fuck," she finally whispers, her voice hoarse. "That was..."

"Yeah," I agree, unable to form more coherent thoughts. I'm still inside her, still holding her against the tree, unwilling to break the connection just yet.

When I finally pull back enough to look at her face, what I see nearly stops my heart. Her eyes are wide, pupils blown, a flush spreading across her cheeks and down her neck. Her lips are swollen from my kisses, her hair a wild tangle around her shoulders. She looks thoroughly claimed—and fucking gorgeous.

"You okay?" I ask, my voice gentler than I'd intended.

She laughs softly, the sound vibrating through where we're still joined. "I think you broke me a little," she admits, wincing slightly as I ease her down. "In the best possible way."

I help her straighten her clothes, my hands lingering longer than necessary. She watches me with those knowing blue eyes, a small, satisfied smile playing on her lips.

"What?" I ask, tucking myself back into my jeans.

"Nothing," she says, but her smile widens. "Just... I didn't expect tonight to end like this."

I pull her closer, my thumb tracing the mark I left on her shoulder. "Who says it's ending?"

Lust settles in his eyes at my words, that flush deepening across her skin. I can feel her pulse quicken beneath my fingers.

"Take me home," she whispers, pressing a surprisingly gentle kiss to my jaw. "Your home. I want to see where you live"

Something possessive and primal surges through me at her request. The thought of her in my space, in my bed, surrounded by my things— it sends a fresh wave of hunger through me despite having just been inside her.

"Are you sure?" I ask, giving her one last chance to walk away from whatever this is becoming.

She tangles her fingers in my hair, pulling me down so our foreheads touch. "I'm sure, Dom. Take me."

The ride back to the city is different—her body molded to mine not from fear or excitement, but from a deeper connection, her hands wandering deliberately over my chest and stomach as we cut through the darkness.

By the time we reach my building, I'm hard again, my control

hanging by a thread. Her hands have been wandering the entire ride, teasing me, testing me. Every red light has been torture, her fingers dipping dangerously close to my waistband.

I pull into the private garage beneath my building, parking the bike in my reserved spot. The moment I cut the engine, I'm off the bike and pulling her with me.

"Someone's eager," she teases, her voice husky as I drag her toward the private elevator.

I don't respond with words. Instead, I push her against the wall, pinning her hands above her head with one of mine while the other fumbles for my access card. Her body arches into mine, seeking friction, seeking more.

"Patience," I growl, though I have none myself.

The elevator doors slide open, and I pull her inside, pressing her against the mirrored wall as soon as the doors close. My mouth finds hers, hungry and demanding. Her hands tug at my shirt, slipping underneath to feel my skin.

"Which floor?" she gasps between kisses.

"Penthouse," I mutter against her lips. "Where else?"

She laughs, the sound mingling with a moan as my hands find her ass, lifting her again. "Of course it is."

The elevator ascends silently, the only sounds are our ragged breathing and the rustle of clothing as we touch, taste, tease. When the doors open directly into my foyer, I carry her through the dimly lit space, her legs wrapped around my waist.

"Jesus," she breathes, catching glimpses of my apartment as we move through it. "You actually live like this."

Floor-to-ceiling windows frame the Seattle skyline, the city lights glittering below us like fallen stars. Modern furnishings, sleek lines, everything in shades of black, gray, and white. Minimalist. Controlled. Expensive.

"Disappointed?" I ask, pausing in the hallway that leads to my bedroom.

She shakes her head, those blue eyes drinking in every detail. "It's exactly what I expected," she says, her fingers tracing along my jaw. "Beautiful but cold. Like you're afraid to leave a mark."

The observation hits too close to home, and I silence her with another kiss, rougher this time. I don't want her analyzing me. I don't want her seeing too deep.

I kick open my bedroom door and carry her inside, finally letting her feet touch the ground beside my bed. The sheets are dark gray, the headboard a sleek black leather. More windows, more city lights, more of the same carefully controlled aesthetic.

She turns in a slow circle, taking it all in. Then her eyes find mine again, and there's a challenge in them that makes my blood heat.

"So proper," she teases, kicking off her shoes. "So neat. I bet you've never made a mess in here."

Before I can respond, she's peeling off her jacket, letting it drop to the floor. Her shirt follows, revealing a black lace bra that makes my mouth go dry. Her eyes never leave mine as she shimmies out of those tight pants, standing before me in nothing but lace and confidence.

"Your turn," she challenges, crossing her arms beneath her breasts, pushing them up in a way that makes my cock throb painfully against my zipper.

I strip efficiently, methodically, watching her eyes widen as more of my skin is revealed. The tattoos that trace my ribs, the scars that tell stories I'll never share with her. When I'm finally naked, I stand before her, letting her look her fill.

She closes the distance between us, her small hands splaying across my chest, tracing the lines of muscle and ink. Her touch is reverent, curious, and it sets my skin on fire.

"I want to taste you," she whispers, looking up at me through those long lashes. "All of you."

Before I can process her words, she's sinking to her knees in front of me, those blue eyes locked on mine as she takes me in her hand. The first touch of her tongue against my cock nearly brings me to my knees. She works me with surprising skill, taking me deeper with each bob of her head, her hand working what she can't fit in her mouth. I groan, fisting her hair, fighting the urge to thrust deeper. She moans around me, the vibration sending shockwaves of pleasure up my spine.

"Fuck, baby," I hiss, watching her take me. "Just like that."

Her tongue swirls around the head before she takes me deep again, her throat relaxing to accommodate my size. My hips buck involuntarily, but she doesn't pull away—she takes it, those blue eyes watering slightly but never leaving mine.

The sight of her on her knees, mouth full of my cock, looking up at me like I'm everything she's ever wanted, sends me over the edge faster than I'd like to admit. I tighten my grip in her hair, a warning.

"Octavia," I growl.

She doesn't pull away. Her hands grip my thighs harder, taking me deeper as I lose control completely. I cum with a shuddering groan, my release hitting the back of her throat. She swallows everything I give her, her eyes never leaving mine, a wicked satisfaction in her gaze as she watches me fall apart.

CHAPTER TWELVE

Octavia

I can't believe I just did that.

I've never wanted a man like that—never felt the need to take him into my mouth, to taste every last drop like I couldn't get enough. But with Dominic?

I *craved* it.

The way he loses himself in the moment—head thrown back, muscles tight, voice ragged with my name — God, it has me soaked and aching, like my body's still begging for more.

Like I'll never stop wanting him.

I'm still on my knees, catching my breath, when Dominic's fingers tilt my chin upward. His green eyes are dark, hungry—a predator who's had a taste but isn't nearly satisfied.

"My turn," he growls, pulling me to my feet effortlessly.

Before I can respond, he picks me up and puts me on the bed, pulling down my panties in one swift motion, tossing them aside like they're nothing but an obstacle between him and what he wants. My breath catches as his large hands spread my thighs wide, exposing me completely to his hungry gaze.

"Look at you," he murmurs, his voice thick with desire. "Soaked for me." His thumb traces the slick seam of my pussy, making me shudder. "All this from sucking my cock?"

I should be blushing because of how wet I am, but there's no room for shame with Dominic. Not when he's looking at me like I'm a feast and he's been starving.

"What can I say?" I manage, my voice breathier than I'd like. "You have that effect on me."

His lips curve into that devastating smile. "Oh, little minx… we're just getting started."

He lowers his head between my thighs, and the first hot stroke of his tongue has me arching off the bed. My hands find his hair, pulling without direction—torn between begging for more and needing a second to breathe.

"Dominic," I gasp as he circles my clit with painstaking perfection.

He looks up at me, his mouth still against me, and the sight alone has me teetering on the brink—this powerful man between my thighs, those green eyes locked on mine as he tastes me.

"You taste so fucking sweet," he growls against my flesh, the vibration of his words sending new waves of pleasure through me.

His tongue is relentless, alternating between broad strokes and precise flicks that have me writhing beneath him. When he slides two fingers inside me, curling them to hit that perfect spot, I cry out, my thighs trembling around his head.

"That's it," he murmurs, his breath hot against my sensitive skin. "Let me hear you."

I'm not usually loud during sex—years of thin apartment walls have trained me to keep quiet—but Dominic draws sounds from me I didn't know I could make. When he sucks my clit between his lips while pumping those thick fingers inside me, I practically scream.

"Dominic, I can't— I'm so close—" The pressure builds impossibly fast, my body tightening, right on the edge.

"I know exactly what you're going to do," he says, increasing the pace of his fingers. "You're going to cum for me. Hard."

His mouth and fingers work in perfect rhythm, and I can feel something building inside me that's different from any orgasm I've experienced before. The pressure is more intense, more concentrated, making my entire body tremble.

"Dom, wait—I don't—something's happening," I try to warn him, but he only growls against my flesh and doubles his efforts, his fingers curling more firmly against that spot that makes me see stars.

"Let go," he commands against my skin. "Give it to me, Octavia."

The orgasm crashes through me with such force that my vision blurs. I feel a rush of wetness as I cry out his name, my body arching off the bed as waves of pleasure radiate outward from my core. I'm vaguely aware that I'm soaking his fingers, his chin, the expensive sheets beneath us, but I'm too lost in sensation to care.

"Fuck, yes," Dominic growls, there's a raw, ruthless satisfaction in his gaze as he watches me come apart. "That's my good girl."

I collapse back onto the bed, trembling and disoriented, my chest heaving as I struggle to catch my breath. "I've never—that's never happened before," I admit, a flush of embarrassment coloring my cheeks.

Dominic rises from between my thighs, his mouth slick with my arousal, his eyes blazing with a mixture of pride and hunger. He wipes his chin with the back of his hand, a gesture that should be crude but somehow seems erotic when he does it.

"You've never squirted before?" he asks, his voice rough with desire. "Never had a man make you lose control like that?"

I shake my head, still too breathless to form coherent sentences. The intensity of what just happened has left me feeling vulnerable and exposed in a way that has nothing to do with my physical nakedness.

"Good," he says with that unyielding growl that sends shivers racing down my spine. "I like being your first."

He moves up my body, those powerful arms caging me beneath him as he claims my mouth in a kiss that tastes of me. I should find it off-putting, but there's something filthy and erotic about tasting myself on his tongue, knowing how thoroughly he enjoyed devouring me.

When he pulls back, there's a dangerous glint in his eyes. "Get dressed," he orders, surprising me.

"What? Why?" I'm still dazed from my orgasm, confused by the sudden command.

"Because," he says, dropping a quick, hard kiss on my mouth, "I want to take you somewhere."

"Now?" I glance at the clock. It's nearly midnight.

"Now." The authority in his voice brooks no argument, but I can't help myself.

"In case you haven't noticed, I'm not exactly dressed for a midnight excursion," I gesture to my naked body, still glistening with sweat. "Unless you're planning to take me to a nudist colony."

A slow smile spreads across his face, appreciating my sass even as his pupils dilate, swallowing the color until there's nothing left but heat. "Five minutes."

"Are we going hiking at midnight?" I ask, pushing myself up on my elbows. "Because I should warn you, my outdoor skills are limited to finding the best patio bars."

Dominic chuckles, the sound rumbling through his chest as he reaches for his own clothes. "Just trust me, little minx."

Trust. Such a loaded word between us. But as I watch him pull on those dark jeans that hug his thighs in all the right ways, I realize I do trust him—perhaps more than I should.

I slide off the bed, still wobbly, and start gathering my scattered clothing. "You know, most men just order pizza after sex," I tease, pulling on my bra and shimmying into my jeans.

Dominic's eyes flash with that dangerous heat as he tugs the V-neck into place, the dip of the collar teasing just enough tanned tattooed skin to make it impossible not to look. "I'm not most men, Octavia. I thought you'd have figured that out by now."

I roll my eyes, tugging my top over my head. "Trust me, your uniqueness has been thoroughly established." I gesture vaguely at my still-trembling thighs. "My body's gotten the memo."

He crosses the room in two long strides, backing me against the wall before I can react. His hand cups my face, thumb brushing over my bottom lip. "And I'm going to make sure it never forgets."

My breath catches in my throat. The intensity in his eyes should frighten me, but it sends a fresh wave of heat pooling between my legs.

"Five minutes," he repeats, his voice a low command that makes my skin tingle. He steps back, giving me space to finish dressing, but his eyes never leave me.

I quickly run my fingers through my tangled red curls, wincing at what I can only imagine is thoroughly smudged makeup. "I look like I've been thoroughly debauched," I mutter, catching a glimpse of myself in his bedroom mirror.

"You have been," Dominic replies with unrepentant satisfaction. "And will be again before the night is over."

The promise in his voice makes my stomach flip, heat blooming low in my belly.

I slip on my shoes—thankfully, I wore the tennis shoes he told me to.

"So, where exactly are you taking me?" I ask as he leads me out of the bedroom.

"Patience, little minx." His hand finds the small of my back, guiding me through his penthouse. Even this simple gesture makes every nerve light up in response.

We take the private elevator down to the parking garage, where Dominic leads me past his Porsche to something I hadn't noticed before—a sleek black boat sitting on a trailer.

"You're kidding," I say, stopping in my tracks. "A midnight boat ride?"

His lips curve into that devastating smile. "The lake is perfect this time of night. No one around for miles." He leans closer, his breath hot against my ear. "No one to hear how loud you get when you cum."

Heat floods my cheeks, but I can't deny the thrill that courses through me at his words. "Pretty confident in your abilities there, Mr. Callahan."

"With good reason," he counters, his hand sliding lower to cup my ass possessively. "The evidence was all over my face a few minutes ago."

I should be mortified by his crude reference to how I came apart for him, but instead, I feel a surge of boldness. "Maybe that was just beginner's luck."

His eyes darken with challenge. "Let's find out, shall we?"

Before I can respond, he's helping me into his truck, the one he apparently uses to tow his boat. It's a stark contrast to his usual Porsche—all rugged power and utility—but somehow it suits him just as well. The man contains multitudes, each one more intriguing than the last.

As we drive toward the lake, Dominic rests his hand on my thigh, his thumb tracing lazy circles that make it impossible to focus on anything else. His touch is casual, possessive, like he's reminding both of us that my body belongs to him tonight.

"You're awfully quiet," he observes, glancing at me as we turn onto a winding road that leads away from the city lights. "Second thoughts?"

"Just wondering if I should be concerned that you're taking me to a deserted lake in the middle of the night," I quip, though there's no real worry behind my words. "Very serial killer of you."

He chuckles, the sound rumbling deep in his chest. "If I wanted to kill you, I wouldn't need some lake or forest cliché. I'd handle it myself—and I have people to make sure your body disappears without a single trace."

"That's... not as reassuring as you might think," I say, but I can't help the smile that tugs at my lips. There's something freeing about his darkness, the way he doesn't pretend to be anything other than what he is.

"You're not afraid," he observes, his hand tightening slightly on my thigh.

"Not of you," I admit, meeting his gaze.

The corner of his mouth lifts in that half-smile that makes my stomach flip. "Good."

We arrive at a private dock on the edge of the lake, the water a vast expanse of black glass reflecting the moonlight. Dominic backs the trailer expertly to the ramp, I'm mesmerized as he efficiently prepares the boat for launch. There's something undeniably sexy about the way he moves—confident, purposeful, his muscles flexing beneath his shirt as he works.

"You just going to watch, or are you going to help?" he calls over his shoulder, amusement coloring his tone.

"Definitely watch," I reply, crossing my arms. "The view's too good to waste."

He laughs, a genuine sound that makes my heart stutter. "At least you're honest."

Within minutes, the sleek vessel is in the water, bobbing gently against the dock. Dominic extends his hand to help me aboard, his grip strong and sure as I step onto the polished deck.

"Ever been on a boat before?" he asks, leading me to the passenger seat beside the captain's chair.

"Does the Ferry count?"

He snorts, shaking his head. "Not even close."

The engine comes to life with a low vibration that seems to resonate through my entire body. Dominic navigates away from the dock, gradually increasing speed as we slide across the dark water. The wind whips my hair around my face, and I tilt my head back, savoring the sensation of freedom as we race across the lake's surface.

I sneak glances at Dominic, captivated by the sight of him at the helm. His strong hands grip the wheel with casual authority, his profile sharp against the moonlight, jaw set in concentration. The wind ruffles his dark hair, and there's something almost boyish in his expression—a rare glimpse of joy that makes my heart squeeze in my chest.

"What?" he asks, catching me staring.

"Nothing," I say, smiling. "Just thinking that you look different out here."

"Different how?" He cuts the engine, letting us drift in the middle of the lake, surrounded by nothing but water and starlight.

I consider my words carefully. "Less... controlled. Like you've let something go."

His eyes hold mine for a long moment. "Maybe I have."

He stands, pulling me to my feet and leading me to the back of the boat where a plush seating area awaits. The cushions are surprisingly comfortable as I sink down. Dominic is immediately beside me, his thigh pressed against mine.

"It's beautiful out here," I murmur, gazing up at the canopy of stars spread above us. Away from the city lights, the sky is alive with them, more than I've ever seen before.

"Yes," he agrees, but he's not looking at the stars. His eyes are fixed on me, hungry and intent. "Beautiful."

"Well, you haven't tried to murder anyone or bury a body tonight, so yeah. We're dangerously close to *normal people* territory."

His laugh is sharp—too sharp.

A quick exhale, tight and wrong. It cuts through the air and vanishes just as fast.

I glance over, and his profile has already hardened. Jaw clenched. Eyes forward. That relaxed version of him I was just starting to enjoy? Gone like a light switch flipped.

"Right," he says, voice flat. "Normal."

The word hangs there—like it tastes bitter coming out of his mouth.

I don't press. But I feel it. The shift. The weight.

He's hiding something. I've known that since day one.

But right now, whatever it is, it's *close*. Like it's still clinging to him.

The wind blows a strand of hair across my face, and I use it as an excuse to look away—giving him the space he clearly needs. But inside, my thoughts are racing.

He didn't just tense because of a bad memory.

That reaction? That was *fresh*.

Something happened tonight. Something I wasn't part of.

I stay quiet, but I don't forget it.

He laces his fingers through mine a few seconds later like nothing happened. Like he's still here with me.

And I let him.

But somewhere, deep in my chest, that spark of curiosity—the one that's always been a little dangerous—flares hotter.

Because whatever Dominic's hiding?

I want to know.

Even if it ruins everything.

The silence between us stretches, comfortable and tense all at once. The water laps gently against the boat, a rhythmic soundtrack to my racing thoughts.

"What are you thinking about?" Dominic asks, his thumb tracing circles on my palm.

I consider lying. It would be easier. Safer. But something about the night air, the isolation, makes me brave.

"You," I say simply. "The parts you show me. The parts you don't."

His hand tightens around mine. Not painful, but a warning.

"Octavia—"

"I'm not asking," I interrupt, turning to face him. The moonlight catches the sharp angles of his face, shadows pooling in the hollows beneath his cheekbones. "I'm just... observing."

His eyes search mine, looking for something. Fear, maybe. Or judgment. He finds neither.

"Most people don't," he says finally.

"Don't what?"

"Observe." His voice is quiet, almost contemplative. "They see what they want to see. What I let them see."

I can't help but smile. "In case you haven't noticed, I'm not great at following expectations." His jaw clenches. That smile I tossed at him doesn't stand a chance. It dies in the air between us.

"No," he says, voice low. Controlled. For now. "You're not."

He stares out across the water, the stars reflected in his eyes like ghosts, like memories he can't scrub clean.

Then, without warning—

"She trusted them."

The shift is instant. The weight of those three words pulls the air out of the boat.

"Who?" I ask, though I already know.

"The doctors. The company. The ones who made promises they never intended to keep."

His grip tightens on my hand until I feel the tremble in his fingers. He lets go abruptly, like he can't stomach the contact while he says this out loud.

"My mother was dying, and we found this trial—her Hail Mary. Expensive, but promising. We bought time. Hope."

He shakes his head, jaw locking again.

"Until the money disappeared."

The way he says it—quiet, deadly—I already know where this is going. But I let him continue. I need to hear it. *He* needs to say it.

"One man stole it. Tom Fletcher. Westfield's CFO. The fucking coward siphoned money from the joint venture fund. Funneled it through shell companies, sent it offshore. Buried it like he wasn't burying people with it."

His voice breaks on that last word—*people*. But he pushes through, teeth clenched.

"She deteriorated so fast without the meds. She was gone in weeks."

He pauses. The boat creaks in the still water like it's listening.

"I found him. I gave him an out—admit what he did, leave the company, disappear, stay quiet. That was mercy."

Then he turns to me, eyes black in the moonlight, empty of remorse.

"Tonight, he threatened to go public. Said he'd tell the board I threatened him. That he'd drag me through the mud, ruin everything I've built."

He leans forward, voice flat. "So I shut him up. Permanently."

A silence stretches, jagged and breathless.

"You killed him." I don't ask. I *know*.

He doesn't blink. "I ended him."

He leans in, close enough I can feel the heat rolling off of him like a storm just barely contained.

"I didn't flinch when I pulled the trigger, Octavia. I didn't hesitate. And I don't feel guilty about it."

I hold his stare, heart pounding. Not in fear. Not exactly.

There's a fine line between morality and instinct, and right now I'm standing on the razor edge of it.

"Good." My voice is steady. Cold. Honest. "He deserved it."

He blinks like he wasn't expecting that.

"You don't think I'm a monster?" he asks, but there's something desperate in the way he says it. Something broken.

I shake my head slowly. "I think monsters don't give second chances. You did."

His breath catches, just slightly.

"And I think," I continue, voice softening, "you'd do it again if you had to."

He leans back like that truth cuts deeper than the rest of it. Like maybe it's the only part that scares *him*.

"I would." His voice is a vow. "I fucking would."

And in the cold dark of the water, with stars above and blood still on his hands, I realize something I can't unknow:

He's not just broken.

He's *dangerous*.

But he's *mine*.

CHAPTER THIRTEEN
Octavia

I should be scared.

That thought rolls over and over in my mind like waves against the hull of this boat, quiet but constant. It brushes up against everything I've seen tonight—everything he's *told* me.

I'm sitting beside a man who confessed to killing someone not even an hour ago, and my pulse isn't screaming in fear—it's steady. Low. *Calm.*

What the hell is wrong with me?

I glance at Dominic, his face shadowed in the moonlight, hands resting on his knees. His expression is unreadable—maybe exhausted, maybe just hollow. He hasn't spoken since those last words:

"I fucking would."

He didn't mean it as a threat.

He meant it as a promise.

I swallow hard, folding my arms around myself against the chill, though I'm not sure it's the cold making me shiver.

"You've done this before." I don't even realize I've spoken until the words are out. But I don't take them back.

He doesn't look at me right away. Just nods once. "You knew that."

"You told me." I hate how breathless I sound. "Back in your office, when you said people who crossed you didn't walk away."

He turns his head, gaze sharp and unreadable. "I did."

And it clicks. That moment. That warning I brushed off as bluster.

I thought he was being dramatic.

I thought it was all part of the persona.

But he wasn't trying to intimidate me.

He was trying to *warn* me.

"Why am I okay with this?" I ask, more to myself than to him.

It comes out as a whisper, like saying it louder would crack something in me wide open.

He doesn't answer. Just watches me like he's trying to solve the same puzzle I'm asking out loud.

"You're not shocked," he says finally. "You're... processing. But you're not pulling away."

"Should I be?"

He exhales, slow and heavy. "Yes."

Silence stretches between us again, the kind that feels like standing at the edge of something steep.

"But you're not," he adds, almost to himself.

I look at him again—really look—and something sharp twists low in my stomach.

"It doesn't scare me," I admit, my voice soft but firm. "Not the way it should. Not the way *you* think it should."

His eyes darken at that, but there's no arrogance in it. Just hunger. Worry. *Regret.*

"You don't know what that means."

"I know enough," I say.

And I do.

Because I've seen what he's capable of—in the boardroom, in the bedroom, and now in the dark.

And instead of running, I find myself wanting to dive deeper.

What kind of person does that make me?

Maybe I don't want the answer.

But I want him.

We don't say anything when Dominic starts the engine and turns the boat back toward the dock.

The ride is quiet.

Not uncomfortable—just... different. Like something's settled between us. Or maybe unraveled. I'm not sure which.

The water laps against the hull, and the wind has lost its bite, but I feel the chill anyway. He doesn't reach for my hand this time. I don't reach for his.

We just sit in the silence—together, but alone with our thoughts— as the lights of the dock slowly grow closer.

By the time we tie off and step back onto solid ground, my chest is tight with questions I'm not ready to ask. He hasn't said a word since his confession. And I haven't asked him to explain.

Maybe I'm afraid he will.

We walk side by side to the car. No small talk. No tension either. Just... space.

When we get back to his place, I kick off my shoes in the entryway while he disappears into the kitchen like he needs something to do with his hands. I wrap myself in the oversized hoodie he handed me, still smelling faintly of him and wind and lake water.

Now, I'm curled up on the far end of his couch, my fingers playing with the hem of my sleeves while he pours himself a drink in the kitchen—silent, focused, too still.

His penthouse feels different now. Not just cold. *Haunted.*

And I can't tell if it's his demons I'm feeling...Or mine.

I pull my knees up, arms hugging them close. Dominic's hoodie is drowning me, but I don't care. It's warm. It's safe. Safer than I've felt in a long time.

The silence stretches, thick and charged. His drink sits untouched on the counter. I can feel the weight of his eyes on me even when he's not looking.

I shift, and the words slip out before I can second-guess them.

"So... hypothetically—if I had an ex who was a complete piece of shit—lied, cheated, hit me once or twice when he was drunk, tried to get his hands on me even when I said no—what would that earn me?"

Dominic's glass clinks softly against the counter. He doesn't move. Doesn't speak.

So I push, because humor is easier than honesty.

"Do you offer a 'revenge package'? Or do I need to join some sort of loyalty program first?"

Still nothing.

I glance up—and the look on his face makes my mouth go dry.

His jaw is set, his shoulders tight, fists braced against the edge of the counter like he's physically holding himself back.

"What did you just say?" His voice is low. Dangerous. Measured. Like he's walking the line between control and combustion.

I shrug, trying to play it off. "It's not a big—"

"Don't," he cuts in, voice sharper now. "Don't do that. Don't shrink it."

I blink. "It was a long time ago."

"How long doesn't fucking matter." His knuckles are white. His entire body's vibrating with something cold and brutal. "He hit you?"

I nod, slower this time. "Mostly when he was drunk. And when I fought back, he'd cry, say it was a mistake, tell me he loved me. Then he'd do it again."

He's across the room before I can process the movement.

Not toward me—but away.

Pacing like he needs the space to keep from tearing something apart.

Or someone.

"You told me he just made you feel small," he mutters. "You didn't tell me he put his hands on you."

He stops. Turns. His eyes lock onto mine, and whatever's in them? It's not pity.

It's *rage*.

He stares at me like I've just handed him a loaded weapon and told him where to point it.

"Where is he?"

His voice is low. Steady. No yelling. No theatrics.

Just quiet, calculated promise.

I hesitate.

"I told you, I haven't kept tabs—"

"Try again." There's no edge to his tone, but it slices clean through me anyway.

I sigh, "Last I heard, he got married. Moved somewhere in the suburbs—Bellevue, maybe. His wife's name is Melissa. They have a baby now."

I wait for that to soften him.

It doesn't.

If anything, it makes it worse.

Dominic's mouth pulls into a razor-thin line. "He's married?"

"Yeah. To someone who probably has no idea what he's capable of." I swallow hard. "I almost feel sorry for her."

Dominic stands. Not fast. Not angry.

Just *decided.*

"I'm going to find him."

My heart lurches. "Dom—"

"No," he says, looking down at me with eyes that are far too calm. "You don't get to protect him now. You already lived through him once. That's more than he deserved."

I shake my head. "I'm not protecting him."

"Then let me handle it."

I rise to my feet, wrapping my arms around myself. "You can't just... show up and kill someone because of me."

His expression darkens.

"Watch me."

I stare at him, pulse skittering, every instinct warring inside me.

And the worst part?

It's not fear I feel.

It's *relief.*

"He has a child now," I whisper, more to remind myself than him. "What if he's changed?"

Dominic steps closer, his voice cold and sure. "Men like that don't change. They just find new victims."

The silence between us hums, loud with everything I don't want to admit.

"You really would do it, wouldn't you?" I say, voice barely above a breath.

He nods.

"For you?" He meets my gaze with steel. "Every time."

And I realize—

I'm not shocked.

I'm not begging him not to.

I'm not even trying to convince him he's wrong.

I'm just standing here... wishing someone had said those words to me back then. He watches me like he's waiting for me to flinch.

I don't.

I should.

But I don't.

Dominic steps even closer, and the air around him feels charged — not wild, but *precise*. Like a weapon that's already been drawn and is waiting for a reason to be used.

"I can find him with just one phone call, Octavia."

His voice is calm. Too calm.

"I don't even have to kill him." A beat. Then his mouth twists into something far too close to a smile. "Not yet."

My breath catches.

"But I do have words. And maybe—just maybe—I'd like to wrap my hands around his pathetic fucking throat and make him think he's about to meet whatever god he believes in."

He tilts his head slightly, like he's *considering it* in real time.

Like he already knows what the man looks like now.

Like he's *already seen* the outcome.

"Make him piss himself first. Make him understand what fear actually feels like. And then maybe I let him walk away... with the knowledge that next time, he won't."

I should say no. I should stop this.

But I don't.

Because hearing those words — that quiet, terrifying promise — doesn't scare me.

It makes me feel *seen*.

"Dominic," I whisper, stepping close enough that I have to tilt my head to look up at him. "What if I said... I don't want to forget what he did? That I don't want to let it go?"

His gaze sharpens. "Then I wouldn't let you."

I nod, slow and quiet.

He brushes a strand of hair from my cheek, jaw still tense, eyes still dark.

"You deserve revenge," he says, and there's no softness in it. Only *certainty*. "And if I can't give you peace, I'll give you fear—in his eyes. Pain in his voice. Regret in every breath he takes after I'm done with him."

My stomach flips. Not in fear.

In *want*.

Because I believe him.

And somewhere deep inside, buried under the parts of me that still flinch at my own reflection—I want it, too.

"Okay," I say, my voice steady now.

And that one word?

It seals it. And I know he'll follow through.

But not tonight.

Not now.

I step even closer, slipping my fingers around his wrist, grounding myself in the quiet tension thrumming just beneath his skin.

"Tomorrow," I murmur, voice low and certain. "Make the call tomorrow."

His jaw ticks, but he nods. He'll wait. For me.

"Tonight..." I pause, letting the silence wrap around the words I haven't said yet. The ones I'm *about* to. My thumb traces a slow circle on the inside of his wrist.

"Tonight, I want you to make that dream I told you about come true."

His eyes narrow. Heat flickers in the space between us.

"The one where you fucked me while I was sleeping," I say, tone hushed, hungry. "Where I woke up soaked and aching and half-drunk on the way you touched me."

His breath hitches. The restraint in his eyes starts to fray at the edges.

"That's what I want tonight," I whisper. "I want to fall asleep knowing you're there… and wake up with you inside me. No words. Just you and me and everything we've been holding back."

His fingers wrap around my wrist, grip firm but reverent, like he's holding something sacred. Or dangerous. Or both.

"You don't know what you're asking for," he says, but it comes out ragged, like a man already unraveling.

"I think I do," I whisper back, stepping into him, chest to chest. "And I want *you* to give it to me."

He doesn't answer.

He just moves.

His mouth crashes into mine with a ferocity that steals my breath. It's not gentle—it's claiming, consuming, like he's trying to devour whatever hesitation might be left between us. His hands slide down my sides, gripping my hips with bruising intensity before lifting me effortlessly. My legs wrap around his waist automatically, my arms around his neck, and I'm clinging to him as he carries me toward the bedroom.

"Say it again," he growls against my throat, teeth grazing the tender curve of my neck. "Tell me what you want."

"I want to fall asleep in your arms," I breathe, my head falling back as his lips trace a burning path down my neck. "And wake up with you inside me."

He makes a sound—half groan, half growl—that vibrates through my entire body. He sets me down by the edge of the bed, not gently, but with purpose. I stumble back a step, my hair falls messily around my shoulders as my eyes are drawn to his. Desire is coiled in his eyes as he drinks me in.

"Take it off," he commands, voice rough with need. "All of it."

I sit up slowly, holding his gaze as I reach for the hem of the hoodie and pull it over my head, tossing it aside.

Next, I unbutton my pants—slowly, deliberately—and slide them down my hips, letting them pool at my feet before stepping out of them. His eyes follow every movement like he's memorizing each second.

Now I'm standing in just my bra and panties, bare legs exposed, pulse thudding under my skin as the cool air brushes across me.

My fingers trail up my sides, then dance along the lace edge of my bra.

"This too?" I ask, tilting my head, voice playful with a dark edge.

Dominic's jaw flexes, his restraint slipping by the second.

"All. Of. It."

I reach behind my back, unclasp the bra, and let it fall from my shoulders, the straps slipping down my arms before I drop it to the floor.

Then, with one final look at him, I slide my panties down, letting them join the growing pile of clothes at my feet.

Naked now. Exposed. Unflinching.

His eyes rake over me, slow and hungry, as he takes a step forward.

"Get in the bed, Octavia," he growls.

I don't hesitate. Don't question. Don't even pretend to resist. I slide onto his sheets, feeling the cool fabric against my heated skin as I settle into the middle of his bed. There's something deliciously vulnerable about being completely naked while he's still fully dressed, watching me with those predatory eyes.

"Like this?" I ask, my voice huskier than I intended.

Dominic doesn't answer. He just stares, his gaze dragging over every inch of my bare skin.

Then he begins to undress—unhurried, deliberate—each movement laced with restraint. First his shirt, revealing the sharp lines of his chest, the ink I've come to know by heart. His hands move to his belt, then his pants, until only his boxer briefs remain.

And when those drop, he's standing in front of me—bare, powerful, unapologetic.

My breath catches.

He doesn't have to say a word.

He already owns the moment.

My mouth goes dry.

No matter how many times I've seen him stripped bare, it never stops hitting me like a punch to the chest, how fucking perfect he is. All lean muscle and coiled power, dark ink slicing across golden skin like a warning and a promise.

And between his thighs—hard, thick, *aching* for me.

It's obscene, the way my body reacts. The way I throb just looking at him. Like my body already knows what's coming and is begging for it.

I bite my lip, heat blooming low in my belly, and think—

God help me, I want him feral.

He joins me on the bed, his weight making the mattress dip as he moves over me. His hands are everywhere, tracing patterns on my skin that make me arch into his touch.

"You're sure about this?" he asks, his voice a dangerous rumble against my ear.

I nod, already breathless, but he doesn't move.

"Use your words, Octavia."

I meet his gaze, steady and burning. "Yes, Dom. I'm sure."

I swallow, letting every word land with intent. "I want you to fuck me while I'm sleeping. I haven't stopped thinking about that dream—I *need* to have it. I'm yours."

Something dark flashes in his eyes. Control. Desire. He doesn't say a word. Just pulls me into him, his hands rough and reverent all at once, and guides me toward the bed like he's already made up his mind.

I curl beneath the sheets, my body thrumming with anticipation, every inch of me aching for what's to come.

His weight shifts beside me.

And finally, with his presence surrounding me, I let myself drift.

Sleep takes me. And every part of me is waiting for him.

CHAPTER FOURTEEN

Dominic

She falls asleep beside me.

Naked, warm and completely fucking bare.

Her breath evens out, soft and slow, and I know the moment she finally falls asleep. Her fingers unclench, and her body relaxes. She is so vulnerable like this. Laid out beside me like she was made to sleep in my bed, wrapped in my scent.

And still, she asked for more.

Begged me to make her dream real, to take what is already mine.

"I want you to fuck me while I'm sleeping."

And now I'm lying here next to her, every muscle wound tight as a wire, staring at the perfect curve of her ass under the sheet. Her leg is draped over mine. One arm tucked under her head. She's soft and flushed and completely mine in this moment.

And I've never felt more like a goddamn animal.

Because this—*this*—isn't about fucking.

It's about the way my name left her lips as she fell asleep. The way she gave me every inch of herself without hesitation. The way she asked to be taken in a state that demands nothing but trust.

It's woken something inside me. Something I didn't know I craved.

Control.

Reverence.

The kind of brutal intimacy that strips away performance and leaves only truth.

She wanted this.

She's here naked, warm, half-sprawled across me and I'm shaking with the effort it takes not to bury myself inside her and show her exactly what that means.

I press my mouth to her shoulder, breathing her in. My hand grips her thigh, lifting it just enough to slide between.

She doesn't stir.

Not even as I position myself between her legs, my cock hard and aching as I press my thick head against her wet slit. She's already soaked, body begging for me even in her sleep.

I push in.

Slow. Deep. A brutal drag of restraint that has my jaw clenched and every muscle locked tight.

She takes me so fucking perfectly, like she was made for me—tight and hot and perfect. Still unconscious, still dreaming, still fucking mine.

I brace myself on one elbow, the other hand locked on her thigh as I start to move. Long, grinding thrusts deeper each time, burying myself like I've got something to prove.

And maybe I do.

Maybe I need her to know, even asleep, that her body belongs to me. That this isn't sex, it's not softness, and it's not romance.

It's *claiming*.

I fuck her harder, breath ragged, hips snapping against her ass with a rhythm that's getting more brutal by the second.

She still doesn't wake.

Doesn't moan.

Just takes it.

It's driving me fucking insane.

My hand slides to her hip, gripping her tight enough to bruise. I'm close, too fucking close—and it's not enough. I need her to wake up. I need her eyes on me.

I pull back, raise my hand—

Smack.

My palm lands hard on her ass. The sharp sound splits through the silence.

She jolts awake with a gasp, moaning as her body clamps around me like a goddamn vice. Her head turns, eyes wild and glazed with sleep and pleasure.

"Fucking hell," I growl, slamming into her again. "That's it. Wake the fuck up for me."

She cries out, back arching, and I don't slow down. I can't. She's awake now, and I'm too far gone.

This is what she wanted.

And I'm giving her everything. Her breath catches on a gasp, back arching into me as her body clenches again, tighter this time, awake and aware.

"You're... f-fucking me," she breathes, voice wrecked with sleep, disbelief, and pleasure tangled into one broken sound.

"I told you I would," I growl into her neck, teeth grazing her skin. "You begged for this. You wanted me to fuck you while you were sleeping. So I did. And now—now I'm not stopping."

"God, Dominic..." Her hand scrambles across the sheets, fingers curling in the fabric as I slam into her again, harder. "Don't stop. Please don't fucking stop."

"You're soaked," I snarl. "So fucking wet, even in your sleep. You *wanted* this. Your body knew it before you did."

She moans like she's about to fall apart, and I grip her hair, yanking her head back just enough to whisper against her ear.

"You know what it did to me? Watching you sleep next to me like that? Naked. Soft. Spread for me. You knew I wouldn't be able to resist."

She shudders, panting. "I wanted you to take me. Just like this. Rough. Filthy. I wanted to wake up full of you."

"You are full of me," I groan, slamming into her again, dragging a high, fractured moan from her throat. "So fucking full, little minx."

"Yes—fuck, yes—" she cries out, grinding her hips back into mine. "I want more. I want it deeper. Harder. Don't be gentle with me."

I laugh, low and dark. "Gentle? You think I've got that in me right now?"

I slam into her again, punishing, mercilessly.

She chokes out a cry, eyes rolling as her body clutches around me like she's coming undone again.

"This is what you dreamed of?" I hiss. "Me owning you like this? Fucking you so hard you forget your own name?"

She nods frantically, tears brimming in her eyes from the sheer intensity. "Yes—Dominic, fuck, yes its everything. You're everything."

I lose whatever small thread of control I had left.

I fuck her like she's my salvation and my damnation wrapped in one perfect, moaning body, until she's trembling beneath me and I'm buried so deep inside her she won't forget who she belongs to, even in her next dream. Her words are incoherent now, all moans and broken pleas.

"Tell me who you fucking belong to." I growl, my voice ragged.

"You—" she gasps, clutching the sheets, her voice shaking as her orgasm builds again. "You, Dominic. Only you."

That's it.

That's fucking it.

I slam into her and her entire body locks up—legs shaking, spine arching, mouth wide open in a silent scream. She convulses around me, coming hard, soaking my cock as she pulses around me in perfect, desperate waves.

I curse, low, guttural, torn from my chest before I finally let go.

My release tears through me like a goddamn explosion.

I grip her hips, slamming into her one last time and I stay there, burying myself as far as I can go while I empty inside her, heat flooding her, claiming her in every way that counts. Her name leaves my mouth in a snarl, her body taking every drop from me.

My hand slides from her hip to her stomach, flat against her skin, firm as I hold her in place beneath me.

She whimpers softly, still twitching from the aftershocks. I bend low, pressing a kiss on her forehead.

"I meant what I said," I murmur, voice rough. "You're fucking mine, baby girl."

She doesn't argue.

She doesn't move.

She just hums, breath catching as I slide out of her slowly, like I don't want to give up a single inch. My cum slips out of her and onto the sheets, and I fucking love seeing her used, owned, and *marked*.

Wrapping my arm around her, I drag her into my chest. She shivers, but not from cold. From me.

"Sleep," I whisper, brushing her hair off her neck. "I've got you."

I always will.

Sunlight filters through the curtains in slow golden streaks, casting a soft glow across the tangled sheets.

She's still here, wrapped in my arms, her bare back pressed to my chest.. One of her legs is over mine, her body still tucked into me like she knows exactly where she belongs.

And fuck me—*she does.*

Her hair is wild, splayed out over the pillow, a mess of curls and red fire. My arm's locked around her waist, hand resting low on her stomach, holding her there like I'm afraid she might disappear if I let go.

She shifts slightly in her sleep, her hips pressing back into mine.

A low groan escapes me before I can stop it.

Even now, even like this, soft, quiet, content—I want her all over again.

For once, I don't want to get up. I don't want to run, or plan, or bury anything. I just want to lay here with her.

Just for a little while longer.

Because whatever this is… I'm not letting it go.

A quiet hum escapes her lips, her limbs stretching slightly before she melts back into me. She belongs here.

In *my bed.*

In *my penthouse.*

In *my arms.*

Then, without opening her eyes, she murmurs, "You're hard again already, Dominic. I don't know if I'm flattered or in danger."

Huffing out a low laugh, burying my face in her hair. "You're in both. And you sound awfully smug for someone still recovering from being wrecked six hours ago."

She smiles against the pillow, lazy and satisfied. "You say that like I'm not ready for more."

Sliding my hand across her stomach, fingertips dragging low and slow. "You're going to be the fucking death of me."

"Please," she mutters, eyes still closed. "You'll die rich, well-fucked, and deeply in denial about your feelings. It'll be poetic."

A soft growl escapes me, half amusement, half warning. "Careful, little minx. You're in my bed, my space. There's nowhere for you to run when I decide to make good on those threats you keep begging for."

Rolling onto her back slowly, blinking up at me, hair untamed against my pillow. "Good," stretching with a satisfied sigh. "I'm not going anywhere."

Her words hit something inside me. I don't want to name yet. But I feel it, deep.

This is my penthouse. My sanctuary above the city, where no one gets in unless I let them.

And she's *here*.

Wrapped in my sheets. Wearing the marks I left on her skin, smiling at me like she belongs.

I lean down, brushing my lips over hers in a kiss that's surprisingly soft for the chaos between us.

"I'll get coffee," I murmur. "Stay put."

She smirks. "Bossy already? You didn't even get your caffeine yet."

I arch a brow. "You're in *my* bed. Don't push your luck."

She winks. "I already did. Look how that turned out."

Shaking my head as I get up, dragging the sheets back over her just to watch her squirm.

Whatever this is between us... is so damn dangerous.

I've never been more addicted to anything in my life.

I leave her in bed, and walk out to the kitchen, needing coffee and a moment to pull myself back together.

The coffee finishes brewing just as the city wakes.

I take it black. No bullshit creamer. It scalds my throat, grounding me for exactly three seconds before reality claws its way back in.

I press the phone to my ear and stare out at the skyline, watching the sun bleed over the buildings.

Marcus picks up on the second ring.

"Find out where he lives."

There's silence on the other end, the kind that comes with knowing I don't waste words.

"Tyler," I clarify. "Octavia's ex."

More silence. Then finally a quiet exhale, like Marcus is already regretting this assignment.

"I'm not asking you to do anything *yet*," I snap. "I want an address. That's all I need. Married or not, I don't give a fuck. I want to know where he eats, sleeps, breathes. And if I decide he needs a warning... I'll give him one he'll remember."

My fingers flex around my mug, knuckles whitening.

"I won't kill him," I add, though my voice exposes the lie. "But he'll wish I had."

Marcus doesn't argue. Smart man.

Ending the call, I take another sip of coffee, trying to swallow down the fury still burning in my chest.

She didn't tell me the full story, not in detail.

She didn't have to.

The bruises she hides in her memories say enough. The way her voice hardens when she talks about him. The things she hasn't even realized she flinches at.

I will *not* let that piece of shit walk around thinking he got away with it.

When I turn around, she's there.

Standing in the kitchen doorway, barefoot in my shirt, hair a mess, eyes locked on me like she just walked in on something she can't unsee.

My pulse spikes. Not with fear, but with the weight of being *seen*.

"How long have you been standing there?" I ask, voice low, steady.

She doesn't move. She just stares, wide-eyed.

"Long enough."

She crosses the threshold slowly, eyes still locked on mine, the hem of the shirt brushing her thighs with every step.

"You didn't even wait," she says, tone quiet, steady, but laced with something I can't quite name.

"You said tomorrow," I reply coolly, setting my mug down.

She stops a few feet from me. Close enough that I can see the faint pink marks on her neck, the ones I left there hours ago. A reminder, a warning, a promise.

"I didn't think you'd actually do it this soon," she admits.

"That was your first mistake," my voice low. "Assuming I'd give someone like him even one more day to breathe easy after what he did to you."

Her lips part, but no words come out.

I take a step toward her.

"I'm not waiting around while ghosts from your past walk free, Octavia. I'm not sitting back while he lives comfortably, knowing what he took from you."

She searches my face for something. Maybe control, maybe reason. But those are things I've already sacrificed.

"What are you going to do?" she asks, voice barely above a whisper.

My jaw ticks. "That depends."

"On what?"

"On whether I see him first or he tries to see *you*."

A sharp inhale.

Her expression softens, just slightly, but her eyes don't leave mine.

"You scare me when you talk like that," she says.

Nodding once. "It should."

Then I close the space between us completely, my hand curling around her jaw as I tilt her chin up.

"But you should also know I'd never hurt you. *Only* the people who already have."

Her breath hitches.

"I didn't mean I was scared *of you*," she says, voice barely audible. "I meant I'm scared of how easy it is to *want* someone who's capable of doing what you've done."

I lean in, brushing my lips just above hers.

"And I'm terrified of how far I'm willing to go just to keep you." Her eyes wide and locked on mine. One hand rises between us and presses flat to my chest—right over my heartbeat, where it jackhammers against her palm like it wants to escape the cage I've kept it in.

"I don't want you to lose yourself trying to protect me," she whispers.

Covering her hand with mine, I murmur, "I didn't lose myself because of you. That happened a long time ago."

I glance at her, at the way her fingers curl tighter around mine, and something inside me shifts—slow, heavy, undeniable.

"I already lost myself," I say, voice rough. "But with you... I found the man I thought was gone. Buried under blood and silence and everything I swore I'd never feel again."

She starts to speak, but I shake my head, my eyes never leaving hers.

"This... this isn't some noble spiral where I'm sacrificing my soul for you. I already gave that up when I realized I couldn't trust most of this fucked-up world. People are currency. Leverage. Disposable."

Her throat bobbles, but she stays quiet.

"I don't care about 99% of them. Never have. Never will." I let that truth land, heavy and cold. "But there are a *very* select few who get through. And you, Octavia — you're one of them."

Her mouth opens and closes, like she wants to say something, but nothing comes out. Her eyes are still locked on mine, like she's trying to memorize the weight of every word.

I lean in, press a kiss to her forehead. One second. Two.

Then my fucking phone buzzes on the counter, loud, breaking the silence.

Neither of us moves right away. But then she pulls back slightly. "That might be Marcus," I sigh, jaw clenching.

"You're not going to let it wait?"

"No," I admit, reaching for the phone without looking away from her.

MARCUS

Address.

I stare at the word, a low trill building behind my teeth.

"He found him?" she asks.

Nodding my head, "Yeah."

"And now?"

Locking my screen, I set the phone face down.

"Now, I know exactly where he sleeps."

She swallows, but doesn't step back, doesn't recoil. Her eyes are darker now, like she's made her peace with this.

"I'm not asking what you'll do," she says, voice quiet. "But I know you."

Smirking, just a little, I say, "Not yet."

Then softer, more honest, "But you're getting there."

She watches me in silence, the tension still radiating off her like heat. The kind that comes from not knowing if you're safe, or if you've just stopped caring.

Yet she still doesn't run.

She just takes the mug from my hand, her fingers brushing mine, and says quietly, "You're really not going to let this go."

It's not a question.

"No," I answer. "I'm not."

A few seconds pass, and her jaw tightens, but her voice is calm.

"I can handle a lot—but not losing you."

The words hit harder than I expect. Not because they scare me, but because *she* scares me. The way she looks at me like I'm still worth holding onto. Like she sees something underneath all the wreckage.

I don't answer.

I just reach out, hook a finger under her chin, and kiss her slow and deep.

Then, I turn back to the window, stare out at the skyline, and let the silence settle again.

Because I'm going to burn the world for her, and I need to start with the first name on my list.

And now I've got it.

CHAPTER FIFTEEN

Octavia

The mug is still warm in my hands when he turns away from me.

He says nothing. He doesn't offer more promises, more threats, or any kind of reassurance. Just stands there in front of the window, the city bleeding light across his skin like it's trying to paint a man who can't be captured.

For a second, I just sit back and watch him. Tall, unshaken and terrifyingly still.

I should feel something.

Fear, doubt, maybe even guilt, for what I'm letting happen—or worse, *encouraging*.

But all I feel is calm.

This is the part where a normal person would say *you're in too deep*. But I think I passed that line somewhere around the moment I begged him to fuck me in my sleep. Or maybe when I asked if we could find the man who used to pretend to love me and ruin him for sport.

Hard to say, really.

I take a slow sip of the coffee and lean against the doorway, watching

Dominic like he's both the ending and the beginning of something I won't survive unchanged.

Maybe I don't want to.

Maybe that's the whole point.

My phone buzzes on the counter, and I glance down to see Lena's name lighting up the screen.

Shit.

I've been *responding* to her texts… just not like I usually do. Short replies, delayed and vague as hell since Friday.

It's now Sunday… And Lena doesn't do vague well.

I walk down the hall to his bedroom, and I swipe to answer, already bracing myself.

"Hey."

"*Finally.*" Her voice is half teasing, half *where the fuck have you been.* "I was starting to think you'd been kidnapped by the hot billionaire and locked in a sex dungeon."

"Not a dungeon," I say lightly, "Just… distracted."

"Mm-hmm. You've been weird all weekend. Short texts, no snark. Who even *are* you?"

Letting out a deep breath. "It's been a lot, Lena."

There's a pause on her end, then softer, "Are you okay?"

I hesitate. Because the truth is… I don't know what I am. Okay? No. Unraveled? Probably. Recklessly infatuated with a man who killed someone the other night, and will do it again? Definitely.

"I'm fine," and it sounds like a lie even to me.

"Octavia," she warns. "You always say you're fine right before an emotional implosion."

"I'm not imploding," I mutter. "I'm just… trying to figure things out."

Lena sighs like she's not sure whether to press or give me space.

"If you need to talk, I'm here. But just promise me one thing?"

"What's that?"

"If you're going to burn your life down, at least let me bring the wine and hold the match."

A laugh escapes before I can stop it. "Deal."

Walking out of the room, I linger in the hallway for a moment after the call ends, staring down at my phone like it might offer answers that I don't have.

If you're going to burn your life down…

As if I haven't already lit fucking the match.

Shoving the phone into my pocket, I head back toward the kitchen. Dominic hasn't moved.

He doesn't look at me when I approach, but his voice is sharp.

"Friend checking in?"

"Yeah." Pausing beside him, the skyline casts gold across the sharp edge of his jaw. "She's worried. Thinks I've gone dark."

"And have you?"

I don't answer right away.

"I'm still here, aren't I?"

That earns me a glance, like he's assessing how much of me is still *mine* and how much he's already claimed.

"She's not wrong to worry," he says, turning to face me fully now. "This isn't exactly a soft landing."

"No," I admit, holding his gaze. "But I'm not here because it's safe."

I take the last step forward, closing the space between us. His eyes drop to my mouth, then back to mine.

"I'm here because it's *you*."

He just looks at me like he's still trying to figure out how I haven't run yet.

Swallowing hard, "But I need to know what you're planning to do,

Dominic."

His brow lifts slightly.

"With *Tyler*," I clarify. "When you find him. When you show up at his house, or his job, or wherever he's playing pretend now."

A moment of silence stretches between us. Heavy and charged.

"I'm not asking you to change who you are," I continue, "But I don't want to be kept in the dark either. I want to know what you're going to do when you get to him."

His jaw tenses, just slightly, like he was expecting me to avoid this conversation, not demand it.

"I don't need protecting from the truth," I add. "If I'm going to keep standing next to you, I deserve to know where your lines are."

He studies me for a moment, the air between us is crackling like wildfire, until he finally lets out a breath.

His eyes are unreadable. When he speaks, his voice is clipped.

"I don't plan to kill him."

A pause.

"Not unless he gives me a reason."

My stomach tightens, but I don't look away, and he sees that.

"If it helps," he continues with an icy tone, "I don't make a habit of blind violence. I calculate, I watch, I wait, and when the moment comes—if it comes—I make sure the message is permanent."

There's no heat in his eyes, just the chilling calm of someone who's already decided how this ends.

"I want him to feel what he made you feel," he says. "To know he's not untouchable. That there are consequences."

His presence settles over me like a shadow, close enough to steal the air from my lungs.

"But if you're asking me to promise mercy..." His head tilts, and that sharp glint returns to his eyes. "You're asking the wrong man,

Octavia."

I nod slowly, processing his words. My fingers trace the rim of my mug, finding comfort in the clockwise motion.

"I'm not asking for mercy," I finally say, meeting his eyes. "I just needed to know."

Something shifts in his expression—not a softening exactly, but possibly a slight recalibration, like he's reassessing me.

"And now that you do?" he asks, voice deceptively calm. "What will you do with that knowledge?"

It's a fair question. One I've been asking myself since the moment his control snapped and he finally revealed just how dark he can be.

"I don't know yet," I answer honestly. "But I'd rather navigate this with my eyes open than trip around in the dark pretending I don't see exactly who you are."

He makes a sound that isn't quite a laugh.

"Most people prefer the dark, Octavia. The illusion of safety it provides."

"I lived in the illusion of the dark for far too long. I'm choosing you." Our eyes lock, his stare intense, like he can't quite figure out what he wants to say back to me. I shift the mug in my hands and clear my throat, needing something—*anything*—to cut the gravity of the moment.

"Sooo... I, uh... I'm probably going to need to run to the store and my apartment at some point," keeping my voice light, "Unless you're planning to let me borrow your toothbrush and wear your shirt all day."

The corner of his mouth lifts in amusement. It's almost dangerous.

"You're not taking my toothbrush." His voice is dry. "But the shirts..."

His eyes drag down my body, slow and heavy. "...you're welcome to wear that all day."

Heat creeps up my neck, and I pretend to be very interested in the last sip of coffee.

"I'll take that under consideration," I mutter.

When I glance back up, he's still watching me, sharp and calculating. He leans back against the counter, with his arms crossed, like he's playing chess while I'm playing checkers.

"You're not going anywhere unless it's with me."

"Okay," I say slowly, the sass creeping back into my tone because it feels safer than the way my heart is pounding. "Well, you have two choices, then. Either you play chauffeur, or you toss me some keys and let me take one of your overpriced phallic compensation vehicles for a spin."

That gets a reaction.

His shoulders tense for a second before a slow, dangerous smile curves on his mouth.

"Overpriced phallic compensation vehicles? I think we both know I have nothing to be compensating for, little minx."

I shrug innocently. "You drive a Porsche that probably cost more than my mom's house, and that is just one of god knows how many vehicles you own. I feel like the label's accurate."

He closes the distance between us with slow, meticulous steps, and somehow it feels like the whole room spins.

"You're real fucking mouthy this morning," his voice a soft threat wrapped in velvet.

"And you're real bossy," I counter, tilting my chin up. "We all have our flaws."

Something dark flashes in his eyes, something that makes my pulse stumble over itself.

"You want to drive one of my cars?" he murmurs, voice dropping lower. "Fine."

He reaches into his pocket and pulls out a key fob, tossing it to me.

I catch it instinctively, heart lurching.

"But I want to know where you are going," he adds as his voice hardens. "No point in hiding it, my cars all have tracking systems in them."

I hold the keys, pretending my hands aren't shaking just a little.

"Are you going to stalk my every Target run now?" I tease him, even though my voice wavers.

"If that's what it takes," he says simply.

And I believe him.

I swallow slowly, fingers tightening around the fob. "Noted."

He steps even closer now, so close I have to tilt my head up to meet his eyes.

"And if anyone even looks at you wrong," he murmurs, so low I can feel it more than hear it, "they won't ever have the chance to look again."

The words should feel suffocating.

They don't.

They feel like oxygen.

God, help me, I think I'm already past the point of being saved.

I'm dressed in last nights clothes—wrinkled , clinging with the scent of him and everything we did. I tuck the key fob into my pocket I head for the elevator, the weight of it feeling heavier than it should.

When the doors slide shut behind me and I'm finally alone, I let out a breath.

Okay...

Now all you have to do is not crash this man's ridiculously expensive car and pick up a few essentials.

Simple.

I slide into the driver's seat a few minutes later, the car smells like him: warm, mysterious, exotic, expensive. The second the engine roars to life, I can practically hear Lena's voice in my head.

"You're being vague, Octavia. I know you're hiding something."

Which is probably why, halfway to my apartment, I give up and call her.

She answers on the first ring.

"About damn time. Spill. All of it."

I laugh, easing onto the freeway. "I'm not hiding anything."

"Bullshit," Lena snaps. "You're hiding everything. I've been pacing my living room like a deranged toddler waiting for answers. And you owe me, bitch."

"Technically, I called you," I point out.

"Yeah, because your guilt finally kicked in. Now talk."

I hesitate, because once I say it out loud, there's no putting it back in the bottle.

Fuck it. If I'm going to spiral, I'm not doing it alone.

"I have been with him all weekend," I say carefully.

There's a beat of silence.

"Is it who I think it is?"

"Depends who you think it is."

Lena groans. "Don't make me say it."

I grin, biting my lip. "Boss man."

"Oh my God." she shrieks so loudly I know everyone walking along the sidewalk can hear.

"Please tell me you're joking. Tell me you're not out here raw-dogging a man who could literally fund a private island."

"I'm not joking," I say, laughing despite myself. "And technically, we haven't discussed islands yet."

"Octavia! I can't even. Is it serious? Is it a one-time 'whoopsie weekend' situation? Are you locked in his penthouse right now?"

"...Possibly."

She gasps. "You little slut."

I'm grinning so hard my cheeks hurt. "It's not just sex, Lena. It's... it's complicated. But it's real."

There's a pause on her end.

"Is he good to you?"

I swallow hard. "Yeah," I say, my voice steady. "In a way I didn't even know I needed."

Another pause. I can practically hear her breathing through the phone, processing.

"And he let me take one of his cars today," I add, trying to sound casual but probably failing miserably.

Silence.

"...What!?"

"I'm just grabbing some stuff from my apartment, and going to stop at the market on the way back to his place." I say, pulling off the exit ramp. "He tossed me the keys and everything."

"I... you... you took a rich mans car?" she screams. "You're not just sleeping with him. You're fucking *owned*, babe. Congratulations, you're a kept woman."

I laugh, heart hammering too fast in my chest. "It's not like that."

"It's exactly like that!" she yells. "Next thing you know he's going to microchip you and buy you your own penthouse!"

"I mean... I'd be a very affordable pet."

"I hate you," she says dramatically. "But also, I'm living for this." I laugh, shaking my head as I turn into the parking lot of my apartment complex.

"Listen," I say, easing the car into a spot, "I just pulled up to my place. Let me grab a few things and we'll talk later, okay?"

"Fine," she huffs. "But don't think for a second this conversation is over."

"It never is with you."

"Love you, bitch."

"Love you more."

I hang up, and shut the car off.

For a second, I just sit there, hands resting on the steering wheel, letting the quiet settle around me.

Then my phone buzzes.

I glance over. Of course, it's Dominic.

DOMINIC

Checking in. I'm going to handle some things this morning.

I am almost to Tyler's. Keep your location on.

I stare at the message, heart thudding louder now.
Handle some things.
Already almost to Tyler's.
There's no anger in his words, just cold intent.
Somehow, that's worse.
I type out a quick reply, fingers trembling slightly.

ME

Got it. Just grabbing a few things and getting out. I'll be quick. Location is on.

Another buzz immediately.

DOMINIC

Good girl.

I toss my phone into my purse and grab it as I get out of the car. Walking up to my apartment feels weird after being in his penthouse all night. The air feels heavier here. The hallway smells like old carpet and someone's burnt attempt at breakfast.

The lock sticks when I turn the key.

Pushing the door open, and tossing my purse on the couch, I head straight for the bedroom.

Everything is still the same and undisturbed. Opening the dresser, I take just the basics, sleep shorts, underwear, leggings, and socks. Tomorrow is coming too soon and I am not ready to go back to the office. I turn to the closet and choose a dress I have yet to wear and pack everything neatly in my bag.

I sling the bag over my shoulder, and I pick up my phone and fire off a quick text.

ME

Just finished packing my things, jumping in the shower real quick.

Also going to stop at the market on the way back to your place.

I want to make you dinner.

Before I can even set my phone down he responds.

DOMINIC

I just left his house.

He wasn't home.

His wife answered the door, covered in makeup and still couldn't hide the bruises.

Her eyes were down the whole time. She wouldn't even speak until I said your name.

He's doing it again, Octavia.

I stop walking.

The air leaves my lungs like a gut punch.

Bruises.

Eyes down.

Wouldn't speak until he said my name.

My fingers tighten around the phone until they ache.

ME

Shit. Is she ok?

He doesn't answer right away.

DOMINIC

Not even fucking close.

Staring at the screen, my chest burning, bile rising in my throat.

Because I remember what it felt like to be her.

To be careful, small and quiet.

Always hoping someone would say something.

Always hoping someone would *see*. But I always hid everything so well. I buried everything deep down, covered every bruise. No one ever knew. No one even speculated.

And now someone did.

Dominic did.

CHAPTER SIXTEEN

Octavia

I don't know how long I stand there, staring at the last message.

Not even fucking close.

His words burn into my brain long after the screen goes dark.

Like he's already planning what happens next.

I shove my phone into the bag to get moving, because if I stay still any longer, I'm going to spiral.

The market's only a few minutes away, and it's quiet when I pull in, just a few cars scattered across the lot, an old man putting a bag of oranges into the trunk of an old Civic.

I take a deep breath to ease the ache in my chest. When I open the door, the cold air hits me like a slap. Thank god for close parking. Grabbing a small basket, I walk down the aisles.

Garlic.

Butter.

Fresh herbs.

Chicken thighs.

Lemons.

Simple and something I can actually do well.

I'm reaching for a bottle of olive oil when I feel it,

a presence behind me. Too close.

My stomach knots.

I turn slowly, basket in hand, breath caught halfway in my throat.

But no one is there, just a woman looking at pasta sauces a few feet back and an employee on his phone, sitting on a pallet of canned beans.

I exhale too fast.

My pulse still doesn't get the memo.

Shaking it off, I drop the bottle into my basket and move on.

By the time I get to the self-checkout, my shoulders are still tight.

I help bag my items, say thank-you to the cashier, and head for the door.

My boots echo on the sidewalk as I step outside. The air bites at my cheeks, and for a second, I focus on my breath, trying to tame the nerves still clawing at my insides.

I barely take two steps toward my car before I feel it… a hand.

Rough and tight, yanking me back.

I'm off the sidewalk before I can react, being dragged into the narrow alley beside the market, my bags slipping from my hands as I hit the wall.

"Thought I might find you here," Tyler snarls, his face inches from mine.

His breath reeks of cheap liquor and bitterness, and his grip on my arm tightens, fingers digging into my skin.

"You've been busy, huh?" he hisses.

I shove at his chest, but he barely moves.

"Let go of me."

"You disappeared," he says, ignoring me. "Didn't even say goodbye. That's not like you, baby. My wife isn't nearly as fun as you."

"I'm not your anything," I snap, voice sharp. "Get your fucking hands off me."

He laughs, low and mean. "You always did get mouthy when you felt cornered. It always makes my dick hard when you fight back."

I try again, harder this time, an elbow to his ribs, my fingers clawing at his shoulder, but he grabs my wrist, slamming it back against the brick.

"You really think he can protect you?" he growls. "You think that rich prick's gonna save you when he's not even here?"

My heart's pounding as I bite back tears, but I keep my chin up.

I won't let him see me break.

"Yeah," I breathe. "I do."

His jaw twitches.

And then his hand goes to my throat.

Not hard yet, just pressure, a warning.

The kind that says *I could*.

"I told you that you would never get anywhere in life," he breathes, leaning in close. "Look at you. You really had to get on your knees like the whore you are to get a better job."

I claw at his wrist, nails digging in. "I'm not scared of you anymore."

He leans in closer, voice rough in my ear. "You should be."

Then I snap. I drive my knee up, hard.

He grunts, stumbling back, and I take my chance, slamming my palm into his chest and twisting free of his grip.

"Back the fuck off!" I shout, my voice cracking as I stumble away.

But he's already lunging again.

His hand tangles in my hair, yanking me back toward the wall.

"You stupid fucking bitch," he growls, teeth bared. "You think that man makes you untouchable?"

I twist, trying to break free, panic and adrenaline slamming through me.

I scream. Loud. Raw.

For someone.

For *anyone.*

And then

a voice cuts through the air.

Low and fucking furious.

"Let. Her. Go."

The words land like gunshots.

Tyler stiffens. His hand is still tangled in my hair, fingers twitching like he can't decide if he wants to tighten his grip or run.

I don't have to look to know who it is.

I can feel Dominic's fury humming through the air like a live wire.

Slowly, Tyler turns his head.

Dominic steps into the alley, his green eyes burning with something I've never seen before. Not anger. *Annihilation.*

"I said," he growls, each word sharper than the last, "let. her. go."

Tyler laughs. A broken, ugly sound.

"What's the matter?" he sneers. "Coming to pick up your little whore?"

He doesn't even get the word out before Dominic moves.

One second Tyler's gripping me—

The next he's slammed against the brick, Dominic's forearm crushing his throat, his feet skidding for traction.

Stumbling back, I gasp for air, my hand flying to my neck.

Dominic doesn't even look at me.

His eyes are locked on Tyler's, cold and lethal.

"You put your hands on her," Dominic says, low and dangerous. "You fucking touched what isn't yours."

Tyler chokes, clawing at Dominic's arm. His face turning beet red.

"You know what happens now?" Dominic's voice drops even lower, so low I almost don't hear it. "You stop breathing."

Tyler gurgles, trying to say something, trying to fight, but it's useless.

Dominic is stronger and ruthless.

Willing to go further.

And he's not letting go.

I see the moment it shifts from a threat to a promise.

Dominic's hand keeps tightening.

Tyler's feet flailing like a fish out of water.

The pure, unstoppable rage pouring off Dominic is palpable.

For the first time in a long time, I'm not afraid.

I'm watching justice. I'm watching retribution. I'm watching Dominic become the monster he warned me he could be.

And I don't want him to stop.

I don't know how long he holds him there.

Long enough that Tyler stops fighting.

Long enough that it's clear Dominic can end it if he wants to.

I just stand there, frozen.

I don't tell him to stop; I don't move. Some part of me doesn't even want to.

But then… he lets go.

Just… lets him drop.

Like he's not even worth the effort.

Tyler crumples onto the ground, coughing and gasping for air.

Dominic steps back, breathing hard, his hands are curled into fists like he's still fighting the urge to go back and finish it.

He doesn't look at me right away.

He's pacing, running a hand through his hair like he can't burn off the anger fast enough.

I stay where I am, heart hammering.

Why did he just… halt everything?

I don't know if I'm relieved or disappointed.

Maybe its both.

Finally, his eyes find mine.

And the look he gives me... it's not the mask he wears for everyone else. It's raw, furious and still dark as hell.

But it's not empty.

It's full of something I don't even know how to name.

"Get in the car," he says, voice low and rough. "Now."

Without arguing, I move fast, grabbing my dropped bags with shaking hands.

And the whole time, I can feel him right behind me, close enough to catch me if I fall.

Close enough to burn the entire world down if I ask him to.

CHAPTER SEVENTEEN

Dominic

I can still feel his puny throat under my hand. Every muscle in my body is tight and burning.

She hasn't said a damn word since we got in the car.

She's sitting next to me, seatbelt on, hands in her lap, her breathing is quiet, but she doesn't seem scared. She seems disappointed.

That's worse.

I grip the steering wheel so tight my knuckles turn white and pop.

I should've killed that fucking bastard right there in that alley.

It would've only taken fifteen more seconds, probably less.

But she was there, eyes wide and still catching her breath.

I just couldn't do it. Not with her watching.

My jaw aches from how hard I'm clenching it.

"This isn't over," I say, finally breaking the silence. My voice comes out rougher than I intend. "He's not getting away with any of this."

Her stare clings to me in silence.

"I'm not done with him," I go on. "I just couldn't do it there. Not in the middle of the street. Not in front of you."

A flicker of connection—that's all I give her.

Her eyes are on me, steady and quiet. Then, finally, she speaks.

"I wanted you to do it," she says, voice small but clear.

I study her face, and for a second, I'm not sure I've heard her right.

"I didn't want you to stop," she goes on. "I've never felt that before. That… need. That ache to see someone fucking end for what they did to me."

Shifting in her seat, she turns toward me fully, and something in her eyes flickers—dark, eager, and honest.

She reaches her hand over, fingers sliding into my hair, gripping tight.

"I want you right now."

She kisses me before I can respond.

Hot and hard, like she's trying to crawl inside me.

I growl against her mouth, grabbing her waist, pulling her over the console because I don't give a shit that we're still in the parking lot.

She moans, and it ricochets through my veins.

I kiss her ravenously.

She is the only thing keeping me grounded.

Her hands are everywhere. My jaw, my shoulders, dragging my coat off like it's in the way, like *everything* is in the way.

I break away just long enough to whisper against her lips.

"You sure?"

She bites down on my bottom lip, hard, breaking the skin and making me groan.

"I've never been more sure of anything in my entire fucking life."

I'm about to fucking lose it.

She's straddling me, mouth on mine, her hands pulling at my shirt like she wants to tear me apart and put me back together in the same breath.

Then, I catch a glimpse through the windshield of an old man.

Standing by a cart staring.

"Fuck," I mutter, dragging my mouth from hers. "There's an old guy watching us."

She turns her head. "Seriously?"

"Yeah. It looks like he's either calling the cops or reliving his youth."

She laughs breathlessly, wrecked, and I steal one more kiss, slow and filthy, pulling myself together.

"Get back in your seat," I tell her, voice ragged. "I'm taking you somewhere better."

She slides back over, still flushed and breathing heavily, eyes locked on me because she's not done.

I grab my phone with one hand, dialing as I pull out of the lot with the other.

Marcus answers on the second ring.

"Hey, Dom. What's up?"

"My bike's behind the market," I say. "Send someone to get it."

"You're not riding?"

"I'm not leaving her alone."

"On it."

I hang up and weave through the traffic.

"Where are we going?" she asks, voice low, teasing.

I glance at her, jaw tight.

"Somewhere dark," I say. "Somewhere I can fuck you without an audience."

Her hand's on my dick before we get to the first light.

"Jesus, Octavia," I grit out.

She looks at me without saying a word, just sliding her palm over me, slow and teasing.

Leaning in, her lips brushing my ear. "Eyes on the road, Dom."

"Not helping," I growl, my hips jerking when her fingers squeeze me. "Are you trying to make us crash?"

Her laugh is wicked and breathless. "Not really."

I grip the wheel harder, trying to focus, but her hand keeps working me through my jeans, steadily, like she's trying to see how far she can push before I break.

By the time I pull into the parking garage, my entire body is strung tight.

I park fast and kill the engine.

Then I turn to her, eyes locked.

"Out," I bite.

She blinks. "What?"

I throw my door open. "Out of the fucking car. Now, little minx."

She scrambles out, her breath hitching when I slam my door behind me and stalk around to her.

I grab her by the hips, spin her, and shove her forward against the hood.

"You wanted this," I growl, bending over her back, lips at her ear. "You started this in the fucking car."

She moans, palms flat against the car, her breath fogging against the paint.

"And now I'm going to finish it," I snarl, hands already sliding up under her shirt, yanking at her jeans. "Right here. Where no one can see, but you'll still feel like they could."

She gasps as I drag her pants down slow enough to tease. Her legs are trembling, and she's already soaked.

"Fuck," I growl, palming her ass, and dragging my fingers through her slickness. "You're fucking dripping."

She moans, pushing back against my hand.

"You are a dirty girl," I breathe the words into her ear, rough and close. "Did you like it?"

She whimpers, hands fisting, trying to grab at anything.

"Watching the life almost drain from that fucking prick's eyes," I go on, voice darker now. "It turned you on. Didn't it, baby?"

She doesn't answer.

So I slap her ass hard, enough to make her yelp and arch back.

"I asked you a question."

"Yes," she gasps. "God, yes. I loved it."

I groan, dragging my zipper down with one hand, and pull my dick out while my other hand holds her hips steady.

"You liked seeing what I'd do to protect you?" I press the head of my cock against her, teasing, not giving her anything yet. "Liked knowing I'll fucking kill for you if you say the word?"

She nods frantically, hips rolling back into me. "I want you to. I wanted you to."

I thrust into her in one brutal stroke, and she screams out loud.

I fuck her hard, each stroke brutal, and relentless, driving her into the hood with the force of it.

Her screams echo against the walls, begging me for more.

She fucks me back, her ass slamming into me, taking everything I give her.

The sound of her, the feel of her, it's fucking obscene.

The raw broken moans tear out of her throat. She's losing herself in it.

I grab her hips tighter, driving myself deeper, watching the recoil of her perfect ass with every savage thrust.

It's enough to make me lose my fucking mind.

Reaching around, my hand slides between her legs, finding her clit.

I circle it rough and fast, not giving her time to think, not giving her a single second to catch her breath.

"Cum for me, baby." I grit out.

She shatters, her body locking up, legs shaking, pussy clenching so tight around me I see stars.

"Dominic," she cries out, voice cracking.

And that's it, that's all I can take.

I crash into her one last time, emptying inside her with a low, guttural growl.

Holding her there, as I spill into her, every muscle in my body gives out at once.

She sags against the hood, trembling, gasping for air, and I don't move.

She's still trembling when I finally pull back, my hands sliding down her sides, steadying her.

I tuck myself away and fix her jeans with shaking fingers, lifting her into my arms without a word.

She doesn't fight it, just wraps her arms around my neck and buries her face in my shoulder.

Carrying her back to her side of the car, I open the door, and set her gently in the passenger seat before getting behind the wheel.

Her breathing has slowed down, but her hands are still shaking a little.

I can still feel her all over me.

The parking garage is quiet except for the clicking of the engine cooling and the dull echo of her moan still playing in my head.

She breaks the silence.

"I meant it," she murmurs, voice rough but certain. "About Tyler."

I glance over at her.

She just stares straight ahead like she's thinking through every outcome and picking the one that ends in blood.

"I want you to kill him," she says. "And I don't want you to wait."

Gripping the steering wheel, something cold and sharp twists in my stomach.

"You're sure?" I ask, even though I already know the answer.

Finally, she turns to me. Her eyes are cool and even. There's no fear there. Just the quiet certainty of a woman who's done pretending everything is ok.

"I want it done tonight, and I want to be there." she says.

My jaw tightens. The monster in me stretches, satisfied. Relieved.

She doesn't want me to be better.

She wants me to be exactly who I am, and she wants to watch.

"Then, it's tonight," I say.

My voice is calm, but inside I'm already moving, thinking through how, where, and how clean it needs to be.

Looking over at her again.

"You are going to stand back," I add. "You don't touch anything. You won't take the fall for this."

She nods.

"I won't."

"But I need to see it." her tone softens.

I give a short nod. That's all I need.

Tyler's fucking done.

I pull my phone from my pocket and call Marcus.

He picks up immediately. "You good?"

"No," saying flatly. "But I will be."

"Fuck."

 He knows what that means.

"I'll track him," Marcus says. "Text you when I've got a location."

"Tonight."

"Understood."

I hang up and set the phone down, then shift my attention to her.

She's still watching me, calm, like this is normal.

My hand drifts to her thigh. "You'll stay back," I tell her again. "No matter what happens."

She nods in agreement.

"I just want to see him fall."

That dark part of me—the one I've tried to bury—wants to kiss her for that, wants to drag her back into my lap all over again.

But for now, I just start the car.

She wants blood and I'm going to give it to her.

CHAPTER EIGHTEEN

Dominic

She stays quiet for a minute, like the words are stuck in her throat.

The only sound is the rumble of the engine and the faint buzz of the city seeping in through the glass.

Then, soft but steady,

"How are you going to do it?"

Not fearful, not hesitant, just pure curiosity.

Like she's trying to picture it.

"That depends on where Marcus finds him," I say while my eyes are still locked on the road. "If he's home, it'll be easier, in and out."

"And if he's not?" she asks, glancing over at me.

"Then, I adjust." I pause, "It might get messy."

She nods like that's acceptable. Like she's expecting that.

"What are you thinking?" she asks next. "Gun? Knife?"

My lips twitch. "Shears maybe."

She tilts her head. "That's… dark."

I glance at her. "What are you thinking?"

She falls silent again, but only for a second. Then, she reaches across

the console and brushes her fingers over my wrist.

"That I don't want it to be quick," she says.

She clenches, fingertips pressing hard against me.

"I want him to hurt," she adds, quieter now. "I want him to know exactly what it feels like to be powerless. I want him to fucking beg like a dog."

My eyes cut over to her.

She's staring straight ahead, jaw clenched, voice calm but there's heat behind it, pure rage.

"I know that's horrible," she says, like she's admitting something she didn't mean to say out loud. "But… fuck him."

She exhales sharply, running her hand down her thigh like she's trying to level herself.

"I don't know what's come over me," she mutters. "I'm not like this."

But she is, I can feel it.

She's just never been given permission to stop hiding it.

"You don't have to explain yourself, not to me."

She levels me with a look, there's something in her eyes I've seen before.

Something close to recognition.

Like she's finally meeting the part of herself she always kept buried. Her gaze flicks away for a second, then back at me with a little smirk pulling at her lips.

"I can't lie," she says, voice light, almost playful. "I kind of can't wait to watch the life drain from his eyes."

She shrugs, casually, like she's talking about a scene from a movie. "I know that probably makes me sound unhinged, but honestly… I think I've earned it."

I raise a brow, lips twitching. She grins wider, unapologetic now.

"I mean, it's not like I'm going to be the one to do it," she adds. "But front row seats? Popcorn in hand? I'll be there in heels."

I chuckle, low in my throat, because fuck… she's perfect.

Not in the sweet, soft way most people mean it. No—she's chaos wrapped in lipstick and confidence. Fire with a sense of humor. The kind of woman who doesn't just survive darkness—she learns how to flirt with it. And somehow, she still looks good doing it.

She talks about revenge with a grin and zero remorse—and all I can think about is how much I want to keep her. Own her. Protect her.

God help anyone who tries to hurt her… because they'll never see me coming.

"I should be disturbed by that," I joke.

She tilts her head, playful and dangerous. "You love it."

She's right. I absolutely do.

My phone buzzes.

MARCUS

He's not at home.

Hotel off 6th. Room 204.

The coward thinks he can hide out in some cheap hotel.

I let out a low breath, fingers tightening on the wheel.

He knows I'm coming.

He doesn't know when, he just knows it's inevitable.

I reroute the GPS silently and take the next turn.

Octavia doesn't ask, she just stares out the window

Twenty minutes later, we're parked down the street.

Second floor. Room 204. Curtains drawn. Lights on.

He's in there.

Octavia leans forward, peering up at the building.

"He's hiding," she mutters, almost to herself. "What a fucking pussy."

Her words hang in the air, unanswered. I'm already watching exits, foot traffic, security cameras, stairwells.

She settles back into her seat with a low exhale.

"I don't know how the hell I'm supposed to go back to work tomorrow," she says after a beat, her voice dry. "Like, how do I just... walk into the office after tonight?"

My eyes drift to her. She's got one leg pulled up, her eyes still on the hotel window.

"You won't have to," I say. "Call in sick."

She snorts. "So do I get murder PTO now? Is that part of the company benefits package?"

I smirk. "Baby, you seem to forget, I own the company. I'll write it in tomorrow."

She grins, but there's heat behind it.

Then she looks back at the hotel and it's there again, that flicker in her eyes.

Not with hesitation. She is anticipating this. I scan the place again, slowly and meticulously.

No front desk, no cameras on the lot.

No one in or out except the two guys smoking outside who look like they've each got at least three warrants.

Perfect.

I grab my phone and fire off a quick text to Marcus.

ME

No security. No eyes. Shitty motel full of criminals. Couldn't ask for a better setup.

MARCUS

You want backup?

ME

No. Just cleanup.

MARCUS

Got it. Text me when it's done.

Setting the phone down, I lean back in my seat, and look up at the glowing light in the window.

He's probably sitting on the bed, watching some trash TV, thinking I've forgotten.

He has no fucking idea.

She's still watching the window, still calm.

But this is different, this isn't the fantasy.

This isn't the moment in the car when she said she wanted to see him fall.

This is *now*. This is *real*.

"Octavia."

She turns her head.

I hold her gaze. "You sure you're ready for this?"

She doesn't shudder, doesn't blink.

"Yeah," she says. "I am sure. I want to see this. I need to see this."

I study her face, looking for even the smallest crack.

There isn't one.

"Ok. You don't touch anything. You stay behind me, and if I tell you to move, you move. Understood?"

She nods. "Understood."

A silence falls momentarily before I speak again.

"You say the word, and I'll stop."

She stares at me for a second. "Don't stop."

Clenching my jaw, I kill the engine, grab the keys, and push the door open.

"Let's go."

The air outside feels heavy. It reeks of stale smoke and cheap beer.

The asphalt under our feet is old, and the flickering neon casts a green glow across the parking lot.

She walks beside me, silently and steady.

The stairs creak under our weight. A door slams somewhere behind us. Someone is yelling, and not one person around cares.

We pass a guy leaning over the railing, cigarette dangling from his mouth. He doesn't give us a second thought.

Good.

Room 204. Faded numbers on a dented door.

Light seeps through the cracks in the curtain.

TV on inside, the volume low.

I stop in front of it.

Octavia halts a step behind me.

Her breath is quiet.

But her body's humming, I can feel it. That same heat from the alley, from the garage. But sharper now, spiteful.

She's fucking ready, and so am I.

I knock once.

Loud enough to be heard but not loud enough to warn.

The lock clicks, then the door creaks open.

He is wearing a stained T-shirt and sweatpants. His hair a mess and his eyes are puffy.

He opens the door halfway and starts to speak.

I don't let him.

One hard shove and he's stumbling back into the room, barely catching himself before he hits the floor.

I follow him in and Octavia is right behind me, closing the door.

He looks between us stunned, and then his face changes.

Recognition. Fear. Panic.

I grab him by the front of his shirt and throw him onto the bed like the pathetic spineless rat he is.

He bounces once, scrambles to sit up, his mouth already running.

"Wait… hey… look, I didn't…"

"Shut the fuck up," I snap.

His jaw shuts on instinct.

I turn to lock the door and drag the chair from the table to wedge it under the knob, just in case.

He's on the bed now, back pressed against the headboard like he thinks it's going to protect him.

He's shaking.

Fucking good.

I zero in on Octavia.

She's by the window. Watching intently. Waiting.

Her eyes lock on his.

Tyler stammers, glancing between us, his voice cracking.

"What is this? What… what the fuck is this?"

I reach into my coat pocket.

I pull out a handkerchief and shove it in his mouth while smiling.

He tries to spit the gag out, but I'm already tying it off behind his head.

"Keep it in," I mutter. "You don't get to scream. No one is coming to save you."

I step back and roll my sleeves up slowly, my eyes on him the whole time.

He's already sweating, shaking harder now, making these little whimpering noises through his nose like that's going to help.

I take the knife from my belt, letting the light hit the blade, but not for him.

For her.

She hasn't moved, she's leaning on the windowsill now, one arm wrapped over her chest, her mouth pressed into a thin line.

Her eyes meet mine when she notices I'm looking at her, and she gives me a small smile.

I turn back to him.

"Legs out," I say evenly. He doesn't move, so I grab his ankle and drag him down the bed. He yelps behind the gag, trying to scramble back up.

"Stop squirming, you little bitch" I mutter. "This is going to be worse if you flinch."

I press the blade to his thigh just enough to break skin.

The first cut is slow. A single clean line.

He jerks hard, then freezes.

His eyes go wide, tears streaking his cheeks.

Then, the front of his sweatpants darkens, and the wet stain spreads down his leg.

He pissed himself.

I smile.

"Did that hurt?" I ask, voice teasing.

I make another cut parallel to the first.

He thrashes and whines through the gag.

Octavia steps in closer, her arms still crossed, and jaw tight.

But her eyes never leave him.

She's not looking at the blood, she's looking at his *fear.*

He used to feed on hers.

Not anymore.

I press the tip of the blade against his inner thigh, dragging it in a slow, calculated line toward his knee.

He flails hard against the bed, gagged screams ripping out of his throat.

I hold him down with one hand.

"Shh," I murmur. "You're going to take this. Like she had to."

His eyes roll, wild as his body convulses.

Piss stains the sheets beneath him.

Pathetic.

I lean in, low and close.

"She flinched every time you raised your voice, didn't she?"

Another slice, not deep. Just enough to sting.

"She kept her head down. Didn't talk back. Did everything you wanted. And you still fucking broke her."

He whimpers more, eyes bulging, gag soaked.

Grabbing his chin, I force his eyes to mine.

"She's not afraid of you now. Look at her."

I tilt his face toward Octavia.

She steps closer.

"Say hi," I murmur. "Or nod, at least be fucking polite."

He gurgles something useless behind the cloth.

I let go and drag the knife down his shin, this one deeper.

A line of blood follows.

He screams more, thrashing again, but I pin his legs and keep going.

"You know what she said?" I say over the sound of his sobs.

"She *wanted* me to do this. She asked to see you fall."

I glance over at her, she doesn't blink.

"She's watching you break," I whisper, right in his ear. "And you know what? She likes it."

He's sobbing harder now, his muffled, broken sounds behind the gag.

He's squirming uselessly against the hold I've got on him.

Then I hear her voice.

"Aw," Octavia says, tone light and cold.

"That little whimper almost sounded familiar."

I glance back. She's standing at the foot of the bed now, a brow arched.

"Is this what it felt like for you?" She tilts her head. "Being the one with all the control?"

She steps closer, slowly, until she's just out of reach.

She crouches slightly, meeting his wide, terrified eyes.

"You used to love it when I cried, didn't you?" she says softly. "You'd say it meant I was learning."

His body jerks again, and she smiles.

"Well," she says, standing again. "Consider this your final fucking lesson."

She looks at me.

"Make it count."

I slide the blade up across his stomach, shallow at first, just enough to make him bleed.

He jerks, still trying to twist away, but I press a hand to his chest and shove him back down.

"You remember the belt?" I murmur.

His eyes widen.

"You used it, didn't you? When she didn't answer fast enough, when she tried to stand up for herself."

Another slice clean, just above his hip.

"She didn't tell anyone, didn't let anyone see what you did."

He lets out a pitiful gargled plea.

Octavia watches it all like she's watching trash burn.

"You made her feel small," I growl. "You kept her scared, quiet, walking on glass."

I press the tip of the blade just beneath his ribs.

He freezes.

"And now you're the one crawling."

Leaning in real fucking close, "You should've begged her for mercy when you had the chance. Now, it's too late."

Octavia steps in beside me. Her voice is soft, but lethal.

"I used to think I was weak for letting you break me," she says. "But look at you."

She gestures to the soaked sheets, the blood, the shaking, gagged mess in front of us.

"Look who's weak and pathetic now."

She looks at me, voice low and certain.

"Don't stop."

He flails again, violent and desperate.

But he's already broken. His limbs don't work right, his body's bleeding too much to fight.

The bed frame creaks beneath him.

He tries to speak again.

Frantic, guttural noises come out behind the soaked gag.

Like if he just pleads hard enough, he might wake up from this.

News flash, he won't.

I reach down and tear the gag from his mouth.

He gasps, spitting blood and slobber, chest heaving.

Eyes wide and glassy.

"Please," he chokes. "Please... fuck—please, don't.... don't kill me..."

His voice cracks.

"I'll leave... I'll disappear... just please..."

I backhand him across the face as hard as I can.

He cries out, head snapping to the side, blood flying out of his mouth, hitting the curtains.

"You had your chance," I growl. "And you wasted it."

He tries to crawl back, shaking his head. "No, please, I swear I was fucked up. I didn't know what I was doing."

"You knew *exactly* what you were doing," Octavia snaps.

Her voice cuts sharper than the blade.

"You knew when you grabbed my throat. You knew when you dragged me down and told me it was love."

He freezes.

"You just didn't think anyone would ever hold you accountable."

I press the knife to his chest, just below the collarbone.

He bellows.

"Dominic," Octavia says, firmly.

I don't need to look at her, I know what she's telling me.

I plunge the knife in deep.

Right beneath his rib cage, angled up.

His mouth opens wide, but nothing comes out. Just a wet, choking sound.

I twist the blade. Slow and cruel.

His whole body seizes once—twice—then finally goes still.

I pull the knife free and let him drop.

I wipe the blade on the ruined sheets and stand.

Octavia hasn't moved. She stands, watching him, fixated. Breathing slowly, lips parted and cheeks flushed.

Her gaze meets mine and she fucking *smiles*.

Dark and satisfied, maybe a little wild. My little killer minx fucking *smiles at me*.

And I swear to fucking god I've never wanted her more than I do right now.

CHAPTER NINETEEN
Octavia

He doesn't even hesitate, just pulls out his phone, blood still drying on his hands.

"Marcus," he says. His voice is composed and firm, like he just filed a report instead of murdering a man.

"It's done."

That's it.

No emotion, no follow-up, no explanation.

Just *it's done.*

I stare at him, heart still pounding, pulse thrumming in my ears like a drum, and I realize something I probably should've admitted hours ago.

I liked it.

Not just the part where Tyler died, not just watching the fear bleed out of him.

But the part where *Dominic* did it, for me.

Because I asked.

I watch him tuck the phone away like it was just any other regular day.

And I feel this sharp, coiled thing in my chest.

Not fear or guilt.

Just... power.

God, I might actually be a little fucked up.

Letting out a breath, I lean against the wall, arms crossed, feeling my smile tug at the corner of my mouth.

"Well," I say, voice light, "that was cathartic."

He glances over at me, one brow arching up.

"Do I get a punch card or something?" I go on. "Like, you know, kill nine abusers and the tenth one's free?"

He huffs a laugh, deep and dark.

I'm joking.

Kind of.

Maybe.

Okay, not really, because I'm not sorry, not one bit.

He watches me for a second, his eyes roaming over my face like he's still trying to figure out what part of this broke me.

Joke's on him.

He takes a step closer, slow, like he's stalking his prey.

"You know what's sexy as fuck?"

My eyes snap to his, perplexed. "You mean besides the blood on your hands and the body on the bed?"

He smirks, that dangerous, *devour-you* kind of smirk.

"You didn't hide," he says. "You didn't cry, and you didn't pretend to be okay while secretly judging me."

He reaches for me, hand curling around the back of my neck, pulling me just close enough to feel his breath on my lips.

"You looked me in the eye," he utters, "and you told him exactly how you felt, and then you watched me kill him."

His thumb strokes along my jaw.

"That's not messed up, baby. That's fucking honest."

My breath catches and my pulse spikes.

Because he's not wrong, that's what scares me.

I *did* look him in the eye.

I *did* tell Tyler how I felt.

I *did* watch him die.

And somewhere between the blood and the begging and the look on Dominic's face as he carved that piece of shit apart…

I got wet.

Fucking soaked.

Right now, standing in a fucking motel room with the body of my ex on the bed, blood on the floor, and Dominic's fingers curling possessively around the back of my neck, I want him. So damn badly it hurts.

What the hell does that say about me?

How am I supposed to go back to pretending life is normal?

Drink coffee like it doesn't taste better after watching justice?

Smile and be the same sweet girl everyone thinks I am?

Respond to Lena's texts with emojis and bullshit like *"lol I'm fine"* when all I can think about is how it felt to see Tyler piss himself?

How am I supposed to lie to the one person who actually gives a shit?

Fuck, I'm broken, and I don't even care.

I swallow hard, trying to get a grip, and blurt the first thing that comes to mind.

"So when you said 'call in sick tomorrow' earlier… you actually meant it?"

He looks at me like I just said the dumbest thing imaginable.

"No shit," he deadpans. "If you want, I'll stay home too."

I scoff at him like it's the most obvious thing in the world.

"Please. You think I *don't* want you glued to my side after that level of murder-turned-foreplay?"

He looks at me quizzically, but there's the tiniest smirk playing on his mouth.

I nudge his chest lightly.

"Of course I want you to stay, Dominic. What kind of psycho asks for a post-kill cuddle and then sends the man home?"

His eyes drag over me, lazy and loaded.

"Cuddling isn't the only thing we'll be doing tonight."

The heat in his voice hits me low and hot, like a match against gasoline.

But then his hand brushes my hip, grounding me.

"We need to go, though," he adds, voice dipping to a serious tone again. "Can't keep standing here with a body on the bed. Clean-up team's already on their way."

I glance over at Tyler's corpse. The blood, the ruined sheets.

Right.

Dead men don't make great décor. Dominic's hand slips into mine.

"Let's go home," he says.

And then, without warning, he grabs me and *throws* me over his shoulder like I weigh nothing.

"Dominic!" I shriek, laughing as my hair flies and the world flips upside down.

He smacks my ass playfully.

I squeal, kicking my feet, still giggling. "You absolute menace!"

"You say that like it's new," he rumbles, his palm sliding up the back of my thigh. "You love it."

He's definitely not wrong, not even a little.

He sets me down just long enough to open the car door, then pushes me inside with a grin that says *this isn't over*.

I barely get buckled before he's sliding into the driver's seat, door slamming shut, and the silence between us practically *crackles*.

His hand drifts to my thigh.

"You think I didn't see it?" he says, voice thick with need. "The way you looked at me when I finished him."

His fingers press a little harder.

"I could feel it, Octavia. You were practically vibrating."

I swallow hard, heat rushing up my chest as I turn toward him.

"I—"

But I don't finish. Because he kisses me.

Hard.

I'm crawling over the console in seconds, straddling him, one hand fisted in his hair, the other practically ripping his shirt.

He groans into my mouth, hands all over me, now under my jacket, under my shirt, fucking *everywhere*.

I grind down, feeling him already so hard for me, the friction driving me insane.

My phone rings, buzzing like it's possessed.

I let my forehead thunk against his.

"Of course."

He laughs, breathless. "You're popular."

I fish the phone out of my pocket and glance at the screen.

Lena.

"Oh, *shit*."

I sigh and swipe to answer. "Heyyyyyyyy…"

"Oh THANK FUCKING GOD," she screams. "Where the *hell* have you been?! You said you'd call me hours ago! Are you dead? Are you kidnapped? Are you getting railed in the Porsche?!"

Dominic looks at me amused.

I stare at the dash, trying not to laugh.

"…I am not getting railed in the Porsche. That was earlier."

He is biting back a grin now, like he's already planning *round two*.

On the other end, Lena lets out a *dramatic gasp*.

"You did it in the Porsche?! You little whore. I've been over here worried, and you've been playing Grand Theft Auto: Erotic Edition?"

"I said I was grabbing stuff from my apartment," I say, grinning.

"I want details. Blood type. Safe word. Do you have a safe word?"

"Lena."

"Noted. Also, I want to meet him."

"What!?"

"I want to meet your hot boy toy," she says, completely unfazed. "Properly, sober-ish and in a public place where he can't kill me if I make fun of his haircut."

Dominic snorts beneath me, loud enough for her to hear.

"Was that him?" she hisses. "You tell him I'm funnier than you and I drink whiskey straight, so I'm already likable."

I side-eye him. He's full on grinning, as if this is his favorite version of foreplay now.

"She wants to meet you," I mutter.

He shrugs. "Alright."

"Oh my god," Lena says. "Set it up. I want a date, a location, and a glass of wine bigger than my damn head."

Then, without missing a beat,

"Also, ask him if he has any hot, single friends. Preferably ones with big hands, and a mysterious past. It's been *a minute* since I've been laid and I'd rather not play third wheel while you two eye fuck each other across the table."

Dominic smiles wryly. "I've got someone in mind."

My eyes narrow. "Marcus?"

His smirk is pure chaos. "Could be fun."

I give him a look. "You *want* Lena to break him?"

He shrugs, completely unfazed. "If he can't handle her, he doesn't deserve her."

From the speaker, Lena's still rambling. "...I'm just saying, if he's emotionally stunted and has a neck tattoo, I will bring condoms and a flexible attitude."

"Oh my god, *goodbye,*" I say, cutting her off mid-sentence.

She cackles. "Love you!"

"Love you back!"

I hang up and drop my phone in the cupholder.

Dominic's watching me, lips still twitching.

"Marcus has no idea what's coming."

"None," I agree. "And honestly? I can't wait."

The drive back to his penthouse is quiet.

Not uncomfortable, just... electric, like everything unsaid is hanging in the air, thick and waiting.

His hand rests on my thigh, thumb brushing back and forth like he's not thinking about it, but I know better.

By the time we pull into the garage, my body is buzzing again.

He parks, shuts the car off, and looks over at me wordlessly. Giving me the look that says *you're mine,* even if he doesn't say it out loud.

We ride the elevator up together, his hand never leaving me.

When the doors finally open into his penthouse, our silence breaks.

But not with words.

He's on me in an instant. No hesitation. Just pure heat, his mouth claiming mine like he has been waiting for *hours.*

He scoops me into his arms, my legs wrapping around his waist instinctively.

"Shower," he growls against my throat. "I want the blood off your skin."

My nails dig into his shoulders. "Then wash it off."

He carries me through the penthouse like he's forgotten what it means to walk without me on him, bringing me into the bathroom and turning the water on high.

He sets me down only long enough to rip my top over my head, dragging his palms down my sides, peeling away my jeans. Everything's wet, and none of it matters except him.

He drops to his knees in the steam.

Water crashes down behind me, plastering my hair to my skin.

And he *devours* me.

One hand grabs my thigh, pulling it over his shoulder, opening me up, grounding me as his mouth finds my center.

His tongue is hot. Slow at first, taunting.

Just the tip, teasing my clit with featherlight flicks, circling just enough to make me shake.

"Dominic—" I gasp, head falling back against the tile.

He groans into the sound of my voice feeding him.

Then, he drags his tongue lower, flat, broad strokes, licking me slow, and filthy like he's trying to memorize every inch. He does it again, *deeper* this time, sucking softly, just enough pressure to make my legs tremble.

My hands tangle in his wet hair, hips already rolling against his mouth like I've lost control of my body.

"Fuuuuuck" I cry out, thighs twitching.

He locks me down with both hands now, one squeezing my ass, the other anchored on my hip.

He is no longer teasing, no more slow torturous licks, just raw and relentless.

His tongue punishes me like he wants me sobbing.

Sucking, licking, circling my clit with precision, like every moan I give him is a goddamn reward.

I'm panting and shaking.

Each flick of his tongue pushes me closer. Each moan from his throat vibrates through me like thunder.

He doesn't stop when I start to come undone.

"Dominic, I—" My voice cracks, legs almost giving out, one hand slapping against the tile to keep myself upright. "I'm… oh my god…"

He groans, satisfied because that's what he's been waiting for.

And I cum *hard*.

It explodes through me, my whole body locks, thighs squeezing around his head, every nerve in my body is on fire and he doesn't stop until I'm whimpering his name, over and over, too shattered to breathe.

Only then does he pull back, licking me slow, like a final kiss goodbye.

Then he stands, his chest heaving, eyes dark.

He grips my chin, tilting my face up to his.

"Taste what I do to you," he growls, kissing me hard.

I do as he says, tasting myself on his tongue.

"Such a good fucking girl for me."

His words still echo between us, but I don't say a thing.

I just drop to my knees.

Steam clings to my skin as the water pours over both of us, and I watch the way it rolls down his stomach. I take him into my mouth as deep as I can.

He groans, raw and desperate, his thighs flexing, abs tight. His hand braces against the tile behind me, the other threading into my soaked hair. Not forcing, not guiding, waiting.

"Fuck, baby."

I suck him deeper, tongue swirling, lips stretched wide as I work him with slow, deliberate pulls, savoring every inch. His cock twitches against my tongue, his hips shaking under my hands, his curse echoes, "Fuck… I'm close."

But before he can fall over that edge, before I can finish what I started, his hand tightens in my hair and pulls me off him with a wet pop.

"Not like that," he growls, eyes blazing down at me.

I barely have time to breathe before he hauls me to my feet.

One second, I'm standing.

The next, I'm *slammed* against the shower tile, mist swirling around us like smoke.

His mouth crashes into mine, wild and ravenous, tasting himself on my lips.

Tongue tangling with mine, teeth grazing my bottom lip as he groans like he's seconds from losing it.

He grips my ass, lifting me with one arm, pinning me to the wall with his body.

"Wrap your legs around me."

The second I do, he thrusts into me in one brutal, perfect stroke.

I cry out, head falling back, body arching as he fills me completely so deep and thick, every inch of him slamming into me like a fucking promise.

He groans, strained and desperate.

"Fuck, you're so tight," he grits out. "So wet. So ready for me."

I moan, clawing at his back, legs trembling as he moves.

Hard, fast and relentless.

His hips snap into me over and over, the sound of skin on skin mixing with the slap of water and our ragged, desperate breathing.

The steam fogs everything around us, but I see *him*.

The look on his face.

The wildness.

The *need*.

Matching it, I rock my hips to meet every thrust, nails digging into his shoulders as he slams into me.

"Mine," he growls, biting at my neck, hips bruising against my thighs. "Fucking *mine*."

"Yes, Dominic…"

"You love this, don't you?" he snarls. "Being taken like this. Pinned to a wall while I fuck you like I've got nothing left to lose."

I cry out, breaking apart beneath him, clenching around him, cuming.

"That's it baby, cum all over my dick," He says as he finds his own release.

We're both gasping, the sound of water slamming against tile, our harsh breaths, the wild rhythm of his heartbeat pressed against mine. It's all I can hear.

He holds me there, still inside me, and for a moment, neither of us moves.

His hand runs slowly down my thigh, soothing now, not desperate, like he's trying to remind himself I'm real–that this is real.

I cup his jaw, thumb brushing the edge of his lip

He leans into it, eyes half-lidded, still catching his breath.

"We should probably actually wash ourselves now," I murmur, teasing. "You know, since this was technically supposed to be a shower."

He huffs a laugh, forehead dropping to mine. "We're not exactly known for multitasking."

I grin, dragging my fingers through his wet hair. "Let's just stay in here all week. No clothes, no work, just water, steam, and occasional food deliveries."

His hand slides up my back again, possessively. "Sounds fucking perfect."

I blink. "Wait… are you serious?"

He shrugs, completely unbothered. "You think anyone's gonna question why we both disappeared for a week and came back glowing?"

I laugh, loud and unfiltered, heart still racing.

"Okay," I say. "But I'm not sharing my sushi."

"Deal," he murmurs, kissing me again, softer this time.

Starving, but full of promise.

CHAPTER TWENTY
Dominic

"Let's just start the ordering in now." I say while grabbing my phone off the counter, still damp, and only half-dressed.

Octavia's across the room, towel draped around her, hair dripping, mouth pulled into that wicked little smirk she uses when she knows I'm looking at her like she's dessert.

"Oh, we're committing to the shut-in lifestyle now?" she teases, grabbing one of my t-shirts and tugging it on. She looks better in it than I ever did.

"We've earned it," I say. "Besides…"

Flashing her a grin, I scroll to Marcus's contact.

"It's time."

Her brow lifts. "Time for what?"

I hold up the phone, shaking it back and forth. "To inform your best friend's future emotional support boyfriend, he's been selected."

She bursts out laughing. "You're actually doing it?"

I nod. "We planned the date. She's already prepped. Now, he gets the honor of being hunted."

She flops onto the couch, grinning like a gremlin. "You're an evil,

evil man."

I tap the speaker icon and wait.

It rings twice before Marcus picks up.

"What?"

"Good to hear your voice too," I say.

"I'm busy."

"You're free tomorrow."

"Why?"

"You've got a date."

"... Excuse me?"

"With Lena," I add. "Octavia's best friend. Whiskey drinker, enthusiastic over sharer, might already know your blood type."

"Dominic."

"Marcus."

A slow sigh leaks through the speaker. "You're doing this to punish me, aren't you?"

"Not at all," I say, deadpan. "This is me being generous."

Octavia's doubled over on the couch now, silently wheezing into a pillow.

Marcus sighs again, heavier this time. "Fine. What time?"

"Seven. Wear something she can compliment while she insults you."

I hang up before he can argue again and toss the phone onto the table.

"Done," I say.

She's wiping tears from her eyes. "You're the devil."

"Only to people I like."

There are takeout boxes scattered across the coffee table and Octavia's curled up next to me on the couch, wearing nothing but my t-shirt and a pair of underwear that I've been trying not to stare at for the last twenty minutes.

She's eating Lo Mein straight from the carton, legs draped over mine, foot bouncing lazily like she doesn't have a single care in the world.

"I probably shouldn't say this," she says between bites, "but I think I've gotten used to being chauffeured around in your overcompensating rich guy car."

I raise an eyebrow. "That so?"

She hums, licking the sauce off her chopsticks. "Mmhmm. Kinda feels like a letdown to go back to my, you know, no car situation after this week of crime and orgasms."

I smirk. "So don't."

She glances at me. "What, you offering to drive me everywhere now?"

"No," I say. "I'm offering to buy you a car."

She chokes on a noodle.

I reach over, gently patting her on the back while she wheezes.

"I was *joking*."

"I wasn't."

She stares at me, incredulous. "You're not serious."

I meet her eyes, completely calm. "Tell me what you want and we'll pick it up tomorrow."

Her mouth opens, then closes. Then… yep, there it is, her hands flailing slightly.

"You can't just—people don't just *buy* other people cars because they're fucking!"

I lean in, lips brushing her ear. "This isn't just fucking, baby."

She stills.

I kiss her jaw. "This is because I want you to feel like you belong—like you're taken care of."

Her breath catches.

"Well, then," she says, sitting up straighter, eyes flashing with mock confidence, "I want the *same* Porsche. The exact same one. Color, trim, all of it. I want to see you write a check for three hundred grand just to watch me drive away from you with the radio too loud and the seat settings all fucked up."

I grin. "Done."

She blinks. "What?"

I stretch an arm across the back of the couch, completely unfazed. "You want the Porsche, you get the Porsche. Or you can get something flashier, if you're feeling dramatic."

"Dominic…"

"Or understated," I go on. "You could go vintage. I'll fly one in if the dealer doesn't have it."

She's staring at me now, and the sarcasm is cracking. "You can't just *buy me a car.*"

"I can."

"You can't *actually* mean it."

"I do."

Her voice climbs. "You are not buying me a whole-ass car like it's an appetizer off a tasting menu!"

Watching her unravel in real time is quite comical. "Would you prefer I order you two? One for weekdays, one for dates?"

"*Dominic!*"

"I'm kidding," I say.

She exhales in relief.

"Three max."

She groans, dragging a pillow over her face. "I hate you."

Laughing, I tug the pillow down so I can see her flushed cheeks and wide, panicked eyes.

"No, you don't. You just don't know what to do when someone means it."

Her breath stutters.

But she doesn't deny it.

She just lays there on my couch, still flushed from laughter.

Fuck.

I'm in love with her.

Not the safe kind, not the easy kind.

The kind that brands itself into your ribs and makes you *ache* for more, and I don't know what to do with it.

No one's ever known this version of me. Not really, not even Sophia.

She saw the surface. The carefully curated edges.

The part of me that looked good in a suit and remembered to smile when it counted.

But Octavia?

She saw the whole goddamn monster.

She watched me torture and take the life of a man, watched me lose all control, watched me spiral into that place that I never let anyone near and she didn't flinch.

She kissed me after, told me she wanted it.

That she actually *understands it.*

Now she's fucking lying here like all of this is normal, like it's not terrifying to give that part of myself to someone and know she won't run.

Shifting closer to her, "I meant what I said. I'll take care of you. Whatever that looks like."

She doesn't joke this time. Doesn't smirk or throw out some line to avoid what she's feeling.

She just presses her hand to my chest, right over where my heart is slamming hard enough to hurt.

"That's the part that scares me," she says, voice soft.

"It should."

I pause.

"But what scares me more?"

My voice is quieter now—raw and exposed.

"You didn't just survive my darkness… You walked into it. Looked it in the eye and stayed."

Her breath catches, but she doesn't look away.

"No one's ever done that."

Octavia's thumb moves in a slow circle over my chest, right above my heart.

"I'm not going anywhere."

Her words hit me hard. Not loud or dramatic, they sink in slowly, right into places I rarely let people reach.

I cover her hand with mine, pressing it tighter against my chest like maybe that will calm the chaos underneath it.

"I've never really wanted anyone to stay before," I say, the words barely above a whisper. It feels like ripping something open. "Not like this."

She shifts beside me, propping herself up on one elbow, eyes locked on mine. "Like what?"

I could tell her.

That I'd set the entire world on fire if she asked.

That I'd give her anything, do anything, just to keep her smiling.

That the idea of not having her next to me makes my chest physically ache.

But I don't say any of that.

I just pull her in close and bury my face in her hair.

"Like I don't know how to wake up without you anymore," I whisper.

She goes still, and for a second, I wonder if I messed it all up, if I pushed too far.

But then I feel her lips against my neck.

"Good," she whispers. "I meant it when I said I'm not going anywhere."

Her hand slides down my chest, fingers splaying lightly across my stomach. It's innocent, kind of, but my body reacts instantly, heat flaring under my skin.

She feels it. Of course, she does.

A smile curves at the edge of her mouth—the one that means *trouble*.

"Although," she murmurs, her voice dropping to that low, teasing tone that undoes me every damn time, "I might need a little more convincing on this whole 'being taken care of' thing…"

I move before she can finish the thought, flipping her onto her back with a growl that vibrates through my chest. Her gasp punches straight into me, and she's already smiling, wild and breathless—like she knew this would happen the second she opened her mouth.

I settle over her, caging her in, one hand braced beside her head, the other dragging up the inside of her thigh slow enough to make her squirm.

"You want convincing?" I murmur, voice low and dark, brushing my mouth along the shell of her ear. "You'll fucking get it."

She arches into me, teasing. "Then stop talking and do it."

My mouth crashes into hers, wild and unrestrained, like I've lost the thread of reason.

My hand finds her center. She's already wet, already aching, and I groan against her mouth.

"Fuck, baby," I breathe. "You're soaked for me."

She shivers, legs parting wider. "Maybe I enjoy being taken care of."

"Yeah?" I slide two fingers inside her, slow and deep, curling just enough to make her whimper. "Then let me take care of you."

I devour her reaction, drinking in every sound, every tremble. Her hands claw at my back, nails dragging down, ripping into my skin as I thrust my fingers deeper, faster, working her until her hips are bucking and her head's thrown back against the pillow.

Her body clamps down around me, so close already.

"Dominic—fuck—"

I pull my hand away, and she gasps like I've ripped the air from her lungs.

"What—"

I yank her to the edge of the couch and drop to my knees.

"I'm not done," I growl.

My mouth crashes into her in one deep, unrelenting stroke. I pin her hips down and work her slowly at first, with long, dragging licks that make her shudder, then faster, rougher, until she's thrashing under me.

Her fingers twist in my hair, nails biting into my scalp. Her cries get louder, more desperate, her thighs trembling against the sides of my face.

"Dominic—oh my God—don't stop, don't stop;"

I don't, I *can't.*

She trembles. Hard. Her breath catches on a broken sob as her body goes stiff, her back arching off the couch.

Then she completely unravels.

She screams my name–high, wild, breathless–and her whole body bucks, crashing into the peak so hard I can feel the rush of it flooding against me—slick and hot. It spills down my chin, on to my chest, soaking me.

I groan into her, licking her through every second of it, refusing to let up until she's trembling, twitching, gasping for breath.

Only then do I finally pull back, my mouth and jaw glistening.

She's wrecked.

Eyes glassy, lips parted, body still trembling in the aftermath.

Fuck. Seeing her like that?

Completely undone because of me?

I've never been harder in my life. "Still need convincing?" I rasp.

She doesn't answer, just grabs me by the neck and pulls me down into another kiss, tasting herself on my tongue.

"I want all of you," she whispers. "Now."

I yank the V-neck over my head, shove my jeans down—my cock springs free, thick and hard, already glistening at the tip for her. There's no hesitation. No build-up. Just raw, violent need.

I slam into her in one brutal thrust, and she cries out, clawing at my back as I bury myself, hitting her cervix.

This isn't soft. This is desperate.

I drive into her repeatedly, pinning her wrists above her head, owning every gasp, every moan, every shattered breath.

Her walls clench tight, and she's close again.

"I'm going to brand you," I growl against her throat, each thrust harder than the last. "Mark every inch of your body, so no one ever forgets who fucking owns it."

She cries out, clawing at my back, completely unraveling beneath me. I squeeze her thighs, rough and relentless, knowing I'll leave fingerprints behind. I want the evidence. I want her body to remember.

"Say it," I demand, voice rough. "Say you belong to me."

"Yes—fuck, yes, Dominic—I'm yours," she cries, breathless and shaking. "Only yours."

My hand fists in her hair as I drive into her, losing all control.

"Damn right you are."

She breaks apart beneath me and I'm right behind her, teeth sinking into her shoulder, piercing her skin as I cum with a breathless groan, spilling inside her.

I settle into the cradle of her hips, not pulling out, hands shaking where they frame her face.

She's completely ravaged beneath me. I've never seen anything more beautiful.

I press a kiss to the curve of her shoulder, the same place I bit her, soft and slow. My hand slides down her thigh, then back up again, soothing where I've left bruises.

"I didn't mean to be that rough," I murmur, my voice ragged..

She hums, barely able to form words. "Mmm... You did."

I can't help the crooked smile that tugs at my mouth. She's not wrong.

I shift off of her gently, pulling her close so her back is to my chest. My arm wraps around her waist, anchoring her there. She sinks into me, quiet and content.

Her breathing slows. I listen to it, counting the seconds between each one like I'm trying to hold on to something fragile. She's already drifting.

I should sleep, too. I should let my body rest.

But I stay there, watching the way her breathing slows against my chest, her body soft and limp with sleep, her skin still flushed where I marked her.

She's out cold.

Carefully, I shift beneath her and stand, lifting her into my arms. She stirs only slightly, a soft sound catching in her throat, but doesn't wake.

I carry her to the bedroom, past the floor-to-ceiling windows where the city still glows like it's watching us.

I pull back the sheets with one hand and lay her down gently, tucking her in before sliding in beside her. She rolls toward me automatically, finding my chest like she always does, like she's wired for it now.

And I hold her, like if I let go, she might disappear.

I stare at the ceiling in the dark, listening to her breathe, thinking about how she has seen the darkest parts of me and didn't walk away.

CHAPTER TWENTY ONE

Octavia

I wake up sore in places I didn't even know could get sore.

Like… deliciously-fucking sore.

Everything aches in the best kind of way: my thighs, my back, my neck, my *soul*. The sheets are twisted around my legs, and there's an arm locked around my waist like a steel bar.

His hold tightens slightly when I try to shift, like, even asleep, he's not letting go.

Not that I want him to.

I blink slowly, the early morning light just slipping in through the windows. The skyline glows outside, and for the first time in forever, I feel... safe.

My shoulder throbs faintly—just enough to remind me of what happened on the couch. I reach up, brushing my fingertips over the skin, and hiss. There's a mark there. *An actual fucking bite mark.* He broke skin; he wasn't lying when he said he was going to brand me.

And the sick part?

It turns me on all over again.

I should be freaking out, I should be analyzing every word he said

last night, every bruise on my hips, every dangerously sweet thing he whispered in my ear as he ruined me. But I'm not. I just... lay there. Letting it settle. Letting myself *feel* it.

The weight of what this is.

Whatever this is.

Then he stirs behind me.

"Mmm. You awake?" His voice is low and hoarse.

"Barely," I mumble.

"Good." He places a kiss to the back of my shoulder. "We're getting you a car today."

That snaps me out of my haze.

Wait.

"What?"

Another kiss. "I told you last night. You pick what you want and we'll go get it."

I twist to look at him, eyes wide. "You were actually serious?"

He gives me a lazy smirk. "Dead serious, little minx."

Panic. Full-body panic. "Dominic, you don't just *buy* people cars."

His hand slides up my side, teasing, slow. "I do."

"Oh my god," I groan, covering my face with my hands. "This is *so much*."

"Pick one that's fast," he mutters against my throat. "That way, I'll still have an excuse to stalk you with GPS."

I let out a strangled noise. "You're insane."

He grins. "You love it."

Do I? ... Yeah, I kind of do.

But, still.

I need help processing this. I need backup.

"I need Lena," I mutter mostly to myself, already reaching for where my phone is buried in the blankets.

Dominic stretches behind me, lazy and smug. "She gonna talk you out of it?"

"She's going to remind me that normal people don't wake up post-sex haze and get handed a car."

He hums, completely unbothered. "You're not normal people."

"Oh, my God." I roll onto my back, staring at the ceiling like it might have answers.

He shifts up on one elbow beside me, brushing hair from my face with the back of his fingers. "What about a convertible?"

I blink. "What?"

He shrugs. "Something flashy. Fits your attitude."

"My *attitude?*"

He grins, wide and wicked. "You're a menace. Might as well drive like one."

I throw a pillow at his face. He catches it midair and tosses it aside like its nothing.

"A convertible," I repeat. "You want me to *sashay* around Seattle with the top-down, like a billboard that screams 'kept woman'?"

"Yeah," he says simply, arrogant as ever. "But hotter."

I groan, grabbing the pillow again and flinging it over my face. "This is too much."

His laugh is low, rough. "You're not saying no."

I lower the pillow just enough to peek at him. "I haven't decided if I'm calling the cops or Lena first."

"Call Lena," he says, sitting up and stretching again like a goddamn Calvin Klein ad. "She'll be easier to handle than the cops. Maybe."

"Oh, *definitely* maybe," I mutter.

He kisses my forehead like this is all perfectly normal.

Somehow, that's the part that messes with my head the most. Because for him? It is.

He's already up, walking toward the kitchen like we didn't just talk about *buying me a car* like a casual errand.

I lay there for a second longer, staring at the ceiling like it might give me a sign.

Nothing.

So I grab my phone and do the next logical thing: I text Lena.

ME

Dominic is taking me to a dealership

like. today.

TO BUY ME A CAR.

It takes about three seconds.

LENA

IM SORRY WHAT.

WHAT.

YOU DID NOT JUST SOFT DROP "BUY ME A CAR" LIKE IT'S A MUFFIN.

I snort, biting my lip as I type.

ME

I didn't ask for this.

he just said it like itwas a normal thingpeople do.

LENA

WHAT KIND OF CAR

TELL ME IT'S SLUTTY

TELL ME IT GOES VROOM

ME

He said convertible; he said it would match my attitude

LENA

WELL HE'S NOT WRONG.

Do you have Stockholm Syndrome???

Are we calling this love or are you being recruited for a cult???

Also, I want to see it before you do anything drastic like NOT pick the sexiest one on the lot.

ME

Ok, but when I show up at your place later

you're doing my makeup

I'm too emotionally unstable for eyeliner right now

LENA

You are living my dream, and I hate you.

Bring caffeine, I'll bring wine and scissors

(you know. In case you need bangs)

I laugh, typing one last reply before I throw the covers off and head for the shower.

ME

Heaven help me.

The water's already steaming, and I'm halfway through rinsing shampoo out of my hair when I hear the bathroom door open.

"Dominic," I warn, squinting through the water. "I need a second to accept that this is my real life now."

He steps in like he owns the place—which, okay; *he does*—and wraps an arm around my waist, pulling me into the heat of his body.

"You said you needed help getting through the day," he murmurs, mouth brushing against my wet shoulder. "This is me being helpful, baby."

His hands are already moving, slowly, teasing, sliding soap over my hips like he's mapping the curves he ravaged last night.

"This isn't fair," I breathe, leaning back against him. "You can't distract me with your abs and your… everything."

"I can and I will," he mutters into my neck, nipping lightly. "Especially when you're like this. All warm and wet and pretending like you don't love that I'm spoiling the hell out of you."

"I didn't *ask* you to buy me a car," I snap, even though my pulse is doing backflips.

He slides his hand between my thighs and grins when I gasp.

"Didn't have to," he says. "And just so we're clear, we're not browsing for some sensible mid-tier car."

I glance over my shoulder, suspicious. "How expensive are we talking?"

"Hundreds of thousands," he replies smoothly. "Depending on what you pick."

I choke on nothing. "*Hundreds of thousands?!*"

He spins me to face him, eyes dark, water pouring down his body like a sin.

"Would it make you feel better if I wrapped a bow around it?" he asks, completely deadpan.

I slap his chest. "You're unbelievable."

"And you're mine," he says, kissing me slow and deep, steam curling around us like smoke.

By the time we're done in the shower, I'm too distracted to be anxious.

Until we're in the elevator.

Then, the panic starts all over again, like a new wave crashing down.

The moment the elevator doors slide open and we step into the parking garage, my palms are sweaty.

By the time we're sliding into his car, I'm two seconds from hyperventilating.

I buckle my seatbelt too quickly.

Dominic climbs in like he's taking me to brunch, not casually dropping six figures on me like its pocket change.

I stare at him. "Where are we even going?"

He glances over, one hand on the wheel, the other already shifting into gear.

"The Porsche dealership," he says, like it's the most obvious thing in the world.

I blink. "I thought you were *joking* about that."

His mouth curves into that dark, dangerous smirk. The one that says *he's not joking about anything today.*

"Nope."

"Dominic," I hiss, twisting in my seat. "You are not buying me a *Porsche.*"

"I am," he says, pulling into traffic like this isn't a crisis. "You said you liked mine."

"I like *ice cream,* too. That doesn't mean I want to own a Ben & Jerry's fucking franchise!"

He laughs under his breath, eyes on the road. "Too late, baby."

I groan, sinking lower into the seat like I can disappear into the leather. "If you actually buy me something that costs more than my childhood home, I swear to God—I'll change my name and disappear into the woods."

His hand slides over to my thigh, warm and grounding. He gives it a slow squeeze, gaze still locked on the road.

"You could try," he says quietly. "But I'd find you."

It's not a threat, it's the truth.

One that settles deep in my chest like gravity.

I believe him. Every single word.

We pull into the dealership and it's exactly as intimidating as I imagined. There's a lineup of cars that look like they belong in a movie, not on regular roads with potholes.

Dominic parks like he owns the place.

Of course he does.

I'm halfway through another internal monologue about how I'm not emotionally equipped for this when I see it.

Parked right in front, like the universe wanted to throw gasoline on the fire of my panic.

A convertible.

But not just any convertible.

Purple.

Deep, glossy, the rich color that looks like it was poured from a bottle of overpriced wine.

My breath catches.

"Holy shit," I whisper, half to myself. "It's purple."

Dominic cuts the engine and glances at me. "You like it?"

"It's my favorite color," I say, stunned. "Like... *actual* favorite. Since I was eight. I had a bedspread in that exact shade."

He shrugs, already getting out of the car. "Must be fate."

I narrow my eyes. "You *knew.*"

That damn smirk curves at the edge of his mouth. "Lucky guess."

Fucking liar.

He opens my door before I can argue, and I step out slowly, heart hammering like this is some sort of high-stakes test I didn't study for.

The sales associate's already approaching, polished smile firmly in place, clipboard in hand.

I whisper to Dominic as he slips an arm around my waist, "If I pass out, tell them it's from excitement and not cardiac arrest."

He chuckles low, lips brushing my temple.

"You're going to look so fucking hot in that car."

And just like that, I'm completely undone.

The salesman is in the back and talking too much.

I can't focus on half of what he's saying—something about torque and engine specs and the stitching—because I'm currently sitting behind the wheel of a six-figure sports car in my *favorite color* while my maybe-boyfriend-possibly-psychopath sits beside me like this is all very casual.

"Go ahead," the guy says, gesturing toward the empty loop behind the dealership. "Take her for a spin. You've got a nice stretch back there. Feel the power."

Feel the power.

I grip the wheel, staring at the glossy purple hood like it might bite me.

"This feels illegal," I mutter.

Dominic leans back in the passenger seat, with a smug composure. "You haven't even hit the gas yet."

My foot hovers over the pedal. "I can't drive this. What if I hit a fence? What if I sneeze and crash into a pole? What if I die and haunt this car forever?"

He chuckles. *Chuckles.* Like this is cute.

"You won't crash," he says smoothly. "But if you do, I'll just buy you another one."

My jaw drops. "What is *wrong* with you?"

"I'm rich," he replies without missing a beat.

And I can't help myself, I laugh.

Then, I take a breath, grip the wheel tighter, and ease out of the dealership lot.

The engine *growls*. That's the only way to describe it, like it's just waiting to be bad.

Dominic watches me the way a man watches a lit fuse, entertained a little, and completely unbothered.

"Foot down, baby," he says, voice low and coaxing. "Let her show you what she can do."

I bite my lip, and I do it.

The car *roars*—no, *screams*—as I hit the gas. My heart launches into my throat and I shoot back into the seat like I just engaged warp speed.

"OH MY GOD," I yell, gripping the wheel like it owes me money. "WHAT THE HELL IS THIS ENGINE"

Dominic's laughing, full-on, head tipped back like this is his favorite thing he's ever seen.

And maybe it is. Maybe me, behind the wheel, half-panicking and half-euphoric, is exactly what he envisioned.

I circle the back lot too fast, shriek once, nearly miss a cone, and ease back into the dealership like I didn't just experience an out-of-body moment.

My hands are shaking.

"I can't own this car," I gasp. "It's *possessed*. I think I blacked out."

Dominic leans over, kisses my cheek, and murmurs, "That was the hottest thing I've ever seen."

I turn to him, breathless. "I hate you."

"You love me."

I don't respond.

Because the worst part?

He might be right.

The test drive ends, and I'm still breathless.

The car hums as we park back in front of the dealership, and the next thing I know, I'm sitting in front of a desk with a folder in front of me, a shiny pen, and a man in a suit saying something about processing and registration.

I can't hear a word of it.

Because *this is happening.*

Dominic's beside me, relaxed. He doesn't even glance at the price sheet before handing over his black fucking AMEX.

"Wait," I hiss, my hand darting to his wrist. "You're really doing this?"

He looks at me, calm, steady and a little smug. "Of course I am."

"No haggling? No discussion? You don't want to at least pretend this is a hard decision?"

"I saw your face when you drove it," he says, low and sure. "That was the only decision that mattered."

I blink at him.

Then I blink at the pen.

My name's already printed on the forms like this was inevitable.

"You're sure you want to do this?" I whisper, still half-expecting him to wake me up from this fever dream.

He smirks. "You've been mine since the second you mouthed off at me in my office. This is just paperwork."

I nearly choke, but my hand moves anyway.

Signature. Date. Initial.

The moment the pen hits the last line, the sales rep lights up. "We'll get her detailed and prepped right away for you, Sir."

"Great," Dominic says, already sliding his arm around my waist.

I just stare at the pen like it betrayed me.

He leans in, his lips brushing my ear. "You look so fucking sexy when you're overwhelmed."

"I hate you."

He grins. "No, you don't."

He is abso-fucking-lutely right. I don't.

CHAPTER TWENTY TWO
Octavia

The sun hits my new car like a spotlight, the deep purple paint gleaming like it knows it just became the most dramatic bitch in the parking lot. I can't stop staring. Or smiling. Or, apparently, breathe properly.

Dominic unlocks the doors with a click and tosses me a look like he's still debating whether to toss me over the hood or make use of the back seat.

I elbow him lightly as we walk toward the lot exit.

"Don't even think about it," I say, grinning. "I have somewhere to be."

He raises an eyebrow. "Oh?"

"I'm going to Lena's. She's doing my makeup for tonight."

I tug my phone out of my pocket, already picturing Lena's over-caffeinated chaos. "She threatened to give me bangs if I show up without caffeine."

Dominic chuckles low. That dark, dangerous sound always makes my knees go stupidly weak. "So, you're leaving me for a girl with scissors?"

"She's not the dangerous one," I mutter, nudging him again. "And besides, you're the one who set up the date night."

He stops at my door and pulls me close, fingers skimming my waist. "You're gonna look like sin by the time she's done with you."

I smirk up at him. "That's the idea."

His fingers tighten slightly on my waist, eyes sweeping over me like he's memorizing this moment, this version of me—the one who's standing next to him with a brand-new car and barely concealed chaos in her chest.

"Don't be too long," he says. "If you look at me like that when you come back, I might skip dinner and take you straight upstairs."

My breath hitches, and I roll my eyes just to keep from melting into a puddle. "We can survive one damn dinner without you sliding my dress up and fucking me against a wall."

He leans in, lips brushing my temple. "You say that now."

I take a step back, sliding into the driver's seat, gripping the wheel. The leather is soft, and it smells like power and recklessness–like him.

I raise my head and find him still watching me, arms crossed, leaning casually like he doesn't know he's making it impossible to breathe.

"Dom..." I start, my voice catching a little. "I—"

He tilts his head, raising a brow.

I swallow hard. What was I going to say? *I love you?*

No, no, no, too soon. Too much.

"I'll text you when I get there," I finish lamely.

He smiles at me like he knows what I almost said. "Good girl."

My chest flips.

I shut the door, start the engine, and pull away before I can ruin it by saying something that'll set everything on fire.

But as I glance in the rearview mirror and he's still standing there, arms crossed, jaw tight, watching me like I hung the damn sky and I know I meant every word I *didn't* say.

I'm two blocks away from the dealership when I hit the call button.

Lena answers before the first ring even finishes.

"Please tell me you're on your way and that the car is slutty."

"She's a whole ass mood," I say, grinning. "Top down, ego up."

Lena squeals. "Yes! I want to lick it. You better be pulling up soon because I already laid out three dresses for you, and one of them is borderline illegal."

I laugh, turning onto her street. "You always dress me like I'm about to commit a felony."

"You *are*, a crime against single women everywhere. And also, I plan to make Marcus weep."

I choke on my own breath. "What?!"

"Nothing. I am just excited, so hurry up and get here, sugar tits. I've got lashes, caffeine, and a curling iron hotter than your boyfriend."

"I doubt that. Plus, he and I haven't even said we are official or anything."

"Official? Are you kidding me!? He just bought you a car. I think that counts as official."

I shake my head, a smile stuck on my face. "I'm pulling up now. Try not to murder me with makeup brushes."

"No promises."

I hang up just as I spot her on the porch, barefoot, coffee in one hand and a lipstick dagger in the other.

She sees the car and *barrels* off the porch like a feral raccoon, high on espresso.

"Oh my *fucking GOD!*" she shrieks, skidding to a stop beside the car, eyes wide. "You didn't say it was a whole *Batmobile* with tits!"

I'm laughing before I even get the door open.

"She's dramatic and curvy. Like me."

Lena circles the car like she's inspecting it for holy relics. "I'm not saying I'd fuck this car, but I'd *definitely* let it buy me dinner first."

"Get in the house, you crazy bitch," I say, grabbing my caffeine bribe from the passenger seat.

"I can't. I'm emotionally attached now. You've ruined me for all other cars. I'm going to have to text my therapist."

"You don't *have* a therapist."

"Exactly."

She finally tears herself away from the car like it physically hurts and stomps up the porch, yanking the door open with one hand while dramatically cradling her coffee in the other.

"Inside. Now. We have cheekbones to carve and I am ready to interrogate you on your sex life."

I follow her in, laughing as she practically skips to the kitchen counter and starts laying out makeup like she's about to summon a glam squad from hell.

"Do you want sultry, smoldering, or 'please ruin me over dessert'?"

"Uh… somewhere between sultry and ruin."

"So 'I might let him finger me under the table' vibes. Got it." She grabs her brushes like they're weapons.

I drop into the chair and let her work. "We only have like ninety minutes."

Lena snorts. "That's at least forty minutes for makeup, ten for mental spiraling, and another forty for me to ask about every single dirty detail you've refused to text me."

I grin. "You really want to know?"

"Octavia, I am voluntarily applying false lashes for you. If you don't give me the dirty details, I will cry into your bronzer."

I bite back a laugh.

"Well," I say, dropping onto the stool in front of her vanity, "he took me up to Snoqualmie Falls and almost fucked me over the railing."

Lena drops her coffee so fast it sloshes over her hand. *"I'm sorry—what?!"*

"Don't worry, he didn't. He drove us up some private road instead," I say casually, pulling a hair tie off my wrist. "Bent me over his bike first, then fucked me against a tree."

Lena is just standing there, frozen, mouth wide open.

"You let him take you into the forest like a horny cryptid *and* you got railed in nature? That's—shit, I don't even know what that is. That's the hot girl version of hiking."

I grin. "It was a lot."

"Bitch, that's not *a lot*, that's National Geographic meets Pornhub. *Was there moss?* Were you nude in the ferns?"

"Lena."

"I'm picturing it. I can't *not* picture it!"

I snort and hand her the coffee. "Drink. Breathe. Blend. You're supposed to be making me hot."

"You're already hot! You're basically a post-orgasm forest nymph who just rolled in here with a brand new car and god knows how many orgasms under your belt!"

"Oh yeah," I say, grinning.

"You're going to rupture something."

"I hope so. At least I'll die knowing true romance still exists."

Lena's already dragging out her arsenal like we're going into battle. Eyeshadow palettes hit the vanity dramatically. Lipsticks lined up like bullets, and the curling iron is heating like a weapon of mass destruction.

"Okay, slut," she says, clipping my hair back. "We're going full face, no mercy."

She dabs foundation while mumbling to herself. "He's hot, he's rich, he fucks you in the woods. You are living my literal dream."

"You good?" I ask, watching her mix highlighters like she's conjuring magic.

"Thriving," she says. "Now, close your eyes, I'm about to give your eyelids their villain origin story."

I do as she says, trying not to laugh. "I feel like I need to emotionally prepare."

"Too late," she says, blotting concealer under my eyes. "I've already committed to 'bad bitch with a secret.' We're leaning in."

"What if I cry?"

"Then the setting spray wasn't strong enough and we riot."

She finishes my eyes and starts working on a smokey liner that could kill. The whole time, she's muttering little affirmations like, "He's gonna choke on his steak," and "Men have died for less."

Finally, she steps back and surveys her work like she just built a nuclear weapon out of liner and contour.

"Okay," she says, dramatically. "Look."

I open my eyes and catch a glimpse in the mirror.

"Oh, damn," I blurt out.

Lena smirks. "You're welcome. Okay, before we pick the outfit that's gonna make you look hotter than hell, I need to ask, what does the hot friend look like?"

I snort. "You mean Marcus?"

"Yes, Marcus. The tall, broody, potentially emotionally unavailable man who might be my soulmate-slash-bad decision. I need visuals, babe. I need to know if I should wear the good bra."

I pull out my phone and text Dominic.

ME

Can you send a pic of Marcus?
Lena's planning her outfit and emotional expectations.

Almost instantly, he replies with a photo. It's Marcus in black slacks, and a white button down with the sleeves rolled to the elbows, tattoos peeking out, leaning against a car with that sharp, don't-fuck-with-me expression.

I show her the screen.

Lena freezes mid-rummage. "Oh… oh, hell yes."

"You like?"

"Bitch," she says, breathless. "He looks like he owns a nightclub and a gun. I want to ruin his credit score."

I laugh so hard I almost drop my phone. "That's your takeaway?"

"Yes," she says, eyes still locked on the photo. "Also, I need to wear red. I want to be unforgettable, like a warning."

"I'll get the dress," I say, shaking my head.

"You get the dress. I'll get the tequila and possibly my entire personality together."

Lena practically skips into the kitchen, already shaking a bottle of tequila like she's prepping for a halftime show.

"Alright," she announces. "Let's make poor decisions and fantastic memories."

She hands me a shot glass shaped like a skull.

"To forest sex and reckless infatuation," I say.

"To hot rich men and hotter outfits," she counters.

We clink and down the shots. The tequila burns all the way down, but it's the good burn, like confidence in liquid form. My cheeks are already warm.

By the time we're shimmying into dresses, Lena's playing DJ, blasting our Bad Bitch playlist. There's glitter, hair spray, and I grab a pair of heels to put on.

"You're wearing those?" she says, one hand on her chest. "Octavia

Moore, you're gonna commit crimes with those legs."

"Just light felonies," I wink, zipping up her dress. "Maybe one act of public indecency."

Before she can respond, my phone buzzes.

DOMINIC

I want you to sit on my face tonight.

First thing. No delay. Just your thighs and my mouth.

I choke on a laugh and show her the screen.

She reads the text, blinks once, then grabs the bottle of tequila and takes another shot.

"Jesus Christ," she mutters, wiping her mouth. "You're in trouble."

I snort. "Tell me something I don't know."

"You better reinforce those heels. That man's got intentions."

She points at me, and I know instantly she is up to something. "Okay. Full glam: complete. Vibes: dangerous. Hair: slutty. All that's left is a text so unhinged it haunts him at dinner."

I laugh, slipping on the silk black dress she demanded I wear. "You're really enabling this."

"Oh, I'm not enabling. I'm encouraging it. There's a difference. Now pick up your phone and make that man sweat."

I open my messages, biting my lip. "What if I told him I wasn't wearing underwear?"

Lena gasps. "Iconic. Evil. Send it."

ME

Hope you're hungry. I'm not wearing anything under this dress.

Lena lets out a full-body gasp and hits the floor in a dramatic kneel. "My queen, my emotional support harlot."

The reply comes in almost instantly

DOMINIC

I'm always craving that sweet fucking pussy.

"Jesus," I mutter, trying to hold in my grin.

Lena's eyes light up like she just got a hit of pure serotonin. "You *have* to hit him back."

"What do I say?"

Lena grins, eyes gleaming. "Text him back and tell him if he wants you that bad, he better be ready to earn it."

I smirk, already typing.

ME

If you want that, you're going to work for it. Unless, you just make me.

Lena nearly chokes on her wine. "That's the energy I like to see."

My phone buzzes almost immediately.

DOMINIC

Oh, little minx... are you giving me permission to take you exactly how and when I want, whether you're ready for it or not?

Heat rushes to my face, and I feel myself throb in anticipation. I take a steadying breath.

"I'm so screwed."

"No," Lena says, while she looks for perfume, "but you're about to be."

CHAPTER TWENTY THREE

Dominic

My phone buzzes, and the moment I glance at the screen, my cock twitches.

OCTAVIA

I'm giving you full permission, baby. Take me whenever, however you want. Especially when I pretend I don't want you to.

Fuck.

I shift in the chair, jaw clenched.

She's not just playing. She means it, every unhinged, perfect word.

I stare at the message a little longer, then lock my phone and set it face-down on the counter. I need ten seconds to get my pulse under control, and even that feels generous.

She doesn't even realize what that kind of permission does to a man like me.

Full surrender.

I push off the counter and walk to the bedroom, grabbing a clean black button-down and roll the sleeves up to my forearms. My watch clicks into place with a snap. I stare at myself in the mirror. Calm, controlled, predatory.

But inside?

I'm counting the minutes until I can get her alone again.

I'm going to wreck her tonight—in all the ways she likes.

She wants to play dangerous? Good.

So do I.

The soft chime of the elevator cuts through the quiet, followed by footsteps.

Marcus steps out like he owns the place, hands in his pockets, a lazy grin spreading across his face.

"You really live like a Bond villain, you know that?" he says, glancing around the penthouse.

"Coming from the guy who drives a matte black Aventador with illegal tint?" I arch a brow, pouring two fingers of whiskey into a crystal glass and sliding one across the counter.

He takes it without question, settling into the barstool. "Fair. But I don't have a skyline view, a private elevator, and a redhead who looks at me like she wants to eat me alive."

My mouth twitches, because *fuck*, he's not wrong.

"She's a lot," I say, sipping. "But she's mine."

Marcus leans back, swirling the drink in his hand. "So, Lena. What am I walking into?"

"A hurricane in heels," I tell him. "She drinks tequila like water and doesn't care who hears her opinions."

His smile grows. "Sounds like my kind of hell."

"You say that now."

He clinks his glass against mine. "You ready?"

My phone buzzes again. Another message from Octavia, and feel every inch of my self-control unraveling.

Marcus smirks at me. "That her?"

I nod, pocketing my phone before I do something reckless.

"You're in deep, Dom."

"Yeah," I mutter. "And I'm not coming back up."

Marcus tosses back the rest of his drink. "Then let's go meet our doom, shall we?"

I grab my keys and jacket. We take the private elevator down, the silence between us comfortable, but focused. I can feel the night shifting already, the weight of what's coming humming under my skin.

Marcus slides into the passenger seat. "So, what's the over-under on us behaving tonight?"

I smirk as I start the engine. "Nonexistent."

He laughs. "Good."

We hit the street, and the drive is quick. The steakhouse is high-end, black windows and gold trim. Valets in pressed suits. We pull up, hand off the keys, and head inside.

The maître d' gives a polite smile and a nod of recognition as soon as he sees me. "Mr. Callahan. Your guests haven't arrived yet, but your table is ready."

"Perfect," I say, slipping the man a bill as he leads us toward the corner booth, secluded, upscale, dimly lit. Strategic.

Marcus scans the place, grinning lazily. "Damn. You really aren't messing around this time."

"You say that like you don't already know this," I say, pulling out my phone.

Nothing from Octavia yet, so I check her location. She is close.

Marcus leans an elbow on the table. "You going to survive the appetizer round without dragging her into the bathroom?"

"No promises."

"God, you're worse than I thought," he says, grinning. "She really has you by the balls."

I smirk, pocketing my phone. "It's not about being whipped."

Marcus raises a brow, intrigued.

"It's about finding the one person who makes you want to burn the entire world down just to keep them safe," I finish, leaning back in the booth.

He whistles low. "And here I thought *I* was the dramatic one."

I don't answer, because it's not drama. It's truth. And Marcus knows that he just hasn't had his world tilted sideways yet.

But he will.

I glance toward the front of the restaurant again.

There she is, walking in, dressed in confidence. Lips my favorite shade of berry, eyes sharp enough to cut. And Lena's right behind her in a red dress—fiery, and a wicked grin to match.

Marcus sits forward slowly, his jaw ticking. "Holy shit."

"Told you," I mutter, already rising to my feet.

Because there's no way I'm staying seated when my little minx is walking toward me like that.

Like she's the reward *and* the punishment.

Like she already knows I'll spend the entire night trying not to fuck her any chance I get.

She reaches the table and I can already tell—tonight's going to be a fucking test of restraint.

"Hey, handsome," she says, voice low and smoky, like she knows exactly what she's doing to me.

She leans in to kiss my cheek, but I catch her jaw and kiss her properly instead—slow, possessive, right in front of the maître d' and half the dining room. Her fingers dig into my shirt, and for one reckless second, I almost forget we're not alone.

When I pull back, her lips are slightly parted, cheeks flushed. That look on her face? It's already testing my limits.

"Hi," Lena says brightly, snapping the moment in two as she slides into the booth next to Marcus. "This place is swanky as hell. Love that for us."

Marcus is still staring at her like he's been punched in the gut by Aphrodite herself. "She cleans up all right," I say flatly, more for Marcus's sake than hers.

Lena grins. "And you've got 'bad idea' written all over you—but at least you wear it well."

I stifle a laugh as Octavia slides into the booth next to me, thigh pressed tight against mine. I'm not sure if she's doing it on purpose, but if she is—well, it's working.

A waiter comes by to take drink orders. Octavia leans forward, and I already know she's pushing her tits up to drive me fucking insane.

"I'll take the cherry mezcal sour," she says, sweetly.

"Same," Lena says, glancing at Marcus and he tips his glass in her direction. "I knew you had taste."

Once the server walks away, Octavia turns toward me, barely above a whisper. "You look like you want to drag me under the table."

"I'd flip the damn table," I mutter, jaw tight. "You wore that dress on purpose."

She shrugs, smug. "Guilty."

Marcus clears his throat. "So, Lena—"

"Oh no," Lena says, raising a hand. "You don't get to start small talk. I want to know what you do, what your star sign is, and if you've ever been in jail."

He laughs.

"Business development."

She narrows her eyes. "That's vague."

"Intentionally so," he says, sipping his drink.

I chime in impassively. "He handles the messes. The stuff we can't put in a quarterly report."

Lena perks up. "So you're the muscle."

Marcus raises a brow. "I'm the guy who makes sure things don't go sideways. And if they do, I tell Dom, and we make them disappear."

She grins. "Hot, but you skipped two questions."

Marcus leans back in his seat, swirling his whiskey like this is the most fun he's had all week. "Star sign is Scorpio. Never been caught."

Octavia nearly chokes on her drink. Lena's eyes light up like she just hit the jackpot.

"Oh, I *like* you."

Marcus grins. "Most people do… until they don't."

Lena cocks her head. "You always speak in riddles, or is that just for me?"

I watch the exchange, amused. Marcus doesn't flirt like a normal person—he circles, pokes, waits for you to step closer. And Lena? She'd walk into the ring with a mouth full of matches and a gas can in each hand.

"You two are going to kill each other," I mutter, "or end up married by summer."

Marcus smirks. "I've had worse odds."

Lena raises her glass. "To terrible decisions."

We all drink.

Octavia leans into me, lips brushing my ear as she whispers, "They're perfect."

"I'm not disagreeing," I murmur, sliding my hand across her thigh under the table.

She shivers slightly, but doesn't pull away, just parts her legs the tiniest bit, like an invitation.

My dangerous girl.

I run my thumb along the inside of her thigh, slow enough to tease, just enough pressure to make her squirm. She's trying so damn hard to act normal, lips pressed together like she's fighting a smile. Or a moan.

Marcus doesn't seem to notice. He's too busy locked in verbal combat with Lena, who's currently dissecting the ethics of tequila shots on first dates.

"I'm just saying," she insists, waving her fork. "If I'm going to embarrass myself, I'd rather do it efficiently. One shot, ten minutes, no regrets."

"Is that your dating philosophy or your strategy for global diplomacy?" Marcus asks.

"Yes."

He laughs, actually laughs—short and sharp, like it caught him off guard. "Jesus Christ."

Octavia turns her head slightly, whispering, "We really did something here."

"They're going to burn down the bar," I whisper back. "Possibly the whole block."

She grins, then presses her thigh harder into my palm. I let my hand slide a little higher.

The food arrives—a perfectly timed interruption, or maybe divine intervention. I pull my hand back, reluctantly, and straighten in my seat.

Octavia's flushed now, pink creeping up her throat.

The server plates everything quickly and professionally, no small talk. He knows better than to linger.

Once he leaves, Lena leans over her steak, peering across the table. "So. Are we doing real questions now, or do we keep pretending we're all normal people out for a civilized evening?"

Marcus wipes his mouth with a linen napkin. "Define 'normal.'"

She points her fork at him. "Have you ever been in love?"

He doesn't flinch. Just meets her gaze head-on. "Once."

The mood dips for a second—quiet, almost too quiet—but Lena doesn't retreat. She softens just a fraction. "What happened?"

Marcus sips his drink before answering. "Didn't work out."

Lena nods slowly. "Same."

And just like that, the match is relit.

They lean toward each other, low conversation slipping beneath the noise of the restaurant. It's quieter now—just the four of us in our little corner of chaos, but something's shifting. Calmer, deeper.

I watch Octavia cut into her food, composed as ever, but I know better. Her legs are still pressed close, her breathing just slightly off.

When she glances at me, it's like a spark shoots down my spine.

She's wound tight, desperate to unravel, and I'm the only one who can do it.

She presses her foot against my ankle under the table and drags it slowly up my calf.

Game fucking on.

I let my fingers drift just beneath the hem of her dress again, slow and deliberate, brushing that soft skin like I've got all the time in the world.

Octavia's chewing, nodding along to whatever Lena's saying about airport security and sex toys, but I feel the slight twitch in her thigh. The way her breath catches when I trace a line higher.

She shifts in her seat.

I do it again—just a whisper of a touch—dragging my fingertips dangerously close to where she's already warm and ready for me.

She clears her throat and reaches for her drink. Her hand trembles slightly, just enough for me to notice. No one else would, but I know her now. Every tell, every weakness.

I dip my fingers under the edge of her panties, just barely skimming where she's already wet.

She exhales a soft, broken sound.

Marcus glances over at her. "You alright?"

She startles. "What?"

Lena smirks. "You're flushed."

Octavia grabs her napkin and dabs at her face, eyes darting to mine like she wants to kill me and kiss me all at once. I offer her a small, smug smile.

"My drinks just really strong," she says, voice just slightly too high-pitched. "I, uh—I'm going to run to the bathroom."

She slides out of the booth quickly, smoothing her dress down as she goes. Her heels click against the marble, that perfect sway in her hips giving her away.

I watch her the whole way.

Marcus follows my gaze, then turns back, eyes narrowing. "You touched her under the table, didn't you?"

I don't say a word.

But my smirk says plenty.

He groans, tossing back the rest of his drink. "You're unhinged."

"She started it."

He snorts. "No. You've just met your match."

CHAPTER TWENTY FOUR
Octavia

My heels are far too loud as I make my way down the hall, my pulse still trying to settle from Dominic's fingers on my thigh and that look he gave me like he wanted to devour me right there.

I needed to get some damn air.

Or a mirror to talk some sense into myself might do the trick.

The bathroom is empty when I first push the door open. Dim lighting, marble countertops, and far too much gold, not trying to be subtle about being expensive or anything. I head straight to the sink, gripping the edge, and exhale slowly. My reflection staring back at me is flushed and a little wild-eyed.

"You're fine," I mutter under my breath trying to calm myself. "It's just dinner. With your maybe-boyfriend, who wants to eat you alive, bought you a car, makes you lose any normal function with a simple fucking look—"

The door creaks open behind me. I glance up and then freeze.

Because the woman walking in looks like she just stepped off the

cover of a god-damn fashion magazine. Long, blonde hair, legs for days, skin ridiculously smooth and a waist that makes me irrationally annoyed at all genetics everywhere. She's wearing something simple, elegant, and stupidly expensive-looking. She moves like she knows every single person in any room is already watching.

She glances at me briefly and turns toward the sink to wash her hands.

I try not to stare, try not to compare, try not to shrink.

But I do. Of course, I do.

Because I'm curvy, bold, loud, scarred, and even though I know Dominic worships every single inch of me, even though I know he's never looked at another woman the way he looks at me, this one moment, standing next to *her*, I feel… small.

The blonde finishes drying her hands and gives me a faint, polite smile in the mirror before strutting out of the bathroom like she's walking the runway.

As the door swings shut behind her, my jaw is clenched so tight it hurts.

I don't know why she got under my skin. She didn't even say a word to me. She barely even acknowledged my existence. But there's something about women like that, effortless, polished, the kind of pretty that makes you suddenly question every inch of yourself. Even though you were feeling damn good about yourself five minutes ago.

With a deep breath, I check myself in the mirror one more time.

My dress still hugs all the right places. I look fucking hot.

Still, that tiny, poisonous whisper in the back of my mind won't shut up: *What if she's more his type?*

Shoving it down, I know Dominic isn't the type of man who would play that game. He's brutally honest and absolutely fucking feral about me. And tonight? Tonight he couldn't keep his hands off me if he tried.

I turn to leave, ready to get back to the table, back to him. Back to the fire that started this whole damn night.

The bathroom door swings open and I step back into the low light of the restaurant, the sharp click of my heels swallowed up by the hum of clinking silverware and mumbled conversations.

I'm still flushed, still recovering from the smug, too-perfect blonde who barely acknowledged me at the sink. The one with cheekbones you could slice bread on and a walk like she's never known rejection a day in her perfect fucking life.

Whatever. She wasn't even worth—

I stop.

Dead.

My heart doesn't just skip a beat—it claws its way up my throat and freezes there.

There she is.

The same damn blonde from the bathroom.

And she's got her arm draped across *Dominic*.

I can only see the back of her at first, those waves of perfect icy blonde hair, the curve of her ass as she leans in, way too close, but I don't need her face to confirm it. My body knows before my brain does.

The same bitch who smiled at her reflection like she was better than everyone in the room.

The same bitch who's now laughing at *my* table with her hand on *my* man's chest like she never left.

A slow, cold fury builds in my gut. Not fire. It's ice, sharp, dangerous, and climbing fast.

She glances over her shoulder.

Sees me and smiles.

It's small, barely there. But it's a smile, like a pin being pulled from a grenade.

Like she knows exactly who I am, and she doesn't give a damn.

Oh, *hell no.*

My hands ball into fists at my sides as I take a breath. I don't feel; I don't move, not yet. I lock eyes with her across the restaurant, letting that smile curl into something vicious—feral, almost, like I'd rip her apart with my bare hands and lick the blood off my fingers.

Because the moment I get to that table?

I'm going to make sure that smile *never* finds her fake plastic ass lips again.

The closer I get, the clearer the scene becomes.

Marcus looks like he's about two seconds from flipping the table. His drink is in his hand, but his knuckles are white around the glass. He's not saying anything, just watching, tense, unreadable, but definitely not amused.

Lena? Lena is sitting so still it's unnatural for her. Her lips are pressed into a thin line, one perfectly arched brow raised like she's already drafting the eulogy for this blonde bitch's funeral. Her hand slowly reaches for her drink like it's a weapon and I'm honestly surprised she hasn't thrown it yet.

And Dominic?

He's not touching her.

That's the first thing I register.

But he *is* pissed. I know that jawline—how it ticks when he's holding himself back. His arms crossed, shoulders coiled so tightly it looks like he could snap in half. He's saying something low, sharp and clipped.

But she's not listening.

She's leaning in like a gnat that just won't buzz the fuck off. Like she knows her time's up, and she's trying to cling to any last bit of attention she can get.

She doesn't see the way Dominic's eyes keep darting toward the entrance.

Toward me.

Lena's gaze snaps up and locks on mine. There's a silent *thank fuck* in her expression, followed by something that looks suspiciously like *do not hold me back if shit goes down.*

Oh, there will be no holding back.

My heels hit the floor harder now, louder, with purpose.

Because *I'm done walking.*

And that stupid bitch?

She's about to know exactly who he belongs to.

As I approach the table, she turns toward me, all fake lashes and a smug ass smirk. She's still draped on the edge of the booth like she owns the damn thing, like she hasn't just stepped into the lion's den wearing pheromone perfume.

"Oh, hi," she says sweetly, eyes raking over me like she's already decided I'm nothing. "You must be the new assistant. I'm Sophia."

The word assistant hits like a slap, but my smile is already spreading, sharp, cold, and bloodthirsty.

"Assistant?" I echo, stepping right up to the table, planting both hands on it as I lean in slightly. "That's cute. Really, really cute."

Sophia's smirk falters for half a second, but she doubles down, tucking a strand of perfect hair behind her ear and looking at Dominic like I'm invisible. "I just wanted to say hi, baby. It's been so long. We should catch up."

Dominic doesn't even blink. "Get your damn hand off me."

But she doesn't. She turns toward Marcus instead, like she's trying to recruit allies. "Marcus, don't you remember when we all used to hang out? God, those were the days. You must be so confused seeing him with someone like this—"

I grab a fistful of her hair before the next word even leaves her lips.

The gasp that leaves her throat is loud enough to turn a few heads nearby, but I don't care. I *want* them to look. I want witnesses. Because this is the moment Sophia learns that I'm not like her. I don't play fucking nice. Not anymore.

"Let me make something real fucking clear," I hiss, yanking her back just enough to make her eyes water. "You ever touch him again, you ever *speak* to him again, and I will show you exactly who I am."

Sophia is trying to scramble out of the booth, but I've got her. One hand still in her hair, the other on her shoulder now, and I'm pulling her back just enough to make her heels slip on the floor.

Lena lets out a low whistle. "Oh, shit."

"S-Someone better stop her," Sophia gasps, finally trying to push my arm off of her.

Dominic doesn't move, and Marcus sips his drink.

I lean down, lips by her ear. "What's wrong, baby? Not used to someone pulling your hair without moaning your name after?"

Then, I throw her, literally toss her, like the piece of trash she is.

She lands hard, squealing, her purse scattering across the floor. Gasps erupt from nearby tables and someone's already calling security—

or the cops, maybe both—but I don't give a single fuck.

Sophia scrambles to her feet, face red, eyes bulging, mascara already running.

"This isn't over!" she shrieks at me as she gathers her shit.

I adjust my dress, smooth my hair, and level her with one final look.

"It is for you."

Dominic's hand is at my back as I turn. The heat of him is grounding, and he leans in, lips brushing the shell of my ear.

"My little killer minx," he mutters, proud and possessive.

"As sexy as that was," he mutters low in my ear, "we really need to get out of here. Right. Now."

I glance around and realize the entire restaurant is staring. Not in awe, not in confusion.

But judgment, whispers, and cameras.

Shit.

"Marcus, take Lena," Dominic says, already steering me toward the exit. "Take my car. We'll meet you at the penthouse." He says as he tosses Marcus the keys to his car.

Lena nods immediately, grabbing her purse with a grin that says she's never been more proud to witness a felony.

Marcus downs what's left of his drink in one swallow and throws a stack of hundreds on the table. "On it."

We slip out fast, adrenaline still buzzing in my bloodstream.

The second we're in the car, I explode. "I swear to God, Dominic, if she so much as breathes your air again—"

"She won't," he says, voice razor-sharp.

"No," I spit out, turning in my seat, fury hissing down my spine. "She looked me in the eye like she *wanted* me to see her hands on you.

Like she knew it would break me. The worst part is she's not going to stop. She's going to try again."

He doesn't answer right away, and that silence says more than any words, because I'm right.

She's not going to stop.

"I'm going to make sure she does," I whisper, voice trembling, but certain. "She's not getting near you again. Never again."

When we pull into the parking garage, I'm out of the car before he's even turned the engine off.

Inside, Lena and Marcus are already waiting, both halfway through glasses of whiskey, like this is some kind of party.

Lena turns when she sees me. "Okay, someone better start talking, because I just watched you drag a walking pap smear to the floor by her $1,200 extensions, and I've got soooo many questions."

I glance at Dominic, then back at her.

"No more secrets," I say. "You deserve to know what you're walking into."

Because this isn't just some petty girl drama anymore, and Lena is in the middle of it now.

I lean forward, elbows on my knees, fingers twisted together so tightly my knuckles go white. Across from me, Lena is curled into the arm of the couch, holding her whiskey like it's an anchor.

She's watching me, carefully, but not like she's afraid. More like she's bracing herself. Which is good because what I'm about to say isn't easy. Once it's out, there's no putting it back.

"I know I've told you tiny bits and pieces," I begin slowly, voice low, "but there's more. A lot more."

Lena doesn't interrupt, just gives a tiny nod, encouraging me on.

"Dominic and Marcus… they didn't get to where they are by shaking hands and filing paperwork. What they've built, their company, their money, their influence, it wasn't just strategy. It was survival, it was power." I pause, glancing at her. "And there's blood behind it, literal blood."

She stiffens, just barely, but her expression doesn't change.

"They've done things," I say, a little quieter now. "Handled people, removed threats. You don't become someone like Dominic Callahan by playing it safe. You become him because no one's ever willing to go as far as you are."

Silence stretches between us.

Lena's lips part, but she doesn't speak. She takes a long sip of whiskey instead.

I shift forward. "Sophia, that bitch? She didn't know. She was his fiancé. She cheated on him, and even then, he never told her who he really was."

Lena blinks. "But you know."

I nod. "I know everything."

She leans back slowly, exhaling hard. "And he trusts you with it?"

My eyes flick to Dominic, who hasn't said a word since this entire conversation started. He's still standing, jaw clenched, arms crossed—but not in the way he does when he's angry. This is restraint. He's letting me be the one to tell it.

"Yes," I say. "He doesn't try to hide it with me. He knows I can handle it."

Lena finally breaks the silence, voice calm and oddly casual. "So what you're saying is… I've been drinking whiskey in a penthouse with two actual, real-life crime bosses and didn't even notice?"

That breaks the tension just enough to make me laugh a little. "Basically."

"Okay," she says, setting her glass down and crossing her legs. "So what now? You just keep dating your murder daddy and pretend the rest of us live in the same reality?"

I grin, but there's something raw in my chest. Because as funny as she's trying to be, there's truth behind it. This life isn't normal and once you're in, you're in.

"I'm telling you because I trust you," I say seriously. "And also because if you keep seeing Marcus, you need to know. He's not the kind of man you just date casually."

Lena's gaze sharpens slightly, but her lips twitch into a smirk. "Good, because neither am I.

CHAPTER TWENTY FIVE
Dominic

Lena is laughing like this is a joke, but she has no fucking clue what she's signed up for.

Not really.

She saw the hair-pulling, sure. The chaos, the rage on Octavia's face that would've sent most people running. But that was just surface level.

She's sitting on my couch, drink in hand, half-amused and half-curious, thinking this is just a messy dinner gone sideways. And maybe she's right—for now. But that won't last, because Octavia just made it clear she's pulling Lena in. No more secrets. No more protection.

Which means Lena's going to learn what it costs to stay close to us, and she's going to have to decide if Marcus is worth the fallout.

I lean against the bar, watching them. Octavia's explaining things slowly, carefully, but her voice is steady. She's not second-guessing this. Not anymore. She's chosen her side, and it's mine—ours.

Fuck, I've never been more certain that I'd level the world if anyone tried to take her from me.

Marcus catches my eye from across the room, a knowing flicker

passing between us. We've been through hell and back to build what we have. The reputation that makes people hesitate before they breathe our names.

But it wasn't just business that got us here.

It was blood; it was choices most men wouldn't come back from.

Now? Now we've got two women sitting on that damn couch who don't cringe in the face of it. Two women who hear the worst and still stay seated, still stay curious.

Octavia... she's already proven she's willing to go further than most of the men I know.

And Lena? If Marcus plays it right, she might just be crazy enough to thrive here, too.

I push off the bar and step closer, glass still in my hand. The burn of the whiskey is doing nothing to settle the way my blood's still burning hot.

Octavia's curled up on the couch beside Lena, her legs nestled under her, and she's watching me with that look—the one that says she's still wired, still coming down from the fire of it all.

Lena doesn't look scared. If anything, she looks more fascinated than anything else. Her brow is arched, the edge of her lip curled like she's still processing, secretly impressed.

I sit on the arm of the couch and rest my hand on Octavia's thigh, just so I'm touching her, anchoring her, or maybe, anchoring myself.

"You alright?" I murmur low enough that only she can hear.

She nods. "I want to go back to work tomorrow."

That catches me completely off guard.

"You serious?"

"I need the distraction," she says. "I need something that doesn't involve stalking or assault or luxury car purchases. Just... something fucking normal."

My lips curl, and I lean in, mouth brushing her ear. "You want normal? Bad news, baby. The second Lena and Marcus leave, I'm going to fuck you so hard you'll forget what your job even is."

She lets out a quiet breath, legs shifting under my palm. That soft, sharp moan she always makes when she's torn between being flustered and turned on.

Across from us, Lena's laughing at something Marcus just said, shaking her head like he's already earned a second date. He's leaning back in the chair, one arm draped lazily over the side, but his eyes haven't left Lena once. Every sarcastic word out of her mouth only makes him smirk harder.

"Are you always this cocky?" Lena asks, taking another sip of her whiskey.

Marcus shrugs. "Only when I'm right."

"And how often is that?"

He grins. "Often enough that you're still sitting here."

Lena rolls her eyes. "God, your confidence is insufferable. I'm going to have to knock you down a few pegs."

"Looking forward to it," Marcus says, tipping his glass in her direction.

Octavia leans into my side, and for just a second, everything is still. No chaos. No fallout. Just four people—two of them battle-scarred, and the other two brave (or reckless) enough to dive into the fire, anyway.

She's quiet again, but this time it isn't tension—it's focus.

And I know her well enough to see it. She's planning.

Something's still simmering in her.

And if it's what I think it is… Sophia has no idea what's coming.

Marcus takes a sip of his drink, eyes still locked on Lena. "You always this feisty, Doll face?"

Lena blinks slowly. "Did you just 1950s pet name me?"

He smirks, unbothered. "Would you prefer, sweetheart? Princess?"

She laughs as she drinks what's left in her glass. "Keep going, and I'm going to call you 'finance bro' unironically."

I nearly choke on my whiskey.

"Touché," Marcus says, chuckling. "But I'm not a finance bro. I'm worse."

"Oh, I know," Lena replies, sitting back. "You've got that look, like you invest in crypto and have a burner phone for reasons you refuse to explain."

Octavia snorts beside me, and I feel her body relax just a little more. The tension in the room is still there, buzzing under the surface, but the sharp edge of it softens with every round of banter Lena volleys back.

"Alright," Marcus says, raising his glass again. "Since I'm already being roasted, might as well go all in. Dessert? Or do you ladies plan to keep dismantling my self-esteem while sober?"

Lena tilts her head. "You're assuming I have any interest in your self-esteem?"

Octavia grins at that, her hand sliding over my knee as she leans in closer.

Marcus lets out a short laugh. "I knew I liked you."

The energy in the room is different now, lighter, yes, but it's the kind of light that flickers just before burning brighter. Like every single person in this penthouse is holding a lighter to gasoline, waiting to see who ignites it first, and from the look on Octavia's face, I already know she's the one holding the match.

Lena leans forward to refill her glass, but something catches her eye.

She squints at Octavia's shoulder, then does a full double take. "Hold on… is that a fucking bite mark?"

Octavia freezes.

My lips twitch.

"Oh my god, how did I not notice this earlier!?" Lena says, setting her glass down dramatically. "Did you get *bitten* during your post-murder sex?"

Octavia groans, dragging a hand over her face, but there's no real shame in it. Just exasperation, and a hint of heat rising to her cheeks.

"I knew it," Lena says, grinning like she just cracked a code. "I knew you had that glow. You've got 'feral CEO turned me into a puddle' energy radiating off you."

"Lena—"

"Do *not* try to downplay this. That's a *bite mark*, and it's not a little one. Jesus, did he *break skin?*"

Octavia cuts her a sharp look, but I answer before she can.

"Yes," I say simply, swirling the last of my whiskey. "And she liked it."

Lena makes a high-pitched noise and flops back drastically against the couch. "This is like a spicy ass telenovela and I am living for it."

Marcus looks at her, amused. "That's what does it for you?"

She grins without missing a beat. "I like violence and emotional unavailability and now, apparently, dental aggression."

Octavia sighs, flopping against my side with a groan. "You're never allowed to speak again."

"Sorry, sweetheart, but I have questions," Lena fires back. "Is that the only one? Or are you secretly a walking crime scene under that dress?"

"She's got marks," I say, voice low, threading my fingers through Octavia's hair and tugging gently. "Plenty."

She shivers under my touch.

Across from us, Lena's grinning, enjoying every last detail. "Good, I hope you branded her. We don't need any more bleach-blonde cockroaches crawling out of the shadows."

That cold glint returns to Octavia's eyes, but there's control in it now.

She's not spiraling anymore—she's strategizing.

And me? I'm just trying not to fuck her senseless on this couch in front of our friends.

Octavia's laughing softly at something Lena says, but I lean in close, brushing my lips over the curve of her ear. My voice is low, meant only for her.

"I can't wait for them to leave," I murmur. "I'm going to chase you down, pin you to the floor, and fuck you hard. You can run, baby, but I know your pussy will be dripping for me."

She sucks in a breath, her thighs pressing together. I feel it, the shiver that runs through her body, the way her pulse flutters hard on my hand.

Good.

But before I can press further, Lena's voice cuts through the moment, wild and amused.

"Oh, yeah?" she purrs. "Bet you won't pull back."

I glance over just in time to see her crawl into Marcus's lap like it's her throne, a wicked grin on her face. She takes a slow sip of whiskey from her glass, then leans forward and lets it spill from her mouth into his.

Fucking hell.

Marcus doesn't blink, doesn't hesitate. He grabs her hips, pulls her tight against him, and swallows every drop like it's nothing. His grin is sharp as he looks up at her, eyes blazing.

Lena licks the corner of her mouth. "Told you. I'm unforgettable."

Marcus's voice is raspy. "That wasn't a lie, Doll face."

Octavia exhales a stunned laugh beside me, eyes wide. "Okay. I think she just broke your friend."

I smirk. "He's not broken, baby. He will be, though."

Judging by the way Lena's fingers are curling into Marcus's shoulders now, hips grinding ever so slightly, they may burn the whole damn place down.

But not before I get my hands back on my little minx.

Lena's straddling Marcus like she's been there a hundred times, his hands gripping her hips, her mouth brushing dangerously close to his. They're wrapped up in each other, and for a second, it feels like the world is slipping sideways into something almost…normal. Chaotic, yes, but comfortable. Like maybe we could all exist like this a little longer.

Then my phone buzzes.

One short, quick vibration.

Normally, I'd ignore it, but it's late, and that usually means it isn't anything good. But something in the back of my neck prickles.

Octavia shifts beside me just as I reach for it, curiosity pulling her gaze to the screen.

I see it hit her like a fucking freight train.

Because there it is.

Sophia.

Her name lighting up my screen like a goddamn warning flare.

No message preview, but it doesn't matter.

Octavia stiffens so fast it's like the air's been sucked out of her lungs.

Her voice is eerily calm. "She texted you?"

Clicking the lock button on the phone. "I haven't opened it."

"That's not what I asked."

Fuck.

"Octavia—"

Her jaw tightens, and I know that look. I've seen it when she's cornered. When something inside her breaks past the point of reason. This is different from the rage in the restaurant. That was explosive.

This is meticulous.

"I'm not mad you didn't delete her number," she says, standing up slowly, every movement conscious. "I'm mad that she had the audacity to message you. *Again.* After that stunt. After I dragged her in front of half the city."

Lena, finally noticing the shift in energy, slides off Marcus's lap and stands. "Uh... should I be pouring more whiskey or calling an exorcist?"

Octavia doesn't answer.

Her eyes are locked on me.

Not in accusation, but in *challenge.*

Like she's waiting to see what the fuck I'm going to do now.

I already know there's only one answer that will cut it.

I hold the phone up, unlock it, and delete the entire thread without hesitation. Gone, no hesitation, no pause.

"I didn't respond and I'm not going to. She's dead to me."

Octavia watches my thumb hit delete, watches the name vanish like vapor.

"I don't want her dead to you," she says coldly. "I want her *dead,* Dominic. Real life fucking *dead.*"

The silence that follows is deafening.

Lena slowly backs toward the kitchen, mouthing *what the actual fuck* at Marcus, who just downs the rest of his drink like he's preparing for what's coming next.

I step toward her, my voice low and pointed. "Then we'll make it happen."

Her lashes flutter, and for a second—just a second—I see that tension in her shoulders loosen.

But the damage is already done.

Whatever moment of levity we had is fucking gone now.

Octavia turns to Lena, serious. "You should go with Marcus."

Lena blinks. "Are you… are you okay?"

"I will be," Octavia says, voice flat. "But I need to plan."

Lena stares between the two of us, and to her credit, she doesn't argue. "Okay. But if you start a murder cult and don't invite me, I'll be personally offended."

Marcus touches her elbow. "Let's go, Doll face."

He gives me a long look, part warning, part understanding, then walks her to the elevator.

The doors close behind them, and then it's just us.

Octavia, me, and the ghost of a woman who just signed her fucking death certificate with a text.

CHAPTER TWENTY SIX
Octavia

The second the doors shut behind Lena and Marcus, it's like a switch flips in my brain.

The silence feels too loud, my pulse too fast.

I'm still standing where I was, staring at the screen of Dominic's phone like it seared me. Like it branded something into my chest I can't tear out.

She messaged him, she actually fucking messaged him.

That bleach-blonde, silicone-stuffed, Botox-brained knockoff Barbie had the *fucking audacity* to text *him* after tonight. After she laid her skanky hands all over him, like I wasn't five seconds away from peeling her like a damn grape, and now she's still trying?

My breath saws in and out of my lungs as I pace the living room, every step more feverish than the last. My body's thrumming, the kind that doesn't end in a cute kiss or another orgasm against the windows. No, this one ends with blood under my nails and that bitch's scream echoing off the pavement.

"Octavia—"

"Don't."

I spin around and glare at Dominic. He hasn't moved, but he's watching me, calm like always, except for that sharp edge in his eyes. He knows. He can feel it.

"I'm not calm," I snap before he can say it. "So don't ask me to be."

"I wasn't going to." His voice is steady, but low. "I know what this is."

I stop pacing and face him dead-on. "Then you know what comes next. You know I'm going to find her."

He exhales through his nose like he expected that. "What are you planning to do when you do?"

My fingers curl into fists. "Whatever I have to."

I mean it, every single word.

She doesn't get to keep popping back up like this. Doesn't get to play games like this is some love triangle and not my fucking life. She doesn't get to smile at me in the mirror like she's better and then throw herself at *my* man like I'm not carved into his goddamn DNA.

No.

I don't know exactly how this ends yet—but it's not with her still breathing.

The silence pulses between us—thick, electric, waiting to detonate.

I see it in his eyes, permission.

He moves to me fast.

One hand wraps around my throat, firm, just enough pressure to still every thought in my head. He walks me backward until my back hits the wall with force, his body caging mine in completely.

His eyes are molten, dark, reckless, and locked on me like I'm not just the only thing he sees, but the only thing keeping him sane.

"You want blood?" His voice is low, rough. "Say the word."

My breath catches.

"You want revenge?" he growls, his hand tightening slightly. "Want her erased?"

My thighs clench.

"Whatever you want," he murmurs, voice sharp as a knife and just as deadly, "you can have. There are no rules anymore, Octavia."

The way he says my name, it's a promise, a vow wrapped in fire.

He leans in closer, lips ghosting mine but not touching. His breath is warm and lethal.

"You want her gone, baby?" he whispers. "She's gone. Just tell me how you want to do it."

I moan, actually moan, like I'm already unraveling beneath the weight of it all.

Because this isn't just being wanted. It's being owned in a way that scorches. Like if the world got in the way, he'd rip it apart and leave the ashes at my feet.

My hands slide up his chest, over his heart, until I'm gripping the collar of his shirt like I need it to breathe.

"She smiled at me," I whisper, teeth gritted. "Like I didn't matter. Like she'd already won."

Dominic tilts his head, eyes burning. "Then let's make sure she understands exactly how wrong she was."

He kisses me then, hard, brutal, unforgiving.

He's hard, unrelenting, pressed against me, and it sends a pulse of heat down my spine. My breath hitches, hands still clenched in his shirt.

He growls low against my ear, voice vibrating with tension like a fuse about to snap. "Run, little minx."

Before I can even gasp, his fingers hook into the neckline of my dress and *rip*—the fabric tears like paper, seams splitting under his grip, falling in shreds to the floor.

My skin is bare, goosebumps rising instantly.

He steps back, watching me. Eyes burning like he's holding back a storm just for me.

"Go," he says again, low and lethal. "You wanted this. So, run."

My pulse explodes.

I hesitate just long enough for his smirk to curve into something darker. Then, I bolt.

The sound of his steps chasing me echoes in my ears before I make it halfway down the hallway.

Adrenaline and arousal mix into something wicked, something barbaric.

I duck into the guest room, sliding behind the long curtains just as I hear his footsteps thudding down the hall.

Then, silence. Too quiet.

"Where are you, baby?" His voice drips like molasses, slow and feral. "You can't hide from me for long."

I press a hand to my mouth, trying not to breathe too loud. My thighs are already trembling from anticipation, my skin hot and aching for his touch.

"I can smell you," he says, and fuck, I know he's smiling. "Dripping wet and trying to hide? Naughty fucking girl."

The door creaks open. Every nerve in my body is a livewire.

I see his shadow move across the room. He steps slow and predatory.

"Take me when I want, you said."

My lungs seize when the curtain is ripped aside.

He finds me instantly.

His hand wraps around my throat, pinning me to the wall, thumb brushing my lips.

"I should punish you for running," he whispers, eyes blazing. "But first—" he lifts me effortlessly, one hand already between my thighs "—I'm going to fucking *devour* you."

Then he's on his knees.

His fingers thrust inside me, curling delightfully until I cry out, writhing in his grip. His palm presses down against my lower belly, trapping me in place.

And then his mouth.

Hot, relentless, his lips sealing around my clit and sucking me into madness.

The scream that tears from me is pure, raging pleasure.

My back arches, heels digging into his shoulders as his tongue flicks and circles, sucking me back into that dizzy, pulsing edge.

"Oh, my god—Dominic—please,"

His fingers curl again, pressing hard as his mouth sucks my clit and that tidal wave of release comes fast, fierce, unstoppable.

But he fucking stops.

Everything.

Fingers gone. Mouth gone.

I sob his name, desperate, eyes flying open finding his.

But he just stares up at me with that wicked, unforgiving smirk.

"Did I say you could cum?"

"Are you… are you serious?" My voice is strangled, shattered. My body is trembling, aching, my pulse thrumming in my ears.

"You thought you could hide that sweet little cunt and still get rewarded?"

He stands slowly, towering over me, dragging his fingers along the inside of my thigh. "Not yet, baby. You'll cum when I say. Not a second before."

His hand fists in my hair and pulls my head back, eyes locked on mine.

"Understand?"

I nod, frantic. "Yes… yes, I understand."

He leans in, breath hot against my lips, almost kissing me.

"Good," he whispers. "Now, get on the bed. On your knees."

I scramble toward the bed, heart pounding, skin flushed, still throbbing from being dragged to the brink and denied like a filthy, disobedient thing. I barely make it onto the mattress before he's behind me, one hand gripping the back of my neck and pressing me down until my cheek hits the sheets.

"Good girls don't pull away from me," he growls. "You want to act like prey? Then I'll hunt you like you are."

He drags the head of his cock through my slick folds, slow, torturous. Not pushing in, just *there*. Teasing, as if I'm not already begging to fall apart.

My hips jerk, desperate for more friction. For him.

"Please—"

He grips my ass hard, spreading me wider, exposing every part of me.

"Please, what?" he snarls, the tip of his cock pressing just barely against my entrance. "You think you get to disappear and still get fucked like my good little whore?"

"Dominic…" I gasp, but it comes out cracked and broken.

His hand lifts and *smack*—a sharp slap against my ass makes me cry out.

"Beg for it. Tell me how fucking sorry you are for being a bad girl."

"I'm sorry," I whimper, breath caught. "I shouldn't have, fuck…."

He presses in slowly, thick and straining, but still holding back. I sob into the sheets.

"You feel that?" he mutters darkly, inching in just enough to make me shake. "My cock is the reward. Not the punishment."

And then he pulls back again.

I lose it. "No… no, please…"

He grabs a fistful of my hair, yanking my head back so I'm arched. His lips graze my ear.

"Not until you break for me, baby. Not until I see you beg like you *mean* it."

"I'm sorry," I gasp again, voice cracking. "I shouldn't have made you chase me. I just… I needed you to find me."

He groans low, that feral sound I've come to crave, the one that means I've flipped some kind of switch inside him. His grip on my hair tightens just a little, holding me in place, unrelenting.

"You needed to be hunted?" he growls.

He releases my hair only to pick me up and shove me down to my knees at the foot of the bed, towering over me, his cock flushed and hard, right in front of my lips.

"Show me," he says, a growled order that makes my knees threaten to give out. "Show me how sorry you are."

My eyes find his, pupils blown wide, lips parted. My hands tremble as I reach for him, but he doesn't let me touch, not yet.

"No hands," he mutters darkly. "Use your mouth, little minx."

I nod, swallowing hard. I lean in and take the tip of him into my mouth, slow and reverent at first, like worship. He hisses through his teeth, one hand tangling in my hair again, guiding me down further.

"Eyes on me." He rasps.

I do as he says, keeping my gaze locked on his while I take him deeper, feeling the thickness against my tongue, the weight of him on my throat.

"That's it," he groans. "You're so fucking good at sucking my cock"

I moan around him; the vibration making his grip tighten, hips twitch.

"Yes," he growls. "Just like that. Fuck, you're perfect."

I pull back with a pop, licking my lips, breathless. "Did I earn it yet?"

He stares down at me, wild and undone, chest heaving. "Not even close."

He hauls me up again, spinning me back onto the bed.

"I'm going to ruin you."

I barely have time to gasp before he's on me, hands gripping my thighs, shoving them apart.

"Spread wider," he growls, eyes devouring me. "I want to see everything."

I obey, breath catching as he kneels between my legs, dragging his gaze over every slick, desperate inch of me.

"You're soaked," he murmurs darkly. "Dripping, all for me."

Then his hand slides down, two fingers pushing inside of me again in one swift, merciless thrust.

I cry out, arching off the bed, thighs trembling as he curls them just right, hitting my g-spot, making my vision blur.

"You like that, don't you, baby?" he mutters.

I'm panting, gasping, choking on a moan as he fucks me with his fingers, curling them up again and again, the pressure from his palm making every thrust more intense, more unbearable. My body's trembling, strung tight and desperate, so close I can taste it—and he knows. The bastard knows.

He's making up for earlier, when he pulled away and left me soaked, aching, clenching around nothing. He said I wasn't ready, said I'd have to wait, like I wasn't already falling apart for him.

Now? He's breaking me. On purpose. Drawing it out like he's trying to make me feel everything I begged him for and then some. And God, I do. I feel all of it. The stretch, the pressure, the way his fingers hit just right, like it's his calling to make me beg for more.

And I want it—I want all of it. Every filthy, perfect second.

"Yes," I gasp. "Fuck, yes… I love it. Don't stop… please, don't stop."

His eyes blaze, mouth twisting into a dark grin.

"Then, give it to me," he growls. "Cum all over my fingers, you filthy little minx."

It hits me hard. My entire body snaps tight, then shatters, pleasure detonating behind my eyes as I scream his name. My walls clamp down around his fingers, soaking him, soaking the bed, the sheets, my thighs, everything.

But he doesn't even give me a second to breathe.

Before I can fully come down, he's flipping me onto my stomach, dragging my hips up beneath him. I barely manage a dazed breath before he's slamming into me from behind, deep and rough.

I cry out, half from the aftershock and half from the stretch of him, the way he fills me completely.

"Fuck," he snarls, grabbing a fistful of my hair and yanking my head back. "You're so fucking wet, baby."

His hand wraps around my throat from behind, holding me in place as he drives into me over and over, hips colliding with the backs of my thighs in punishing rhythm.

"Every inch of you is mine," he grits. "This cunt—this body—it's all fucking mine."

"Yes, Dominic… yours," I sob, nails clawing at the sheets, barely able to hold on.

He bends down, lips brushing my ear.

"My perfect little mess," he mutters, dragging the words out. "So greedy for it. You break so fucking pretty for me."

His grip tightens just enough to make my breath catch, my head tipping back as I whimper beneath him.

A filthy sound rips from his throat, half groan, half praise. His free hand slides down the front of my body, until he finds my clit rubbing in fast, relentless circles, exactly the way he knows will drive me over the edge.

My entire body tenses, the build-up unbearable. Pressure winding tighter until I'm choking on a sob.

"Dominic, I.."

"Do it," he demands, not stopping. "Cum all over my cock, baby."

That's all it takes.

I explode, screaming his name into the sheets, my whole body locking up as I cum so hard I see stars. The pleasure rips through me, wave after wave, my thighs shaking as I pulse around him.

He groans like it's the sexiest thing he's ever felt.

"Fuck, that's it," he snarls, hips stuttering. "You're fucking dripping for me, dirty fucking girl."

He drives in one final time, burying himself deep as he cums with a low, guttural moan, his entire body pressed against mine like he can't get close enough.

His lips graze the back of my shoulder, over the bite mark from the other day. "You good?" he murmurs against my skin.

I can't even form real words, "mmmhm" I smile at him, completely spent.

CHAPTER TWENTY SEVEN

Octavia

My body aches in places I didn't even know could ache.

Every inch of me feels used, claimed, still humming with the aftermath of last night. My thighs are sore, my back is stiff, and I'm pretty sure I have a faint bruise on my hip where he dug his fingers into me. But it's the good kind of ache. The kind that makes me bite my lip when I stretch and feel it all over again.

Sunlight spills in through the tall windows, painting streaks across the disheveled sheets and the long line of Dominic's back as he stands by the window, already in slacks, shirt unbuttoned, coffee in hand.

I stay there for a second, admiring him.

I should feel unsure about today, about the mess still ahead of us. But all I feel is this low, burning drive under my skin.

Because I haven't stopped thinking about Sophia.

About her voice. Her hands on him. Her text.

The more I let it simmer, the more the rage sharpens into something lethal.

I push off the sheets, wincing a little, and walk to the bathroom. My reflection stops me. My lips are swollen, my hair is a mess, and on

my shoulder, the bite mark he left is still very visible.

I turn on the water, splash my face, and start pulling myself together. Clean, tailored slacks, my favorite blouse, twist my hair up into a messy bun, and do light makeup.

By the time I step back into the bedroom, Dominic's buttoning his shirt. He turns, eyes raking over me slowly.

"You look amazing, baby," he says, voice still sleep-rough.

"I don't know about that," I mutter, grabbing my phone and sliding it into my purse.

He watches me a moment before walking over and brushing his fingers down my arm. "You doing ok?"

I nod once. "Better than ok."

And I am. Because now I can't stop imagining it, what it will feel like when I finally get my hands on her. When I get to choose how she goes.

Strangled? Stabbed? Shot?

There's something appealing about each of them. The intimacy of wrapping my fingers around her throat and watching the life drain from her eyes. The visceral satisfaction of watching her bleed. The quick efficiency of a bullet.

I haven't decided yet, but I will.

Soon.

Dominic tilts my chin up with two fingers. "You're thinking about her again."

"Can you blame me?"

He smirks. "Not even a little."

He grabs his keys, checks his watch, then steps in close. "We've got twenty minutes. You want coffee?"

I nod, lips twitching into something close to a smile. "Only if you're making it."

Dominic gives me a look, that slow, amused one he does when he's trying not to be smug. "A little demanding for someone who can barely walk."

I roll my eyes and follow him to the kitchen. "I'm walking just fine, thank you. Well, mostly."

He chuckles under his breath as he grabs the kettle, pouring water with the same intense focus he gives to everything else. Like making coffee is a mission and not just… making coffee.

I lean against the counter and watch him move. It's stupid how domestic this all feels.

But it's also kind of nice.

He slides the mug toward me and leans on the counter, sipping his coffee like we do this every day.

"You sure you want to go in today?" he asks.

"I need to." I take a small sip. "If I don't go now, I'm just going to sit around all day thinking about her, and I'll end up doing something stupid."

His gaze sharpens a bit. "Define stupid."

"Showing up at her apartment. Maybe slashing a few tires. Maybe her throat."

He laughs. "You wouldn't go alone," he says, like it's not up for debate.

We fall into silence again. This time it's heavier, laced with things we're not saying.

He finally sets his mug down and steps closer. "We should go soon or traffic will be shit."

I down the rest of my coffee, grimacing a little. It's strong, probably intentionally so.

He grabs his keys and slides on his jacket, watching me like he's waiting for something.

"Don't start," I warn.

He smirks. "Wasn't going to."

"Liar."

He leans in and presses a kiss to my cheek. "You look delectable."

I grab my bag and head for the door before the moment can get too heated.

We take the elevator down to the garage in silence. It's colder down here. The air is stale, humming faintly with the sound of the overhead fluorescents. Dominic unlocks his Porsche with a soft beep, and I slide into the passenger seat, suddenly hyper aware of everything: my breathing, my posture, the way my pulse kicks up when he gets in beside me.

The engine rumbles to life, and he doesn't say anything as we wind our way up through the garage, the world outside still hidden from view. It's like we're suspended in limbo, between floors, between realities, between what happened last night and everything tocome.

But then we break through.

As the car rolls up the ramp and out into the open, the city greets us with a different face than the one I remember from earlier. The sun is gone, swallowed up by thick gray clouds. Dampness clings to the edges of the windshield.

I blink, surprised. "Wasn't it sunny, like, thirty minutes ago?"

Dominic gives a soft huff. "That's typical Seattle, for you," he mutters. "The only place you can get all four seasons before lunch."

It makes me smile, just a little. That weird shift, sun to clouds, warmth to chill, it feels weirdly appropriate. The calm is over and the storm is about to be raging.

We drive in silence for a few minutes, the tires hissing over damp pavement.

My phone buzzes in my lap. It's Lena.

LENA

So... last night. Wild. Are you still breathing?
Did you kill that bitch?

I snort and tilt the screen away.

ME

I'm breathing. No murders. Yet.

LENA

Yet? Oh god. Do you need backup? Tell me
everything.

ME

Can't. Headed into work. Try not
to summon a demon while I'm
gone.

LENA

No promises. Love you.

I lock the screen and Dominic glances at me.

"Lena?"

"Who else?" I murmur. "She thinks we killed Sophia already."

He smirks faintly. "Not yet."

The word *yet* hangs between us.

The car slows as we approach the building, rain streaking down the windshield in thick, erratic lines. It's no longer just a drizzle, it's full-on pouring now, the sky opening up like it's been holding back all morning.

By the time Dominic pulls into the executive garage, the rain has turned to heavy hail. It pelts the car in staccato rhythms, tapping against the roof and hood like impatient fingers. It's loud, jarring, like the day's already started throwing punches before we've even stepped inside.

Dominic kills the engine and glances at me.

"You ready?" he asks.

No, but I nod anyway. "Yes, let's go."

We get out quickly, the sound of hail hammering the concrete above echoes through the garage in warning. The air is cold, and I can feel the shift in pressure like a weight on my chest.

The elevator ride to the lobby is quiet, but I can tell he's switched into CEO mode, the sharp-edged version of himself that runs the world like it's a chessboard.

The doors open, and the contrast hits me immediately. Warm air, soft lighting, and Derek.

He's already waiting, coffee in one hand, his other tucked into his jacket pocket like he's been standing there no more than a minute. He's calm, composed, professional as hell in a tailored navy suit.

"Morning, boss, glad to have you back," he says to Dominic with a nod. Then to me, "Octavia. Good to see you as well."

"Morning," I say, trying to sound like a normal human being and not a woman who was just contemplating how to kill someone forty minutes ago.

"I've got the revised numbers from Hartwell," he says, already falling into step beside us. "Design team's making fast progress on the updated visuals."

Dominic nods. "I want a full walkthrough this afternoon. Nothing skipped."

"Already noted." Then, glancing at me, "You're in the strategy sync at ten. It should be light. Just timeline and rollout projections."

"Sounds good," I lie. Because nothing feels light.

Derek offers a half-smile. "No pressure, everyone's still in scramble mode. You'll look like a rockstar just for showing up."

"Clear my calendar after one. No calls, no drop-ins." Dominic states.

Derek doesn't ask why. "Done."

Dominic doesn't touch me, doesn't say anything. He just heads straight for his office with that purposeful, don't-fuck-with-me stride. Derek follows a few steps behind, rattling off something about a vendor call as the glass doors swing shut behind them.

I'm left standing there, suddenly hyper aware of how alone I feel. This shouldn't hurt, but it does. I know he can't kiss me in front of everyone here.

I head to my desk, trying not to think too hard. Just one foot in front of the other, keep my face neutral, keep my posture relaxed. Normal. Like I didn't spend the weekend wrapped in the arms of my boss, killing my ex and fantasizing about cutting out the heart of the woman who crawled back into his life like a maggot.

A few heads glance up as I pass, but no one says anything. Just the usual nods and polite smiles. There's something weird about coming back into the office after a weekend like that—like I'm wearing a secret no one else knows about.

I sit down, pull my chair in, and start my computer like it's any other day.

My phone buzzes once beside me.

UNKNOWN NUMBER

Hope you got some rest. You'll need it.

Unknown Number

I'm sure he enjoyed his weekend with you. But I bet he's not the only one on his mind.

My stomach churns, that cold knot tightening.

I glance around the office. Nothing looks out of place—just the usual hum of conversation and the quiet sound of keyboards while people pretend to work. No heads turn. No one's looking.

But I feel it.

That prickling sensation at the back of my neck, like someone's watching. Like eyes are on me, just out of sight. Her words still hang in the air, clinging to my skin like static.

UNKNOWN NUMBER

You might think you've won. But you haven't. Not yet.

I grip the edge of my desk. The words are simple, almost playful, but there's no mistaking the message behind them. She's toying with me, she's daring me to snap. Pushing me until I can't take it anymore. She wants me to break.

I inhale slowly, fighting the urge to smash my phone into the wall. It would feel good, it would feel *right* to let it all go, to finally lash out.

I try to ignore it, my hand shaking slightly as I type up a response to the report sitting in front of me.

The phone buzzes again.

I can't stop myself. I pick it up.

UNKNOWN NUMBER

You won't be able to keep hiding behind him.
Sooner or later, he'll see that I am better than you,
and he will leave you.

The words slice through me like a knife.

I can feel her smirk behind the screen. I can see her, the way she lingers in the shadows, watching me, pushing, trying to make me crack under the weight of her presence.

I slam the phone face down on my desk, fists clenched.

I stare at it like it's tainted. My pulse is beating so loud I can barely hear anything else. The drone of the office fades into a dull, useless background. Phone's ringing, keys clacking, voices rising and falling. It's all white noise compared to the way my blood is screaming beneath my skin.

I try to breathe. In, out. I try to focus on the report in front of me, but the words blur.

Because she's in my head again, and now she's trying to twist the knife.

He'll leave you.

The thought alone makes my vision go red.

No. No, he won't.

She doesn't know what we've done. What we are.

I sit still for a few more seconds, hands shaking, chest heaving with the effort it takes not to hurl something across the room. I clench my jaw so hard it aches. I want to scream; I want to tear this building apart with my bare hands. I want her fucking *gone.*

Instead, I pick up the phone, slow and calm. My thumbs hover over the keyboard.

I don't think. I just type.

ME

> You used to have him. But now he's mine. And he fucks me every. Single. Night.

I stare at the message. Let it sit, let it burn and I hit send.

The three dots pop up and disappear multiple times.

For a second, the world itself holds its breath.

Then the adrenaline hits. I want her to see it. I want her to read it repeatedly, stewing in the reality she can't rewrite.

She lost.

She's not used to someone being better than her.

And Dominic Callahan? He's mine now.

I lean back in my chair and cross my legs slowly, letting the satisfaction settle deep in my gut.

The three dots blink again.

Disappear.

Blink again.

And then finally, it lands.

UNKNOWN NUMBER

Cute. But he said that to me once, too. I was there when he built his empire. You think you know him? You're just a version. I was the original.

My breath catches in my throat. Not pain—but pure fucking rage.

She's scrambling, trying to rewrite history. Trying to convince herself she mattered in a way she never did.

But it's not working, because I've seen the parts of Dominic no one else has. The soft, the unhinged. The parts that bend only for me.

This is a pathetic attempt of trying to get under my skin.

I exhale, slow and steady. My hands shake from the heat crawling up my spine—the urge to finish this once and for all.

I press the side button on my phone, holding it until I can swipe to power the damn thing off.

She doesn't get another second of my energy.

Not when she's already lost.

I set the phone in my desk drawer, close it, and I run my hands over my face, taking a breath.

Ten o'clock meeting, strategy projections.

I need to focus.

Let her rot in her little world of delusion and recycled memories. I've got other shit to handle, not deal with her skanky ass right now.

I double-check the file I need for the meeting, forcing my mind to click back into place. This is business. Get through this, and then I can show Dominic the texts. From there we can decide what comes next.

The moment I step into the conference room, the conversation softens. A few people glance up and nod, familiar, friendly. No tension, just a team getting ready to do what we're here to do.

I offer a quiet "good morning" as I take my seat near the front, flipping open my folder and glancing through the latest projection updates. Numbers, charts, rollout timelines—all things I should normally care about. But right now, my mind keeps going back to that drawer. To the silence of my phone, the words I won't let myself reread.

The door opens and Dominic walks in and he owns the floor. There's always something different in the air when he steps into a room. The way conversations ease, the way focus shifts. He has gravity, presence.

He greets the group, expression unreadable, and takes his place at the head of the table.

Our eyes meet for a split second. Just enough for him to register that something is off.

I drop my gaze and flip to the next page like everything's fine. Like I'm not seconds away from climbing out of my own skin.

I can hold it together just a little longer.

CHAPTER TWENTY EIGHT

She's already seated when I walk in, front row, folder open, pen resting neatly on the table.

She looks up, just for a second.

It's enough to register me, to acknowledge I'm in the room. But it's not the look she usually gives me. There's no fire. No spark. Just a flicker—tight, cautious—and then she's back to pretending her notes are the most interesting thing in the damn world.

My jaw tics. Something's off.

Octavia doesn't do guarded with me. She doesn't pull back unless she's pushing down something darker, something she doesn't want me to see.

I can feel it crawling under her skin.

She hasn't touched her pen since I sat down. She nods along with the conversation, but there's a delay in it—just a second too slow. Like her mind is somewhere else entirely.

I force myself not to reach out and ask her if she is ok, keeping my expression blank as the team cycles through rollout projections and updated campaign budgets. Nothing registers beyond the pounding certainty that she's coming apart at the seams.

And I don't know why right now, but I will.

As soon as this meeting's over, I'm locking the door behind us, and she's going to tell me exactly what the fuck is going on.

The meeting ends, finally, after what might as well have been an eternity.

Every minute that ticked by, every fucking slide on that screen, all I could think about was her—how stiff she sat, how silent she was, how that one-second glance she gave me at the start said everything and nothing at all.

People stand, gathering laptops and papers, casual small talk picking up around the table.

I don't move.

She starts to get up, collecting her things like everyone else.

"Octavia," I say, voice low, just loud enough for her to hear.

She pauses.

I tilt my head slightly toward the hallway. "Office. Now."

She doesn't argue. She just nods and falls into step beside me, her face unreadable.

I don't speak as we walk. I wait until the door shuts behind us, the click of the lock sounding louder than it should in the quiet.

Then I turn to face her.

"What the fuck happened?"

She stiffens, just barely. But it's enough to tell me I'm right—something definitely happened.

"You were fine this morning," I say, stepping closer. "Now, you're wound tighter than a tripwire and acting like you're trying not to shatter in front of the whole damn company."

Her jaw tightens.

"Don't say you're fine either," I warn, a little softer. "Don't lie to me."

I watch her carefully; she hasn't shut down.

Not completely.

She's just trying to hold it together long enough to tell me what I already fucking know—I'm going to want to kill someone when I hear it.

She doesn't answer, just stands there, arms crossed, breathing too evenly like she's trying to keep herself from coming apart. And that silence?

It pisses me off more than I want to admit.

"I need you to talk to me," I say, low and hard. "Right now."

Her arms still folded across her chest, like she's trying to contain herself. Her eyes flick away, toward the window, the floor, anywhere but me.

Something inside me snaps.

"I'm not asking as your boss, Octavia. I'm not even asking as the man who's been inside you more times than I can count this weekend. I'm asking as someone who gives a fuck about you. Who's already picturing which corner of the city I'm going to burn down based on whatever the hell's got you this broken."

Her jaw tightens. Finally, she exhales and crosses the office, opens the door just long enough to disappear around the corner.

When she comes back, her phone is in her hand.

That tells me everything I need to know.

She had to walk away from it. Shut it off. Hiding it from herself.

She powers it back on in front of me.

When the screen lights up and the messages load, she doesn't say a word—just holds it out to me.

I take it, and I read.

Unknown Number

Hope you got some rest. You'll need it.

He said that to me once too. I was there when he built his empire. You're just a version. I was the original.

A slow, cold fury rolls through me.

I hand it back and walk behind my desk, pressing my hands flat against it like it'll keep me from putting my fist through the goddamn wall.

"She sent that today?"

Octavia nods. "Right after I sat down."

I stare out the window for a second, jaw locked so tight it feels like I may break a tooth.

"She's grasping at straws," I mutter. "Throwing out whatever she can to stay relevant."

I turn back toward her.

"She doesn't know what we are. She never will."

Octavia just stares at the floor like part of her still wants to crawl out of her skin and tear someone apart.

"She's pushing you," I say. "Trying to crack you open just enough so you'll fall apart in public. So she can prove you were never strong enough to have me."

I move around the desk again, closing the space between us slowly.

"But you already have me, baby."

She lifts her head slowly.

There's something different in her eyes now. Still wild, still furious, but focused. Like the switch has flipped.

"I'm ready," she says, voice low. Steady. "I want to plan this out. I want her gone."

I don't ask if she's sure.

"Okay," I say. "I'll call Marcus."

She shakes her head. "Not just Marcus."

Her voice sharpens. There's no hesitation. No second-guessing.

"I want Lena in this, too."

I study her for a second. Not because I'm doubting her, but because I'm weighing what it means. How far she's willing to go, how far we'll all have to go once this starts.

"You trust her with this?" I ask.

Octavia meets my eyes dead-on. "I'd trust her with my life."

That's enough for me.

"Alright," I say, already pulling my phone out. "Then we bring them both in."

I scroll to Marcus's name and dial.

He picks up on the second ring.

"Tell me this is about something more interesting than Hartwell projections," Marcus says dryly.

"It is," I say. "We've got a problem."

"Sophia?"

"Yeah."

"How bad?"

"She's been texting Octavia. Found a way to rattle her at the office. Playing mind games, trying to drag her into some delusional pissing contest."

"Bold," Marcus mutters. "Stupid."

"She's pushing too hard. I think she knows she's out of time."

"Okay," he says, instantly shifting gears. "What do you need?"

I glance over at Octavia. She hasn't moved.

"We're going to plan something," I say.

"Say less," Marcus replies. "I'm in."

"And Octavia wants Lena involved."

That catches him off guard.

He exhales, slow and low. "Does Lena know what she's signing up for?"

"She will," I say. "Octavia trusts her."

"Alright. I'll loop her in. Where are we meeting?"

I look at the clock.

"Tonight. My place. Eight."

"I'll be there," he says. "And I'll bring her."

The line clicks off.

I slide the phone back into my pocket and look at Octavia.

"Eight o'clock. They're coming to the penthouse."

She nods once. No smile, no relief.

Just that same fire burning behind her eyes.

"Good," she says. "Because I'm fucking done waiting. This bitch has gone too far."

"You want to stay here?" I ask quietly. "Keep working like nothing happened?"

She doesn't answer right away. Her shoulders are still locked, her breathing shallow. I know that look—she's barely keeping her cool.

So I move in closer, drop my voice low.

"Or..." I murmur, "I can bend you over my desk and *really* make you forget."

Her eyes snap up to mine, wide for just a second, and there it is, that flicker of fire I've been waiting to see. Her mouth opens like she might say something, but nothing comes out right away. Just a sharp breath and a flush in her cheeks that makes every part of me tighten.

I smirk.

"There she is."

She blinks once, then shakes her head slightly. "You're ridiculous."

"And you love it."

She doesn't bother denying it. That tension in her shoulders finally eases—not all the way, but enough to breathe again.

I lean back a bit, giving her room. "But seriously. We can leave. Reset. No distractions. No noise. Just us—getting clear before we do this right."

She holds my gaze for a second longer. "Yeah. Let's go."

I walk to the door and crack it open.

"Derek," I say, just loud enough for him to hear across the hall.

He looks up from his desk immediately. "Yes, sir?"

"In my office. Now."

There's no hesitation. He grabs his tablet and follows me inside, closing the door behind him. His eyes dart between me and Octavia, reading the tension in a heartbeat.

"Something wrong?"

"We're leaving," I say, voice calm but clipped. "I need you to handle the office, everything. Meetings, follow-ups, press filters, all of it."

His brow furrows just slightly. "May I ask why?"

I meet his gaze dead-on.

"Sophia."

That's all it takes. His mouth presses into a tight line, posture shifting like he just clicked into a different mode.

"She's been harassing Octavia all morning. Texts. Manipulation. Trying to destabilize her."

Octavia says nothing, she doesn't need to. The silence around her says enough.

Derek nods once, jaw tightening. "Understood. Do you want me to start a digital trace?"

"Not yet. I don't want to spook her. Let her think we're off balance."

He gives another nod, more subtle this time. "I've got it covered."

I glance at Octavia, then back at him. "Keep your phone on. I may need you later."

"I'm ready," he says simply, as he steps out, closing the door behind him without another word.

I look back at Octavia as I grab my jacket off the back of my chair. "Let's go, baby."

We leave the office in silence, the hallway unusually still around us. She walks beside me, all tension and intent, every step coiled like a loaded spring. I can feel it building in her—the pressure, the weight, something steady and dangerous.

We step into the elevator, and I press the button for the garage. The second the doors close, I turn to her.

She doesn't move. Her arms are still at her sides, her eyes forward like she's trying to hold herself together.

I pin her to the wall with one hand and take her mouth with ruthless control. No warmth. Just command. No warmth. Just command. A silent claim she can't ignore.

All that tension between us, all that fire just under the surface—I let it break through.

My hand finds her hip. Not to anchor her, but because I *need* to touch her. I need her to remember exactly where she stands in this storm.

She responds instantly, her hand fisting in the front of my shirt, and for a few seconds, the whole world pulls tight around us.

When I pull back, I press my forehead to hers.

"She won't get near you or me again," I say. "It ends tonight. However, you need it to."

She doesn't say anything, but her fingers tighten slightly against me.

"I love you." the words slip from my mouth, but I don't regret it.

The words hang between us, heavier than anything else I've said today.

CHAPTER TWENTY NINE

Octavia

For a second, I forget how to breathe.

He says it so easily. Like it's always been sitting on the tip of his tongue, waiting for the moment to come out.

I love you.

Three words.

Dropped like a bomb between us, right there in the elevator.

I don't know what I was expecting when he kissed me—maybe some release, some twisted comfort in the middle of all this madness. But not this, not something so... *real.*

I blink, trying to steady myself, but my thoughts scatter.

My fingers are still curled in his shirt, knuckles white. I feel his breath against my cheek, warm and steady, like he's giving me time. Not pushing, just waiting.

I pull back slightly, enough to see his face.

There's no panic in his eyes, no regret. Just that same brutal, unwavering focus.

He meant it and that scares the shit out of me.

Because I thought I was the one sinking. I thought I was the only one falling. But he's already there.

Now he's pulling me with him—with softness, with fury, with love.

I swallow hard, but my throat feels like it's closing.

"Dominic," I breathe, and it's all I can manage.

Because if I say anything else, I might fall apart.

And I can't—not yet.

His thumb brushes just barely over my hip. Still close, steadying me. "You don't have to say anything back," he murmurs. "That's not why I said it."

I blink up at him, throat still raw, heart pounding so hard it almost hurts.

"I mean it," he adds, voice lower now. "Whether you're ready to say it or not, it doesn't change a damn thing."

The elevator descends like nothing's happened—like my whole world hasn't just shifted sideways in my chest.

I look at him, really look, and my stomach clenches like it's bracing for impact—because loving him feels a lot like falling off a ledge.

I press my forehead back to his, just for a second. I still don't speak, but the way his breath catches tells me he understands.

When the doors slide open, we step out together. The air is cool, sharp, but it barely registers. All I can think about is how tonight we're planning to kill someone—and somehow, *this* is what has me trembling.

Not the blood, not the crime.

But *him*.

The way he loves me without expecting anything in return.

The car is quiet. Dominic's hand rests on the wheel, steady as ever. The city passes in a blur outside the window—gray skies, wet pavement, that constant drizzle Seattle wears like a second skin. I should say something. But I'm still trying to process the three words he dropped like a grenade with the pin already pulled in the elevator.

I love you.

He said it simply. Like it wasn't something I've been terrified to admit.

My phone buzzes in my lap, and for once, I'm grateful for the distraction.

LENA

So... we still meeting at Dominic's tonight or did things go nuclear after dinner part two?

I stare at the message for a second, then type back.

ME

Yeah. Eight. Bring whatever you want. Just be ready.

Three dots pop up for a quick second.

LENA

Cool. Should I bring wine, snacks... or, like, a shovel?

A laugh slips out of me before I can stop it.

Dominic glances over. "Lena?"

"Mm-hmm."

"She's asking about snacks or body disposal?"

"She's leaning on shovel."

He nods, like that's the most reasonable thing in the world.

I turn back to the window, smiling faintly despite the storm still crawling under my skin.

ME

Bring both. It's time.

She doesn't reply right away, but a minute later a gif pops up—someone dragging a suitcase with chaotic determination.

God, I fucking love her.

I tuck my phone away and let my head fall back against the seat.

The hum of the engine, the rhythm of the rain, Dominic's presence beside me—it's the first time all day I've felt like I could breathe without shaking.

But I don't let myself relax too much. Because tonight isn't just about planning, it's about delivering the final blow.

I stare out the window as the city slips by in blurred streaks of gray and light, my reflection faint in the glass.

I can't believe I'm really about to go through with this.

Killing someone, actually ending a life.

The worst part about it is that it should scare me. But some sick, twisted part of me is *excited*.

Not just because Sophia deserves it—though she does.

But because I've never felt this kind of clarity before.

Like my rage finally has somewhere to go. Like all the fear and helplessness that's been choking me since the moment she slithered back into his life is about to be erased with one final decision.

I don't feel sick about it; I don't feel guilty.

I feel fucking *ready*.

Like I've been heading toward this moment since the second she touched what was mine.

I glance over at Dominic, his profile sharp as his free hand drifts over and squeezes my thigh gently.

He hasn't said a word, hasn't tried to talk me down. He just drives, like he knows I need the silence to keep building this thing inside me. He trusts I'll come to him when it's time.

And I will. Because this isn't just revenge, it's *closure*.

And I'm going to enjoy every second of watching her fall apart.

We pull into the garage beneath the penthouse just as the clouds start to break. The last of the rain slides down the windshield in slow, heavy streaks, giving way to slivers of light.

Dominic parks in his usual spot. The engine cuts off, and we sit there for a second—both of us staring straight ahead, wrapped in the weight of what we are doing tonight.

He gets out first, rounding the car without a word. When he opens my door, I meet his eyes for half a second—steady, unreadable—before stepping out. My heels click against the concrete as we make our way to the elevator, the silence between us saying more than either of us will.

By the time the doors open into the penthouse, the storm outside is fading, and a pale golden light is filtering in through the windows, casting everything in a strange, almost calm glow.

But there's nothing calm about what I feel.

I kick off my shoes the moment I step inside and toss my bag onto the couch like I'm shedding the last layer of whatever I used to be.

Dominic heads to the bar, pouring a glass of whiskey. "You want one?"

"Maybe later."

I pace toward the window, arms folded, tension still pulsing under my skin.

He takes a sip and watches me carefully. "We need to talk about how you want to do this."

"I've been thinking about that," I say quietly.

He waits.

"Shooting her would be easy, right?" I ask, turning toward him.

He nods. "Clean. Fast. Low risk. Easiest to control."

I tap my lips, contemplating. The idea of ending it quick... it's tempting. Logical.

But it just doesn't feel right.

"I'm not sure I want easy," I say.

His brow lifts slightly, but he doesn't interrupt.

"I have years of rage in me, Dominic. From Tyler. From everything

I've swallowed just to survive. And now she's here, pushing every fucking button, thinking she can crawl back into your life like she didn't already get discarded like the pile of dog shit she is."

I walk to the center of the room, suddenly restless.

"I don't want it to be simple. I want her to *know*. I want her to feel fear. Regret. Pain."

My voice is flat, not emotional. Not loud.

He nods once, slow and steady.

"Then we'll do it your way," he says. "Whatever you need, however far you want to take it, we'll make it happen."

I pace, words tumbling out before I can even think to filter them.

"Maybe I hang her from the top of the fucking Space Needle. Upside down. Naked. Broadcast it live."

Dominic chokes on his drink.

I keep going, too wound up to care.

"Or I rent a damn billboard downtown—plaster it with photos of her screaming while I carve every lie she ever told into her skin. Let everyone see what kind of person she really is."

He's full-on laughing now. Low, amused, head shaking.

"What?" I snap, even though the edge in my voice is mostly for show.

He sets his glass down, smirking. "You really spiraled past practical homicide and landed in a villain origin story."

I fold my arms. "I'm just spit balling."

"Yeah, well, unless you've got a black market harness rig and a helicopter budget, the Space Needles off the table."

I crack a smile despite myself. "I don't have helicopter money, but you do," I say sarcastically.

He steps closer, more serious now, voice soft but steady.

"I do, baby, I have the money to buy the damn helicopter, but that is beside the point. If you want her to suffer," he says, "we don't need theatrics. We just need time. Somewhere private. Somewhere she doesn't see coming."

I nod slowly; the rage cooling into something more consuming.

"I want her scared," I say. "I want her to *know* she's not getting out."

"Then we take her alive," he says. "We can sedate her. Move her somewhere remote. Let her wake up to you. Just you. No escape. No help. If that is the way you want to do it."

I look up at him. "And what do I do then?"

He holds my gaze. "Whatever the hell you want."

I sit on the couch, heart still thrumming, slightly slower now.

Whatever I want.

The words settle under my skin, warm and alive. My fingers twitch against my knee. My mind's already spinning—timing, logistics, the quiet satisfaction of being in complete control.

She has no idea what's coming. But I do.

And that's the part I like best.

"You already have somewhere in mind, don't you?" I ask, eyes narrowing on him.

Dominic doesn't even hesitate. "Yeah."

Of course he fucking does.

He walks around the couch and drops into the seat beside me, leaning forward, elbows on his knees.

"There is an old safehouse just outside of the city. Hardly anyone knows it exists, and the people who do... know better than to ask questions. Soundproof, isolated. No cameras. No neighbors. No cell signal."

I stare at him.

"That's terrifyingly convenient."

He shrugs. "Wasn't meant for anything legal."

I nod slowly, tension settling deep in my spine like something ready to be unleashed.

I grab my phone off the coffee table, unlocking it without thinking, and I text Lena.

ME

Can you and Marcus come early? I need your crazy ass here before I start thinking I'm the only lunatic in the room.

She replies so fast, I wonder if she was already holding the phone.

LENA

Bitch, I knew you would need me to be there early. I am already dressed. Marcus is almost here. Be there in twenty.

I stare at her message, and finally—finally—feel like I can breathe.

Because if anyone can make murder feel like a group bonding activity, it's Lena.

I look over at Dominic. "They're on their way."

"Good."

Dominic leans back, resting his arm along the back of the couch, eyes still on me, unreadable in that way that only he can pull off.

"This won't be like Tyler," he says quietly.

I glance at him, pulse stuttering just a little.

"What do you mean?"

"You watched me kill him," he says, voice low, even. "You didn't hesitate. You didn't back away. But you weren't the one to end his life."

He doesn't say it like he's doubting me. There's no judgment in his voice. Just a fact.

"This time," he adds, "it's going to be *you*."

The room feels heavier suddenly.

I sit with it, that weight. Let it press into me, sink down to the marrow of my bones. Because he's right.

This won't be the same, it isn't watching.

This is doing.

Seeing the blood, hearing her voice go quiet, taking her last breath and knowing *I* made that happen.

I want the blood on my hands. I want the scream. The silence after. The proof that I'm not the same girl who used to lie there while Tyler fucked me when he came home wasted and I would tell him no. The girl who bit her tongue through the bruises and let him turn her body into his personal outlet, who scrubbed blood off the bathroom tile like it was just another chore.

I never expected this to feel like clarity. But it does. Like I've been waiting my whole life to *finally* let all of this out. The rage. The ache. The parts of me I had to swallow just to survive.

And the best part?

Lena's in. She didn't even ask why.

She just nodded.

Ride or die. Literally.

What the fuck kind of life is this?

And why does it feel so good?

"I know."

He studies me for a moment longer, then gives a small nod.

The elevator dings, and a second later, the doors slide open.

Marcus steps out first, calm and composed in that lethal way that always makes him seem like he just left a board meeting *or* a body behind. Lena's right behind him, hair up, combat boots on, her jacket half-zipped and eyes already scanning the room like she's looking for blood splatter.

"Didn't think we'd be back here so soon," Marcus says casually, tossing a glance toward Dominic.

"No one ever does," Dominic mutters.

Lena makes a beeline for me, arms open like she might hug me, but she grabs both my shoulders and gives them a squeeze.

"You good, babes?"

I huff. "Good enough."

She tilts her head. "You ready to kill this fucking plastic barbie bitch?"

"More than ready."

"Yesss, that's what I am talking about. Love that for you."

Marcus walks toward the kitchen, dropping a black duffel bag onto the counter. It lands with a heavy *thump*. "Alright," he says, unzipping it partway to reveal... rope, gloves, duct tape, and a couple things I don't even want to ask about yet. "What's the plan?"

Everyone looks at me.

It hits me that I'm not following someone else's lead. This is *my* plan.

I take a breath and look at Dominic, who just gives me the smallest nod—solid, steady, like a silent I've-got-you.

Then, I turn to them.

"We're going to take her somewhere quiet," I start, voice steady. "Somewhere no one will find her. Then, I'm going to make her regret ever fucking with me."

Marcus pulls out a tablet from the bag, tapping the screen a few times as he logs into whatever surveillance he has access to. "Give me a sec," he murmurs. "let's see if our girl's been stupid enough to leave a trail."

I cross my arms, pacing slowly. My phone buzzes on the counter.

UNKNOWN NUMBER

You looked so confident at work today. Almost like
you forgot who he used to come home to.

My blood runs cold.

I pick it up with a hand that's way too steady for what I feel churning under my skin.

Dominic is already walking toward me. I hold the screen up without a word.

He reads it, jaw clenching hard enough to crack stone.

Lena leans over my shoulder. "This bitch for real has a death wish."

Marcus glances up from the tablet. "Got her."

We all turn to him.

He tilts the screen toward us. A small map with a blinking dot.

"She's at a spa in Bellevue. One of those 'wellness retreats' that's really just cucumber water and overpriced body wraps."

My heart pounds in this calm, calculated way I've never felt before.

"That's her last stop," I say.

And I mean it. Dominic's already moving.

He crosses the room without a word, disappears down the hall toward one of the back rooms where he keeps the real shit in the safe—stuff that's not legal, no serial numbers, and never meant to be found.

Lena's beside me. Her grin is gone now and has been replaced with something more serious, calculating.

"You sure you don't want to rough her up first?" she asks lightly, cracking her knuckles. "Or do I wait until you're done with her?"

I almost smile.

"You'll get a turn to torture her. But I am going first."

She gives a mock bow. "As you wish, execution queen."

Marcus snaps his tablet case shut and grabs the duffel. "I'll drive, Lena rides with me. Dom, you're taking Octavia."

Dominic reappears, calm as ever, gloves in one hand, and a handgun holstered under his jacket, just in case things don't go according to plan. Seeing him like this stirs something in me. It's so damn sexy.

I don't need to ask what else he grabbed. I know we will have everything we need.

He walks right up to me, holds out a knife. It's not pretty or flashy. This one's brutal. Serrated, made for pain, not mercy.

"You ready?" he asks.

I take the blade, feel the weight of it settle in my hand. Cold. Heavy. Real. My grip tightens, knuckles whitening as something hot crawls up my spine—slow, mean, familiar. Rage, sharp and unfiltered, pressing against my ribs like it's been waiting for this.

"Yeah," I say, meeting his eyes. "Let's end this."

Without another word, we move.

No turning back.

CHAPTER THIRTY

Octavia

The knife sits in my lap as Dominic drives, tucked neatly beneath a folded towel, like we're heading out for a weekend getaway and not a fucking execution.

The city lights blur past the windows, and I can feel the tension rolling off him, thick and crackling, but he doesn't say a word.

This isn't the kind of moment that needs conversation.

This is the kind you *feel*—in your teeth, in your bones, in the steady beat of your heart as you barrel toward something that will change you forever.

I catch a glimpse of Lena and Marcus in the SUV behind us from the side mirror. Marcus is driving like a man with nothing to lose, and Lena's probably bouncing in her seat, high on the thrill of impending violence.

It hits me that I'm not scared, not even in the slightest.

I've never been more ready for something in my life.

Dominic changes lanes fast, taking the exit toward Bellevue. The spa's tucked behind rows of manicured hedges and overpriced silence. The place that women like Sophia pretend to find peace when all they're

really doing is hiding from the people they stepped on to get to the top.

Dominic pulls around to the back lot, the tires crunching softly over the wet gravel.

I lean forward, peering through the windshield.

"S-Class," Dominic murmurs, nodding toward the silver Mercedes parked near the far corner. "It's hers."

Marcus pulls in behind us, cutting his lights. He steps out first, scanning the lot before walking to my side of the car.

"She's still inside," he says. "Checked in under her alias. She's booked for a two-hour facial and massage. Room 6B, back hallway. Private entrance. We're not pulling her here."

Dominic leans over the steering wheel, voice quiet but certain. "We will wait."

The calm in his tone is colder than any threat.

Lena's leaning against the hood of Marcus's SUV, arms crossed, chewing gum like she's got all the time in the world and nothing better to do than witness a murder.

I glance at her. She catches my look and grins.

"You wanna key her ugly ass car while we wait?" she offers.

I snort. "Tempting."

But I'm not here for petty.

I'm here to paint the walls with her regret.

We wait in silence.

The sky's cleared now, the clouds splitting open just enough to let in a sickly sort of twilight—a faint, golden moon, almost peaceful.

The clock ticks.

Dominic remains beside me, still and quiet, eyes trained on the spa like a predator waiting for the moment to strike.

I feel every second crawl over my skin.

My heart is steady, but inside, I'm already playing it out.

What I'll say, what I'll do.

How she'll look when it hits her that I'm not just angry anymore, when she realizes she is already fucking dead.

The door swings open and Sophia steps out into the glow of the moon, sunglasses on despite it being dark, phone pressed to her ear, and she's laughing.

Fucking *laughing*.

Her hair's up in some effortless looking fucking pony tail, her bag hanging off one elbow like a fashion statement. She tells whoever is on the phone she has to go. Then she is holding her phone up, looking at herself in the forward facing camera, adjusting her jacket with a self-satisfied little smirk.

I don't even feel my nails biting into my palms until Dominic touches my arm, grounding me with just one look.

"Wait," he murmurs.

I hold.

Sophia gets to her car and that's when Lena peels off from the SUV, casual, hands in her jacket pockets as she strolls right toward her.

"Heyyy," Lena says, voice chipper. "Aren't you the bitch who caught hands at Canlis the other night?"

Sophia freezes.

Whips her head up, brows knitting as she turns to face her.

"What the hell—"

That's as far as she gets.

Marcus comes up behind her in complete silence, the syringe already primed. One quick jab at the base of her neck and it's over.

Sophia's eyes go wide. She tries to turn, but her knees buckle first.

Dominic's already moving.

He and Marcus catch her before she hits the ground, smooth and practiced. No one even sees. No one hears.

She's out fucking cold.

Dominic throws open the back of the SUV, and they haul her in like luggage—efficient, quiet, deliberate.

Lena circles back toward me, all grin.

"God, that was so satisfying," she mutters. "She went down like a deflated blow-up doll."

I stare at the crumpled, unconscious body now stretched across the backseat.

My pulse doesn't spike, my stomach doesn't turn.

All that fills me is this dark, rising calm.

"Let's go," I say, voice like steel. "It's time."

We follow behind them.

Marcus's SUV stays just ahead on the highway, taillights glowing red through the soft mist clinging to the road.

Dominic drives, one hand on the wheel, the other resting loosely on the center console between us. The drone of the tires on the pavement is the only sound for a while. The city's long gone now—replaced by towering evergreens and darkness that's stretched out in every direction.

He glances at me, then back to the road.

"How are you feeling?"

The question cuts through the silence. He already knows the answer, but he asks anyway.

I stare at the SUV ahead of us.

"Calm," I say. "Too calm, maybe."

"You expected panic."

"I expected *something*. A voice in my head screaming that this is insane. That I've crossed a line I can't come back from."

He's quiet for a second.

"And?"

I exhale slowly. "I don't hear a thing."

He nods once, like that tracks.

I rest my elbow on the window and press my knuckles to my mouth, watching the way the trees whip past in the headlights.

"There's no guilt," I say softly. "No hesitation. Just this cold… certainty."

He says nothing, but I see it in his profile. He understands that feeling better than anyone.

The drive stretches on, and we say nothing more.

Ahead of us, Marcus takes the final turn down a side road that disappears into thick forest.

The gravel crunches under the tires as Dominic pulls in behind Marcus and Lena. His SUV's already parked outside the safehouse—if you can even call it that. From the outside, it looks like an abandoned cabin swallowed by trees. No windows out front. No lights. Just wood, shadow, and silence.

"You want to see it first?" he asks, his tone unreadable.

I nod.

He doesn't follow me right away, just hands me the keys and lets me take the lead.

The air is sharp and cold as I step out. Pine needles scatter under my boots, the faint scent of damp earth rising with every step. The forest is watching—like it already knows what's about to happen—like it's seen it many times before.

Lena meets me on the front porch, arms crossed, chin lifted like we're casing a crime scene instead of prepping for one.

She smirks. "Babes, this place practically screams, 'no one will hear you.' It's fucking perfect."

I unlock the door and push it open. The hinges groan.

Inside, it's dim. The walls are bare wood, the floor cold concrete. There's a single metal chair in the center of the main room and a heavy steel table pushed against the far wall. A drain in the floor catches my eye. There are hooks bolted to the beams overhead. For what, I can already guess.

I walk a slow circle through the space, each step echoing louder than I expect. My fingers trail across the edge of the table, across the back of the chair. The air in here is still thick.

It's quiet, *too* quiet.

I hear Lena's boots behind me.

She whistles low. "Girl. I've seen horror movies start like this."

I glance back at her. "And?"

She grins. "Can't wait to see how this one ends."

She leans in the doorway, arms crossed, watching me with that casual sort of chaos only she can pull off.

"So," she says, "do we have a murder playlist, or are we just going full ambiance and letting the blood and torture do the talking?"

I glance at her, brow raised. "What would even be on a murder playlist?"

She taps her chin. "Something dramatic. Cinematic. Maybe Halsey's villain era or some angry underground shit with a beat that says *bury the body.*"

I snort. "Please don't make this an aesthetic."

She grins. "Too late, babes. You're giving main character energy with a side of war crimes."

I shake my head but can't help the way the corner of my mouth twitches up.

She steps further into the room, giving the place a slow once-over. "Honestly? Ten out of ten murder vibes in here. You did fucking good."

"I didn't pick it," I murmur, half distracted by the space.

"Still. The atmosphere is killing it. No pun intended."

I glance back at her, my voice quieter. "You think I've lost it?"

She scoffs. "Octavia, you dragged a woman by her extensions in a five-star restaurant without hesitating. I knew you had it in you."

I bite back a real smile.

She moves closer, voice softening just a little—just enough to slip past my walls.

"You're not crazy. You're just done playing nice. And for the record? I'm here to help you bury the body, and I brought snacks."

I look at her, really look at her.

She'd never talk me down, never ask me to stop—she'd just hand me the knife and say, "don't miss any arteries."

And right now, that's exactly what I need.

The silence settles for maybe ten more seconds before the door creaks open behind us.

Dominic steps inside, his expression unreadable. "She's coming to."

Everything in me goes still.

"She's restrained?" I ask.

He nods. "Hands secured, ankles too. Marcus is keeping her steady for now. You ready to bring her in?"

Lena glances at me like she already knows the answer, but she waits anyway.

I straighten my shoulders.

"I'm ready."

Dominic holds my gaze for a second, then turns and walks back out.

Lena stretches her arms and cracks her neck like she's getting ready for a yoga class. "This is so much better than therapy."

I let out a breath that mimics a laugh.

But it doesn't last.

Because the moment I step into that hallway, everything intensifies.

Marcus is waiting just outside the door, standing next to the slumped, half-conscious form of Sophia.

I stand above her, arms crossed as I stare down at the mess she's already becoming—mascara smudged, hair plastered to her cheek, drool collecting at the corner of her mouth.

She mumbles something incoherent, barely more than breath and vowels. Her eyelids flutter but don't quite open.

"She goes in the chair," I say.

Dominic and Marcus exchange a glance, but no one questions it.

Marcus grabs her under the arms, Dominic takes her legs, and they lift her like dead weight. She's limp, still floating somewhere between sedation and panic.

Lena holds the door for them, eyes flicking over Sophia with the disgust usually reserved for roadkill and ruined shoes.

"Careful with her," Lena mutters. "Wouldn't want her to bruise before the main event."

I step aside as they carry her in, every footstep echoing like a countdown. The chair waits in the center of the room, and they lower her into it.

Sophia groans, sluggish and dazed, head tipping forward.

Marcus and Dominic move quickly, checking the restraints around her wrists and ankles, cinching them tighter with an efficiency that has my stomach fluttering.

She jerks weakly, still half out of it.

"Wha...what is...?"

Her voice cracks. Muddled and slurred.

Dominic crouches beside the chair, securing the final strap around her thigh.

"She'll be alert in a minute or two," he says, glancing up at me. "And she'll feel *everything*."

"Good." I step forward, right in front of her. "Let her wake up."

CHAPTER THIRTY ONE

Octavia

She wakes up slowly, eyes fluttering, a twitch of her fingers.

A groggy sound that might be a question—might be her trying to remember what her own name is.

She shifts in the chair and immediately stiffens.

The restraints bite hard before her brain catches up. Ankles locked down, wrists strapped tight, the cold metal of the chair presses against her skin.

Her head lifts, sluggish and uneven, like her muscles forgot how to work.

Then she sees me, and I see the exact second recognition snaps into place.

"Wha—" Her voice is dry, cracked. "What... the fuck?"

I take a slow step forward, one hand on my hip, while my other hand twists the knife around.

"You look confused."

Her eyes dart around the room. No windows, no light but the one overhead and no one else to come to her rescue.

Just me and her.

She swallows and tries to sit up straighter. Tries—and fails—to look unbothered.

"What is this?" she rasps.

I smile, slow and hollow.

"Closure, baby."

She blinks again, like she's trying to process the word, make it mean something else.

Her voice wobbles. "Wait... look, the texts... they were *jokes*, okay?"

I raise an eyebrow.

She thrashes around, trying to pull her arms free, panic rising. "I meant nothing by them. I was pissed, sure, but it wasn't serious. Just stupid jokes."

I circle the chair slowly, the knife still twirling in my fingers.

"Right," I say flatly. "Just jokes."

She swallows. "Yeah. I was just messing with you. I didn't think you'd... I mean, I don't even *know* you."

"No," I murmur. "But you wanted me to break anyway."

Her eyes widen slightly, and I stop behind her.

"And now," I add, voice dropping, "you're the one that is going to be breaking."

Sophia's eyes widen, pupils dilating with fear.

"Octavia, this isn't... this isn't funny," she stammers, her voice trembling as she pulls against the restraints. "Dom will—"

"Dom, will *what*?" I step in, the knife catching the overhead light as I twist it in my fingers. "Call the cops? What, like you're some tragic little fucking princess locked in a tower—hoping your knight in shining armor shows up before the dragon gets hungry?"

Her face drains of color.

"He's the one who helped me set this up."

She blinks. "You're lying."

I smile, slow and cruel. "Am I?"

I take another step, circling the chair, my eyes never leaving her.

"You know what he did when he saw the texts you sent me? When he read your pathetic little attempts to get under my skin? *Hope you got some rest. You'll need it. He said that to me too. I was there first.*"

She flinches.

"He laughed," I say. "Then he kissed me and told me he'd *never* go near your whore ass again."

Her mouth opens like she's going to protest, but nothing comes out.

I lean in, slowly, until I'm right beside her ear.

"He's not thinking about you, Sophia. He's not angry, he's not even bothered, he's fucking *done.*"

She tries to shrink away, her shoulders curling in towards herself.

I step around to face her again and I grab her by the cheeks, making her look right at me.

"You keep calling them jokes," I say. "The texts, the threats, that desperate little stunt at dinner like you were auditioning for a sequel no one asked for."

I slam the knife down onto the metal table beside her—*clang.*

She jumps so hard it pulls her face from my grip and almost tips the chair.

"Let me be clear," I whisper. "You don't get to laugh at me. You don't get to crawl back into his life after everything you've already ruined."

Tears spill down her cheeks. "I didn't mean—"

"You meant every word," I snap. "You just didn't think I'd *answer back.*"

I pick up the scissors from the table and Sophia's sobs turn frantic when she sees them, body jerking uselessly against the restraints.

"Please," she whimpers. "Octavia, please—don't—"

I walk behind her, slow and deliberate, staring at the bun twisted at the back of her head.

I reach out and grab the tie at the base of her skull.

Then I *yank* hard.

Her head jerks back violently with the force of it, a sharp cry ripping out of her throat as the elastic snaps and her hair falls in tangled, sweaty waves around her face.

She's breathing hard now, mouth open in shock.

"See," I murmur, stepping closer, "that's better."

I fist a handful of it and twist it tight in my grip, forcing her head to tilt to the side, exposing her neck.

"You walked out of that spa like you owned the world," I whisper. "Like you were still someone he'd want."

The scissors glint in the light as I lift them.

"Let me fix that for you."

Snip.

The first chunk lands on the floor.

A jagged, uneven, ugly fucking mess.

She screams, voice cracking. "No…no! Please! Don't—"

Snip.

I keep going, vicious and meticulous, tearing through every perfect strand until what's left is a butchered disaster of uneven cuts and exposed scalp.

Tears streak her cheeks, and now she's shaking, not from the cold—but from the weight of it.

I drop the scissors, and her breathing is shattered. I lean in close, mouth just above her ear.

"Now," I whisper, "we can begin." I pick up the knife.

Sophia's eyes follow it like prey spotting a predator's teeth.

She whimpers. "Please—please, I'll disappear, I swear, I'll never go near him again—"

"*You* don't get to decide when this ends," I say flatly.

I crouch in front of her, and she flinches like the air itself might hurt.

"You think because you used to spread your legs for him that it meant something?" I ask, voice low, steady. "That you had some kind of right to try to weasel your way back in?"

She shakes her head, tears falling fast now, chest heaving with every broken sob.

"You know what I should do?" I tilt my head, knife resting on her knee. "I should fuck Dominic right in front of you."

Her face crumples.

"So you can finally see what it looks like when he actually *wants* someone."

She sobs like it's torn straight from her ribs.

I smile coldly and press the tip of the knife into the inside of her thigh, just enough to break skin.

She jerks, screaming, the sound bouncing off the walls like music.

I drag the blade slowly, letting it kiss her skin, carving a thin line down the soft, sensitive flesh. Blood wells in its wake.

"You're fucking pathetic," I say, quiet but venomous. "You had your chance, and you decided to fuck everyone else behind his back, and got jealous when he finally moved on."

She sobs harder. "Please, Octavia… I'm sorry—"

"Shut the fuck up," I snap, slapping her cheek with the flat of the blade.

She recoils as much as she can, bound to the chair, trembling so hard her teeth chatter.

"Let me be clear," I say, voice calm again. "This isn't revenge."

I press the blade to her again, her side this time, just under the ribs.

"This is *balance*."

I'm still crouched in front of her, blood on the knife, her tears dripping down onto her butchered hair scattered on the floor, when the door creaks open behind me.

Lena walks in like she's arriving at a fucking brunch.

"Holy *shiiiiiiit*," she says, dragging out the syllables with a grin. "Look at you. You look like someone shaved a poodle and gave it trauma."

Sophia whimpers, body jerking weakly.

Marcus is right behind her, calm and silent, setting a small kit down on the side table. I don't ask what's in it, I already know.

Then Dominic steps in.

Sophia lifts her head the second she sees him. Hope flashes across her face.

So fucking pathetic.

"Dom," she sobs, voice hoarse and shaking. "Please… please make her stop… she's gone insane, you have to,"

He doesn't even look at her. His eyes are on *me*.

"You doing ok, baby?" he asks, voice even.

I nod once. "Yeah. Just getting started."

Sophia's breath shudders. "Dom," she tries again, louder. "Please! You know me! This isn't… you can't let her—"

He finally looks at her and something in his face goes still.

"I don't know you," he says.

That breaks her more than the blade ever could.

Her mouth opens like she wants to argue, but no words come out.

Just air, just a soundless, broken sob.

Lena steps forward and crouches beside me, not touching, just watching.

"Damn," she whispers. "She's really not taking this well."

"No," I murmur, eyes still locked on Sophia's face. "But she asked for it."

Lena leans over to me, elbows resting casually on her knees like this is a goddamn sleepover and not a torture scene.

"She's a damn mess," she says, nodding toward Sophia's face. "But you know what'd really fuck with her?"

I glance at her. "What?"

Lena grins sadistically.

"You should cut off her fucking nipple."

Sophia screams instantly, wordless, pure panic.

Lena ignores her and continues. "Deadass. Leave her with just one. Real uneven, symbolic."

I actually pause, because that was *impressive*, even for her.

"Damn, Doll face, you are so damn sexy," Marcus mutters from the corner, admiring.

Dominic doesn't say a word. His expression unreadable, but he's not stopping anything.

Sophia thrashes in the chair, screaming louder now, tears and snot running down her ruined face.

"No… no, please! Please, don't… Octavia, please! I'll do anything! I'll disappear, I promise! You'll never hear from me again!"

"Should've done that in the fucking first place," Lena says sweetly.

I reach for the knife again, dragging the tip across Sophia's collarbone.

"No one's hearing from you after tonight," I say.

Her cries hitch—she knows it's real now.

I press the tip of the knife into Sophia's collarbone again, but this time I don't stop.

I *drive* it in.

Her scream shreds through the room, piercing and raw. The metal sinks in deep, sliding through soft tissue with a sickening resistance.

Her body jerks so hard the chair rattles beneath her.

"Oh, fuck yes!" Lena howls, clapping once like she's watching the finale of her favorite show. "There she is! That's my girl!"

I twist the blade slow—*mean*.

Sophia shrieks again, her whole body convulsing. Blood spills down her chest, warm and slick, soaking into the straps across her.

She sobs between gasps, mouth hanging open in broken shock. "Stop, please, *please!*"

I yank the knife out, and she wails like a wounded animal.

"Beg louder, bitch," I hiss, dragging the blade down her stomach now, leaving a long, shallow trail behind.

Lena leans in from behind, her eyes wide, delighted. "Carve something into her. Leave a signature."

That makes me grin.

I dig into the point just above Sophia's navel and start cutting slow, calculated letters.

S.

L.

U.

T.

She screams with every line.

Dominic steps in close behind me, his voice in my ear, dark and calm.

"You're magnificent."

I glance up at him, blood on my hands, chest heaving.

"I'm not done," I whisper.

He nods. "Good."

I press the blade to her thigh and stab again. She bucks hard in the chair, another ragged scream ripping from her throat. Blood spatters across my forearm.

Lena's breathless, pacing now. "This is *art*. I'd hang this shit in a gallery. Fuck."

"Do it again," she urges. "Cut her down. Bleed the bitch dry."

I do.

Again.

And again.

Sophia's barely upright, her body's limp, drenched in blood, trembling from the pain. She's whimpering now, no more screams, just these broken little sounds like she's running out of voice. Of fight.

I crouch in front of her, gripping her chin in my blood-slicked hand and forcing her face up to meet mine.

Her eyes flutter, she's fading.

But she sees me.

"You should've stayed gone," I whisper.

She tries to speak, lips barely moving. Another plea? Another excuse?

Too. Fucking. Late.

I raise the knife and slide the tip under her chin, dragging it up her throat with just enough pressure to make her pulse jump under the blade.

"You wanted to remind him who you were," I say, voice shaking with rage. "So let me show you what it looks like when he wants someone else."

Then I drive the blade straight into her throat.

She gurgles, choking on her own blood as it pours down her chest, thick and hot.

Her eyes go wide for one last second.

Then they glaze over, and just like that, she's gone.

I breathe hard, watching the last flicker of her disappear.

Then, I let go. She slumps in the chair, blood pooling fast under her feet.

The room is silent now, except for the dripping.

Drip. Drip. Drip.

I step back, covered in blood, shaking from adrenaline.

Lena exhales behind me, almost reverently. "Holy fuck."

Marcus nods once. "That was... thorough."

Dominic steps forward, slow and deliberate, and he reaches out to wipe a streak of blood from my cheek with his thumb.

His voice is low, rough. "That was the hottest fucking thing I've ever seen."

Each inhale tastes like iron. My lungs burn, chest rising and falling in shallow bursts, hands slick and dripping red—but all I feel is light. Euphoric. Like I just clawed something dark and rotten out of my chest and left it bleeding on the floor.

He steps closer, eyes burning into mine like he's ready to devour me right here, in the middle of this goddamn crime scene.

"I mean it," he murmurs, voice dark and reverent. "Watching you ruin her? *Perfect.*"

I stare at him, chest heaving.

And then I smile.

A slow, wicked smile, because I've never felt more wanted.

CHAPTER THIRTY TWO

Dominic

She stands there, drenched in blood, knife still dangling from her fingers, and all I can think about is how fucking beautiful she looks.

Ruthless. Unflinching. Unapologetic.

And she's all fucking mine.

Marcus steps up beside me, phone in one hand, calm as ever.

"Cleanup's already on the way," he says, voice low. I nod, eyes still locked on Octavia.

She hasn't moved. Her chest rises and falls with slow, measured breaths, like she's coming down from something wild. Something holy.

I step toward her, slow and deliberate. Blood streaks down her arms, painting her like something untouchable and holy. She doesn't look at me, she doesn't need to. I see it all—the tremble beneath the adrenaline, the quiet aftershock settling into her bones. I guide her back into me, her body hitting my chest like muscle memory.

"I've got you," I murmur.

I hold her close for a long minute, her body pressed to mine, her breath warming the side of my neck. Her skin's still tacky with blood, but I don't care.

She did it, and she didn't break.

She fucking *became.*

Lena's pacing off to the side, still buzzing.

I lean down, press my mouth to Octavia's temple. "Let's go home."

She nods against me, silent.

I guide her out, past the wreckage we left behind, past the chair, the blood, the body, and into the cold air. She doesn't look back.

Marcus glances up as we approach. "Derek got the car handled."

I nod and open the passenger door. Octavia climbs in without a word, curling into herself in the seat like her body's just now registering everything.

As soon as I'm in the driver's seat, I shoot off a quick text to Marcus.

ME

I need to get a ring.

Something good. Something her.

Have Lena find her size for me.

It's quiet in the car except for Octavia's breathing. She stares out the window, dried blood crusted on her cheek, hands in her lap.

I reach over and grab one of them, squeezing gently.

By the time we pull into the garage beneath the penthouse, the blood on her skin has fully dried and darkened. Her eyes are still distant, her body slack with exhaustion and the comedown from adrenaline. But she hasn't let go of my hand once.

I kill the engine and walk her to the elevator, keeping her close. Her steps are slow but steady.

When we get inside, she peels off her jacket and drops it in the entryway like it's too heavy to carry one second longer.

"You're covered," I murmur, stepping in behind her. "Let me take care of it."

She doesn't speak. Just nods.

I carry her to the bathroom, flipping the light on low, letting it fill the space. I set her in front of me, reaching in to turn on the water, waiting until the temperature's just right.

Then, I face her again. She looks wrecked, but *gorgeous*.

I reach for the hem of her shirt and pull it up slowly.

She doesn't stop me.

She lifts her arms and lets me strip her down, piece by piece. The bra goes next. Then, the pants. Her underwear's streaked with blood, but her skin underneath is perfect.

I undress next, fast and quiet, and step into the steam-filled shower first, holding out my hand.

She takes it.

The water hits us like heat and relief. She tilts her head back, eyes closed as it rushes down her face and over her shoulders, rinsing the blood down the drain in slow, red rivers.

I grab the soap and start at her neck, washing her gently, carefully, like she's something precious and worn thin, and only I know how to hold her right.

She watches me the whole time, her hands resting on my chest, her eyes unreadable.

"I love you," she says, so quietly it almost gets lost under the water.

My hands stop and my eyes snap to hers.

But she doesn't look away.

"I love you," she repeats, louder this time, steady and certain.

And fuck me—I've never wanted her more.

I say nothing, I just lift her.

One fluid motion—her legs wrap around my waist like muscle memory, her arms around my neck, and I pin her back gently against the shower wall.

Her lips crash into mine before I can speak, desperate and wild, like she's claiming me the same way she claimed *everything else* tonight.

I let her; I *want* her to.

I kiss her back like I need her to breathe, like the only thing keeping me sane in this fucked-up world is the way she tastes.

She pulls back for a second, panting, her forehead resting against mine.

"I've never felt more alive," she whispers, breath catching in a laugh. "Like... ever."

Then her voice drops a little, softer but unflinching.

"How fucked up is that?"

I stare at her, water cascading down her face, her skin still warm from the adrenaline and aftermath.

I press my mouth to hers again, slower this time, deeper. Then, I murmur against her lips, "It's the hottest fucking thing I've ever heard."

She grins, and I swear it goes straight to my chest and my cock at the same time.

"You're mine," I say, kissing along her jaw, down her neck, biting lightly. "All of it. Every dark, messy, perfect part of you."

She moans when I shift my hips forward, pressing her harder against the tile, her back arching, breath shuddering.

"Then, take it," she whispers. "Take *me*."

I don't wait. I slam into her.

She gasps—head tilting back, fingers digging into my shoulders as her body clenches around me.

So fucking tight. So fucking ready.

The water rushes over both of us, steam curling around her moans as I set a punishing rhythm, hips snapping forward again and again.

Every sound she makes goes straight to my dick, my grip tightening as I drive into her—fast, hard, unrelenting.

She doesn't ask for slower.

She meets me stroke for stroke, teeth biting into my neck, nails raking down my back.

I growl into her ear. "This pussy is fucking mine."

She whimpers, breathless. "Yes… fuck… Dominic,"

"This is what it means to be completely *wanted*."

Her mouth crashes into mine again, all tongue and hunger and fire.

She's shaking and so am I.

Her body tenses, and she gasps my name like it's the only thing she knows, *Dom, Dom, Dom*—and then she breaks apart around me.

It's fast. It's filthy. It's fucking perfect.

I follow her with a low groan, spilling into her as she shudders in my arms.

We don't move at first.

Just stand there—soaked, panting, tangled up in each other like we'll never let go.

Eventually, I reach out and shut the water off.

She leans against me, quiet, eyes half-lidded, chest rising and falling in steady rhythm. I wrap a towel around her and guide her out of the shower, kissing her temple as we move.

We make it to the bedroom slowly, dripping and warm, still flushed from everything we left behind tonight. I toss a towel onto the mattress and pull her down with me, both of us sinking into the softness like our bodies finally remember what rest is.

She curls into my side, one hand on my chest, the other tracing lazy circles across my skin.

For a while, neither of us says a word.

Then, I break the silence. "I want to take you somewhere," I murmur, voice low. "Out of the city, maybe somewhere tropical. No blood. No distractions. Just you and me."

She shifts, looks up at me, eyes soft but sharp. "A vacation?"

I nod. "Yeah, I need it. You need it."

A small smile tugs at her lips. "Can we bring Lena and Marcus?"

That catches me off guard. "Seriously?"

"They need it, too," she says, looking at me innocently before settling back against my chest. "Whether they admit it or not."

I think about it—Marcus trying to pretend he's not fucked up in his own quiet, detached way. Lena's mouth never stopping, always running, always covering. She's not wrong.

"Fine," I say, brushing a damp strand of hair behind her ear. "They can come. But I get you to myself every morning."

She grins, eyes glinting. "Greedy."

I kiss her shoulder. "Always."

She falls asleep against me, curled into my chest like she finally feels safe enough to let go.

Her breathing evens out, soft and steady, one arm draped across my stomach. I run my fingers through her damp hair, letting the silence settle around us.

I reach for my phone, careful not to wake her.

A message from Marcus is already waiting.

MARCUS

Lena got the size. She didn't even have to be subtle about it. Girl's bold as hell. Size 7.

I smirk.

ME

Thanks. And start prepping for a trip. Octavia requested you and Lena join us and she won't take no for an answer.

I swipe over to my browser, scroll through a dozen rings—none of them right. Too flashy. Too soft. Too impersonal.

Then I find it.

Clean design. Vintage cut. A little dangerous around the edges—just like her.

Perfect.

I snap a screenshot and fire off a quick message to Derek.

ME

Need this ring. Get it first thing tomorrow.

I lock the screen and set the phone down on the nightstand.

Then I turn back to her, pull her in closer, and close my eyes.

Tomorrow starts everything new.

CHAPTER THIRTY THREE

Dominic

I'm up before the sun. The city outside the windows is still dark, still quiet, just the occasional passing of headlights down below.

Octavia's still asleep, tucked under the sheets. She didn't stir when I slipped out of bed, just rolled onto her side and pulled the blankets tighter around her like the weight of last night had finally let her rest.

I grab my phone and step into the other room, closing the door behind me.

There's already a text from Derek waiting.

DEREK

Picked up the ring. Locked and secured. Want me to drop it today or hold it for after the trip?

I glance at the photo he sent—*Her* ring.

It's even better in the photo he took than it looked online.

ME

Bring it to me. Octavia is still asleep.

I open the travel app and scan through the itinerary again.

Booked. Private villa, oceanside, three nights—no obligations. Just us.

And Marcus and Lena, because, of course.

I click on Marcus's text thread and shoot off a quick message.

ME

The place is booked. Tell Lena, and for the love of God, don't let her overpack.

He responds instantly.

MARCUS

No promises. She's already got a full suitcase.

I smirk, pocket the phone, and glance down the hall toward the bedroom.

She doesn't know it yet, but by the end of this trip, I'll be on one knee.

And nothing—not the past, not Sophia, not Tyler, not a goddamn thing—is going to stop me this time.

There's a faint ding from the elevator, it has to be Derek. The doors open and he steps inside, dressed like he's heading to a board meeting and not delivering a fucking engagement ring.

He pulls a small black box from his coat pocket, discreet and unmarked, and he hands it to me.

"Got it," he says quietly. "No issues."

I pop it open with my thumb and look at it.

It's perfect, simple and timeless. *Her.*

Before I can say anything, I hear soft footsteps behind me.

I snap the box shut and slide it into my back pocket just as Octavia walks into the kitchen, rubbing sleep from her eyes, wearing one of my t-shirts and nothing else.

She pauses when she sees us, blinking. "Everything okay?"

Derek doesn't miss a beat. "Just dropping off some paperwork," he lies smoothly.

She frowns slightly, still half-asleep. "This early?"

He shrugs. "No time better than bright and early in the morning."

Derek catches my eye with a subtle nod.

"Text if you need anything else," he says, already heading for the door. "I'll be on standby."

I give him a tight nod. "Appreciate it."

Octavia pauses when she sees me alone.

"Drink up, buttercup. You need to pack." I say easily, already pouring her a cup of coffee.

She stares at me over the rim of the mug. "Pack?"

"Our flight leaves in three hours."

Her eyes narrow. "Flight to where?"

I lean in and kiss her cheek. "Somewhere without bloodstains and body bags. It's a surprise, little minx."

She freezes at first, then—*explodes.*

"You're taking me on a fucking vacation? Like actually? You only just brought it up last night! How do you already have it all planned out?" she gasps, nearly spilling the coffee in excitement.

Before I can even nod, she's bouncing in place, bare legs, wild hair, one of my shirts hanging off her like she's forgotten what pants are.

"Oh my God, oh my *God*—what do I pack? What do I *wear*? Are we going fancy or casual? Is there swimming? Hiking? Am I going to need boots or a bikini or both—"

I grab her by the waist mid-jump and kiss the side of her neck. "Expect it to be hot," I murmur. "Bring whatever you want to or nothing at all."

She pulls back just enough to narrow her eyes at me, already flushed and glowing.

"You're lucky I love a man who plans in chaos," she mutters, then bolts down the hall. "Where the *hell* are my sunglasses?"

I lean against the counter, watching her disappear, grinning like an idiot.

She reappears five seconds later, holding one shoe, her phone charger, and a tangled mess of hair ties like she just robbed the bottom of a junk drawer.

"Oh my *God*," she mutters, spinning in place. "I don't have shit here. Like—*none* of my real stuff. All my makeup, my flat iron, half my damn wardrobe. It's all at my place."

I lean against the counter, watching her spiral. "Do you need to run there?"

She whirls on me, eyes wide. "Yes. I need, like… everything. I packed three outfits and none of them match. Also, I don't know where my sunglasses went."

"You lost them in the ten minutes since you found them?"

"Don't come for me right now," she warns, already heading back toward the bedroom. "I'm fragile and *extremely excited*."

I grab my phone, glancing at the time. "You've got about thirty minutes before we need to leave. The driver's coming in forty."

Her head pops out from around the doorframe. "We have a *driver*?"

"Of course we do."

She grins. "You're really giving me the full villain's girlfriend experience."

I walk over and smack her ass. "You're not the villain's girlfriend. You're the fucking queen pin."

She pauses, visibly swooning for a second before snapping herself out of it.

"Okay, okay, I am going to go. I'll be fast."

"You?" I say, raising an eyebrow. "Fast?"

She flips me off but smiles as she runs to the elevator.

About twenty minutes have passed and Marcus walks in, casual as hell, duffel bag slung over one shoulder and a coffee in hand like we're heading out for a weekend conference—not flying to a villa with two emotionally volatile women and a ring burning a hole in my goddamn pocket.

Lena's right behind him, dragging a bright pink leopard-print suitcase that looks like it's packed for a month, sunglasses already on.

"You're early," I say, setting my mug down.

Marcus shrugs. "Figured we'd beat the chaos."

"She's not here?" Lena asks, glancing around.

"She went to grab stuff from her place. Didn't have much here."

Lena drops her bag and dramatically collapses onto the barstool. "So, we're really doing this. You're giving us sun and booze and emotionally unstable hot people. I could cry."

I laugh. "The driver's set to pick us up in, like, ten now. Octavia should be back soon."

Marcus walks to the counter and taps the side of the coffee pot. "So... are you doing it there? Or after?"

I give him a what the fuck look.

Lena perks up immediately. *"Doing what?* Oh my *God.* Wait. *WAIT."*

I don't answer. Just slip my hand into my pocket, pull it out and show her.

Lena practically levitates off the stool. "Shut the *fuck* up, Callahan. Ahhhhh!!!"

"Not a word," I mutter.

She zips her lips and acts like she is throwing the key over her shoulder, then immediately turns to Marcus and hisses, "This is going to be *so good."*

Octavia comes barreling in, out of breath, hair a mess, sunglasses crooked, tote bag slipping off her shoulder, and her other bag is hardly zipped.

She stumbles over the threshold—trips—*actually trips*, and lands hard on her knees with a muttered, "Son of a bitch!"

Lena *howls*.

Full-body, doubled-over laughter that echoes through the penthouse.

"Oh my God, you're like a baby deer on rollerblades," she wheezes. "You good, sweetie? Need a helmet?"

Octavia flips her off from the floor, face flushed. "I *was* doing great until gravity betrayed me like the bitch she is."

I shake my head, and lift her into my arms.

"Maybe I'll just carry you until we get to where we're going," I murmur, brushing a strand of hair out of her face. "So you don't injure yourself before the trip even starts."

Her arms wrap around my neck as she exhales. "That might actually be safer."

"You're ridiculous," I mutter.

She grins up at me, breathless. "Don't forget, adorable."

Lena's still laughing as she wheels her suitcase toward the door. "You two are going to be disgusting this whole trip, aren't you?"

Marcus deadpans, "They already are."

The black SUV is already waiting at the curb when we exit the building, engine idling, our driver standing by.

The driver opens the back door gesturing towards it. "Mr. Callahan."

Lena immediately claims the far window seat. "This seat is mine. Everyone else can fight for scraps."

Marcus slides in beside her without a word and I help Octavia into the middle, her bag dropped at her feet, and then climb in beside her, shutting the door as the driver rounds the front.

As we pull away from the curb, Octavia leans into me, her head on my shoulder. "I still can't believe this is real."

I kiss the top of her head. "Believe it. We're leaving everything else behind."

Lena kicks her feet up onto Marcus's lap. "If I don't come back with a tan, an orgasm, and at least one illegal souvenir, I'm suing."

Octavia laughs. "You're not allowed to steal anything live this time."

"No promises."

Marcus sighs. "This is going to be a long flight."

The car settles into a smooth rhythm as we cut through the city, the early morning sun just beginning to climb through the clouds. Octavia plays with the hem of my sleeve while Lena's already scrolling through vacation playlists on her phone.

"By the way," Lena says, glancing up. "Tell me you didn't fucking book coach."

Marcus gives her a look. "Do you see this man? He wouldn't survive commercial."

I smirk. "Private jet. No security lines, no screaming toddlers, no strangers. It's the only way I fly."

Octavia perks up. "Wait, *seriously?*"

"Dead serious, baby," I say. "I'm not flying you to paradise and cramming you next to some weirdo digging toe jam out of their sock mid-flight."

She laughs, fully leaning into me now, visibly relaxing. "Okay, I take it back. You do plan things well."

Lena stretches her arms overhead. "I love rich people. I love when my friends are rich people. And I love when my rich friends let me mooch."

Marcus doesn't look at her. "You didn't even offer to split snacks for the car ride."

She kicks his leg, grinning. "You'll miss me when I'm gone."

He glances sideways, dry as hell. "I'm counting on it."

She raises an eyebrow, lips twitching.

The corner of his mouth tips up, just barely.

Yeah. That spark's getting harder to ignore.

Octavia nudges me lightly. "If they start making out mid-flight, I'm blaming you."

"I'll take full credit," I murmur.

The SUV rolls to a stop on the private tarmac, pulling around to where the jet is already waiting. Dark and sharp-lined.

Octavia leans forward, pressing her hands to the window. "Wait… *that's* ours?"

Lena practically throws herself across her to get a better look. "Shut up. Shut up. That is not real."

I smirk. "It's real."

The driver opens the door, and both of them launch out like it's Christmas morning.

Lena spins in place, sunglasses still on, wind tossing her hair everywhere. "I swear to God, if there's champagne on board, I'm never flying commercial again."

Octavia stands frozen at the bottom of the stairs, staring up at the jet like it's a trick. "You planned all this?"

"I wasn't playing when I said we should go on vacation," I say, grabbing her bag.

She turns to me, mouth open like she's about to say something, then closes it and grabs my face instead.

"Okay," she whispers. "That's insane. And amazing. And you're… you."

"I try," I murmur, brushing a kiss against her mouth.

Lena's already halfway up the steps. "I need a drink. It's party time, bitches!"

Marcus trails behind her, dragging both of their bags. "I should've stayed home."

I help Octavia up the steps, her fingers laced tight with mine.

She glances back over her shoulder, still wide-eyed. "I can't believe this is real."

"You better," I say. "Because you haven't seen anything yet."

CHAPTER THIRTY FOUR
Octavia

I swear to God, this isn't real. The moment I step into the jet, it's like walking into some alternate universe where people like me get flown across the world in private planes with leather seats and built-in bars.

I pause just past the door, trying not to stare. The lighting is soft; the seats are massive, and there's chilled champagne already waiting like someone read Lena's mind.

"Holy shit," I whisper.

Dominic brushes past me, casually placing my bag in the storage area like he does this every day. Like this isn't completely over the top.

Lena's already kicked off her boots and claimed one of the recliners, stretching out like a damn cat. "Okay, yeah. We live here now."

She grabs a glass of champagne and lifts it like a toast. "To surviving, thriving, and excessive wealth."

Marcus slides into the seat across from her, silent as ever but not hiding the faint grin that pulls at his mouth when she bumps her foot into his knee like she's daring him to react.

Dominic gently guides me toward one of the window seats and sits

beside me. "How are you doing?"

"I'm somewhere between crying and having a full-body orgasm," I say honestly, still looking around. "You didn't have to do this."

"I know," he says, eyes steady on mine. "But I wanted to."

Something in my chest squeezes. Hard.

I lean my head on his shoulder as the engine roars to life.

"Thank you," I whisper.

He kisses my forehead. "We're just getting started."

Before I can say anything, he adds, "And don't look at me like I just handed you the moon. I'm a rich asshole, baby. Booking a jet's basically the same as ordering takeout at this point."

I snort, and he grins, brushing my hair back like it's nothing.

"You really think I'm not going to spoil the woman who literally killed for me?"

That makes me laugh—loud, real, a little unhinged.

"You're the worst," I mutter.

"Rich and the worst," he says, leaning back like he's already won. "Deadly combo." He winks and kisses my head.

"Alright," Lena calls from across the cabin. "I've decided something."

Marcus doesn't even look up. "God help us all."

She ignores him completely, already rummaging through the mini bar. "We're doing shots. We just got away with murder and we're on a private jet. This calls for tequila and questionable decisions."

"I don't think shots are a great idea mid-flight," Marcus mutters.

"That's because you're boring," she says, holding up four tiny bottles like she's just found buried treasure. "C'mon. One round. Celebrate the fact that we're not in jail." She pouts.

Dominic leans in close, his voice low. "You in?"

"Do I look like I'm going to be the only one sober while Lena yells about vibes and fake crimes?" I say.

He grins and stands. "That's my girl."

Lena passes out shots like we're in a club, not thirty-thousand feet in the air. She clinks glasses with me dramatically. "To hot people doing unhinged shit."

"To survival," I add.

Marcus raises his glass last, sighing. "To peace and quiet, may it find me again someday."

The tequila burns on the way down, but I don't care. I feel light, spinning, free.

The rest of the flight passes in a blur of music from Lena's phone, half-drunk banter, and the steady warmth of Dominic's hand on my thigh. At some point, I stretch out across two seats and fall asleep with my head in his lap, his fingers tangled in my hair.

For the first time in what feels like forever... I don't dream about blood.

Just sun and salt on my skin.

Fingers brush against my cheek. Soft and warm.

"Hey," Dominic murmurs, voice low and close. "We're here."

I blink slowly, eyes adjusting to the light filtering through the jet's windows. The sound of the engines has quieted, and everything feels still, like the whole world just paused.

I sit up groggily, rubbing at my eyes. "Already?"

He smiles, helping me up with a hand under my arm. "Welcome to Bora Bora, baby."

I glance out the window—and it hits me.

Bright turquoise water. Lush green in the distance. Thatched-roof bungalows stretching out over the sea like something off a postcard I never thought I'd actually step into.

Lena lets out a full-body gasp. "Are you fucking *kidding* me right now?"

Marcus, already pulling bags down from the overhead storage, just mutters, "Here we go."

Dominic watches me as I take it all in, that subtle smile tugging at his mouth like he's been waiting for this moment.

My eyes lock with his, heart stuttering just a little.

"You really did all this?"

He shrugs. "I did, baby. Now, let's go. Your ocean throne awaits."

The heat hits me the second we step off the jet, thick and sweet with salt in the air. The staff is already waiting with cool towels, cold drinks, and polite smiles that make me feel like royalty, or maybe like I accidentally became someone important.

The ride to the villa is short—too short, honestly. I want to soak in every second of it. Crystal-clear water, palm trees swaying like they know they're sexy, and those overwater bungalows that don't look real even when you're standing right in front of them.

Ours is tucked at the very end of the dock–secluded and private.

I walk in and stop cold. Glass floors in the living room show the ocean beneath us. Open walls, a king-size bed that might as well be a cloud, a private deck with a plunge pool and stairs that go straight into the water.

Lena walks in behind me and makes a sound that can only be described as a feral screech. "We're staying here?"

"I don't even want to unpack," I whisper. "I want to burn my life and move in permanently."

Dominic sets our bags down, "Settle in. We've got the whole place to ourselves for three days."

Marcus raises an eyebrow. "Are you going to let her settle in, or are you just going to stand there and stare at her the whole trip?"

Dominic just smirks. "I promise, I didn't fly us to paradise just to watch you stress out."

Within ten minutes, Lena and I are in bikinis, racing each other down the deck stairs into the water like we're ten years old and this is a summer camp for crazy adults.

I dive in; the water is surprisingly warm.

When I come up, Lena's floating beside me, her hair slicked back and her sunglasses barely hanging on. "You think the boys are plotting something?"

I glance back at the deck, where Marcus is sipping a drink and pretending not to watch Lena, while Dominic leans against the railing, unreadable.

"Always," I say.

Lena floats onto her back, arms spread wide as she stares up at the perfect sky.

"This might be the best decision you've ever made," she says.

I laugh, water dripping down my nose. "You mean me telling Dominic to have you come or swimming with me instead of unpacking?"

"Yes," she says simply, then flips onto her stomach and starts paddling in lazy circles. "This is, like, peak main character energy. Private villa. Crystal-clear water. You with your crazy CEO boyfriend. Me with a suitcase full of bad choices, and maybe a vibrator or two."

I grin and duck under again, letting the warm water wash over me. When I come up, I glance back toward the deck.

Marcus is sitting with a drink in hand, legs stretched out. He's looking out toward the horizon—definitely not at Lena. Not at all.

Dominic's still standing there, arms crossed, eyes locked on me.

The way he watches me makes my whole body feel like it's on fire.

I turn back to Lena. "You think we're gonna be able to relax for real?"

She shrugs. "Not sure. But this? This is a damn good start."

We stay in the water until our fingers wrinkle and the sunlight turns to a beautiful honey, the golden glow that makes everything feel a little too perfect to last.

Dominic's voice carries from the deck. "Dry off, little minx. I've got something I want to show you."

I blink up at him. He's leaned back, looking all relaxed and powerful, but something in his voice is a little too casual. It makes my stomach flip.

Lena looks at me. "Want me to go up with you?"

I shake my head. "Nah. I'll go up in a minute."

She nods once and swims back toward the villa, humming some off-key pop song as she goes.

I tread water for a second longer, letting the air hit my skin and the nerves settle.

Then, I climb the deck steps, wrapping a towel around myself as I reach him.

Dominic just offers me his hand.

"Come on," he says. I let him lead me through the villa, past the glass walls, past the bed still untouched, past Lena's sandals kicked into the corner, and out to the end of the deck where the sun's kissing the horizon.

Everything is glowing. The water, the sky, him.

And then he stops.

Right there, at the edge of everything.

Turns to face me and drops to one knee.

My breath catches.

"Dominic…"

He doesn't give me some rehearsed speech. No long monologue. He just looks at me like I'm the only thing he's ever needed and says, "I've done unspeakable things in this life. But loving you? That's the only thing I've ever been sure of. I don't want anything else, baby. Just you. Forever. Will you marry me?"

For a second, I can't breathe.

Not because I'm shocked—some part of me always knew we were heading here—but because it's *him*, on his knees, asking me to choose him when I already have a thousand times over.

My hands fly to my mouth, and I nod so hard I nearly knock myself off balance.

"Yes," I gasp. "Yes—*Dominic*, oh my God, *yes.*"

He slides the ring onto my finger, and my vision blurs instantly with tears that I refuse to wipe away. Before I can even finish blinking them back, he's on his feet, pulling me into him. His mouth crashes into mine, hungry and full of something raw and real.

We're still locked together when the door swings open behind us.

Lena steps out with a bottle of tequila in one hand and four shot glasses in the other.

She stops short, eyes locking on my ring, and her whole face lights up.

"Holy shit!!!" she yells. "You're *engaged?* Someone pour me a drink!"

Marcus follows her out, more reserved, as always. His gaze flicks to my hand, then to Dominic, and he just gives a small, approving nod.

Dominic doesn't let go of me. His arm stays firm around my waist.

Lena's already lining up the glasses on the edge of the railing. "To love, murder, and good taste in rings. Let's go."

I laugh, breathless and half-floating, as we all raise our glasses.

And just like that, this version of our story begins.

EPILOGUE
Octavia

It still doesn't feel real most days.

The quiet, the sunlight streaming through windows we picked out ourselves.

No constant buzz of a city outside. No elevators. No whispers in hallways. No cameras.

Just space, him and our home.

I step onto the back patio barefoot, coffee in hand, and look out at the view. Trees, the view of Mt. Rainier peeking out and our pool. The scent of cedar and something soft in the breeze I haven't figured out yet—but it smells like peace.

Inside, I can hear Lena yelling at Marcus.

Again.

"If you *touch* my playlist one more time, I swear I will light your stupid socks on fire!"

"You have *six* versions of the same song, Lena. That's not a playlist. That's a cry for help."

I take a sip of my coffee and smile. They're supposed to be here for brunch. They've been here for three fucking days.

They're also supposed to hate each other.

But I heard them in the guest bathroom last night. Again.

Dominic steps up behind me, shirtless and warm, wrapping an arm around my waist.

"Murder or makeup sex this time?" he asks against my neck.

"Hard to say. Could be both."

He chuckles, low and quiet, and kisses my shoulder.

"You're not going to stop them, are you?" I ask.

He shrugs. "I'm just glad they're not setting anything on fire this week."

I lean back into him. We worked for this. Bled for it. Burned down everything that didn't fit the life we wanted. Now, it's ours.

The wind stirs gently through the trees, and somewhere in the distance, a bird chirps like this is all perfectly normal. Like the people inside aren't deranged and dangerous and completely mine.

"You sleeping, okay?" Dominic murmurs against my neck.

I nod, slow. "Mostly."

"Nightmares?"

"Less." I pause. "Not about her. Not anymore."

His arms tighten slightly, just enough for me to feel it.

It's been three months. Three whole months since we ended it. Since we ended *her*.

I still see it sometimes, but it doesn't shake me. If anything, it grounds me.

Because that was the moment everything shifted.

That was the moment I finally became someone who could never be broken again.

I turn in his arms and press a kiss to the base of his throat. "Thank you."

His brows crease. "For what?"

"For letting me become who I needed to be. For not trying to fix it."

"You didn't need fixing, baby," he says, brushing a knuckle along my jaw. "You just needed someone who wouldn't look away."

God, this man. This *infuriating, loyal, reckless* man.

I'm about to say something else when the sliding door bursts open and Lena storms onto the patio in a flowy black romper, sunglasses, and absolutely zero chill.

"I swear to God, if that man breathes near my playlist one more time—"

Marcus steps out behind her, calm as ever. "All I said was that playing the same artist fifteen times in a row doesn't count as variety."

"It's called a *mood*, Marcus."

"It's called a hostage situation."

I sip my coffee and watch them, amused. "You know you don't *have* to stay the whole weekend, right?"

Lena waves a hand. "Please. I love it here. You have hot water, no neighbors, and a fridge that never judges me."

Marcus raises a brow. "You ate half a jar of whipped cream at two a.m."

She flips him off without turning around. "And I'd do it again."

Dominic leans into me, whispering just loud enough for me to hear, "They're seriously either going to kill each other or get married."

"I'm betting both," I whisper back.

Dominic kisses the side of my head before letting me go. "I'll get breakfast started."

"You're cooking?" I tease.

He shoots me a look over his shoulder. "Don't act surprised, little minx. I made you pancakes the morning after I fucked you for the first time."

Lena chokes on her coffee. "Jesus *Christ,* warn a girl."

Marcus doesn't even blink. I laugh into my mug and follow them inside, my heart feeling full in a way that has nothing to do with sunshine or expensive countertops.

The kitchen smells like fresh espresso and vanilla. Dominic's already pulled out eggs and fruit like he's done this a thousand times, sleeves pushed up, tattoos on full display, wedding ring glinting in the light.

We haven't set a date yet.

I'm not in a rush.

Because this? This is already everything I ever wanted.

Lena opens the fridge like she lives here and grabs a bottle of champagne. "Mimosas, anyone?"

Marcus raises his hand without looking up from his phone. "Only if you don't splash orange juice on the stove again."

"That was an ambush pour."

"Sure it was."

Dominic cracks eggs into a pan as if he's tuning them out, but I can see the small smile playing at his mouth. His knuckles brush mine as I pass him a plate.

He leans in low, voice deep in my ear. "You happy, baby?"

I glance around the kitchen—at the man I love, the chaos we invited in, the life we built from the ashes of something darker.

"Yeah," I say, without hesitation. "I really am."

Later that night, the house is quiet.

Lena's passed out on the couch with one leg hanging off and a throw blanket tangled around her like she's lost a fight. Marcus is in the guest room pretending he doesn't care that she's here—even though he hasn't stopped checking the hallway all night.

I step outside barefoot, wearing one of Dominic's shirts and carrying a glass of whiskey.

He's on the back deck, staring out at the trees. The moonlight catches the side of his face, silvering the edges of him, softening something that doesn't soften easily.

I hand him the glass and sit down beside him.

He takes it without a word, sipping once before setting it on the table between us.

"Everyone alive?" he asks.

"Barely. Lena threatened to stab Marcus with a cheese knife, then passed out mid-rant about lizard names."

He hums low in his throat, amused but unsurprised.

We sit in silence for a while. Like everything in the world has finally stopped spinning.

"I used to think peace would feel like silence," I say eventually. "Like nothingness. Boredom, maybe."

"And now?"

I glance over at him. "Now, it feels like this."

He turns, eyes locking with mine. "Good."

I study his face, the one that used to intimidate me, the one that I now know better than my own. "Do you ever think about how far we've come?"

"All the time," he says. "But I try not to dwell on it."

"Why not?"

He reaches for my hand and laces our fingers together. "Because what we have now is better than anything I ever imagined. And I don't want to miss a second of it looking backward."

That tightness in my chest hits again, but this time it's soft.

I lean in and kiss him, slow and deep, letting it say what words can't.

And for once in my life, I don't feel like I'm surviving anymore.

I feel like I'm finally living.

THE END.

ACKNOWLEDGEMENTS

Writing a book is a solo act... until it's not. This story might have poured out of my own slightly unhinged brain, but it never would've made it to these pages without the people who kept me sane, inspired, and caffeinated.

First, to my husband, Nate—thank you for supporting me, even though spending money makes you cringe and reading isn't exactly your thing. You asked how it was going, listened when I rambled about plot twists, and didn't once run for the hills when I said things like "I think she might kill someone in this chapter." That's love.

Skye—thank you for always cheering me on from afar, for being a constant source of encouragement, and for somehow always knowing the exact thing I need to hear (even when I wish you lived closer so I could shout it at you in person). Your love and unwavering support have meant the world to me, especially on the days when I doubted myself the most. I'm so incredibly grateful that you're a part of my life, and I honestly don't know what I would do without you. You've been my sounding board, my hype girl, and my safe place—always showing up in ways that remind me I'm never truly alone. I love you more than words can say, and I'm so lucky to call you my best friend.

Bailee—you've been my "this is going to be amazing" girl from the very beginning. Thank you for always being the one who believed I could actually do this, even when I was spiraling and second-guessing everything (which, let's be honest... was more often than not). Your excitement and confidence in me made me feel like maybe I wasn't totally crazy for chasing this dream.

To my sister Tiffany and my friend Kristin—thank you for reading, for cheering, and for making me feel like this wild thing I created actually makes sense. Your feedback, love, and support meant everything.

Mandi—thank you for being my wonderfully chaotic friend. You're real, you're loud, and you always know how to make me laugh at just the right time. I adore you.

To my editor, Alexis—

You're honestly a wizard. A brilliant, patient, ridiculously talented wizard who somehow took my chaotic mess of a manuscript and helped turn it into something I'm actually proud of. I don't even know how you do it, but your compassion shows in everything—how you treat people, how you read between the lines, how you make characters and scenes feel right.

You didn't just clean it up—you cared. You encouraged me when I doubted everything, hyped me up when I needed it, and never made me feel like I was asking too much. You gave this book structure without losing the heart of it—or the smutty, possessive ;) chaos I live for. Seriously, without you, this book would be nothing but characters yelling spicy nonsense into the void.

I'm just so damn grateful our paths crossed. You're not only an amazing editor, you're one of the most genuinely compassionate, badass humans I've met. Thank you for everything—for the late-night messages, the deep dives into messy scenes, and for making me feel like maybe, just maybe, I actually know what I'm doing.

I love the hell out of you.

To my PA, Misha—thank you for being the behind-the-scenes magic and for making my life just that little bit easier when I really needed it.

To all my bookish friends—you know who you are.

Thank you for letting me ramble, scream, and obsess through every stage of this process. Whether you were reading snippets or just sending love when I needed it, your support meant more than I can ever say. I'm so lucky to have a community that truly gets it. You made this journey feel a little less lonely and a whole lot more fun.

I love each and every one of you. If I didn't have your support, I wouldn't have made it this far. This book is as much yours as it is mine.

With love and probably too much caffeine,
E.A. Harper

ABOUT THE AUTHOR

E.A. Harper lives in the beautiful Pacific Northwest with her husband, four adorable (and occasionally chaotic) kids, two dogs, and a cat who may or may not be plotting something. Fueled by Monster Energy, a little mayhem, Sleep Token, and a steady diet of smut, she finally gave in to the lifelong dream of writing books—despite years of doubting she was good enough. When she's not lost in fictional worlds, you can find her camping and riding quads at the dunes with her family, chasing adventure and stories wherever she goes.

9 798999 127495